The Porcelain Menagerie

Jillian Forsberg

The Porcelain Menagerie © copyright 2025 Jillian Forsberg. All rights reserved. No part of this book may be reproduced in any form whatsoever, by photography or xerography or by any other means, by broadcast or transmission, by translation into any kind of language, nor by recording electronically or otherwise, without permission in writing from the author, except by a reviewer, who may quote brief passages in critical articles or reviews.

NO AI TRAINING: Without in any way limiting the author's exclusive rights under copyright, any use of this publication to "train" generative artificial intelligence (AI) technologies to generate text is expressly prohibited. All rights to license uses of this work for generative AI training and development of machine learning language models are reserved.

ISBNs: 978-1-963452-18-1 (pb);
978-1-963452-19-8 (hc);
978-1-963452-20-4 (eBook)

Book Cover Design: The Book Cover Whisperer, OpenBookDesign.biz
Interior Book Design: Inanna Arthen, inannaarthen.com
Library of Congress Control Number: 2025930861
First Printing: 2025
Printed in the United States of America

Publisher's Cataloging-in-Publication
(Provided by Cassidy Cataloguing Services, Inc.)
Names: Forsberg, Jillian, author.
Title: The porcelain menagerie / by Jillian Forsberg.
Description: [Minneapolis, Minnesota] : [History Through Fiction], [2025]
Identifiers: ISBN: 978-1963452-19-8 (hardcover) | 978-1963452-18-1 (paperback) | 978-1-963452-20-4 (ebook)

Subjects: LCSH: Augustus II, King of Poland, 1670-1733--Fiction. | Artists--Fiction. | Women
household employees--Fiction. | Porcelain--Germany--Dresden--History--18th century--
Fiction. | Meissen porcelain--History--Fiction. | Menageries--Germany--Dresden--18th
century-- Fiction. | Survival--Fiction. | LCGFT: Historical fiction. | BISAC: FICTION /
Historical / General. | FICTION / Places / Europe.
Classification: LCC: PS3606.O748661 P67 2025 | DDC: 813/.6--dc23

Dedication

To my women.
Those here: Phoebe, Bennett, Beth, Claire, Betty, Annika.
Those gone: Lindsey, Kerri, Vicki, Juanita.

"God forgive me, my entire life was one sin."
- Augustus the Strong, on his deathbed, 1733

"The King will yearn for golden fruit,
Which the feeble hand yet cannot present.
On this account it proffers now but crystals of porphyry and borax
before the King's throne in place of those sacrifices.
Yes, the hand extends even the heart in vessels of porcelain
and as an offering here tenders both."
- Johann Friedrich Böttger, in a letter to the King, 1709

Reader, beware.

The truth of history is people come across things we'd rather close our eyes to. In this book, based on truth, is a cruel sport called fox tossing. I wish it weren't real.

There is also a woman who cannot escape the reality that women are seen as objects, even today. I wish that weren't real either.

If you find yourself needing to close your eyes, skip chapter 30. If you find yourself wanting to feel the fire I did when I uncovered these unfortunate realities, read it all.

Chapter 1
Johann
1718

Horse bells jingled outside the four-paned window, waking two brothers, ages twelve and six, from a sleep warmed only by each other. Johann and Herman shared a narrow bed, nestled snugly in the slanted eaves of the one story Lutheran parsonage. It was Christmas Eve Day, but too early, too dark, to call it a day yet.

"What's that, Johann?" Herman said. He sat up, leaning over Johann, his orange hair colored gray in the predawn light.

Johann pushed himself up on his elbows and rubbed the window, but the frost was on the outside. "Someone's probably on their way to the Christmas market near the palace." The muffled neigh of a horse followed the shaking of a mane. The bells tinkled, louder this time, then a man's voice, low and soothing, rumbled through the walls.

"Probably a problem with the harness and he'll be on his way again," said Johann. He tried to push Herman to lay back down. It was far too early to be up, and Da had a big day at the church with the services.

But Herman wouldn't budge. He knee'd Johann in the gut clambering over him, pressing his nose and hands to the cold pane. Frost trickled up the windows, and Herman stood to see, his feet sliding precariously close to Johann's face.

"Brother!"

"I want to see!" The boys grappled for a moment, one trying to urge the other back to his sleeping place, the other eager to see the cart, certainly full of luxurious gifts or fur or copper ore, all destined for the Christmas market.

Johann overpowered his brother, as he always did. Herman weighed no more than a newborn goat, with bony elbows for horns. Da always told

The Porcelain Menagerie

Johann to be careful with his brother, stressing that his body did not work like Johann's did. Johann was careful, especially with the tender raised shoulder that spread wide and broad up to Herman's jaw and uneven smile. But Herman fought, and wiggled from Johann's grasp. Though he looked different, he did not act differently than other six-year-old boys.

"It's a snow white draft horse!" And like a mouse, Herman was gone from the bed and down onto the uneven planked floor. From the back of a chair, he grabbed Da's large brown coat, the one with pewter buttons and fur-lined pockets. Da loved that coat, and Herman dragged it across the floor and was soon out the door and into the snowy, sludgy street.

Johann ran after him, pulling his own coat from the hooks that were too high for Herman to reach, and hopped into Da's leather boots. Da's coat. Da's boots. Might as well grab his black preacher's robe and his Bible, Johann thought. He closed the door, hoping it would delay their fate.

Silver faded the edges of the horizon not blocked by Dresden's wood framed buildings. The church spire, freshly installed and ready for its debut this winter, gleamed. A biting wind hit Johann's face. His eyes watered. Even with his unusual gait and uneven legs, Herman had somehow made it all the way to the white horse's nose and the fogged breaths of boy and horse met in a warm cloud.

The driver let the large, feathered hoof of his animal drop. The silver shoe flashed and he stepped around to Herman's side. Johann flinched and in two large steps came between his brother and the man. The old man had a white beard and an elaborate multicolored Turkish coat. He leaned down to Johann. Johann could not help but flicker his eyes to the covered wagon, packed full of trade goods, too dark to see. But still, things bathed in shadow glistened and gleamed. Large things. Treasured things.

"Boys," the man said, his voice a strange cadence. "How convenient to have stopped in front of your home on this cold morning. I'm on my way with my wares to the Christmas market, I'm sure you know the way."

Herman elbowed Johann in the ribs. "As I said!" he whispered, sounding loud as a yell in the empty street.

The horse stomped and sent the bells jingling again. A click of metal sounded on the cobbled streets, a flash of silver shone. The horse had a loose shoe.

"Is your father awake?" the old man said. He peered at the parsonage. Johann nodded. Perhaps his father would be merciful to them if he knew they were helping someone in need. And it would give the brothers a chance to carefully replace their father's clothes.

"I shall fetch him," said Herman, unsteady on his feet as he rambled back to the house. His unusual movements made the horse put its ears back. It raised a hoof. The horseshoe clattered to the street and Johann ran after his brother, hoping to shield him from the prying eyes of the stranger.

The people around old Dresden knew Herman well enough to be unaffected by him. They usually watched out for the boy. But strangers, as Johann learned from many years of stepping into their lines of sight to protect his brother, could not be trusted.

The man stayed put. Johann turned, put his back to the parsonage and his face to the overflowing cart. What were the objects? Some so large their shrouds shrugged from their shoulders like they were giants. The cart's belly sagged. Johann crossed the threshold and ran out of his father's shoes.

Herman's voice sounded, then Da's. Next came Da's heavy steps. Johann made sure the boots were in place and shoved his feet into his own. He'd grown this winter and his smallest toe crunched inward.

"Da, there's a man outside with an unshod hoof, surely we can help..." Johann began.

"Your brother's told me. Grab my boots, son. Herman's brought the coat. A good deed this cold Christmas Eve morning is a fortunate thing, the Lord must want me awake to see the dawn."

Marten Kändler's black curls draped forward over his eyes. He was the opposite of his fair-skinned, strawberry-blonde sons. Coarse black hair covered Da's body, and his eyes were deep, russet brown, sometimes gold-cast when sunlight or joy struck him in the right way. *These boys look like their mother, may God rest her soul*, he'd say to the curved-spine, elderly women of the church when he pulled Johann close on one side and Herman on the other.

Da clapped Johann on the back and leaned out the door, giving a wave to the old man. The horse huffed. Steam rolled from its nose.

Johann and Herman did not wait for their father. They ran out again into the lightening morning, determined to comfort the horse who had no need of the boys, but accepted their warm hands on its chilled coat anyway.

The pastor and merchant shook hands and spoke, and Da led him around where a lean-to in the side yard held more than chicken cages. The family mule perked her ears, silent in the cold. Where the garden grew in the summer, now only the rosemary was green. Workers who put the new church tower together had left a small anvil, a pile of wood and tools the church might need. The boys played often with the leftovers, wielding wood hammers and scavenging nails from the project to bang into whatever they could find.

The Porcelain Menagerie

Soon after surveying the available materials, the merchant was back at his cart, rattling until he found his desired wares. Johann's fingertips and nose lost their feeling as he watched the merchant and his father prepare a new shoe for the horse. The jingling of the horse's bells signaled to Johann that his brother was no longer by his side. He snuck away to find him.

Herman was holding the horse's hoof in his hand, brow furrowed, crouched low. Lord! If that horse decided to bite him, his head would be gone in one crunch. Johann hurried to him and hissed: "Herman! That's dangerous!"

"No, he's a gentle thing. See?" Herman dropped the hoof and the horse gingerly touched the broad tip to the stone street. He paid no mind to the small boy.

"Well, be careful. Come watch them work on the shoe. Warmer over there."

"Doubt it. This horse is what's warm."

"What's...what's in the cart, Herman?" Johann tilted his chin.

"Haven't looked. Waiting for you." Herman gazed at the horse like he'd met a new mother.

"Come on, then."

Herman showed small bright teeth and held his hands to Johann, who picked him up and put him in the driver's seat of the cart. He toppled through the small window behind the seat and into the cart's bed with a clatter. The horse turned to watch, the bells harmonizing with the hammering from the side yard. Herman's gasp set Johann's belly flickering with excitement.

"What? What's in there?"

"Oh, you must come up! Treasure! Exotic and rare, no doubt meant for King Augustus himself! Far better than the normal wares at the fair!" Herman's meandering smile appeared, the dawn becoming whiter now. Johann's throat warmed as his brother held a gently-curved, ornately-carved teapot.

"A beautiful teapot, brother, not likely meant for Augustus himself. But you're wise to be careful anyway." Johann could not help himself, he clambered up and into the cart, although at twelve years old, he knew he was supposed to act more like a man.

Inside things were packed tightly, though a narrow aisle between man-sized, covered objects provided plenty of space for the boys. The smell of some fragrant herb, a strange perfume or oil mixed with woodsmoke, overpowered Johann. Legs of furniture and stacked crates created a cityscape of its own. Herman was right. The shrouded treasures felt larger and more special than any Johann had imagined. They accidentally loosened one of the many shrouds to show the face of a cherub, carved from dark marble.

"Oooh," the boys said in unison. Johann reached out and touched its face. His fingers, already cold, were chilled even more. How could something so lifelike not be warmed by blood? Its face was perfectly detailed: dimpled chin, thin brows, heavy cheeks. Johann curved his hand around its head, feeling the curled, carved hair.

Herman poked it in the eyes.

"Herman!" And though he tried to be serious, Johann laughed. He pulled the next shroud, revealing an angel. Herman poked it in the eyes, too, and a game of reveal and poke began. Soon all of the statues were unveiled and Herman's small fingers had prodded every marble eye. Next the boys uncovered the golden gleam of many Turkish pots, then rugs, then wooden boxes nailed shut, then bright white dishes painted with blue flowers the likes of which Johann had never seen.

But at the jostling of the cart, the horse whinnied loudly. Herman covered his small ears. His right hand could not reach his head. The horse gave away the boys and their treasure game.

The pastor and the merchant unlatched the back door of the wagon. A roll of steam billowed out into the street. They'd been in there far too long. Johann's fingers were no longer cold; his belly shrank to his spine and he grimaced. Herman laughed and held his arms out to his Da, ready to be picked up from the cart. Da grabbed him and set him down. Johann expected a scolding from the merchant, but the merchant crawled inside.

"What's your name?" the merchant's voice had a trilling lilt.

"Johann Kändler, sir."

"Johann, this is my livelihood. Your father's livelihood is in that church across the street, where he's told me they put that new cross up so high. You know who made that cross?"

Johann shook his head.

"A man like me. Someone who can melt metal and curve stone and bend wood to my liking."

"You made all of this?" Johann motioned to the faces of the statues, who looked suddenly wary of his presence in their wagon.

"Not all of it. Most of it I did, but other things I traded for my sculptures or woodwork. The point is, boy, I would not destroy your father's church or harm it in any way. I know you would not harm my livelihood either."

Johann shook his head. "No, herr merchant, I would not."

"Herr merchant. I like that. Very respectful. Let's climb out, now."

The Porcelain Menagerie

Johann grabbed the hand of the merchant and it felt like a hand that had lived a thousand lives: hardened and calloused, warm and strangely sharp on the edges of his fingers, as if his skin had been melted to a point by all of the fire and chisels he'd wielded. Johann's eyes went from the man's white beard to his hands and back again.

"These hands were earned." The merchant crinkled his eyes as he smiled.

Herman and Da had already had a little chat, as was apparent by Herman's snot-streaked face. The people of Dresden were waking, and the horse stomped, impatient, still waiting for its new shoe.

"In you go, Herman." Da picked Herman up and put him in the cart. "All of them, understood?"

"Yes, Da." Herman began covering the statues and packages with the shrouds they'd torn away. Johann opened his mouth to speak. It could be hard for Herman to reach over their heads. But as he turned to tell his Da this, Herman poked the cherub in the eyes again and Johann could not speak.

"You'll help the merchant with the new shoe," said Da. Then he turned to the merchant and said, "I have to prepare for services, but I shall be close by. Best of luck to you, and may God bless your journey. My sons will attend to your needs."

"I am grateful for you, Pastor Kändler, and shall stop again on my way out of Dresden. I hope your Christmas Eve with your new church tower is pleasing to God."

Da smiled and Johann followed the merchant sheepishly to the white draft's front left leg. With simple instructions to follow, he helped the merchant reshod the horse. By the time Herman was done covering the wares, the merchant and Johann were done as well. Johann felt he hadn't done much. Herman cried out for help to get down from the wagon. He rubbed his shoulder after Johann released him. Herman had the damp, sweet smell of winter sweat.

"Farewell, boys. Perhaps I'll see you again, or tonight, at the fair."

Johann twisted his mouth. They didn't go to the fair, not with the risk of losing Herman in the crowd, or the risk of his brother being taken and sold by a collector of the strange, or simply being seen at all. They stayed here, safe in the shadow of the new church tower.

Herman kissed the horse on the nose, patting it with a furrowed brow as if he'd known it all his life and had to bid farewell to a longtime friend. Johann and the merchant smiled knowingly at each other and the merchant snapped the reins. The bells of the draft horse chimed. Dawn revealed the horse's gray spots, like fingerprints in frost.

The streets were no longer empty, and Johann led Herman, who cried openly now, back to the parsonage for warmth and bread and perhaps more sleep. Their Da waited inside, straightening his black pastor's coat, which reached all the way down his long legs and nearly skimmed the floor. On the table was a bent and dirty horseshoe, the one the horse had lost.

"The merchant thought you boys might like to have it."

Johann and Herman grinned at each other. Herman wiped his nose on his sleeve and picked the horseshoe up, holding it to Johann with a wicked grin.

"From the horse that pulls the King's treasure!" he said. Johann reached out to touch it and felt a zing of shared excitement. Treasure indeed.

Several months passed, and the springtime birds returned to Dresden. After months of carrying the horseshoe around like it was a shield or a goblet or a crown or a halo or whatever small play adventure Herman came up with, he asked Johann to nail it above the bed.

"I want to look upon it every day and remember my horse."

"The merchant's horse, Herman."

"I am the merchant, Johann," Herman said, turning his voice into a deep bass that mimicked the merchant's.

Johann grabbed the hammer and a wooden nail from the side yard, stepping around the chickens and the newly-sprouted vegetables in the garden. Once back inside, he stood on a stool and hammered in the horseshoe tight. Wielding a hammer felt natural and good and he hopped from the stool and admired his handiwork. Herman, hands on his hips, showing how truly uneven he was, nodded his approval.

A string of misfortunes had struck the Lutheran Church. Johann stamped his boots outside the parsonage door, but the grave dirt stuck fast. The dust, which clumped and crumbled after it dried, wafted to the horseshoe and made a thin film of brown. The Kändlers did not notice.

Fall had come, and with it, early dark, and problems with Leichendiebe, the body snatchers, in the church's graveyard. Herman slept, but Da and Johann were home from yet another incident.

"They're getting bolder."

"I thought the cage would work," said Johann, his breath a harsh whisper.

The Porcelain Menagerie

"I did, too. We'll have to try something else. These people, they depend on us to keep their loved ones safe. I am unsure of what to do."

"We'll petition the King? Ask for assistance?"

Da laughed. "The King cares not for stolen corpses, Johann. The anatomist works for him after all, and if he has no bodies to open, he has nothing to show King Augustus for his advancements in natural philosophy."

"Why take bodies from the graveyard? Why not use the criminals or the bodies that wash up in the Elbe?"

"I am not an anatomist nor am I a thief. I do not know. But we'll go to the family in the morning, tell them..."

Johann suddenly felt sick. "Tell them what, Da? That their loved ones are gone again? Taken from them in death and now...?"

Da pursed his lips and grabbed Johann gently by the shoulder.

"This is the work of a pastor."

"I know," said Johann. "And you know I do not desire to be a pastor."

Da let Johann go and nodded. Johann's hands itched. What did he want? To be a maker. Not a mourner, a bad news giver, a baptizer, a marrier, a speaker. He wanted to be a maker.

Herman stirred. Da and Johann parted from each other to their own respective chairs at their table.

"Johann, you know I've spoken to the stone carver," Da said.

Johann lifted his head from his hands. "Thomae?" Benjamin Thomae was in the church last week, installing a new marble baptismal font. Johann did not leave his side.

"Thomae. He's agreed to apprentice you. You'll not stay here much longer. You'll be there three years as an apprentice, room and board taken care of," his father explained, holding a parchment contract on which Thomae's thick signature dripped. "Then, after that, you might be a journeyman, or perhaps make a living on your own. But for now, you must work your hardest and best. And keep the secrets of Thomae's place to yourself."

"Keep the secrets? But I already know how he works," Johann said.

"No, Johann. You think you know. But he'll reveal things to you that any smaller carver would kill to know. He's the best in Dresden for a reason. Any master, anyone who considers himself the best, keeps his process close to his heart."

Johann's belly quivered with excitement and fear. He would leave his father's house, and Herman, to begin his own life. What a fortunate life! He expected his father to return his smile, but Marten Kändler's face drifted to sleeping Herman. Johann opened his mouth, and quickly shut it.

Johann swallowed, breathing deeply the smell of his brother's hair, trying to memorize the scent. Herman would be well taken care of by their father, but leaving this boy felt like leaving a piece of himself. Though he knew he would return, boys grow and change, and things would be different each time he stepped through his father's threshold.

A small satchel was all Johann had, packed with most of his belongings. He left a few things behind for when he was able to visit. A hollow chasm opened in his chest. How could he leave the only home he'd ever known? He took the place in: warm wood floors, a gray stone fireplace, wood beams dangling with garlic and herbs from the garden, a clean, simple cross on the wall, and the horseshoe, nailed into place three years prior. The memory of that frosted Christmas Eve was a good one.

Johann tied his hair back with a leather ribbon and stocked the pockets of his travel coat with cheese and bread. He tied a soft leather pouch of coins close to his body. Da picked up the satchel and Johann took it, steadying his gaze, though his lips quivered.

"Time to go, then," said Herman slowly, backing away from Johann.

"Time to go," Johann repeated.

Da opened the door. His muddy boots sat outside. Grave dirt from another reburied casket. The morning was bright already, summer upon them. Herman blinked, stepped around a soil-covered shovel, and held his hand to his light colored eyes. Johann bent to him while Da fetched the mule.

"Herman, I..."

"Johann," Herman smiled widely, squinting, "make me something that'll last, yes?"

"Treasure fit for the King."

"For the King!"

Johann picked Herman up in an all-encompassing embrace. Though Herman was nearly ten, he hadn't grown much the last year. His cough was frequent, a rumble that filled the parsonage day and night. Herman laughed and squirmed, cleared his throat. Da and the mule rounded the parsonage from the lean-to and Johann put his brother down and grabbed the reins. Da shook Johann's hand.

Johann mounted the mule, slinging his satchel up with him.

"Maybe, brother, maybe..." Herman said, his little fists flexing, eyes pleading, "maybe I can come with you?"

"Oh, Herman, I..."

The Porcelain Menagerie

"Listen, I can't do much but I can sweep and clean and make the beds and cook a stew! I can get the tools you need and haul small things and mend the fires and..."

Da kneeled to him. "The apothecary says for you to stay calm to rid your cough, Herman. Your brother's journey is his own. All brothers must part, and Johann will return."

"I will, Herman. And maybe someday, when you're old enough, and your cough is gone for good, I can apprentice you myself, in my own workshop. Besides, you need to take care of Da."

At this Da smiled and Johann kicked the mule. He must leave now, or he'd lose the courage to go. He looked away from his family and toward the street beyond. Behind him sounded the small, fumbling steps of his brother's limping run, and when the mule turned a corner he heard the unmistakable wailing of a child.

Wind rattled the panes of the parsonage. An early, cold night fell as Da tapped the last nail into Herman's coffin. It was clean, white wood, a contrast to the black, dirt-covered coffins Johann had helped his father rebury in the church cemetery.

The fire crackled, sending sparks from a smoldering log to the worn floorboards.

"Da. Are you sure? You're sure he's gone?" Johann said, frightened that Herman might wake and claw at the soft pine box.

Da looked up from the coffin, gray circles under his eyes.

"I've buried enough people to know."

"What do we do now? Bury him by Ma?"

"The Leichendiebe will know," his father said. "They linger close by, watching the surgeon and apothecary and waiting."

Johann's gut clenched. The Leichendiebe sought the valuable dead; for study, for knowledge, for *gain*, the anatomists said. But to the remaining Kändlers, Herman was not a body. He was a soul.

The coffins dug up by the Leichendiebe, body snatchers, were often broken, corners smashed, covered in cold spring mud. Herman's was smooth, uninterred. Johann's heart pounded, thinking of the grave robbers who sought the newly buried. In his imagination, the Leichendiebe violently tossed the lid of Herman's coffin aside, and hauled his body to the anatomist for silver coins.

Was there no place safe for his brother? They could bury him with a steel mortsafe over his grave, but Herman appeared in Johann's mind, clutching the bars. Johann pushed the thought away. He stood, grabbed the chair, and reached for the horseshoe hammered in above Herman's bed, faded with age and dust. He pried it from the wall and set it on the casket.

Da sniffed. "When I tell the mourners that their loved ones have been stolen from the graveyard, they wail, Johann. They wail."

Though no cries sounded in the small parsonage, Johann's ears rang as if they did. "We cannot let that happen to Herman."

"They seek the unusual."

The unusual. Johann knew what they preferred, who he'd seen pulled from their graves: pregnant women, children, those who died of uncommon maladies. In darkened corners of Dresden, the Leichendiebe followed the surgeons and slid pennies to the apothecary boys, bidding them to find oddities soon to die. Common men were left to rot.

Johann's legs trembled; he could not shed the childlike fear that rumbled through him, though no one called him a boy any longer. Herman's small body, bent and crooked since birth, grew cold in its pine coffin near the parsonage hearth. Herman had been taken from them once in death, and if they placed him in God's green earth, could be taken again by thieves.

Johann set his jaw and clamped his thighs together to stop their quivering. He was seventeen now; he had to stay steadfast for his father, who had lost everyone. Their mother had taken her last breath as Herman had taken his first. Though years had passed, Johann could not separate the voices that filled his nightmares—both mother and baby had their mouths open wide with screams. His mother was soon dead. Her hair the color of blood-warmed straw, her soft milky smell, the rough feeling of her seamstress' hands and homespun dresses—carried out the door and gone.

But with the grief came Herman. A twisted, small baby, Herman had wailed and wailed. He had a tuft of reddish hair curled around his head like a blood smear. As a result of the traumatic birth, the baby had one shoulder higher than the other and legs that would not unbend. The wiggling baby replaced their mother's place of warmth and soft breath in the family bed.

What would happen to Da, now alone? Gooseflesh erupted on Johann's arms. He turned his face to the yellow-cast firelight. Dawn was far away. Was Da right? Did grave robbers wait in the shadows?

"Da," Johann said. "Do we bury him? Make a cage...a mortsafe?"

Marten Kändler did not respond.

"They are waiting, Da," Johann said. "If you say they've been by the door, they'll know for certain he's gone now."

Da placed his thick hand on the clean casket. The sadness Johann

The Porcelain Menagerie

should have felt was saturated with fear. Herman had gone from his little brother to a body thieves wanted, that the anatomists desired to dissect in a room full of strangers, to bottle and save in pieces. Johann stood and paced. His soft leather shoes scraped the floor of their house. He tried to still his breath.

"In the root cellar," Da said after several moments. "We'll protect him."

Johann turned to his father, though they did not meet eyes. "I will dig it, Da."

Johann opened the front door and stepped into the night. The air was sharply chilled. Cold stars reflected on the golden cross on the tower of his father's Lutheran church. Something moved in the shadows. The boring of strangers' eyes was heartbeat heavy. He grabbed the wooden shovel from the lean-to. A whisper ran up Johann's spine.

Shovel in hand, he put his back to the parsonage door and bravely faced the street. "You'll never have him!" he shouted. He trembled. "He's protected."

The only answer was his own echo. A black ball of worry rolled through his gut. The shadows squirmed. Johann closed the door, opened the floorboards to the root cellar, and descended to dig his brother's grave.

Johann's chest relaxed some knowing Herman was safe, buried with the horseshoe in the parsonage underbelly, but fear did not fade easily. The Leichendiebe still lingered around the church and parsonage, watching for funerals and caskets on dark wagons. For a few weeks, on leave from his apprenticeship, Johann lay alone in the once full bed, hearing muffled voices outside. Despite the state his delicate brother's body was in, decomposing in the cellar in his bright wood box, the anatomists still wanted him.

Johann's imagination drove itself into the body snatcher's thoughts. They must have wondered where the boy with the unbending legs went? What happened to his fragile frame? Johann's mind wrapped itself tightly around the secret of the cellar, around protecting his aging father. But the dirt on the shovel washed away, and the creaking floorboards around the trapdoor settled.

Everything settled. The days of gut-wrenching grief lessened their hold on him, and he started a life without his brother. The loss of Herman: his shuffling steps, his too-loud laugh, his wracking, familiar cough, weighed heavily on the two remaining Kändlers, but eventually in waves, no longer drowning. Life continued, even after death.

After Herman's passing, Johann found himself doubting the God his father preached about, who took mothers from young boys and made brothers whose legs wouldn't straighten. But he stayed steadfast and prayed and took communion anyway. The congregation shared their pain with Da and Johann and wept alongside them. They did not know Herman rested in the root cellar of the pastor's house, horseshoe pried from the wall and placed between dirt and casket.

Johann was expected back at the workshop.
"Father," he said. Da clapped him on the back.
"Come back to me when you can, son," Da said. "Don't miss the Holy Days in this church."
"I won't. And I'll write. And I'll bring you a sculpture for the church, the finest you'll ever see."
Da smiled and exhaled gently through his teeth.
"This house will be empty now," he said.
"I'll make sure you're not alone all the time." Johann's eyes welled.
An eagle called from high above them, wings rustling as it made its way to the church steeple. The Kändlers grew silent, the air heavy with loss and the presence of the boy who lay breathless beneath the floorboards. They embraced, and Johann hoisted himself up on their old mule. A feather had fallen onto the saddle. He pocketed it, kicked the mule, and looked back as the shadow of the cross fell on his father's face. Though he was alone, the memory of Herman, and his father's warm blessing, felt like he had companionship in his heart. Da raised his thick hand. The mule plodded away.

Johann's master, Benjamin Thomae, was red bearded, with shoulders the size of small pumpkins. His hands were curved with strong veins and thick fingers. Months ago, in the church, Johann hung about like a stray cat watching Master Thomae. And now, he was the master's apprentice. His first day, he felt the tools sing in his hand like a songbird, though he was just assigned with cleaning up.

The sound of the workshop made his ears ring: metal on stone, metal on wood, shouts and thuds and hammer blows, whistles of men and whooshes of fire and brooms. The smells of wet stone and sharp metal and the sweet, pungent stench of men hard at work mixed with strange chemicals and paints. The workshop was foreign, exciting, alive.

Johann longed to tap the hammer on the fine-toothed chisel, to indent the years of birth and death on tombstones, to finesse the curls of a cherub. But first he had to learn.

The workshop held wonders far greater than the merchant's cart: altar pieces, gargoyles for Dresden's castles, stone finials, creatures with grotesque faces, angels for new cathedrals. The ceilings were high, the floor dirty and rock strewn, his shoes constantly sparkled with marble dust. Each corner had something half created, draped with cloth, pulled from the earth, waiting for an artist's eye to turn it into something more marvelous than sharp, raw stone.

The workers carved dead rock into art. The carvers put their own hearts into it, making lips and smiles and bodies so realistic that the only clue to a sculpture's lifelessness was the cold temperature of stone. The process for each piece, from ornate fountains to small fixes for crumbling finials, was sharply specific and took great focus.

Johann longed for this structure, this precision, after watching his father's profession have no real shape. When God molded a person, they always came back seeking change. In this place, Johann could create something everlasting. Just as Herman had asked.

But Johann had little skill, despite his itching fingers. So he replenished the firewood, helped haul in stone, picked up dropped tools, swept the floor. Johann's observations and Thomae's instructions blended, and the first time Johann was allowed to take a chisel to marble, the solo, singing tool in his hand became a full song.

Johann proved himself helpful to the stone carver, no longer an eager child but a well-versed young man. The workshop's large windows and wet rock smell, a courtyard for storing new marble and lumber, constant grunts and the tapping of metal on rock, became home. Thomae was severe but kind, and when Johann made mistakes, he was punished by the work instead of his master.

"How's the hand?" Benjamin Thomae did not look up from his careful carving on a medallion for King Augustus' hunting companions. Small things were sometimes more complicated than large ones.

Johann turned his palm. The bruising had faded, but his knuckles were still swollen from a wayward hammer blow last week.

"Better," Johann said. "I imagine I won't be wielding a hammer anytime soon."

"Ah, sorry, not true. I have another project that demands my attention today, and I want you to finish this mold."

"I have not done a bronze mold before," Johann said. His hand trembled at the thought of finishing something for the King himself.

"You've been here a year and haven't? It is time. I've done the front; you finish the back."

Johann swallowed. He could do it, but an acid-sour taste filled his mouth. If he made a mistake, they would miss the King's deadline. Surely there would be inconsistencies—could King Augustus tell the master's work from the apprentice's as he turned the medal from front to back?

"I'm off to the chapel. Installing the altarpiece today," Benjamin said. He dusted his hands, gently placed the clay mold that would be cast into bronze on his workbench, and rose to his feet.

The altarpiece was nearby—a massive, warm gray stone carved with cherubs in the round. The angels were bent at the waist, hands clasped, gilded wreaths around their bellies. Johann had helped with the gilding, laying precious gold leaf with a whisper-thin brush. Benjamin readied the wagon outside, and Johann sat silently at the workbench, staring at the red clay medallion before him.

The profile of Augustus II, called The Strong for his show-like acts of strength, was carved in relief. His curled wig was formed, the lines of his double chin prominent. But when Johann looked at it, he saw what *could* be. The curls could have more detail. The single eye, seen in profile, lacked the liveliness he knew the King possessed. In front of him was no longer a red clay medallion, but a person, waiting for its soul to come alive under Johann's hands. Dare he correct his master's work?

Johann swept the bundle of carving tools closer and felt the world disappear around him. A perfectly clear image came to him, when he had seen the King:

Augustus on a white stallion, the horse prancing through the cobbled streets of Dresden. He was in full armor, a crimson cape wrapped round his shoulders, pinned with a star-shaped brooch. Augustus had piercing brown eyes, sticky-wet, colluded by thick black eyebrows, contrasting his silver wig. Johann held the image of the King in his memory and took up his master's tools.

Johann and Benjamin walked into the King's unfinished Japanese Palace with a box of medals. They wound through maze-like halls filled with treasures. But it wasn't gold or jewels or abalone shells on delicate silver pedestals. There were plates in white and blue, eggshell-thin green bowls, a small room with only five yellow glass pieces glowing like yolks. Thicker pieces rested on the floor, dotted with copper-gold sparkling in the mid-morning sun.

The Porcelain Menagerie

There was one path to the throne room, lined with uncountable amounts of a surprising amount of porcelain. As Johann turned his head to take the place in, he remembered the small teapot from the merchant's wagon. Was it here, meant for the King after all? Was a ceramic worth so much, so enviable that the King had so many pieces? Johann's medals suddenly felt strangely unimportant. Bronze surely held more value than a plate... it could be melted down, turned into a sword, or a coin, and what could this ceramic do, besides shatter with little force?

Benjamin led the way without hesitation, passing by the dozens of gleaming vessels as if they were not held in an unusual place of pride. Johann gaped, pausing and rushing to catch back up.

"How many pieces of porcelain does King Augustus have, Benjamin?"

"I do not know," Benjamin said. "If he craved stone work as he does porcelain, I would be the richest man in Saxony. Instead, he imports Japanese and Chinese pieces, and his own factory makes him these thicker pieces. You can tell right away which ones are from the orient. Seems the artists in Albrechtsburg, at that old castle in Meissen, haven't found the perfect clay to mimic the porcelain Augustus desires."

Indeed, many of the pieces were translucent and delicate, contrasted by thick and sloppy looking things. Johann felt a connection there: a master versus an apprentice.

"How could anyone in Saxony know how to make Chinese porcelain? This does not lack in skill, just in materials, it seems." Johann's gaze shifted from piece to piece.

"You see it with an artist's eye, my boy. King Augustus cannot understand the process. He has the porcelain fever, as many royals do. He wants the real thing, not this imitation made locally."

"Porcelain fever...?"

"The King has obsessions, including some of my own work over the years, that he cannot quench without gaining more and more. Women, hunting, porcelain, animals from far away. Soon there will be no room for more dishes in this Japanese Palace."

"You are making me believe acquiring more will not stop the desire."

They rounded a corner and the place glowed white and blue and brick-red. Shelves upon shelves. Figures, vessels, plates, bowls, strange objects of great size and small tiny things, like a yellow shoe no larger than a thumb, sat. Breakable and fragile, yet strong in their presentation. Johann itched to run his finger down one large green vase, to feel its raised texture. He held his hand still.

"Nothing will stop Augustus' desire. Our many medals and bronzes and altar pieces have not satiated him, no amount of porcelain can, either. But we have an advantage, Johann. We have perfected our trade. Marble yields to me. Porcelain does not yield to those in Albrechtsburg. They have struggled for years to make white porcelain. Many you see here are not theirs."

"Luckily we are not porcelain makers."

Benjamin nodded.

"If we were, I don't know if we'd be invited to luncheon. They have a finicky relationship with the King. I've heard rumors that they haven't been paid in nearly a year, though they keep producing."

They strolled through the rooms more quickly than Johann would have liked, as he wanted now to tap his fingers on the massive porcelain vases on display to hear their ringing. He followed his master, mind filled with the shapes of vessels and teacups and platters and bowls. Eventually, the noises of the King's hunting party echoed in the hallway and two guards stood near an open door, the frame Baroquely carved.

Benjamin turned to Johann and dusted his overcoat. He nodded and his eyes crinkled, though his small smile did not reassure Johann enough to still the quaking of his legs. His first audience with the King. Johann closed his eyes and shook his hands out.

"Stone carver Benjamin Thomae and his assistant, Johann Kändler, in presentation of the honorable medal to the King's hunters." A herald's voice echoed through the hall, his staff rapping on the floor.

The audience chamber took the breath from Johann's chest. The ceiling was painted as if heaven and hell, intertwined, danced above them. Birds, beasts, and all manner of angels pulled clouds to clothe themselves. A lion, a hercules-like man, and dangerous red clouds blended. Power exuded from the corners of the room, golden-painted flowers and berries, recognizable from Thomae's workshop. And there, at the front of the room on a fiery red throne under a canopy of silk, was King Augustus himself.

Benjamin gently shoved Johann forward, a single gleaming bronze medal in his hands. Benjamin held a wooden box in which twenty more identical pieces waited for the hunters. They milled throughout the room, dressed in long overcoats and striped pants. Some carried rifles and horns, some had thin-stemmed pipes dangling from their mouths. All of them were ready for luncheon to be laid out on the long table in the adjacent room, and then a day's adventure in the nearby woods. Were the medals an afterthought?

Despite his broadness, King Augustus the Strong sat childlike, legs open wide, on his throne. Even while sitting, his enormous stature was evident. His feet and hands were twice the size of Johann's. Fox fur draped his thick neck. Though the King lounged casually, Johann's brow beaded with sweat. Johann felt as if his presence was judged along with his work.

Benjamin gently bumped Johann on the shoulder, forcing him closer. Johann bowed. The King cocked his head to the side and smirked, using one finger to beckon him close. Johann swallowed and his scalp prickled. The medal in his hands was his finest ever work. But perhaps the King would think otherwise.

"What have we—come, come." The King shifted in his seat, leaning forward eagerly to see the shining bronze. He was older than Johann remembered from the parade—white wigged, perhaps sixty, his dark eyebrows flanked by deep wrinkles. A double chin protruded from his white lace collar.

"Your Majesty, forgive me, I had never seen you so close up." Johann dropped to a knee, holding out the medal. He focused on his soft brown shoes, handed down from his father. Herman's face flickered. Would he be proud? A presence nestled itself beside him, a whisper in his mind. Johann could not bring himself to look at the King.

King Augustus chortled as he took the bronze from its cloth.

"Ha!" he said. The men gathered in, clapping the King on the shoulder. "Look at it, it is beyond grand! I look impeccable. My hair has never looked better. Lean in, look, look!"

The King is a manchild, thought Johann, his nerves lessening. Augustus' voice was a bouncing, booming ball in the room. Joyful wasn't quite the right word; his mannerisms were too boisterous.

"My boy, this is the finest portrait I have seen. But why do you present it as your master stands behind you?"

"Your Majesty," Benjamin Thomae said, stepping beside Johann. "I claim nothing but the bronze casting. Johann Kändler improved my design from his own memory and created your likeness."

"Ah, and you are *proud?*" Augustus drew the word out long, raising his thick eyebrows and smiling, sickly sweet. A chill dripped down Johann's spine. Something malicious carried the words.

"I am, Your Grace." Benjamin swept to a gentle bow. Johann's mouth went dry. He could not tell if the King was genuinely pleased; surprisingly boy-like, it was nearly impossible to decipher his true meaning.

The King fiddled with the medal. He scratched its surface and tossed it in the air a few times before placing it back in Johann's waiting cloth.

"What else can you make, my boy?" He leaned back onto his throne, tossing the fox fur over his shoulder. The animal's glass eyes bulged, and Johann looked Augustus in the face. Heat filled his belly.

"What do you desire, Your Highness?"

"People are fine. But I have a penchant for animals in white gold."

"White gold, Your Highness?" Johann's heartbeat filled his ears. He felt Benjamin stiffen beside him.

"Porcelain, Kändler," said Augustus. "I own a porcelain factory, you know. There, the porcelain makers hold the only arcanum in five thousand miles."

"Ar...arcanum?"

Master Benjamin inhaled.

"The arcanum is the formula for porcelain," said Augustus. "A secret, held close to this kingdom. The formula and pieces created from it are quite precious. More valuable than everything from your master's workshop."

Augustus leaned forward. He smiled, revealing black gaps in his molars.

"Master Benjamin makes valuable items, of course, but not like the *objets de art* you walked through in my palace. The arcanum is priceless. The formula itself is more valuable than the Chinese porcelain I own, brought around the horn of Africa, or overland to me. Objects of perfect beauty. Fragile yet strong. But they are cups and bowls."

"You desire animals, sire?"

"Yes, something more unusual. The Chinese and Japanese have perfected the bowl, the cup, the vessel. But no one has a lifesize porcelain menagerie. Though I have asked Christian Herold, the current leader at Albrechtsburg, he says no modelers at Albrechtsburg are capable. They have tried and failed."

Johann considered what the King asked of him.

"You'd like me to try?"

The King stuck out his hand to Johann.

"Go to Albrechtsburg, and I promise you, if you succeed, you'll find everlasting glory in making porcelain for me."

Johann looked to Benjamin, who pursed his lips together in a smile and nodded. Johann could not read the pained look in his eyes. Johann cautiously stepped forward and took the King's hand. Scars criss-crossed Augustus' damp, rough palm.

"I would be honored, Your Majesty."

"Brilliant," he said. "Your goal is to fill my Japanese Palace with porcelain animals. A carver like you should find it simple. I'll write to Albrechtsburg ahead of time so they don't put an arrow in you upon arrival."

Johann let out an awkward laugh, unsure if the King exaggerated. He exhaled as he stepped back. Benjamin put his hand on Johann's

The Porcelain Menagerie

shoulder. He slumped with the comforting weight and tried to still the trembling in his gut.

Johann helped Benjamin gift each of the twenty hunters the bronze medal with Augustus' profile. They told him stories of the King: how he bent horseshoes with his bare hands, how he smashed his tennis rackets with sheer force while striking the ball, how destiny brought him to be King as he was not the first born son...

Servants announced the luncheon was ready, and they settled around a long table. First was soup and pickled items, pies filled with carrots and wild game, pastries molded into elaborate shapes and viciously bitten in half by the hunters. Roast meat was sliced into thin portions, served with herbed potatoes. Small loaves of dense black bread steamed. Everything was served on perfect porcelain plates. Johann held back the desire to pick them up and examine them. Instead, he ran his fingers over the edges and tried to imagine how they were made but could not.

The final course was stollen, a sweet bread dotted with jewels of fruit and dusted with white, fine sugar that flaked off the hands of the hunters and the two artists. A rare, dense, black coffee in a delicate cup was savored by the King and the hunters but Johann found the drink bitter and after one luxurious sip, could not finish it. Benjamin twisted his mouth in a hidden smile.

The hunting party's conversation was deafening, but no one was louder than Augustus. Though Johann and Benjamin sat far away from him, Johann still felt it an honor to be at the King's table. A far cry from his father's parsonage.

Just as the group was about to raise from their chairs, they were interrupted. A footman stepped in quickly, followed by two women in matching red travel cloaks. They nervously glanced down the table to Augustus. Though they were richly dressed, their faces showed weariness. They both had dark hair, though the older one had streaks of silver at her hairline, her eyes creased in the corners. The other, younger woman's face was a direct copy to the elder's, though her brows were dark, her hair thick and raven-black. Johann had never seen anyone that looked like her—skin the color of golden sunset, a proud, angular profile. He could not help but stare.

The older woman rushed to the King, signaling to the younger woman to wait. They must have been mother and daughter. The hunting party quieted and Augustus stood. The older woman looked up at him through furrowed brows. He bent to her, nearly twice her height, putting his ear close to her mouth.

Johann leaned up in his chair to see if he could read the situation, but Benjamin put his hand firmly on Johann's forearm. This was not their business. Still, Johann watched. The energy between the older woman and King Augustus lit like a matchlock. Augustus' countenance turned from jovial to wicked-sharp: nostrils flaring, shoulders back. The woman was dwarfed beside him, fists clenched, her throat contracting at every word. Though she was small, she did not shrink away from the King. Who was she to speak to King Augustus like this?

The younger woman, whose skirts were hemmed with dirt, came closer to the table. Johann turned and watched her. Dark shadows circled her eyes. Her jawline was tight, bone-sharp. His fingers itched to carve her angles. As she approached her mother's side, Augustus softened, though his fists were still clenched.

The hushed voices of the hunters sounded:

Katharina, they said. *The King's daughter*. And another word, broken, sliced by whispers: *Divorce*.

King Augustus left the dining hall flanked by the two women, followed closely by a shrew-faced man from the hunting party. Turning to watch, Johann nearly fell from his chair. Both of the ladies had elaborate rope-like braids in their hair, something he'd only ever seen on a horse's mane.

Benjamin nudged him in the ribs with his elbow.

"The King has many women," he said in a whisper. Johann turned back to the table, embarrassed by his lack of self-control. "Though I have not seen Frau Maria in many years."

"Maria?"

"The older one, Katharina's mother," Benjamin said, taking a large gulp of his wine. "Augustus' woman before he married her off to one of his chambermen."

"I thought Augustus had a queen..."

"Augustus' wife, may God rest her soul, refused to return to his side after he converted to Catholicism. Rumor has it he only did that to gain the crown in Poland. After that, and before it, too, the man had many women in his chambers and at his tables. They fought for his attention like rabid she-wolves."

Johann scrunched his nose. "They fought for him? Did they think they'd be the next queen?"

"Can't be a queen while the Queen's still alive. I don't rightly know what they fought for, but every time I presented a new altarpiece or statue for his palace, a different woman hung from his arm. Until Maria."

The Porcelain Menagerie

A member of the hunting party spoke up, slurring his words.

"She was his favorite, for a bit. Swear he might've loved her. Married her off even though she had his child."

"What happened?"

"What always happens," the hunter said with a wink. "Women have but few uses when they're unwed. Augustus wouldn't marry her, so he made a choice to rid himself of the temptation to father more bastards on her, likely to spare himself the gold."

Johann swallowed. He had a suspicion the hunter at the table knew one side of the story. The desperate way King Augustus and Maria approached each other spoke of something more.

"And the young woman?" said Johann, knowing he likely spoke out of turn.

"Katharina. Augustus' daughter. Right fine one. Married away when she was sixteen, a year or two ago. Surprised to see her here, now. Someone down the table said they'd heard a rumor the church was bein' asked for her to divorce her husband, and they said no."

"So she's here..."

"To ask her father, most like. He's the only one can grant it."

"Divorce is legal?" Benjamin said.

"If both parties consent," said the hunter, raising his silver goblet and winking. Johann turned again to the door where the women and the King had exited.

"Welcome to court," said Benjamin. "A never-ending stage drama. You'll see more of it at Albrechtsburg."

"I am unsure if I should go, after what you told me," said Johann.

"You have no choice," said Benjamin. "While I could petition for you to stay with me, the King has made his decision. You can make your own way, you have learned a lot. Though I did not predict you would go there."

"And what am I to do about the plain truth that I have no experience with porcelain?"

"No one new there does, Johann. It's a secret art. One you'll learn, like you learned from me. If the King wants you there, that's where you'll go, even if you may be slow at first."

"What if I fail? And no amount of trying gets him a porcelain menagerie?"

"Then you come back to my workshop, though it may be in disgrace."

"Disgrace?"

"There is no freedom to fail here. Augustus has his eye on you, which means he expects you to succeed for him. His obsessions, Johann, go far enough to drive men mad if there is not perfection in their deliveries."

Johann felt the beat of his heart in his temples. The stollen in his belly felt heavy, the coffee tempting, and he took another bitter sip.

"How do I start to learn a secret art?"

"By studying the finished pieces already. And by going to the menagerie."

Johann perked at that, nodding slowly. Benjamin kept talking. "I'll get you permission to linger in the Japanese Palace. Touch the pieces that are here. And before we leave, we will go to the menagerie. It'll do you good to see what animals Augustus is familiar with. They'll likely be what he will ask you to create."

"He did that with you, didn't he? With the mythology sculptures?"

"Yes," Benjamin said. "When he was obsessed with Greek and Roman myths, my lists grew long. Satyrs, goddesses, Bacchus, Hercules. They call him that, you know, the Saxon Hercules. I had to become familiar with the myths before I created the art. So I studied the myths, and you shall study the animals."

"What if he asks me for an animal I have never seen?"

"Then you'd better pray you stumble upon it, or fake it well enough that it will not matter."

Johann gazed down at the table. The hunters were leaving their seats, drawn to the muskets that leaned against the walls of the room. Augustus had not returned. Johann wondered where the women had gone, and could not shake the image of Katharina's dirt-coated cloak and dark braids from his mind.

The hunters' voices grew louder as they sloshed the silver cups and emptied the wine casks. They would wait for Augustus before they left for their hunt, but Benjamin and Johann were not invited. Benjamin patted his white napkin in the corners of his mouth and tossed it on the table, motioning for Johann to follow him. They left the hunting party, whose bronze medals lay ignored on the table.

Benjamin held a finger up for Johann to wait by his side while he whispered to a footman stationed by the door. The footman nodded and grabbed the gilded door-handle with a gloved hand, extending his arm into the hallway. As Benjamin and Johann slid through, the footman gave Johann a piteous look.

"Porcelain awaits, Johann," said Benjamin. "We can stay here as long as you like with permission, as the guard knows you're headed to Albrechtsburg."

The hallway was brightly lit by the afternoon sun, gleaming on the bright, clean porcelain pieces that marched down the parquet floor like a waiting army.

The Porcelain Menagerie

Johann picked up the nearest piece, surprised by what felt like fragility. He held it to the window. The sun illuminated it, like a garden snail shell he'd held to the summer sun as a boy. He pushed away Herman's noise of exclamation.

"That's a Chinese piece, maybe Japanese," said Benjamin. "Now judge it against one from Saxony."

Benjamin handed him a small porcelain shoe from a shelf. It was dense and felt thick, more like a stone than a snail shell. When Johann held it to the sun, there was no glow.

"This is poorly made in comparison," Johann said. "Seems like the materials are utterly different."

Benjamin picked up a bowl, thin and cloud-white. It was translucent. He flicked it with his fingernail. It filled the hallway with an echoing, bright ring. He beckoned Johann to the next room where a thick, reddish-brown, dull teapot sat on a shelf, surrounded by similar pieces.

"They can't quite figure out how to make it like the Japanese or Chinese. This was an early attempt, from a man named Böttger's formula. Red or white, Johann, which do you prefer?"

Johann leaned in, narrowing his eyes and taking in the delicate design on the red pot.

"This is beautiful carving. Finely done, but it does not compare to the paper-thin porcelain from far away. In fact, I cannot rightly call this porcelain, if that is my example. But why?"

"I wish I could tell you," said Benjamin. "The differences in technique are beyond my knowledge. Something I'm sure you'll learn. The King certainly notices. I remember years ago, when all the artists delivered the King's birthday presents, how he fussed over the red clay stuff brought from Albrechtsburg. They called that porcelain too, but it looked more like a common earth pot."

Ahead lay a smooth clay teapot, reddish-brown and opaque. Johann picked it up. The piece felt cool in his hands, the opposite of its color, and he flipped the piece over. It felt smooth, but he could see the imprints of imperfection: a rough stroke from a thumb, a smudged finger. On the side was a carved face, surrounded by grapes.

"Bacchus," said Benjamin.

"During the god obsession era?"

"Quite right," Benjamin laughed. "And now apparently you're entering into the animal obsession era."

The rays of sun on the parquet floor moved from one side to the other as they examined each piece of porcelain in the hallway. As the light turned golden outside, Johann followed Benjamin to the entrance of the Japanese Palace.

"Beyond the little copse of trees there is the menagerie. I've been there myself to draw the animals. Helpful when I'm ordered to make a thing like a marble boar. We'll go now, as I anticipate your orders to arrive in my workshop in the morning."

Johann noticed a small quiver in Benjamin's voice as he said this.

"Master Benjamin," he said, "are you afraid for me?"

The grasses met their soft brown shoes as they walked across the slight hill of the palace grounds.

"I must admit I am, Johann. You are a talented man, perhaps the only apprentice I think could leave a legacy behind him. But part of me fears that castle and what it does to its inhabitants."

Johann raised the corner of his mouth, though his lip trembled. "The castle is just a place. It's letting you down that I fear the most."

"If that were true, Johann, I would not feel my heart in my chest when I think of you climbing the hill to Schloss Albrechtsburg. Instead, I would fear that you cannot make the art the King desires. But I know you can, and I know you will. I hope you outlive me, boy."

The menagerie was visible through the trees, slender black bars and a gilded gate shone in the dipping sun. A strange, loud caw sounded from the wooded area. Johann startled, thinking of what was loose inside.

Benjamin opened the gate with a shove, which moved a pile of leaves. The gate had not been opened in some time. It creaked and caught on the dirt path. Johann sucked in his belly and pushed through. The place smelled darkly damp, with an overtone of sharp animal piss. Benjamin shut the gate behind them.

The caw sounded again, beyond a small curving path. The place felt like a tree-draped cave, and Johann could not see where the curving path led. Along the sides were black cages, some empty and strewn with leaves, others with pacing creatures.

"A stoat?" said Johann, narrowing his eyes in the dim. The animal disappeared under a log in its cage, white tail flashing.

"Seems to be. Look, a birdcage, look at the parrot."

A bright white bird with a tall feathered crown flipped its head in a wobbling circle, padding toward them with sharp gray talons.

"I've never seen a bird like that," said Johann. He desperately wished he had something to draw with. "You've no parchment on you, Benjamin?"

"No, sadly. You'll be back, Johann, you'll have to be. I imagine every animal in this place will have a porcelain counterpart made."

The Porcelain Menagerie

"How many animals are here?" Johann said. He listened to the rustling around him and began to feel the expanse of the place pressing in. Dozens? More?

Benjamin shook his head. "Not sure, let's keep going. It's getting dark now, and we don't want to be here then."

The trees covered most of the graying sunset. Around the first bend, the cawing sounded again. Benjamin jumped back, putting his arm out protectively. A massive bird, blue and green feathers spread wide in a fan, shook its tail at them.

"I've seen this before," said Johann, crouching down. "The feathers are for sale in the market sometimes. This is a peacock."

The bird shook again, opening its mouth in a hiss. The men skirted by slowly, Johann practically crawling. The bends of the menagerie took them onward, making the small place larger by its waving path. Johann counted thirty cages, twenty more for birds, though half were empty. They strolled down a small hill and around a sharp curve.

In front of a cage the size of two large wagons, two figures in red traveling coats stood, barely visible against a shadowed grove of evergreen pines. The women stood and turned to Benjamin and Johann. Johann looked to Katharina's face. Her eyes were swollen and red, though her mouth was firm and unmoving. Maria stepped in front of her daughter, shielding her from the men. She raised her chin to Johann, and his breath left him.

Chapter 2
Fatima
1706 - 20 Years Earlier

The door to Fatima's small, drab chambers swung open. She startled, sitting straight up in bed. She'd been dreaming of a flock of small bright birds with night-sky heads and silky teal backs, like she'd seen as a child in Buda. The image quickly faded as a ripping sound filled the room.

"You've been summoned," Aurora said, tossing what remained of a letter onto Fatima's lap. "This letter arrived from Dresden."

"Summoned?" Fatima said, delicately picking a fragment up. In large, scrolling script was the letter "A".

"King Augustus wishes to see you and you alone."

"Surely there's been a mistake, Aurora, I..."

Aurora raised her hand to stop Fatima's words. Her mouth was held in a thin line, fingers visibly trembling.

"There is no mistake. King Augustus has requested Fatima the Turk to Dresden's court. There's no mention of me."

Fatima's palms prickled with sweat. She pinched her eyebrows together, gathering bits of the letter to try and fix it. Perhaps Aurora had misread. Surely the King did not want his official mistress' handmaiden, alone?

"What does this mean?"

Aurora tilted her head, pale skin on her double chin wobbling.

"That I've been replaced. Gather your things. Time to go."

"Now? But surely I can make a decision, take a few days and write back."

Aurora scoffed, a glazed look in her eyes.

"You do not get to make a decision, girl. If the King calls, you go."

The Porcelain Menagerie

Fatima ran a hand down her braid nervously. She understood. The replacement of Aurora as mistress in Saxony was not a choice for the women to make. But it was Aurora's choice how quickly Fatima left.

"You no longer want me here," she said. "But what if Augustus changes his mind? Or he calls me to create a surprise for you, something special for his mistress?"

"He does not," Aurora said, pursing her lips. "It was all outlined. I'm dismissed. Eight years his senior, three years in his bed, a child, not a spot of gray on my head. Yet he cannot stop thinking about *you*."

Fatima's body pulsed. She had not asked for this. In her desperation, she skimmed her memory for a moment in which she led King Augustus to this position, one where he decided he wanted her. She shook her head lightly, and remembered his dark brows rising as he drank her in while she stood by Aurora's side. And now it felt like she was betraying her mistress, the only person constant in her life.

"You're angry with me," Fatima said. "I promise you I didn't mean for this to happen."

"It doesn't matter what we mean to have happen," said Aurora. "We are dealt our lot in life when we play the game of mistresses and kings."

"It's not a game, Aurora." Fatima rose from the bed. Pieces of the letter dropped to the rug. "Your son is not a plaything, and neither are you. I only wished to be at your side, never in your place."

Aurora stiffened.

"Understand something about Augustus, Elector of Saxony, King of Poland, Saxon's Hercules, Fatima," she said. "To him, everything is a game."

The next morning, a gray dawn emerged, and Fatima whimpered. She forced herself to quiet. The journey from Goslar to Dresden was familiar, one made with Aurora many times. But never alone. In the carriage, the steep rolling hills forced her body forward, and the velvet pillows slid to the floor. Her dark hair bounced over her shoulders.

Fatima was on her way to Augustus' side, beckoned to court, and his bed. The look on Aurora's face when Fatima packed her things and slipped on her small white shoes was venomous. The arched eyebrow, the trembling double chin as she tried to smile.

"Do you know what to expect from King Augustus in his royal bedroom?" Aurora had asked.

Fatima hesitated. As seen from the chafed skin and green bruises on Aurora's thighs when she helped her mistress dress, she knew Augustus was rough.

"You'll have your own chambers. Lovely ones. And many pretty things. Rings, pearls, diamonds. You'll have time with *him*, in his bed, to do his bidding. You might fight. He won't care. You might scream. He likes it. You'll be his second choice to drink and merriment. Watch yourself when he's drunk. He likes to play with his guns and swords, and cares not who's in front of him."

Fatima's heart raced, thinking of that conversation, and of the promise of Augustus' large body on top of hers. He was big as a bear, looming, with a voice that filled even the largest rooms of the Zwinger Palace and of his many other ornate and maze-like residences. She knew that Aurora got many things from him by acts in the bedchamber—the gleaming pearls and egg sized baubles around Aurora's throat were payment for when she did her duties well. Aurora could not have known that the conversations afterward, in private to her own handmaiden, had taught Fatima what to do with the King.

The lurching ups and downs of the hilly road felt like the ground beneath her could open and swallow her and the carriage whole. Part of her longed for that. To disappear. The ride was hours long. Though the carriage was warm, she trembled with a chill. She'd eaten, and been treated like a princess, although she was not. She was a mistress. Unwed, no title, no voice... at that thought she stopped herself.

When Aurora was mistress, her many whisperings to the King brought her things. Gifts, outings, people, entertainers. Perhaps, Fatima thought, daydreaming despite her fear, she, too, could convince Augustus to give her the things she wanted. She raised the corner of her mouth.

The carriage ride reminded her much of her past. She remembered her mother, left behind in Buda when Fatima was not yet five years old. The lingering smell of her mother's perfume, rich oils blended in a silvery bottle, clung to her skin from their last embrace. Sometimes, the smell filled the air around her, though her mother was now a specter, nothing but a memory, and likely a ghost. Now, as a young woman of sixteen, Fatima understood. The last hug from her mother had included a jingling sound. It was the coin purse in her mother's hand, given to her by the man driving the carriage. Fatima had been purchased like a lamb. A similar thing happened now.

Fatima closed her eyes, longing to wake up in the small, narrow bed in Goslar where she cared for Aurora and Augustus' bastard son, his cries piercing the night. But baby Maurice and Aurora were left in the wake of the dust kicked up by thin wheels and two glossy geldings. With every clop of the horses' hooves, the life she knew grew far away. She dove reluctantly into the depths of the kingdom of Augustus.

The Porcelain Menagerie

She must have slept, for when she woke, the filtered sunlight was bright through the curtained windows. The carriage stopped, and the shouts of footmen and sounds of a city filtered in. Fatima pulled the silver curtain aside at the same time the door opened, nearly careening to the cobblestones. A building cast a cool shadow onto the street. It was so tall the top of the spires were hidden amongst low clouds. A rough arm grabbed her, and she was on her feet, dizzy from lack of sleep, rolling hills, and apprehension.

The building was covered in scaffolding and sculptures, the whole place partially assembled. A woman dressed in blue led her up a shallow, curved bank of stairs. Fatima could not rip her gaze from the naked, sculpted men carved of stone, hanging from the archways leading into the castle. Their faces were mournful, but a powerful emotion rested in their eyes. She could not place it—fear, longing, or torture?

"I've waited all morning for you," the woman said. "You're late."

She put her hand on the back of Fatima's arm, pinching, and directed her inside. The woman had flame-red hair, mouth creased and down-turned.

"Late? I was told to arrive today…"

"We have been waiting for you. For renaming. Christening."

"Christening?"

"When Augustus became Catholic, he insisted the court women become Catholic, too. You're the first Turk in this palace, we can't have you Protestant as well. You'll have no objections."

Fatima furrowed her brow. She had been the first Turk everywhere she went, first in Sweden, then in Hanover, then in Goslar, always with her mistress Aurora. She was used to the stares, the curious looks at her blue-black braids and tan skin.

Inside, the stone floors of the Japanese Palace made papery, sweeping sounds under Fatima's slippers, and more statues glared. Fatima raised her skirts and nearly stumbled trying to keep up with the woman, who urged her onward with the tight claw of a hand on her arm. The palace walls were sand-colored, with dozens of archways and statues of half goat, half men. The last time she was here, she entered through a different, grander door. This back entrance felt reserved for the doomed. She felt a chill creep up her spine and took shuddering breaths.

The back of her arm grew tight and sore. She would bruise. She shook off the hand that led her and stopped. "You are hurting me."

The woman turned, hands on her corseted waist. Her eyes flashed wildly. A smile crept up her face, but Fatima could not call it joyful.

"You will need to strengthen yourself, especially as he has chosen you," the woman said. "He has dismissed me, Marianna, and Aurora, who I hope told you of his preferences. Before that it was Anna Constantia, then Maximiliane, and before then I know not their names. You are no longer in charge of yourself. You are now the official mistress, King Augustus' to do with what he will."

Fatima shuddered, palms damp with sweat. She raised her chin and curled her hands into fists. She had many things to say, mostly about Aurora's talk of his preferences, but was only able to squeak a simple phrase.

"I belong to no one but myself," she said.

The half-smile on Marianna's lips expanded.

"I like that. Maybe you shall keep it. You could do well here. Augustus likes unique things to be part of his collection."

"His collection?"

Marianna gestured to the many objects that decorated the palace, the finely-dressed servants and women who milled around, and to herself. She raised her brows. "We can never tell what the favorite is: the porcelain, the paintings, the animals, the women. When he decides he no longer wants something, he sends it away. Or destroys it. Lucky me, I am to be married to one of Augustus' hunting friends. At least he has a title. Do not ask what happened to Christiane or Anna. Fates worse than death, I tell you. Seems Aurora made out alright. Bastard son, nice little estate."

She grabbed Fatima's arm again, gentler this time, and led her to a room where a cross hung on the wall. A priest in black waited there, with a face like a dripping candle.

"Augustus wants you baptized and renamed," Marianna said. "Then you can join him, in his chambers and at court. And I can leave this godforsaken place forever. I am done with that man."

"What did he do to you?"

Marianna did not answer. Before the priest was a great marble bowl, large enough for a baby to be placed, filled with still, clear water. Marianna pushed Fatima to her knees, and the priest took her by the shoulders. He spoke Latin, which she recognized from the Catholic masses she and Aurora were forced to attend during their last stay in Dresden.

Water cascaded over her black hair, dripping into the pool.

"What will be her Christian name?" said the priest to Marianna. Fatima turned with furrowed brows and opened her mouth to protest. She did not want a new name.

"Maria," Marianna answered. And Fatima's name was taken from her.

Chapter 3
Johann
1732

Katharina and Maria stood in front of a black animal cage, arms extended straight in an identical gesture, one of protection. Johann and Benjamin glanced from each other to the women. Johann opened his mouth to speak but found he could not.

Benjamin stepped forward, bowing.

"Madams, we apologize for the intrusion. We are artisans working for Augustus, who has requested a porcelain menagerie of my apprentice, Johann. We were here simply to see the animals in his care, and we will leave your space."

Johann exhaled, mouth still open. Benjamin grabbed his left shoulder and began to pull Johann toward the leafy path they'd taken earlier. But Maria stepped forward.

"Augustus requests a porcelain menagerie? You are not porcelain makers. I know them all."

Johann looked to Benjamin, who released his hold, and turned to her. Johann's eyes darted to silent Katharina. His heart was in his throat. He'd never felt this pull toward another human before, especially coupled with utter inability to speak.

"I am a stone carver. This is my apprentice. Augustus saw his work with the medals today and ordered him to Schloss Albrechtsburg."

Maria's eyes shone darkly.

"Have you been there, apprentice?"

"No, madam," said Johann, his voice a squeak. He forced moisture to his mouth. "No, I have not, I have merely seen it from afar. Hard to miss the castle on a hill, even if it is an hour's ride."

"It is not a place for..." Maria began, but behind her a rattling noise sounded. She and Katharina turned to the black-barred cage.

Johann stepped back. Whatever was inside the cage was large. The enclosure was not empty, nor void of life. The only thing visible was a large and long dead tree on its side that looked as if it was pulled through a flood, stripped of bark and small branches long ago.

From the bars hung the butchered hind-quarters of some kind of animal. In the growing twilight, a shadowy shape walked forward on massive paws. Johann's underarms prickled at the sight of a beast, large yet slender, who had undoubtedly been watching them, waiting for its opportunity to eat.

"Oh," he managed to say before the lion, mane matted and spiky from age, hip bones showing through its dull golden hide, reared on its hind legs and pulled its meal from the cage bars. A smell like something sweet mixed with the dirt.

Maria collapsed to her knees in front of the cage, a hand's width from the animal, whose yellowed teeth pulled at its dinner. It whumped to the dirt floor of its home, paying no mind to Maria. Johann longed to rush forward and pull the woman back. But Katharina wrapped her arms around her mother. Small whimpers came from the woman, whose dark hair was a contrast to the golden animal.

Benjamin stepped forward.

"What magnificence is this, Johann?" he said. "A lion in Dresden."

Johann took one step, and a branch snapped under his heavy foot. The lion looked up. Its left eye was sewn shut, the other stared at him as if he were prey. A heartbeat of time passed, shuddering through Johann's body. The lion returned to its meal.

"This is my menagerie," said Maria, her back to the men, still crouched to the ground. "I created it years ago."

"What an incredible thing you have done to bring animals to this place. We never would have seen a lion here, nor would Johann be able to see its likeness with such accuracy for the King's porcelain."

Katharina turned, her skirts and dirty red cloak gathering the leaves in a swirling storm around her.

"Being responsible for lives, human or not, is a heavy burden, sirs, and I ask you leave this place. Leave my mother her sanctuary. You can see she is—"

Maria interrupted her. Her cape parted, a bone-thin hand grabbing Katharina's. The women exchanged a look, passed a silent message, and Johann remembered doing the same with Herman. Unspoken things were loud with family. A familiar, aching mournfulness surfaced.

The Porcelain Menagerie

Katharina helped her mother to her feet. Katharina stood a hair taller, and though their faces were nearly identical, Katharina's cheeks were full with the bounty of youth, her mother's sunken. Their chins raised simultaneously—were they immensely irritated, prideful, or stoic? Attempting to define their moods made Johann's palms sweat. Perhaps he was not made for court life.

"May I ask," he said, tripping over his nerves and stuttering, "may I ask, please, to come and sketch here. Otherwise, I fear the King will be stuck with birds and goats and field mice."

"Perhaps," Benjamin offered, glancing sideways at Johann, "we can arrange Johann to be here when you are not. To give you your sanctuary."

"Yes, of course," said Johann. "I am sorry to intrude. This is your place."

Katharina looked to Maria with narrowed eyes. Maria cupped a hand around her daughter's ear and Katharina looked down as she spoke. Katharina pulled away and Maria pursed her lips. Five heartbeats of time passed.

The lion behind them let out a low rumble from its chest, startling Katharina, who took steps away from the cage. But Maria stayed still and close to the one-eyed beast.

"I know what happened to others who have tried and failed in Albrechtsburg, and wish that fate upon no one," Maria said. The lion stood, its back legs quaking with age. It licked its lips and went back to its hiding place behind the fallen tree. Maria turned to Benjamin.

"But my idea might surprise you, stone carver. If your apprentice plans on spending many days here, I will not allow him to be here *without* my presence," Maria said. She turned to Johann. "I wish no harm fall on my creatures nor you, and the only way to make sure they do not attack you or you do not fool yourself into thinking you are safe is to have me or Katharina here. Escorted, of course, so we are not in danger of you in turn, young man."

Johann nodded, his head falling forward in a bow, his shoulders heavy. He rubbed his fingers together. This was his lot, then, to have a continued, overwhelming sense of being watched: by King Augustus, by Master Benjamin, and now, two women who knew nothing of his intentions. He realized he was watched, too, by the ghost of his brother. The pressure to please them all sank him deeper into the damp menagerie path. Proving himself in this place was everything to him, but he was not sure he could survive the pressure.

"I will accept any help I can get," he said. The lion let out a barking cough from its cage.

"We will show you the animals," Katharina said. "Tell you which ones will ruin your carver's hands if you get too close."

"All of them," Maria said. "All of them will ruin him if he gets too close."

Chapter 4
Fatima
1706

In the damp, pre-dawn morning after her arrival, Fatima watched Marianna load into a plain, single-horse carriage with her trunks and parcels. Augustus' resident castle blocked the warming sun, and the cobbles shone with melting frost. Fatima stood at the window on the third story, watching through a parted curtain, her heart a drumbeat of war. Marianna slid inside the carriage, gathered her skirts, and shut the door, giving one last look to the sandstone palace. She did not look up at the third-floor window. Fatima placed her hand on the night-cold pane, leaving a fogged, echoing imprint.

At this point in the day, Aurora's young son, Maurice, would be waking, usually greeted by Fatima. Her heart sank. Aurora was not anywhere near her, and neither was Maurice, whose care had become routine for Fatima. Her guide to this new place, Marianna, was gone, too. Without Marianna or Aurora, Augustus' intentions to make her his mistress were upon her. She'd cared for his bastard child and his former mistress. She knew the stories Aurora told of his behavior. What would happen now?

She felt like a deer exposed in a meadow, clearly seen by a hunter at a wooded edge. She had tightened Marianna's corset strings and buttoned the tiny pearls on her dress an hour ago. Marianna did not return the favor and left Fatima to dress alone, a nearly impossible task.

"A former lady-in-waiting needs a lady-in-waiting," Fatima said aloud, though she was the sole person in the parquet-floored chamber. She sighed.

The room was opulent compared to her small chambers in Goslar, though she knew it was bland compared to other bedrooms in the palace. She'd stayed here before with Aurora.

Her favorite part was the hidden door. It seemed to be cut into the fabric floral wallpaper with a knife blade. Inside was a small room with soft chairs and sofas tucked into the walls. She hadn't ever been there alone, as Aurora always lounged there. She knew the servants were aware of the room, but surely here she could release her straight-backed spine and relax, as if Dresden were not outside the door. She ran her fingers along the seam, opening the door with a gentle click.

The room was dark, in need of a candle, but a crystal chandelier reflected white light from the window behind her. Before she could step inside, a knock on the outer door told her what she knew was coming since Marianna left, heels clacking, leaving Fatima with a roiling, sour stomach. The King summoned her. Fatima shut the hidden door; the wallpaper blended, hinges gone.

She twisted her corset around, pulling its cords tight, and shimmied it back. She contorted her arms to button her red overdress, flaring her ribs and tensing until her forearms burned. The door muffled the voice of a young footman. She was taking too long.

"Frau Maria," he said. She cringed, making fists, her knuckles turning white at the sound of her new Christian name. "King Augustus wishes an audience with you this morning. Make haste. He is planning on leaving for his hunt."

She cleared morning fuzziness and fear from her throat.

"I have a favor to beg of you," she said. "Please come in."

The footman inched the door open, peering inside.

"Are my buttons crooked?" She knew they were. She could not reach them. She turned, satin skirts sweeping the ground, and pulled her black hair to the side. She'd braided several strands, though she'd seen no other woman at any court do so. It was something she had always done. The footman balked, eyes dancing anywhere but her and the gaping, crooked back of her dress.

"They...they are not done properly, madam," he said.

She hesitated, taking a few short steps.

"Would you fix them, please?" But the footman did not move. "I do not have anyone to help me. Please."

Fatima trembled, glancing over her shoulder at the footman. She tried to make her eyes kind but knew they were full of worry. She jumped when he touched her. The footman fumbled through the buttons, his large, flat fingers unpracticed. It took many silent minutes of listening to his exacerbated breathing before Fatima was ready for her audience.

"I will lead you there, Maria," he said. She rolled her shoulders down and stared at him.

"I prefer the name Fatima."

The footman could not have been twenty. Dusty blonde hair, light eyes, a long, mouse-like face, and a chin that melted into his weak jaw.

"I am sure you do, lady," he said softly. He looked down, swept his arm toward the door and walked her into the gray-green painted hallway.

The raucous crew of assembled hunters in Augustus' throne room were heard before they were seen. Fatima held her skirts gently, teetering on narrow heels, and bowed low when she reached the center of the room. The footman stopped at the doorway, backing into his spot along the wall. She was alone in the center of the room. This was identical to Aurora's introduction to the court. Fatima had watched it from the corners. She wished she, too, had a companion waiting to care for her, but she was distinctly alone. The hunting party's eyes were on her.

"Ah, Frau Maria!" Augustus called from his throne. The men surrounding him nudged each other, looking Fatima up and down. She felt like a caged bird surrounded by wildcats.

"Welcome, welcome. It is lovely to see you, though I must admit, a bit strange without Aurora by your side. I now get to know you, alone."

Augustus put a finger to the side of his nose and grinned, showing missing molars. Fatima could not feel her breath. She was unable to move. Augustus arched his thick, black eyebrows, blue eyes shining. His silvered wig settled over his large head, cascading down in curls that reached his chest. He had narrow lips that revealed red wine stains on his teeth, and she counted four black voids when he laughed. His frame cascaded over his chair, shoulders broader than any other man there, though his waist was narrow.

"What do we think men?" he said, leaning into his companions' sight lines. "This one we've talked of for years, and now she's mine!"

His surrounding attendees rocked with laughter. Fatima's mouth went dry, and she attempted to swallow, but her throat only wobbled in fear. They'd talked of her for years... so Aurora did not hold his attention as fully as she'd believed.

"In the meantime, Frau Maria, you'll join me before my hunt today. I have a surprise for you in the courtyard. A proper introduction to being my woman, so others know your place. The world may speak of other kingdoms and cities, but Saxony is the best, aren't we, men? Time for everyone to know you're mine, Maria."

The men cheered. Heat rose to Fatima's cheeks. Everyone would know her by Maria, not her real name. And what position did she hold besides the King's mistress? None. At least with Aurora, she helped with Maurice. She felt singular, and though Aurora was not always kind, and she would've been angry, Fatima found herself wishing Aurora were beside her, holding the attention of the King.

"My job as King of Poland and Elector of Saxony means I must provide for my people. This city was nothing before me. And now, you shall see art, music, life. Women, children, and men of all kinds, provided for. I am their father, their leader, and their patron. Anything you desire in this life, any dream you have, will come true in Dresden."

Any dream she had? She dreamed of being called by her birth name. She dreamed of the narrow bed in Goslar, the simple lullabies she sang to Maurice while Aurora slept. Fatima dreamed of erasing the day she'd been taken from her home as a child in Buda. She knew this ruddy, large, and incomplete man in front of her could not give her anything she desired.

Augustus continued to speak, but Fatima heard little of what he said. The hunters were suddenly busy gathering muskets and short swords and bows and quivers of iron arrows. Her ears rang as Augustus approached, swaying as he walked. He held his arm out to her. With the arm came an onion-sour smell of sweat and the musk of a man who did not know that bathing with water was superior to washing with powder.

Fatima's throat stuck again. Augustus reached down to her hand and placed it on his arm, leading her through a brightly lit doorway where a dewy courtyard glistened. For a few moments, she blinked, absorbing men's low, excited voices as they lingered around large objects organized in straight, clean rows on the grass.

Her eyes adjusted to the sun, now emerging over the gray and tan castle walls, blazing the sculptures in the corners with golden light. Cages. The objects were cages.

As a child, she had a house and yard full of animals. Her brothers brought home baby birds fallen from trees, placed them in soft yarn nests until they flew away. They had dogs and goats that wagged their tails in the grassy yard and puppies that wobbled through her legs, bred for companionship as well as hunting. She thought of the young mother cat outside the kitchens in Goslar, whose orange fur glowed like a fire in the sunspots of the yard. Fatima closed her eyes briefly, remembering the chirping love and half-closed eyes of the sweet cat, and felt a subtle ache in her heart.

The noises of beasts sounded. Warbling foxes, deep, unsettling growls, the squeal of a boar as it was pinched through the cage bars by one of Augustus' men holding a sharp metal poker. Her breath returned to her now, and Augustus must've felt it, for he patted her hand and grinned, the crevices of his missing teeth catching her eye.

"This, my dear, is how we hunt. The servants and townspeople

The Porcelain Menagerie

capture these fine creatures for us, and we release them in my own wood. Some we catch right away, some we don't, and they populate my grounds for hunts. A year ago I had five hundred deer in this courtyard. Can you imagine? It was a great day for the children, easy shots for all. Then we opened the gates and mounted, and the real fun began!"

A caged she-wolf paced, baring her fangs at the men. Fatima's eyes grew wide and she felt her knees would collapse underneath her. She had never seen so many animals. And their fate was to be destroyed, one by one, by this man. She squeezed her hands together.

"The joy this brings to the men, you've no idea. It does something to me, Maria, and makes me realize why men were created. It encompasses power, love, lust, future, money. The hunt here represents everything I have done for Dresden, for Saxony. I have gathered the things we need to thrive and provided for this place."

Fatima smelled animal dung and piss, the fear-filled kind, and Augustus' wine-choked breath. Though she was outside, she longed for fresher air.

"When..." she began, clearing her throat again with a slight cough. "When do you let them go?"

"Now, my dear," Augustus patted her hand, bending over to make eye contact, gaze darting to her lips and hair and every inch of her face. "That's why I've called you. A welcome gift, if you please. You are releasing the animals for the hunt."

A false release, let go only to be slaughtered immediately. He let go of her arm. Fatima swayed in the sunlight. In the cage before her, a small fox whose fur was jagged with stress and illness panted, eyes dull, mouth dry. There was no water in its cage.

Her fingers itched to let it go, to see it run through the fields without a look back at this place, to escape into the woods beyond. Yet the men waited with their carved and expensive rifles, hoisting the guns to their shoulders in mockery and practice.

Even if Fatima let this creature go, it was to its doom. A flickering thought came to her: perhaps this would be the lucky one to escape and avoid the fate of others. Maybe it would make it. Augustus motioned to the crate. The fox trembled, cowering.

Fatima opened the cage, and the animal darted. Augustus raised his arm, signaling to wait, and the fox ran toward the open gate, where the rolling field and woods waited.

The men aimed. Augustus lowered his arm. At the sound of gunshots, Fatima closed her eyes.

Chapter 5
Johann
1732

Johann stepped into Albrechtsburg and immediately began coughing. Inside, the castle was scorchingly hot. The air burned his eyes, acrid-yellow and searing. Beautifully decorated wooden beams, like honeycombs, held up the vaulted ceilings, evidence of once grand halls, but this castle no longer housed royalty.

"We will be followed by the guard at all times," said Benjamin. "Do not be startled by it. The formula for porcelain is priceless, and the factory is the only place in Europe that has made strides in its manufacturing. The formula must not escape these walls. The man we seek is Christian Herold."

Benjamin did not cover his mouth, though he did wipe his eyes. The walls were soot-stained, the sounds of the workers harsh and raucous. The factory breathed like a monster in a cave: bright orange firelight pulsed up a staircase that led downward to the hell-hot kilns. Heat seeped into his thin leather shoes. The floor, streaked with black, was hot like skin.

A man stood under a vaulted ceiling, scowling, his arms crossed in front of his chest. Coppery pink-gold paint dotted his linen clothes. His thin mouth was such that if Johann had carved it, the relief would have been impossible to discern. This must be Christian Herold. His hair was pulled into a low, thick ponytail. Little was remarkable about this man's appearance, minus the glimmers of paint that crusted his hands.

"By royal decree, you're here," he said. "But that does not mean we trust you."

Johann sucked in air through his nose, sinuses lighting with poison. Fear grew like a slow ember. As he stood in front of the guard, a thin man dressed in black, the soles of his feet grew hotter and hotter.

The Porcelain Menagerie

"You know I've been tasked with the King's porcelain menagerie," said Johann. "Though I must say, I have never worked with porcelain before. But I can model anything he may want from clay or wood. I have visited the menagerie on the palace grounds, to begin his project."

"You will make a clay sculpture. We will make it into a porcelain figure." Herold shifted from one foot to the other, likely an effort to withstand the heat rising up through the floor.

Herold's scowl deepened, and he sighed. It was clear the man was far too busy to lead a young protégé through any training. He motioned to Johann and Master Benjamin. They followed him up a curved staircase, where the blustery June wind creaked through open windows. The air was fresher up there, stories away from the opal-orange fire below.

In a room off the long, stone hallway, workers surrounded long tables. Whitish clay covered both tables, some raised higher with deep water-filled wells, some lower set where carvers sat, intimately leaning over their work. Six men used fine tools, not unlike the ones Johann used in Benjamin's workshop, carving plates and cups and vases.

"You shall work here until you are dismissed," said Herold. "You will be shown to your quarters and instructed on delivering your sculptures to the mold makers. From there, you will deliver your molds, pressed or poured with porcelain, to the kilns. You are not to leave Albrechtsburg without permission from the King."

Christian Herold turned on his heel. Johann took in a breath to ask him about attending services on the holy days in his father's church, but the thin-lipped man was out the door and gone.

Benjamin and Johann stood awkwardly, the guard uncomfortably close. A worker with graying auburn hair, broad shoulders, and green eyes looked over his shoulder at them, wiped his hands on a rag, and rose from his stool.

"Hallo, new?" he said with an easy smile. "Come sit and tell me why you're here in Albrechtsburg."

He pulled up two stools near him and sat, taking up his tools again and carving a smooth line on an unfired teacup. The guard stood behind them, silent.

"I've been here years now," said the carver. "I've perfected this specific kind of cup and am asked for little more. It is part of my essence to make this cup on the wheel. They must all be identical, perfect. To make the same thing, but have it feel different each time, is a wonder."

"The same cup?" said Johann, staring at the dexterity of his hand as the small wooden tool he used smoothed the surface.

The carver nodded, a slight smile on his face.

"Do you grow bored?" asked Benjamin.

"Ah, sometimes. I do make other things, but none worthy of the King. But I have proven myself by doing this. Others before me did not make cups to the King's liking. Too thick, too boring, not delicate enough." Johann counted three quick movements of the carver's thumb over the surface of the clay cup. *One, two, swish, one, two, swish* - the cup smoothed over like a deep river.

"That a hand so large should want such a delicate piece..." began Johann.

The carver laughed. "Augustus wants more than these delicate pieces. He wants the world made for him in white gold."

Johann's eyes narrowed as he looked from the carver's hands to his face. Utter concentration. "White gold. Again I hear that phrase."

"The porcelain made here is more valuable than any other ware in Saxony. The King would give his coffers for a porcelain menagerie."

"The porcelain menagerie is my task. Though I am not sure where to begin."

The carver perked at this, putting the cup down. He rubbed his clay-covered hands together. "That's your task, lad? How did you get saddled with such an impossible thing?"

"I..." Johann hesitated, eyes on the lumps of clay on the table before him. "The King has asked me to do this, to carve animals for porcelain. To please the King, I must make his porcelain menagerie."

The carver flicked his tongue over his lips. "What is your name, young man?"

"Johann Joaquin Kändler, son of Marten."

"The pastor? I have heard his sermons."

"One and the same." Johann smiled broadly, thinking of his dark-eyed father in front of the stained glass windows of their church. Herman's body in the cellar flashed in his mind, too. He pushed the thought aside. "My father is proud I am here by order of the King."

Benjamin stepped forward and clapped Johann on the back. "Augustus saw this lad's work in a medal and commissioned him to come here to see what he could make from your white gold."

"You must be proud, as his master. I hope the King is gracious to you. I have seen many come and go in his pursuit for the menagerie."

"Who are you, pray tell?"

"No one." The man looked at his hands. "A whisper of a tool on clay. A conjurer of one teacup. A smoother of lines and broken things. I am here to make this single cup, and before I lose my head, I hope I shall get to leave. Took us years to get this far, with white porcelain instead of red."

The Porcelain Menagerie

The man's deft hands ran the wooden dowel over the clay again. The teacup was precise, perfect. Johann imagined it, finished white-blue porcelain, as pale as a maiden's unblemished hand, painted with the copper rose that covered the apron of Christian Herold.

"Samuel Kirchner."

Samuel placed his teacup down and gathered a heavy lump of clay from the table. He scraped it up and, with an echoing thump, plopped it in front of Johann.

He motioned to the clay, slid over a pewter cup of water and a satchel of tools, and smiled. "Let's see what you can do. You're making a press mold. Porcelain clay is soft, like a melting cheese. Once your molds are done, we press this special clay into them and capture every tiny detail. You must make your sculptures perfect for the molds."

Johann had no earthly clue what the King wanted, but Samuel and the guard were watching him. He grabbed the clay in his hands. It was soft, malleable, cold. His heart pounded, and though he knew no one else could feel it, he felt the clay pulse with him. Johann remembered the eagle soaring above his father's church, wings outstretched. Pressed between the folds of his clothing in his meager belongings was the crumpled feather.

Johann's mind's eye expanded, and the room faded. He saw the bird. His hands began to form its face, slipping water and tools over the clay to carve what he hoped would please Augustus. Samuel smiled at him. Benjamin bid him farewell.

"This is a welcome beginning." Samuel grasped Johann by the shoulders. "Make it *live*, boy."

Each morning, Johann rolled from a small cot in the corner of the modeler's room, not allowed anywhere else in the castle except the large dining room and the privy. He dreamed of the eagle, woke startled and sweating in the night, unable to sleep as images of the eagle's eye or its feet or feathers consumed him.

After several weeks, and much guidance from Samuel, Johann's sculpture was made into a mold, the mold was refined, and it was ready to be filled with porcelain clay and fired. This was the final test.

"It may crack," Samuel said, wiping sweat from his brow as they took the winding staircase into the breathing throat of Schloss Albrechtsburg. Johann reluctantly followed him down the stairs to the sublevel.

Albrechtsburg was alive, a monstrous creature; the people inside it blood and air. Adding wood to the kilns made the castle walls shake and rumble, sending stone pieces to the floor. The heat seeped between the cracks of the crumbling floor like steam rising from a bull in winter. The men who kept the fires going were covered in soot, their hair and eyelashes burned. They smelled of fire and earthy clay and burnt flesh.

The castle heaved at changes in the weather. A driving rainstorm meant the upper levels were soaked through the cracked windows, while the floors beneath dripped slimy water from the teeth of the ceiling, arched above like a cavernous mouth. When the kilns were fired, the place steamed, and Johann felt closer to death than he'd ever been when the doors to the dungeons opened, and the fire belched from below.

But he and Samuel descended all the same. The castle's bowels were blacker and blacker as the stairs took them down, night dark even when warmed with lantern light. Sweat dripped down their bodies, and Johann found it hard to breathe. Samuel brought up the white kerchief he wore round his neck and covered his nose and mouth. It caught his streaming tears.

"The kilns," said Johann. "How hot must they be to fire the porcelain?"

Samuel shook his head and lowered his kerchief.

"That is not something I'm allowed to know, Johann, and if you ask the kilnsmen, they will not answer. We only know our own tasks. To ask questions is to put yourself in danger."

"Why?"

"We are the keepers of the arcanum, boy—the only formula for porcelain in Europe. If someone knew the full order of every step, they'd be targeted, kidnapped, taken. Or never allowed to leave. We have few freedoms as it is. It is best to know nothing but your own work, do you understand?"

Johann nodded, a jolt of lightning crackled through his belly, from the descent or the warning of his new friend, he did not know.

The molds in Johann's hand were heavy, filled in with soft white clay. When assembled, his eagle, spread-wing, would be nearly four feet tall and five feet from wingtip to wingtip. Wings, head, body, and tail were all set in individual molds to be pieced together. They carried each mold carefully, Samuel's strength showing in pale, dripping muscles. Johann heaved down the stairs, his scalp prickled with sweat.

The kilnsmen were dirty, vastly different from the pure white porcelain they heaved out of the hellish fires. They systematically replenished their stacks of coal and wood by pitching shovelfuls of black rock dropped from chutes. Closed molds were visible inside the kiln flames, and Johann wondered how long it took to fire the pieces.

The nearest kilnsman came to Samuel first, scratching his greasy beard with scalded hands. His arm hair was singed, spiky, and gray with ash.

"Gon' to crack, Sam, you know it, same as all of yours did at this size. No reason to even try."

"But try we must, Lucius. It's Johann's first time making molds. I told him where to put the holes and how to make it work. We can repair it during assembly. We'll try, for the modeler sent by King Augustus, won't we?"

A golden coin glimmered in Samuel's hand, subtly passed to Lucius. Johann did not mind the need to bribe the kilnsman. He wanted to succeed here, to avoid a permanent return to his father's church, where Herman's ghost would haunt him, telling him how disappointed he was for the remainder of what could be a plain and ordinary life.

Lucius took the molds from Samuel and nodded at Johann to follow him. The kilnsman's leather shoes had burnt soles. His arms were rock solid sinew, his neck thin, smeared with ash. Johann followed, though his body fought. He did not want to approach the kilns.

They blazed: small brick ovens, large brick ovens, around a dozen of each size. Johann's sweat dripped into his eyes, stinging, but he followed. His heart beat wickedly fast, and in his vast imagination, he found himself in the throat of a beast, approaching its wicked fire rich gullet.

"Drop it here; we'll take care of the rest."

"When can I see if it has been successful?" Johann said, choking and wiping his eyes. "How long does this take? How hot are these fires? What happens after the pieces come out of the kilns?"

Lucius raised a singed eyebrow and looked at Samuel.

"He thinks we're here to reveal all of Albrechtsburg's secrets, does he? Are you a spy, boy? Telling the King who's loyal or dead?"

"No, no, Lucius, he's on assignment. Either prove himself now or crumble. He means no harm."

Lucius stared at Johann, who felt entirely too hot. His breath was heavy in his chest and he longed for the less acrid air that waited up the spiral staircase. His art and his future were in the hands of this black-dusted man. He bit the side of his tongue.

"I'll be sure to tell you when they fail," the kilnsman said.

Chapter 6
Fatima
1706

Spring cascaded into summer and the hunts grew more frequent. Many mornings Fatima watched men tethering and caging animals in the courtyard, setting up for more outings. She considered retreating, pulling back into the wallpapered, hidden door of her chambers to avoid the beastly cries.

But instead she fled to a different wood where the empty cages were stored, and skimmed her slippered feet over a path worn by servants who hauled the beasts to their doom. After many silent mornings there, hidden in the dappled, damp light, she had an idea. One that would mean, perhaps, an unsettling permanence, but with no word from Aurora, whom she often dreamed would arrive in sorrow, begging for her return, Fatima indeed longed for something that could define this place as home.

She snuck through the broad hallway to the King's chambers the night before a hunt. The guards by his door twisted their mouths at her but said nothing. This was normal. They knew her purpose. It was her duty to attend to Augustus' wishes, just as Marianna, and just as Aurora, and the dozen others before them.

At the clicking of the door, the King sat up in bed, blankets wild around him. Fatima went to him, all the while thinking about the creatures in the courtyard, braying and howling and clawing at their cages. She did the same.

She said: "Augustus," the word honeyed, "I *desire* something." Suddenly he was wide awake. He desired something, too. To get what she wanted, she had two choices: make promises, or sacrifices. This time, it was a sacrifice.

She remembered Aurora's stories of how Aurora earned baubles and gowns and a small white dog. Though likely Aurora never knew her salacious tales—told while Fatima scrubbed around her bruises in her bath—would help her own handmaiden please the King, Fatima used the memories well. Fatima doubted Aurora would have told her anything or flashed her thumb-sized jewels at her if she knew she'd be replaced.

Fatima decided to sleep in the King's bed with him, to stay all night long. It was warm there, at least, and the King, tonight freshly powdered, slept quietly. In the morning, before slipping away in the dark hallway to her chambers to dress, she told him her dream.

"Augustus," she said, watching his eyes flutter open.

"Yes, Maria?"

Fatima sighed. "Can you call me Fatima?"

Augustus turned to her, eyes dark.

"Is that the thing you desire? That you spoke of last night?"

"No, not the thing I desire," she said, frustrated. "I want something else."

Augustus swung his legs to the floor. His feet were swollen, no sign of bones showed through the skin. They were puffy, like something recently dead. He wiggled his toes.

"What is it you want, woman?" he cringed, clearly in pain.

"I...I want a menagerie."

He sighed, looked at her sidelong, and blinked heavily. "So earn one."

Fatima was now attended by a chambermaid, by her request, after the chinless, mouse-faced footman spread scandalous rumors of how he buttoned her dress that first morning. Now, the young man could scarcely look at her. Fatima stared at him as she passed into the throne room to watch King Augustus hold court.

Dress done up properly by a woman's hand, Fatima settled in next to Augustus, her thighs sore from the night before. Saxon's leader leaned over to her and waggled his dark eyebrows. It was here that she would learn if her request had come true, perhaps this morning.

She expected to sit through many merchants and local farmers, at the mercy of a skittering Englishman with a funny accent and a wobbling quill, who wrote down every person's comings and goings for the record. But the courtroom was interrupted.

A darkly dressed man pushed through, waving his hands wildly. He looked like he'd rolled in soot. The man had a pouting, full mouth and round-tipped nose, skin filthy. His clothing looked like it had once been fit for a nobleman, but it was threadbare, singed, full of holes. Augustus stood. Fatima looked from one man to the other and held her breath. Augustus stood for no one.

Augustus' fists curled. He exhaled largely and put his chin up, a gesture akin to a bull. Fatima leaned back, gripping the arms of her chair. She did not know who this man was, but Augustus' tension made her shrink.

"Böttger," he said. Fatima's mind flashed. She did not know that name.

She knew most of Augustus' hunting friends, foreign dignitaries, and relatives. She knew the servants—at least their faces were familiar to her by now, even if she did not know their names. She knew the gardener and the blacksmith, the cook and the man who cleaned the guns and kept the armory. She knew the marble carver and his apprentice, a teenage boy named Benjamin Thomae, but she did not know this man named Böttger, and she had never heard Augustus speak of him.

Böttger stepped closer, wringing his hands. "Your Majesty bid me come when the kilns are hot. You must come now. It's happening."

He drew close to Augustus' silver chair and dropped to a knee. He did not lower his face as many did. Instead, he held the King's gaze.

Augustus stepped down the dais. Fatima sat back, feeling as if a hare were about to be snared by a wildcat, that Augustus would catch this man with his teeth.

Böttger kept his eyes up but lowered his face. Through the dirt, he had a strong jaw, sinew of neck muscles leading into a trim if filthy body. His profile was handsome.

"Your experiment finally works?"

"Yes, Your Majesty," Böttger said, his voice nearly a shout at the floor, full of emotion, though Fatima could not tell if it was joy or sorrow. "You will be the first to see it..."

Augustus clapped his hands. The still room startled. "Everyone out! Ready my carriage!" People whipped into a frenzy.

Fatima stood. Böttger stayed on his knee. What strange prisoner was this, who could force the King to leave his court immediately? Panic radiated off Böttger's body. He shuddered, closed his eyes tight, and rose. Fatima met his gaze. He looked away and coughed.

Augustus motioned to Fatima to follow him.

"I will impress you with my alchemist's experiment," he said. "Come." It was not a question.

Fatima nodded. She could not say no to such drama, and joining Augustus would certainly get her closer to her menagerie. But what was this experiment? With the energy pulsing from them both, mayhaps

The Porcelain Menagerie

Böttger had discovered a new type of fire.

She took Augustus' outstretched hand, damp with sweat and wildly hot, and followed him down the steps. Böttger stood amidst the scattering of the court and followed.

Fatima's small steps and narrow heels could not keep up with Augustus and he pulled her quickly. She practically floated over the parquet floor, past trembling treasures in their cases, white-blue porcelain and gilded nautilus shells jingled as Augustus' heavy feet tromped.

Böttger kept up, and soon they were out the palace door, where hurried footmen barely had time to open the carriage door for Augustus, who tossed Fatima's hand and sat himself. Fatima attempted to gather her skirts and step up. Augustus was oblivious to her need for help to get in.

Fatima startled when Böttger grabbed her around the waist, and she felt again as though she were floating. One hand was on her midriff, the other grasped her left hand. Though unlike Augustus', Böttger's hands were cool and left a dusted imprint on her satin bodice. A fluttering filled her belly as he settled her gently into the carriage. Then he caught himself, letting her go abruptly.

"Forgive me, my lady," he said, eyes growing wide. "In my haste I have lost my understanding of what is appropriate."

Fatima's breath caught up to her and she looked him full in the face, merely inches from him as Böttger, too, climbed in. He smelled of earth, burnt in a strange sort of way, and Fatima pressed her back to her seat, between the King and the prisoner alchemist.

The door shut, and the horses pulled quickly to whatever hellish place had dusted Böttger with its soot.

"Böttger, this is Frau Maria."

Böttger looked straight ahead. If he turned, he would be nearly nose-to-nose with her.

"Nice to meet another of your fine ladies, Your Majesty."

Another of Augustus' ladies. Fatima was placed in a category she had no control over. She desperately wanted to be different from the others, but so far, besides her skin not being porcelain white, there was little that set her apart.

The horses tore around Dresden, coming to a stop in front of a wooden pavilion. Augustus exited the carriage first, and lifted Fatima from the wavering steps. Böttger rushed out and stepped lightly down a set of stone stairs. The place was consumed in smoke.

Heat rolled up from below. A cellar door loomed. Fatima balked. Augustus and Böttger descended, disappearing and coughing in the gloom. Birdsong sounded. The horses stamped. A chill climbed Fatima's legs.

The men did not re-emerge. Fatima's breath shuddered in her throat and she gathered her skirts. If the King thought her weak, or disinterested, she might not get her menagerie. If she did not follow... She swallowed and took the stairs.

Heat engulfed her, sending a whoosh to her ears. She was forced to close her eyes.

"Oh, God," she said.

"It is not purgatory, Maria. It is progress!" Augustus' voice sounded from a distance. Fatima opened her eyes in time to be blinded by white light and another wave of heat. "He's opened the kiln! Maria, porcelain is in there!"

But Fatima could not see beyond the blaze and shielded her face with her hands. Though she tried to take a deep breath, no air entered her lungs. She squeezed her eyes shut. She coughed, took a moment, and when she could tell the light subsided, pink-white behind her lids fading to gray, she opened her eyes. Augustus was near an open mouthed stove, the kiln, and Böttger had a pair of tongs. He reached in, his arm disappearing into the white light.

Fatima stepped closer. A teapot, glowing red, was Böttger's desired target. He snatched it with the tongs and tossed it into a bucket of water. The bucket hissed, bubbling, then a loud explosion burst in the chamber and Fatima hit the floor.

Her ears rang. Water droplets, bath-hot, hit her bare hands. Augustus' voice was far away.

"It's broken," he said, though it was muffled and a high pitched sound waved over his words. Fatima looked up.

Böttger leaned over the bucket, rolling up his sleeves, from which dust and ash fell. "No, Your Majesty," he said. "It must withstand this test."

He plunged his hand into the water. Fatima stood, shouted at him, for the water must have been scaldingly hot. But Böttger tilted his face up to the low, blackened ceiling and laughed, withdrawing the pot, whole.

Augustus curled his mouth into a wicked smile, a look Fatima had seen in his large ornate bed. Böttger handed Augustus the pot. Augustus turned it in his hands, still steaming. Böttger watched the King, but then turned his face to Fatima.

She inhaled. Böttger's eyes were kind and blue, though worry creased their edges. His hairline was blackened, but golden hair was pulled at the nape of his neck with a piece of cord. Fatima tried to guess how old he was, and could not. Dare she call him handsome? Her ears still rang.

Augustus opened his mouth to speak, pointing a finger at Böttger, but Fatima spoke first.

The Porcelain Menagerie

"How did you make this?" she said. "It should have burst in the water."

The King and Böttger held their jaws open, then both of them smiled at her.

"My lady Maria, it is a special clay and formula I have been working on for years. The goal, as King Augustus can tell you, is to make our own porcelain. It is priceless. Worth more than gold, more than jewels, more than..."

Augustus cleared his throat. "Don't mention gold to me unless you plan on making it, alchemist."

Böttger settled, and looked to the ground. He put his hand out to Augustus, taking the teapot. He walked to Fatima, held out the pot to her. With two hands, Fatima took it. Their hands touched briefly and her stomach jumped. He held her gaze. The pot was warm, smooth, brick colored.

"I am an alchemist by trade, but my experiments making gold remain unsatisfactory. I believe, with the right materials, I can supply your fine King with porcelain instead. Uniqueness on this continent, something no one else has, something special and foreign; small, breakable, malleable. Something that will last lifetimes beyond us. This one needs to cool completely now."

Fatima blushed as he withdrew, taking the small pot back to the kiln.

"Do you believe this red pot is the special something?" Fatima asked.

Böttger turned to her, about to answer.

"No," said Augustus. "It is not white porcelain. It is not gold."

"Other pieces in the kiln next to it are white, Your Majesty, and my men will do anything for you, to prove ourselves. Trust me." Böttger opened another kiln. The heat burst forward, like a wind gust. Opal colored pieces glowed. King Augustus shielded his eyes, bending to the flames to see, and stood upright once satisfied.

"If you've truly done it," Augustus said, narrowing his eyes, "then your men shall have my blessing and their livelihood. For now, your captivity continues."

Böttger shut the kiln door and knelt at Augustus' feet. Fatima rolled the word captivity in her mind. She felt a kinship to Böttger, who was not unlike the animals in cages in Augustus' courtyard.

"Augustus," Fatima said, surprising herself. "I liked the way that red pot felt in my hands. I was reminded of carrying a baby bird. It felt like it was alive in a way...in a way that felt special and beautiful. Though it is not white porcelain, it is fine."

Böttger raised his eyes to Fatima's. She smiled at him, and watched his face turn the same color as the pot in the kiln.

"You liked it that much, my lady?" said Augustus, turning away from the fire. His face dripped with sweat, starchy under a layer of powder.

Fatima nodded. "I did, and in fact I would like to keep it personally."

Böttger let out a noise like a gasping animal. He put his hand to his heart. "Then it is yours, lady," he said. "Provided the King says yes."

Augustus took Fatima's hand and kissed it. She glanced at him, knowing that her behavior now could help her get what she wanted from him. She lowered her eyelashes and smiled demurely, squeezing his hand. His sweat melted into her skin.

"I want it, Augustus," she said. "Will you give it to me?"

"Yes, yes I will," said the King. She grinned at both the King and the porcelain maker, then her eyes jumped to the floor, head bowing with a small laugh.

Böttger's smile was broad. Augustus looked at Fatima from the corner of his eye, his lips parted. The heat pulsed.

"Thank you," she said.

Both of them replied: "You're welcome, my lady."

Though it was not a cold day, the air outside the kilns felt like diving into cool water. Fatima and Augustus left the porcelain maker and slid back into the waiting carriage.

"What a treasure," Augustus said, sighing in satisfaction. "Though it is still infuriating. Why can he not make gold? Why can he not make porcelain like we import? How can the Chinese make such a thing, so perfect, so delicate? And yet, we cannot?"

"Your porcelain maker has done well. Red is unlike anything else, yes?"

Augustus nodded. "Yes, though I wanted something different. I want gold, and he failed. I want true porcelain…"

"Getting something no one else in the world has *is* different, Augustus. You desire something unattainable, the same as me," said Fatima, choosing her next words carefully. "I hope I can someday get what I desire."

"What is it again that you asked for?"

Could Augustus see the pounding pulse in her neck?

"A menagerie."

"Ah yes, I had forgotten. Whatever you want. Organize it yourself, Maria. I'll assign a few men to help you."

The Porcelain Menagerie

She was confused by his response. Did it not seem a large thing to him? She was asking for money, land, people, wild animals, cages, food. Perhaps he was preoccupied with his porcelain... She would not let the opportunity pass her by.

Fatima leaned into him, wrapping her arms around his large chest. The onion smell of him, mixed with fire from the kilns, touched her nose. She stopped breathing as he pressed his body into hers. Her breath grew short until he let her go. It occurred to her during the embrace that he still had not called her Fatima.

Chapter 7
Johann
1732

"What are you saying, Lucius? It didn't crack?"

The kilnsman's bright teeth cut an eerie slice through his soot-stained face.

"It didn't crack. Off to assembly, then paint, and you have yourself a porcelain piece the Emperor of China would covet."

Samuel clapped Johann on the back, sharing the kilnsman's smile. Johann's heart soared. What would come next if the King loved his spread-winged eagle? Perhaps a complete dinner setting for him to design? A permanent position in the factory? A royal title?

"I don't want it painted," said Johann. "I want it to remain pure white, a true testament to the beauty of Meissen porcelain."

"It will have to have one small dot of paint," said Samuel. "Each piece leaves here with crossed swords, so the world knows it was made in Albrechtsburg. We mark our trade with it."

"Crossed swords?" Johann said.

Samuel nodded, beckoning Johann to follow him. Johann had not been allowed to explore the factory, and the black-garbed guard breathed down their necks as they wound around to what used to be bedrooms in a far off hallway. Porcelain filled the rooms. A fortune lived here. One piece was worth more than anything Johann or his father had ever owned. One piece was worth more than his life.

Tables, shelves, and packed wooden crates gleamed, stacked with creamy white. Samuel picked up a delicate plate and showed Johann the bottom, where crossed swords painted with two blue strokes were no larger than his thumbnail. The rim of the plate was golden pink, shimmering and unusual.

The Porcelain Menagerie

"I noticed this color on Herold's apron," Johann said. "What is it?"

"Ah, the copper-gold," Samuel said. "It took Herold years to develop this color. The King is particularly fond of it. No Chinese porcelain has it, you see. Only Meissen can make it; Herold has the only known formula, and no one knows it but him."

"I'm sure he guards it quite well," said Johann.

"You are correct. Rumor has it there is a book containing all the recipes and formulas for precious porcelain and paints we use. But I have never seen it, perhaps it is not real. Perhaps I am just a lowly modeler without the privilege of it."

"Am I a lowly modeler? Destined to make the same eagle over and over?"

Samuel smirked. "I doubt the King will allow you to make the same eagle again. I wish I could hear his words when he sees your masterpiece."

Johann blushed. A masterpiece? But it was his first one... maybe he had gotten lucky, maybe it would be the only one that wouldn't break in the kiln, maybe he couldn't make another like it, ever again.

The guard harrumphed, a noise of disapproval, and stared at the two men.

"Soon you'll have your own apartment here, Johann," said Samuel, gently replacing the porcelain plate on the stack.

"Samuel, the kilnsman said you tried to make an animal and failed."

"I did," said Samuel. "My animals were deemed not lifelike enough when they made it through the firing. But most of them exploded in the kilns. We didn't have the formulas perfect, yet—I think the clay I used had lobster shells mixed into it. Smelled like rotten cabbage and dead sea creatures. Augustus wants lifesize, you see, and it's nearly impossible."

"Do you think it was luck for me?"

Samuel shook his head. "Perhaps we got a good vein of clay? Perhaps the formula was perfect this time, with egg shells or alabaster, or something else? Perhaps the kilns were at a different temperature? Perhaps you have some skills you haven't told me of? Perhaps you were lucky, and the god of creation smiles on you."

Johann stared at this man with his hands covered in clay, knuckles bulging from use, and did not know what to think. "What if I can't do it again?"

Samuel shrugged. "You'll fail many times, and you may need a break. Then you'll make teacups like me. Or be chained to the floor of your quarters until you produce more, like those in the past. There's no telling why King Augustus does what he does with the workers here. But for now, lad, you're safe."

The summer sun streamed through the windows, reflecting on the white gold cache like snow in a meadow. Safe felt like a complicated word.

"No paint?" said Herold, frowning. He paced, arms flailing, his forearms streaked with gold and deep river blue. "Unfathomable! This factory's pride is in its paint, and I shall not allow the King to see this unadorned!"

Johann stood by his glossy eagle, breath catching in his throat. He did not know what to say.

"It is too late, Herold," said Samuel. He held his hands up defensively, standing between Herold and Johann. "The glaze is set, and you and I both know if we paint it now, it will crack or explode when we refire it. It's too large."

Herold's face grew purple. His hands were set into fists, dangerous devices near porcelain.

"The swords, Mr. Herold," said Johann, gathering all his courage. "If you please?"

"They will fade. Cold painting is not lasting. I should have seen and painted this before its firing to ensure the Meissen swords were permanent."

"Give the lad his damn swords, Herold." Samuel stood, his bumpy hands reaching slowly for the brush.

Herold and Samuel stared at each other, Johann behind them, watching. Pieces filled the painter's studio—beautiful plates, cups, serving dishes, platters, but they did not command attention the way Johann's eagle did.

The blue paint for sword painting was in a shallow dish, freshly mixed from cobalt and lapis, expensive and rare. Johann grabbed a thin brush, dabbed it in the paint, and motioned to Samuel to pick up his eagle. Not letting his eyes leave Herold, Samuel hoisted up the massive piece, and Johann raised the brush.

"Wait!" Herold said. "You'll do it wrong!"

He snatched the brush from Johann and, in four swift motions, painted the crossed cobalt swords on the eagle's base.

"I meant you no ill will, sir," said Johann. "We will try to paint the next one. Perhaps a smaller bird. But this eagle was meant to be white—to show the true purity of Albrechtsburg's porcelain. Surely you understand."

Herold said nothing. He returned the thin brush to the table and waved Samuel and Johann out the door.

The Porcelain Menagerie

The following day, bright blue skies greeted Johann as he journeyed to see King Augustus, the eagle tucked snugly, surrounded by clean hay, in a wooden crate. Master Benjamin met him at the castle gates. The same herald announced them, and the master and apprentice carried the crate into the gilded throne room together.

"Oh hoo!" Augustus leaned forward on his throne. Maria was seated next to Augustus. Katharina was nowhere to be seen.

Johann lifted the crate's heavy lid and nodded at Benjamin to grab one side of the fragile porcelain eagle. He locked eyes with his master and absorbed Benjamin's steady gaze, one that calmed the sourness that filled his mouth. His hands were slick with sweat, and he feared dropping his eagle, but Benjamin's help held it steady. They hauled it out together, its milky white surface gleaming.

The King rose to his feet and, though he limped, was down the stairs of the dais in a heartbeat. He swept his fur-lined cape behind him, the hide of whichever animal it was gleamed with clean slaughter. Augustus' eyes were bright, spellbound. He crouched near the sculpture, knees crackling, thighs bulging in his vibrant blue tights.

Johann expected him to say something, but the King was moving his mouth silently. He rose, rotated, and crouched again until he had circumnavigated the eagle. Sweat dripped down Johann's back.

Frau Maria stood, inhaling through her nose. She descended, her small feet barely filling the steps.

"After all these years, have you found your menagerie maker at last, Augustus?" she said, looking at Johann. Scattered strands of silver in her dark hair sparkled in an elaborate braid.

"Perhaps I have, my love," said King Augustus, eyes still fixed on the delicate yet strong feathers of the eagle's outstretched wings.

Benjamin, eyebrows raised, nudged Johann, urging him to say something.

"I carved this from memory, Your Highness," said Johann, bowing. "I hope it fits your vision of a porcelain menagerie."

"To fill the Japanese Palace," said Augustus, standing. He stepped to Johann, a hand's breadth shorter, and though they likely weighed the same, the width of Augustus' shoulders doubled his.

"The Japanese Palace is full of porcelain of all kinds but has no objects like this. It holds porcelain from China and Japan, redware from decades ago, but most Meissen animals tend to lack..." said Maria, struggling to find the word.

"Life," said Augustus, smiling at Johann with an intensity in his eyes that made Johann's legs tremble. "This is better than the menagerie Maria made, full of living, stinking, hungry animals."

"They lack life, Your Highness?" said Benjamin. "But your porcelain is lifeless sculptural art."

Augustus shook his head, smile broadening. He knelt once more by the porcelain eagle.

"You see this masterwork?" Augustus said. "Look at the knowledge in its eyes. This eagle knows the skies and its nest, knows its mate and its eggs. Knows how to snag a hare from the brush a mile away with talons like knives and a beak sharp as my sword. This eagle could take off, shattering the porcelain shell it lives in, and none of us would be surprised when its feathers emerge from glass and it soars. This eagle is as alive as you and I, master, and your apprentice must've put a beating heart into it or his own incantations cast into the fires of my kilns."

Johann dared not breathe, at the risk of breaking the spell that Augustus wove in the throne room. His words fell upon the white eagle and stayed there, draping it like a precious blanket. The King was more than enamored. He was enchanted.

"Make more," Augustus said, finally looking at Johann, eyes steady but wild under his bushy brows. "Others before you failed, and nothing has disappointed me more, Kändler. But if this was not a fluke, you may be the god of creation I have been searching for."

Johann bowed deeply and dropped to a knee. The gleaming eagle stared at the King, and though it was made of porcelain, Johann could hear an echoing cry of greatness.

Johann and Benjamin exited the throne room, leaving the eagle behind, still hearing the glistening words of the King. Johann nearly bumped into a person on his way out and muttered a quick apology. "Pardon me." It was Katharina.

Worry pinched her face. Benjamin walked on, beckoning Johann to do the same.

But Johann lingered. "You are the King's daughter. Why do you hide in the shadows, lady?"

She smiled cooly at Johann and turned her back to the hallway, pressing against the stone. She was beautiful: dark eyes with draping lashes, a full mouth, a full figure curved under crimson folds.

"I am, but not currently in his favor."

"Did you have an argument?"

"No," she said. "Not exactly. You've heard the rumors by now, they've spread through Dresden like wildfire."

"Albrechtsburg keeps itself closed to Dresden's rumors."

"And many other things. You'll hear it soon enough," Katharina said. "I know about you and where you make your precious wares. I've also heard not everyone in your position survives, held captive there."

"I've worked there for a few months now, and I am still alive. Seems not all rumors are true."

Katharina turned to Johann. Augustus' booming laugh echoed their way, and she cringed. Benjamin tapped his foot down the hallway and hissed a warning. "Johann!" he said.

"Is your rumor true?" asked Johann. "One word kept surfacing the day you arrived. Divorce."

"Quite a bold thing for someone like you to ask, porcelain maker." Katharina dipped her eyes to the ground. Benjamin came back and pulled Johann by the sleeve. Katharina looked up at Johann as Benjamin escorted him away. Johann nodded a curt goodbye, and Katharina stepped into the throne room.

Chapter 8
Fatima
1706

Though Fatima knew a quicker way around after her many trips to the new menagerie site, Augustus, who had never been there, insisted on guiding her. She pursed her lips and let Augustus lead the way, taking four steps for each one of his.

Finally the project was done, and Fatima had organized a gathering of townsfolk and the smaller ranked nobility to accept the King as he opened the menagerie for the first time. Augustus towered over her, and in the mid-morning sun, began to drip with sweat. His jewels sparkled, his curled wig gleamed.

The manicured lawn dipped into waving, tall grasses and eventually into the wooded copse no more than a hundred paces from the palace. Between the woods and the residence was the courtyard that, during hunts, held temporary cages. Beyond the woods and meadows, the city of Dresden spread broadly. The red-tiled roofs of homes and shops pulled Fatima's mind, and she allowed a stream of consciousness to emerge, wondering who was waking there. In the distance, a church bell sounded, and she absorbed it, replaying the pattern in her mind to keep calm.

Being by Augustus' side made her breath grow short. He was unpredictable. She smelled wine on his breath and worried about the animals ahead in their cages. Would they be subjected to his rifles if he didn't like the menagerie? Would she be forced to release them into his woods? Some of the animals were from the surrounding countryside, but some were rare. Surely he would see the value in keeping something exotic, one-of-a-kind, alive?

Ahead lay the black iron gates to the new menagerie. A crowd had gathered, workers and townspeople and palace residents: the cook in her

The Porcelain Menagerie

apron, the Englishman who kept record at court. Children wore their finest play clothes, tugging at their mothers' hands. A cheer erupted, and the crowd parted as Augustus and Fatima strolled forward, arms linked. Fatima kept the church bell in her mind, but acidic tendrils rose from her belly, and she blanched. The vast majority of common people in Dresden had not seen her yet. She did not know how they would respond to her, not a queen, or a royal, but foreign and unknown, by the King's side.

Augustus took a black key from a servant and handed it to Fatima. He motioned to her to unlock the gate. She blinked. This was unexpected. With a trembling hand, she put the key into the lock. The crowd grew silent and the click and subsequent slow opening of the gate was interrupted by a whimpering, distant bark. Fatima snapped her head up at the noise. A peacock emerged on the path.

The crowd made a cooing noise, enraptured, and gathered behind, eager to enter the place. Augustus swept his hand forward, allowing Fatima to be the first to cross the threshold. The menagerie was tree-covered; green canopies let in dappled light, but the place remained cool and damp. The sun strained in but could not find many permanent places between the leaves.

Black cages lined the freshly laid path, which wound around monstrous oaks and elms. Pines stretched upward, their tops unseen, and the crowd inhaled the heady smell of animal and woods. The wandering people narrowed into a line to fit through the gate and on the pathways. The peacock took up much space, shaking his rainbow feathers at the first bend, defending himself from those walking through.

Fatima stopped at each cage. Macaws, red and green, flashed their white eyes at her. The peacock eventually shuffled and pulled his tail feathers in, disappearing into the underbrush. She longed to leave the path to find him but continued onward, leading the people.

A deer, spotted, with twisted horns, brought in by Dutch-speaking sailors weeks ago, stood stock-still in the largest cage ahead. Many shipments of animals arrived daily, and she wasn't able to keep up with all of the deliveries and attend court. Some of them were a surprise to her.

Around two more bends were pairs of pure white doves, love birds in a small swinging cage, and a dark brown eagle with a piercing scream.

Then, the path opened up, and in their cages were more local creatures: a pacing fox, a boar and its partner. The largest cage drew a surprised noise from Augustus, whose dramatic boyish expression livened. A she-wolf lay calmly, front paws crossed, enormous.

"Oh, Fatima," Augustus said. "She reminds me of you."

Fatima turned to the King. He called her Fatima. She raised her chin. "Why is that?"

"She is beautiful. Look at the size of her! Imposing, impossible to tame, a vicious huntress who gets what she wants. But I long to bury my face in her fur."

Augustus turned his gaze from the wolf to Fatima and touched her waist. She flinched. He laughed. Was he describing himself, or was she vicious, like he said? Perhaps she could be...

Fatima and Augustus lingered by the black barred cage, keeping their distance, when a loud, wild scream sounded. A monkey was tied to a post around the corner. Fatima rushed to see, glad for an excuse to rid herself of the King's touch. She felt uncomfortable with the crowds of people watching Augustus with her, knowing she was yet another mistress, knowing what her purpose by his side was. The monkey had a metal ring tightly clamped around its neck and pawed at it desperately.

Fatima fell to her knees and picked up the creature, though it flailed.

"Where is the key to remove this?"

Augustus shrugged, gesturing to the servants that filtered through. Fatima whistled loudly, and a nervous menagerie man hustled forward.

"My lady?"

"Remove this collar. Can you see this animal is in distress?" said Fatima. The servant looked from Augustus to Fatima, who held the screaming white-faced monkey. Augustus nodded at him.

Producing a ring of keys, he freed the creature, which then buried itself in the crook of Fatima's arm. She tried to set it down, but the monkey refused to leave, its child-like fingers pinched her skin in desperation. She looked to Augustus. He was gazing at the milling crowd, seemingly embarrassed by Fatima's whistle and the scene she caused.

"Seems one animal will leave this menagerie today if you choose it, lady." He smiled at her, narrowing his eyes as if offering her yet another favor. "But I will educate you a bit. Animals cannot be in distress. To feel pain is a human quality, Maria."

Fatima blanched. "That is not correct, Your Majesty. From a young age I have known all creatures feel pain and fear. Can you not see that?"

Augustus' smile did not fade. "Animals, my dear, are made for man to do what they wish."

"Animals are living things. If you think that about them, what must you think about children, or women?"

Fatima hoped for playful banter. She smiled at Augustus sheepishly, holding the monkey to her chest. But when she met the King's gaze, her expression dropped. Augustus did not move his eyes from hers. His smile faded and a serious look of superior anger came to his face. He grabbed the back of her arm. It hurt.

The Porcelain Menagerie

"Women are also made for men to do what they wish."
He pinched.

The back of Fatima's arm was bruised—yellow-green, a purple splotch, now five days old. She inhaled through her nose as she slid her day dress over her head. Its blue sleeves covered the mar on her smooth skin. At least it's not a scar, she thought, and it will continue to fade. But the memory of Augustus' Herculean hand, strangling her arm, remained strong. In fact, the memory pulsed.

The monkey she rescued from the menagerie made a chortling sound, tied to a small table, chain around its waist instead of its neck. Fatima's breathing slowed and she went to the creature, which she had named Amar.

"Hello, lovely thing," she said. The monkey pawed at her skirts and Fatima unclipped its golden chain from the table leg. "Perhaps I'll be able to let you roam free today?"

The monkey rested in the crook of her elbow, tiny paw curled where Augustus' hand left its mark. The creature needed her. Her destination this early morning was the kitchens, like the last few mornings, on a quest to find what Amar would eat.

Fatima straightened her dress and checked her tightly bound hair in the warm copper mirror before unlocking her chamber door. Posted outside were two men, including the rat-faced one who still smirked at her, no doubt the memory of buttoning her dress still flaunted to his friends.

Amar squirmed in her arms, and Fatima put her down as she closed the door. The rat-faced guard licked his lips, giving Fatima a long look. The monkey cooed and stopped. The guards stared down at the creature. Amar hopped, paused, and then sprayed a bright stream of urine at the rat-faced guard.

Fatima covered her mouth with her hands and pulled gently on the tinkling chain. Amar skittered toward Fatima, face split open in a human-like smile.

The kitchens were down several sets of stairs; warm with flagstone floors. Fatima saw few people in the early dawn. Most of Augustus' friends in the palace stayed up late playing cards and drinking bottle after bottle of wine from France. Even the guards were lazy, except the ones meant to keep other men out of her chambers and report her comings and goings to Augustus.

The cook was at a steaming stove, hair tied in a loose bun, covered with what could have once been a white kerchief, now damply gray.

"Now, Maria, I don't like that creature in my kitchens," she said.

"I know, Brunhilde, but she's not eating what you're sending, and I need your help."

Fatima stood several steps from the stove, a large stone contraption that was fed logs to keep its fire blazing. Amar clung to her dress, burying her small face in her elbow. "You can call me Fatima, cook."

The cook wiped her hands on her apron and turned to Fatima.

Brunhilde turned up a corner of her mouth and ran her pointer finger along the furry spine of the monkey. The cook's mouth had marionette lines that drooped into low jowls. Gray curls poked out from her bun. She was shaped like a countryside pear, dull clothing clinging to her broad backside.

"You've told me that. Heaven forbid one of my assistants hears me callin' you anything but your Christian name."

"Your assistants aren't here, Brunhilde."

Brunhilde inhaled through her nose and beckoned Fatima to a vast cupboard with a shelf filled with produce. "She didn't eat any eggs? Nor the radishes?"

Fatima shook her head, peeled the monkey from her dress, and took a carrot offered by Brunhilde. Amar sniffed it, refused it. "No, and I fear if she does not eat, she will perish."

"Ach, her spine is showin' through. Try this." Brunhilde uncovered a small basket of forest strawberries, as red as Fatima's new cape.

Fatima took the smallest one between her fingers and bit its small, sour end. The pink flesh showed through. She waved it in front of Amar's face. The monkey grabbed the berry with its human-like paw and took a delicate bite. Then another, and quickly, the berry was gone.

"Meant for a special thing tonight," said the cook, staring at the monkey's working jaw. "But I can say they weren't no good."

"I am in your debt," said Fatima. "No one else could help me like you."

"Not true," said Brunhilde, emptying the berries into a rag and twisting the top. "Your menagerie men are willing, and able, but they're frightened of you."

"I understand why," said Fatima. "I am the King's woman."

"One wrong move toward you, and Augustus will lock them away. Or make them the front lines of his next hunt. I've seen many men brought through that kitchen door, shot clean through in a hunting accident. Always wondered if they're true accidents or if..." The cook shook her head, waddling back to the stove.

The Porcelain Menagerie

"Or if what, Brunhilde?"

"Nothing. Keep yourself out of trouble. Do the King's bidding. Take care of your animals. Go to court. I've seen far too many in your position come down for herbs, claimin' hurts and aches and sicknesses of the female type. Moon tea, sick tea, death tea. Things I shouldn't know, but can't erase from my memory, my girl. Don't fight him, Fatima." She used her name.

The bruise on the back of Fatima's arm pulsed. "And if I choose to fight...?"

The cook picked up a large wooden spoon, stirred a boiling pot. Around the room were jars on wooden shelves, nailed to the stone walls, filled with unlabeled dried greens. Stems hung from every ceiling beam, filling the space with fragrance. How many of them were deadly...?

"May God help you."

Fatima's requirements to be at court disrupted her wishes to be in the menagerie. The people were the most exciting part of the day, but she drummed her fingers on her heavy chair and stared out the window, thinking of what the husbandry men were doing among the black-barred cages. Amar flitted, lighting from one chair arm to the back and around again, clearly annoying Augustus as he kept throwing looks at both Fatima and the monkey. He had not touched her today. For that she was grateful.

"Is it almost done, Augustus?" Fatima said, leaning toward the window. Augustus, too, was antsy, wiggling his large leg. A wooden sinew-bound tennis racket rested at his feet.

"One more, I believe, then off to the game courts," he said. "You'll come to watch me play tennis." It was not a question.

Fatima's mouth parted, and her mind rattled with an excuse to not join him.

But the doors to the long room opened and in stepped Böttger, the porcelain maker, with two crates stacked in his arms. Fatima sat up and gathered Amar's chain. Amar trembled in Fatima's lap as Böttger slid the crates in front of the dais.

Augustus rose. Fatima stayed seated, watching the King and the porcelain maker. Böttger's eyes flickered to hers and she leaned forward, eager to erase the distance between them. Her skin grew hot and Amar shifted, jingling the chain.

"What have you brought this time, Böttger? Gold at last?"

"No, Your Majesty. My many attempts to make gold have proved no more fruitful than your many attempts to make your wife, the exiled Queen, love you."

Augustus stepped down the dais, fists clenched. Fatima curled Amar closer to her, ready for rage. But the King laughed, demonically, a sound that made Fatima jump. She did not understand the relationship the King and the porcelain maker had, and this exchange was surprising.

Böttger smiled. Fatima's palms tingled.

"Instead, Your Majesty, I bring you white gold. At last."

Böttger threw open the larger crate, and inside was what looked like grayish-white mud, the color of a June morning cloud. Augustus unclenched his fists and grabbed a chunk of it. Clay, Fatima realized. Raw clay. The King smelled it. Then, the porcelain maker opened the other crate. From under a pile of straw, Böttger drew out a small, thick teapot. A white one. Augustus dropped the clay and gasped.

Böttger knelt and held the pot to him. A bead of sweat dripped from Böttger's forehead to the gleaming floor. His handsome face shone. His raised knee showed a burned-through pant leg. Augustus took the porcelain.

"What I need now, King Augustus, is the space to make the finest porcelain in the world for you. The kilns must be larger. I need storage for the redware you saw, for the production of the white I promised you. I need a place to make this work, and you and I both know where is best."

Augustus held the pot in the air and remained crouched near the floor. Fatima could only see his back and his broad shoulders, his face was directed at Böttger. Fatima strained to hear the word Augustus spoke to Böttger, wishing he whispered it in her ear.

"Schloss Albrechtsburg."

Chapter 9
Johann
1732

Master Thomae stood at the black gates of Albrechtsburg to say goodbye. Johann's meager belongings were slung in a leather pack on his back. Albrechtsburg, per the King's orders, was now Johann's home. The gate creaked as Johann opened it, and Thomae lingered. It was clear he would not cross the threshold. The echoing words of Katharina rang in Johann's head, *held captive*, but he said nothing to Thomae. His master was proud of him.

"When your menagerie is finished, you and I shall meet at the Japanese Palace and celebrate your accomplishments," Thomae said. He smiled with pride at Johann. Johann smiled back, reluctantly excited to make the King's porcelain animals.

"I am indebted to you, Master Thomae. How can I ever repay you and your kindness?" Johann said.

Benjamin gestured at Albrechtsburg. "By making it here, you have made every moment spent teaching you worthwhile. Continue to make me and your father proud, boy. Don't forget where you came from."

Johann nodded, turned to the castle, and called a final goodbye to his master. Benjamin waved and gave a bow. Johann was truly on his own now, with only the castle and porcelain makers ahead to guide him.

The dark entrance of Albrechtsburg loomed, casting a cold morning shadow despite the warm June sun. Leaning against the ancient stone wall was the thin guard, in black again.

"I should know your name if you're going to trail me constantly," said Johann.

The man in black stood upright, clicked his tongue, and stepped into the sunlight.

His eyes were bright and seeking. His hair shone black-blue out of the shadows. "My name is Chien Haoran. Everyone here calls me Hao. *You* are the King's current favorite modeler. My job is to prevent anyone from knowing the entire porcelain formula. That means I will indeed trail you constantly."

"Call me Johann. Know that I have no intention of stealing the arcanum. It is so guarded here that I couldn't know it, anyway. Besides, I have a mark of writ on its way from King Augustus to make him a porcelain menagerie for the Japanese Palace. It may take me a lifetime, but I intend to finish it and move on, perhaps back with Benjamin Thomae."

"One job will turn into many," Hao said. He stared at Johann with an unmoving expression. "That letter from the King has arrived already." He handed Johann a folded letter sealed with the King's initials.

Johann opened the letter. It was a long list of animals and birds. He scanned it: fox, wolf, parakeet, boar, unicorn, gryphon. He blanched, feeling his chest grow heavy. How could he give all of these animals to the King if some of them were mythical?

"Have any of Albrechtsburg's residents left with the precious formula, then?" Johann said this with a smile, but Hao's stern gaze met him.

"They have, but I find them, my cohorts do, or the King's army. They do not last long. It is easy to trace thieves who quickly earn silver. The formula has leaked, in bits and pieces. Thieves tend to run to the cities that will support their evil habits. You have years of work ahead of you, Johann."

A small black mark of worry grew in Johann's belly. Hao was right. The amount of work that waited for him was enormous. He did not know where to begin but his eagle was so well received, perhaps he should make another bird. He had now practiced a beak and feathers.

Hao led Johann to a narrow stair he had not been allowed to ascend before today. It was on the opposite side of the meandering hall that led to the rooms full of painters and modelers. The narrow stairs led to a series of apartments, connected by a moss-grown hallway, walls slowly dripping with water.

"How are these halls wet, with the fire from down below?"

Hao did not answer. He took a coil of keys from his belt and unlocked the farthest room on the right, shoving the door open for Johann. The room was clean, humid, with a narrow bed, small table, single wooden chair, tall and ancient wardrobe. A wide paned window looked out over the city of Meissen. Albrechtsburg was on a high hill, and Johann felt like a bird here, seeing the extent of the city and countryside that spilled outward. A sparrow flitted by, and Johann breathed in the space.

"These are the nicest rooms besides Christian Herold's," Hao said. "Examine your letter and choose your next menagerie piece. I will be making my rounds."

"So you won't be following me any longer?"

"I always follow, seen or unseen. I know where the secrets are kept, where you are supposed to be, and where you are not. Get to work, porcelain maker."

Johann nodded awkwardly. Home, he was learning, was only sometimes a place of comfort. Below him in Albrechtsburg, fires burned. Below him in his father's home, his brother's body crumbled to earth. Eventually, he must descend the stairs. But today, he ascended to the workroom, where Samuel waited.

"What's this, Johann?" Samuel asked, brushing a clay-dirty hand through his hair. His eyes shone with anticipation staring at Johann's letter. Johann had not considered how interested Samuel would be in the menagerie.

"The King loved the eagle," said Johann. "He wants more. This is his list. I'll start with more birds, as I have experienced feathers once already."

Samuel grinned and slapped Johann on the back. Johann handed him the King's list, and Samuel took a square-headed nail and tacked it to the wall, shaking his head.

"This is quite a list! Mostly birds, for now?" Samuel said. "What's next?"

"Ah, whatever I can see from my window," said Johann. "Seeing as the King loved the eagle so much, I think focusing on the birds from the list will be fine."

"He did not ask for an aviary, Johann," said Samuel. He sat, ran a rough thumb over a sandy edge of the cup in his hand, smoothing it. "You'll need different things soon enough."

"He asked for nearly three hundred birds of thirty varieties," said Johann. He stared at the list and the black pit in his stomach grew a little larger. "I do not know how long it will take me to make those, but the birds are smaller than the bears and lions he requested. Easier, I suppose."

"Make whatever you can, Johann. Your work will be prized, no matter how long it takes you. But if you want a break from the birds, you should venture outside Albrechtsburg."

"Am I allowed to do that? Could I go to the menagerie in Dresden, near the palaces?"

"You are supposed to make everything on this list," Samuel said. "I will not tell you no, and can help distract Hao. When you find a gryphon and a unicorn to sketch there, please tell me. You may find more animals nearby in our small city of Meissen, first."

That afternoon, Johann followed the narrow path down the backside of Albrechtsburg out the kitchen door, nearly tripping over his feet as he ensured Samuel kept Hao busy with a mysterious broken window in the modeler's room. The goat farm down the road would serve Johann's purposes for now.

Johann ran, though his swarthy frame resisted it, and his breeches rubbed on the pink skin of his ankles. The green hill of Albrechtsburg fell behind him, purple flowers trailing down into the broad field beyond, where white blossoms and an apple tree shaded the grasses. Brown goats grazed, and in the distance, a ram.

The goat reminded Johann of Augustus. Horns curled behind it, spiraling powerfully, and its eyes held a certain kind of knowledge, ownership of this herd and this meadow. The kids that played around kept their distance, and the ram regarded them with pride. His kids, his does, his own goat kingdom.

Johann knelt by the stone fence, curling his feet awkwardly underneath him, and pulled out a scrap of parchment, which blew in the wind. He put kohl to it and began to sketch.

He wiped his sweating brow and at the crack of a twig, looked up. The ram was a step away, separated by the fence's stone pillars, rectangular pupils strange. Johann took a deep breath and raised his kohl.

Half an hour later, he had his sketches. The brown and white goat was alive on the page—the texture of its fur and horns drawn in detail, its lashes and delicate mouth conveyed as a husband artist might paint his wife—lively, energetically curved.

He made his way back up the steep hill. The window to his room flashed, and steam rose from the dungeon windows. Two pairs of draft horses pulled a wheel attached to the castle, churning minerals on a great grinding mill. June in Albrechtsburg offered both beauty and brutal heat. The hill climb made Johann's ankles creak, and he could not draw a deep breath by the time the kitchen door came into his sight. He continued climbing to the steep, narrow stairs, through the mossy hallway, and directly into his bedroom, where he placed his sketches on the table and collapsed into a chair, dust clouding around him. He had but a moment to rest before he had to get back to work.

He changed out of his sweaty clothes, donning charcoal gray pants and brown waistcoat over a cream tunic. Johann touched the mossy wall

The Porcelain Menagerie

on his way to the modeler's room and paused by the doorway, catching his breath. Hao and Samuel were talking.

"I'm not sure he will be able to do it again," said Hao. "Beginner's luck. The kiln must have been set perfectly. None of yours have turned out like this."

"He doesn't know how many times I've failed," Samuel said. "It feels like more than luck, Hao. Perhaps this is our relief from the pressure of Augustus to produce. I cannot tell you how free I feel."

Hao laughed, a dull short sound. "Free is a word you use too easily."

"You know what I mean. A noose is no longer around my neck."

"You still have a chain around your ankle, even unseen."

"Böttger's chains are still in his chambers, you know, even twenty years later. And his book is somewhere, hidden in the mess he left behind."

Johann took the opportunity to walk in.

"Johann," said Samuel. "I told Hao you went to sketch. He watched you from the window. Did you get what you needed?"

Hao watched him from the window? Johann was not pleased, but not surprised. "I got what I needed, and more."

"May we see?" said Hao.

Johann flipped through his dry parchment, showing them the goat.

"If you can make this, Johann, you'll have the King bowing at *your* feet," said Samuel.

"The King will be here tomorrow, lads."

Johann and Samuel turned abruptly at Hao's words. Hao stood near the window that showed Dresden in the distance, clear though it was a two-hour horse ride.

"The King is coming here?"

"We are lucky for the warning."

"Does this happen often?" said Johann. He looked around the room at his companions, worried.

"You never know what to expect at Albrechtsburg." Hao turned, swept from the room and spoke from the doorway. "Hopefully you'll have a rough sculpture to show him. He is an impatient man, but remember, without him and his patronage, none of us would be here. He has created this place for us, for you, to make art as your life's work. Do not disappoint him."

Johann swallowed. The King wanted lifesize. The goat was large. A lump of white clay waited in front of him. He raised his tools.

Chapter 10
Fatima
1706

In the hallway near his chambers, Augustus' nostrils flared, staring. Fatima curtsied, aware that her bosom billowed over the seams of her best day dress, a pale blue. She would fight Augustus' hands during their trip to Albrechtsburg. The porcelain factory had been open for six months, and Böttger had invited them to tour. Böttger. Since seeing him in the courtroom and in the old kilns, Fatima had thought of little else.

In the menagerie, she daydreamed he walked with her. In the courtroom, she perked at new attendees, hoping it was him. At the tennis courts, where Augustus walloped counts and dukes and visiting dignitaries, she dreamed Böttger arrived and beat Augustus at his favorite game. During the nightly parties and gambling games, she thought of what the porcelain maker might be doing. She talked to Amar like the monkey was him—though the monkey responded with chattering coos and no words of affection.

In the King's dark chambers nearly every night, Fatima blocked Augustus' image from her mind and replaced it with Friedrich Böttger's. The King enjoyed her more when she let loose to the dream that the porcelain maker took her in his arms. She kept this secret, this fantasy that Friedrich Böttger was her lover.

Today, Augustus was to take her to the porcelain maker's factory. Augustus smiled at Fatima, missing molars like caves. His black eyebrows wobbled. Fatima could not help herself and smiled back at him, ready to go to Albrechtsburg, where she would see Böttger, whose face rarely left her mind.

"I have retrieved our meal from the kitchens," Fatima said. They planned to eat on the grounds of Albrechtsburg, a basket of fine food

The Porcelain Menagerie

prepared. In the kitchens, Fatima also downed, in two large swallows, the moon tea Brunhilde had prepared for her without being asked. Though she imagined the artist, the consequences of her actions with the King were real. Monthly, Fatima frequented the cook's kitchen for moon tea.

"*Our* meal," Augustus repeated. He was childlike, his expression joyful. Bile rose to her throat, the flavor of it matching the moon tea, and she swallowed. She tried to enjoy this moment when Augustus was not touching her, when she didn't have to imagine, when she was so close to seeing Friedrich.

Fatima stood in the doorway to the King's chamber, her body turned sideways to indicate she was ready to leave. Augustus nearly stumbled forward, following her and closing the bedchamber door. Black handle. Two locks. He used two separate keys to close them, taken from a hidden belt wrapped around his bulging middle. She waited, raising her chin, which was carefully powdered. She wore her sky-pale dress not for Augustus, but for Böttger.

Augustus stroked his stubble and led Fatima through the towering, diamond-shaped hall that led to their waiting carriage. The carriage was beautiful, with a red interior and pulled by six white horses. Footmen waited. Fatima relaxed a little. She wasn't alone with Augustus. She could try to enjoy the journey through Dresden and nearby Meissen, which she had not seen much of, despite her living in the city for months.

The two footmen's eyes dipped to her waist, undoubtedly wondering what lay under her pretty frock, and Augustus let her climb in first. She was keenly aware of three sets of men's eyes on her backside. Always viewed as a creature of lust, regardless of the work she did in the menagerie or the input she gave the King at court. As the King's mistress, most people assumed Fatima's only reason for existence was pleasure. She could not fight them on the assumption. It pained her.

Fatima sat down fast, seeking comfort in the window on her left. Augustus climbed in and sat with his legs spread wide, thigh touching hers. She did not move her leg away. Though she did not love him, she accepted her place by Augustus' side. What else could she do? She lived with only specific, secret wants; without hunger, without much risk. Though she did not agree with the King, nor his policies, nor his womanizing, she had no choice. Her risks were her fantasies. But no one saw the complicated visions of Böttger in her mind.

Fatima briefly closed her eyes and imagined how it would feel if the porcelain maker was seated by her side. Her breath deepened. Her spine softened. Böttger's face emerged. She was not surprised by this—he was often in her thoughts, with his white-stained rough hands and blackened clothes. There. That was her risk.

The carriage careened off, rattling wildly on the cobbles, and Fatima asked Augustus to part the gold curtains so she could watch Dresden unfold. He did so grandly, proudly. This was his city, after all, and without his influence, Dresden would have been mild and old. Now, it was ornate and luxe. The road to the small town of Meissen that held the castle-factory, Albrechtsburg, was curved and beautiful—gleaming buildings with copper roofs surrounded them, some piled with forests of scaffolding, some covered in statues, all impressive.

"Each statue was of my choosing, you know," he said. "The craftsmen here make the finest carved marble, and I chose to decorate my city with elements of the ancient world. I have even had my face put on a sculpture of Atlas, holding the world on my shoulders."

"Why not Christian elements, Augustus?" Fatima was genuinely curious. She had noticed from her first arrival in the city that most things were inspired by ancient fantasies—satyrs, gargoyles, dragons, nymphs.

"Christianity is what drove my wife from me. I was foolish enough to think my conversion to Catholicism wouldn't change our marriage. I thought it would even make her happy, as it allowed me to accept the title of King of Poland. But she hates me for it. Religion is everything to her. Good riddance! Never much cared for that woman. Besides, she loves God more than me."

"Is that not what most women are asked to do? Love God, then their husbands?"

"I prefer a woman who will worship the right form of God if I request it. Religion can get you what you want, if you work it into politics. I would not be King of Poland otherwise. You know, religion is how I changed your name."

"I don't like the name Maria," Fatima's tongue said before her mind stopped her.

Augustus smiled broadly, chuckling and waving a thick finger at Fatima.

"You have made that clear. I know there are a few who call you by your old name in the palace. The court is used to accepting a mistress by my side instead of the Queen, but you being baptized and given a Christian name certainly helps them like you, Maria."

Changing her name was supposed to make others like her? Fatima gazed out the window, memorizing the skyline and wishing they would stop to grab a loaf of bread from the bakeries or flowers from the carts in front of Augustus' gold-topped masterpieces. She thought of her past—the days of red and gold tents in Buda, with her promised Muslim husband and his warm laugh. But he was gone, slaughtered in the battle of Buda nearly ten years ago. She was a child. He was a distant memory. She spoke nothing of this to Augustus. The carriage careened on, taking a bridge that connected Dresden to the countryside.

"What will we see at the porcelain manufactory?"

Augustus smiled. "Progress," he said. He lowered his tone. "Wealth. Böttger."

"Böttger." Fatima looked at her hands, then darted her gaze to Augustus' eyes before looking away quickly. She should not have said Böttger's name in that way. The road rolled on for a bit, rocking cobbles beneath them.

"You are not like others who unfold to me. Your refusal of your Christian name. Your origins, your plaintive eyes. The way you try to hide that you desire others."

She blanched, keeping her panicked face to the window. How did he know?

"You cannot hide much from me, Fatima."

Her name. "I thought you'd stripped me of that name."

"You have not *allowed* me to strip you of that name." He sidled closer to her, inhaling deeply, rustling the hair by her ears. A chill spread up her neck. She wished it were not him. She wished he were Böttger. "But I have given you your menagerie and this special attention to go to Albrechtsburg. I have forgiven you the moon tea you drink every month. I am a God here, Fatima, an all-knowing one you do not want to anger."

Panic cascaded down her throat, settling in her belly. She tried to breathe it out, but her breath came too quickly, and beads of sweat dotted her forehead. He had complete control of her.

Augustus laughed lightly. He reached out to her dark hair, tugging one of her braids. He used his large hands to undo it, sighing as he did, gently pulling and wrapping the strands around her ear. He was gentle, for him, but his hands were so large, and Fatima's neck so small… Gooseflesh erupted on her arms. Her pulse echoed in her ears. Albrechtsburg was in the distance, and she pointed, breaking the moment. "Tell me of Schloss Albrechtsburg."

Augustus let go of her hair and straightened, prideful. "Kings of Saxony lived there for generations. Stood empty until I decided to use it."

"For a porcelain manufactory?"

"Mhmm," he said. "No one in Europe knows the formula for porcelain except the men in that castle. But Böttger cannot leave Dresden without permission, not even the twenty miles to Albrechtsburg."

"I thought he lived in Albrechtsburg? At least in Meissen?"

"No, dear. He knows the formula for porcelain and is halfway to getting me alchemist's gold. Can you imagine when we can make our own gold in Saxony? It is a risk to let the man leave. It's a long horse ride for the man daily, as he's shackled in Dresden, but he will be seeing Albrechtsburg's progress alongside us today. Chains wait in the chambers in the manufactory."

"Chains? Surely that's not needed. He told you he cannot make you gold, that he has failed. If you can't trust him to live there and be in charge of the factory, how can he make your porcelain?"

"Ah, you don't understand. The reign of a king is not much if he has nothing new to show for it. No one has this, Maria, no one. It is important to be the king who owns something no one else does. Including a man like Böttger. I cannot let him leave. The chains serve as a simple warning to the man."

She gently shook her head. Black smoke poured from a nearly hidden window near the ground. Albrechtsburg belched, dirtying the crystalline skies.

"What do they do in there to make such smoke? Looks like the mouth of a dragon."

Augustus laughed, an unpleasant rumbling. "A dragon indeed."

"So if the factory is doing well, you'll let Böttger go?" She pushed him.

Augustus narrowed his eyes, his mouth twisted. "Böttger lost his freedom long ago."

"Perhaps that is the way my animals feel in the menagerie." Fatima was unsure of why her mouth kept opening, why she engaged him in such a manner. "Perhaps they are intertwined, Your Majesty."

"Intertwined?"

"The menagerie and your porcelain factory. The exotic animals and Böttger."

Augustus sat up straight, jostling his thigh away from hers—immediate relief.

"They're both caged!" he said in a boyish voice. "That's precisely it, Fatima."

He'd used her name three times.

Augustus leaned forward, and beyond, the castle drew closer, a black spired chapel rising from its center impossibly tall. It felt different than the residential palaces—older, and though it was white, darker, stranger. Fatima inhaled sharply. The outline of a man stood near the arched door. Böttger.

The Porcelain Menagerie

"I hope he will not disappoint me today."

"If the smoke belches like this, they are producing something."

Fatima smiled from her seat as Böttger took steps toward the carriage. Her heart raced. The man she'd dreamed of, in front of her. In his hand was a leather book. He closed it, tucking it under his arm.

"What if..." Fatima offered, vying for Böttger's freedom, "what if Böttger has done more than you think, and today he deserves to lose his chains?"

Augustus opened his mouth, raised a finger, and fell silent, scratching his temples. A flurry of white skin flakes fell to his rough face. He leaned back on the gold seat and put his arms behind his head. A sharp smell of onion-sweat and laundered clothing mixed. Fatima inhaled through her mouth. Böttger waited outside.

"Like your monkey? You command something to be freed and expect to get what you want?"

"Not like my monkey. Like a man who has succeeded at his task."

"Success and freedom are not equivalents," said Augustus. "The chain is mine to tighten until I get what I want, and then, when I get what I want, I tighten it more." He leaned forward and reached out to touch her. She pulled her ribs to her spine.

"Even if you get a god of creation, it seems; who knows how to make every version of gold you desire," she said, doing her best not to breathe him in. "You won't be satisfied. Even if you find someone who can perfectly make something from that white gold you love, the yellow gold that fills the coffers?"

"That should be Böttger," Augustus said, "but he fails. You have that in common, being chained to me, though, yours is light and beautiful."

The whites of his eyes gleamed. He leaned into Fatima, too close. She had nowhere to go. He kissed her; stuck his tongue in her mouth. She kept her eyes open, waiting for the crawling snake to withdraw. Böttger rapped on the door. Her stomach caved in. Augustus leaned back in his seat, satisfied, wiping his mouth with his broad hand. Fatima waited for the door to open, avoiding a glance at Böttger. What did he think of the kiss? She wanted him to show her pleading eyes, to tell her in some small way that he, too, thought of her. She looked up.

But Böttger stood there, brows knitted, book under his arm. He did not meet her gaze, though she leaned imperceptibly forward to take in his face and breathe the air around him. Fatima exited the carriage. Though she often thought of the handsome porcelain maker, once faced with him again, she realized how silly she had been. He thought of nothing but porcelain, Albrechtsburg, the invisible shackles around his wrists. He thought nothing of her, the King's mistress, whose life was one of ease compared to his. No ripples of jealousy entered his body when he saw that kiss.

She retreated, clasping her hands behind her back and settled in step behind Augustus, whose frame created a shadow. Fatima swallowed. The men talked of production numbers and debt and kilns and Fatima's infatuation was crushed, the image of the porcelain maker's hands on her waist instead of Augustus' blown away like the smoke from the cellars.

She shielded her eyes. Ash swept the ground. She could pretend the stinging tears that threatened were the fault of this place, and not of her fantasies with the porcelain maker broken like one of his fine wares. The dragon of Albrechtsburg loomed.

Chapter 11
Johann
1732

"Up, up!" Samuel shook Johann awake. This dawn was dewy, the windowsill slick with morning. Johann nearly fell out of bed.

"We're sketching today, boy. I've arranged it all," Samuel said, the lines in his face creasing into a smile. "Much better than traipsing down the hill. We've permission! Rare, joyous freedom in permission!"

Johann inhaled deeply through his nose and stood, pulling on his worn brown breeches and sliding on the handed-down leather shoes his Da had worn for years.

"I've been tasked with documenting the jobs of Dresden in porcelain. Flower sellers, musicians, actors. Need to get the anatomist's."

Johann blinked awake. The anatomist's? His palms prickled. That was where the Leichendiebe longed to take his brother, Herman. He turned to Samuel to protest, but his companion had already grabbed Johann's kohl pencil and satchel and rapidly escorted him out the door. The white flowers on the moss wall ahead shivered with the men's wind.

Hao waited at the bottom of the wide stairs, hands clasped behind him. He reached an arm out to the open door of Albrechtsburg, ushering the men outside. Johann saw him notate in his ledger their leaving.

"I've no more parchment in my satchel, Samuel," said Johann. "I planned on finalizing five bird molds today, you know, the goat waits, too..."

"Ah, you've plenty of time for that. We'll stop by the menagerie, too, so you can see more animals. We'll find something for you to sketch in. We'll be back before this evening's visit by Augustus. You'll ride, I'll be in the carriage going over some numbers."

Hao waited for them, bent at the waist, expressionless and cool. He extended his hand where the black carriage pulled by a single draft horse and a bay mare waited, saddled, the only ones available for the few trips from Albrechtsburg. Samuel practically leaped into the carriage.

"Why so eager, Samuel?"

"I have rarely left the factory other than to go to the palace and deliver porcelain, Johann. Since Böttger...well, Augustus is hesitant to let any of us leave. Perhaps someday, we'll be allowed to come and go as we please. But it is not that time in the history of Albrechtsburg."

"Böttger?"

"The original porcelain maker. He ruined his life when he decided to..."

Hao shut the door, the carriage jolted, and Samuel's sentence was unfinished.

Johann hauled himself into the bay mare's saddle and blinked the last of his sleep away as the horse descended the steep hill through Meissen, into Dresden, beyond crossed the stone bridge that stretched impossibly onward, beyond the capabilities of a manmade structure. He marveled at it, counting boulders until they melted into the wobbling, wild street beyond where newly constructed buildings of the same quarry rock stood. While makers set out their wares, the clanging tone of his father's church bell sounded. He slowed the mare, pressing his thighs into her back.

There was always a reminder of Herman and Marten, and for that, Johann was grateful. But over the melodious sound of the Lutheran Church bell, he realized that in a few short hours, he would see a place he'd blocked from his mind's eye: the anatomy chamber where the Leichendiebe desired to deliver his brother's body for jangling silver in their pockets. He pushed the idea from his mind, settling his breath, reminding himself that Herman's remains were safe, and likely by now, too far gone for the anatomists to want him. Still, the fear lingered.

The King's palace emerged, its sculptures by Benjamin Thomae mounted on each corner. The castle grew larger, statues glaring, and the bay mare snorted, shaking her head.

The anatomist waited, but Johann's mind was on his brother below the parsonage floor. The ride felt short, though he knew they covered quite a distance. Sixteen miles. The mare sweated. The sounds of the city overwhelmed: clopping hooves, shouts, and animals braying, fiddles from street performers, the river and its stone bed, more church bells, and in the distance, faint singing. Johann tried to still his trembling hands, but they grew pale and damp on the reins.

Smells of the muddy river and its banks rolled over him. He was reminded of the faded smell of decay rising from the cellar door that lasted for months, apparent to him when he visited his father before he left for Meissen. He didn't know if his father noticed. Johann tried to push the smell away. He could not, though the parsonage was far away.

The anatomist took residence in a chalky, gray building in an older part of Dresden. No scaffolding cages waved over the structures here as construction was completed decades ago, and this building appeared ancient.

Samuel clambered out of the carriage. Johann breathed heavily through his nose, unable to move on the mare's back. Samuel's excited smile faded.

"Come, Johann," Samuel said, wary of Johann's lingering. "Are you quite well?"

The past haunted him. Fear of harm coming to Herman was not easily shrugged away; carved into him like a deep scar. He tied his horse and followed Samuel through the dark wooden door.

Inside, the sunny place was clean enough but smelled of sharp herbs and salt, masking something he could taste in the back of his throat. Deeper, earthier, rotten. He pushed his fear down with a swallow.

A thin man with a deeply parted white wig waited for them, a hint of a smile on his face. He clasped his hands behind his back. As they approached, the man bowed. Only Samuel reciprocated. Johann felt as if his feet were the rocks of the Dresden bridge.

"Welcome, gentlemen, porcelain makers," said the man. "I am Gunther, court surgeon. Nice to see you again, Samuel."

Samuel tipped his hand, and Johann stayed still. Gunther swept a navy tailcoat behind him and led the men to a narrowing hallway where curved doors were shut and locked. When they turned into a bright courtyard, Johann realized he'd been holding his breath. Gunther noticed and cleared his throat.

"Here, sirs, we keep specimens in salt, vinegar, and pure alcohol. You may smell rosemary and camphor and aloe, depending on who did the embalming today. We haven't yet got the funding to fully understand what makes a body stay fresh."

Gunther opened a wide double door; the smell overwhelmed. The room was cool, a former church sanctuary, but in place of the pews, tables bore shrouded bodies.

"A child from the poor house, a woman pulled from the Elbe, a criminal, and an unusual specimen, a freak if you will, deformed at birth," Gunther said. Johann cringed. "But surely you don't want these. Tell me, Samuel, what would you like to see?"

"Yes, good question," said Samuel. "I want to sculpt you, Gunther, in the act of a surgery. Imagine the profession captured in porcelain forever. The King desires all of his most special denizens in white gold. You, performing, would be simply delightful."

Johann balked. Delightful? Samuel removed his satchel and drawing tools and motioned for Johann to do the same.

"Samuel," said Johann, leaning into his companion and whispering. "I am not well." Samuel regarded him with widened eyes. Johann's skin grew clammy; sweat dripped down his double chins. The bodies all changed shape, all became Herman, even under shrouds.

"Go sit outside, Knabe. Go on, then. We'll talk for a moment."

He called him Knabe, boy. Johann sighed. Samuel took him by the shoulders, guiding him. He stumbled to the bay mare, who shifted from foot to foot in anxiety of the smell of the place.

"What is it, Johann?" said Samuel. Johann was surprised at his genuine care.

Johann kept his chin lowered but looked at Samuel. "If I tell you something, will you keep it a secret?"

Samuel leaned in and drew the side of his mouth upward. "If I did not know how to keep secrets, I'd be dead by now."

Johann took a breath and raised his chin. "My brother, Herman, was born with a hump on his back, one leg shorter than the other. Killed my mother during his entrance into the world—cruel thing. I loved him. He...he passed recently. The anatomist wanted him and watched the coroner and doctors visit my Da's parsonage. They offered us 500 thalers for his body."

Samuel stood straight, brows furrowed. He absorbed this information abruptly, like a sudden blast of cold wind. "Who offered you?"

"My Da calls them Leichendiebe. He's watched them steal bodies from the church graveyard for a few years now since the anatomist came to Dresden."

"The anatomist's college is not funded. King Augustus won't sign off on it. This is why they take the bodies."

"So, the people in there are stolen?"

"Not people anymore. Bodies. But I hope none are corpses from the Lutheran cemetery…" Samuel bit his lower lip and looked to the building where the anatomist waited. "Where's he buried, your brother? Have you one of those cages over his grave? Surely he is no longer needed, all bones now?"

Johann could not imagine his brother's bones. Perhaps it was true. He hesitated to answer, opened his mouth to describe the small casket under the floor of the parsonage, but looked at his hands instead.

"Say nothing, Kändler. It is safer that way. If I'd have known, I wouldn't've brought you to this place. Why don't you go on? Go to the menagerie without me."

Johann nodded, wiping sweat from his brow, and Samuel left him leaning against the building. The horses watched warily. Johann found his bearings after a few moments and mounted the bay, heaving his thick leg over her, gooseflesh prickling on his arms despite the day's warmth.

He rode the horse to the menagerie. Memories of his childhood, the warm body of his little brother pressed to his side, flooded him. He passed the tailor who'd cut Herman's special clothes, the grocer who slipped the boys sweet small pastries, the flower shop that reminded Johann of his mother, whose milky, lavender smell found him despite the unfamiliar chemicals of the anatomist's chamber still clogging his nostrils. His eyes welled with tears and he had an imaginary conversation with his brother on the back of the bay horse, longing to be back in his father's parsonage where Herman's ghost clung to every brick.

"Why'd you have to be born like that, Herman?"

I couldn't have existed in any other form, brother.

"What's it like, where you are?"

Like air. I can see you and Da here, and Ma is near.

"I wish you were still here, and her too."

We're closer to you now than we were in life. Don't forget that.

The menagerie gates beckoned him inward. Johann swung down, wiping his face and exhaling and realizing he had no parchment on which to sketch. He entered the gates, cursing himself for being sentimental and foolish and sad. His lost loved ones' voices faded. The cages were still. He wound around to the right, where the trees filtered green-white light, and bird caws met his ears.

A peacock feather lay on the path ahead of him and Johann bent to pick it up, holding its flickering shine to the sky. In the distance, something moved. He glanced away from the feather and toward the largest cage, the one that held the lion. Johann took steps around the bend, feather still in his hand. It was her.

"Porcelain maker," said Katharina.

"Katharina." Johann gripped the feather tightly.

"What brings you here uninvited? We made it clear that you were to come here chaperoned." Katharina rose from the ground near the one-eyed lion's cage.

"I...I'm sorry. My fellow sculptor Samuel sent me away when I...I could not handle the terrors of the anatomist."

Katharina pursed her lips and straightened her skirts, blue as the Elbe. They swayed like a belled flower.

"I do not think I could either."

"I am here to sketch, but...in my haste I did not bring paper." It was in the carriage, with Samuel's things.

Katharina had at her feet a basket, and a wooden bucket of what looked like raw meat.

"I grabbed a few books from my mother's old chambers to pass the time after I finished feeding the animals. I can linger here longer, then, avoid that palace, full of men who are desperate to be like Augustus. Perhaps there's a book with a few pages to spare."

"Desperate to be like Augustus?"

"The culture my father has created is one that echoes his own ideas of grandeur. Mostly, it is control they seek. Controlling the women, the men below them, the animals. This is a place of escape for me. The workers here leave me alone."

"And the workers, do they let you take the job, feeding the animals? Seems like that is not a king's daughter's place."

"No. It is not. But I am a bastard. And I like it, so I do it anyway."

"That is rare for a woman to do what she likes in Augustus's palace, is it not?"

Johann bit the inside of his cheek. Had he overstepped? Gossip about Augustus' mistresses loudly crackled through Dresden. Johann could name five just in the last few years. He shifted uneasily. Katarina smirked at him.

"Mr. Kändler, do you spend much time around women in Augustus' palace?"

"No, no, I have never...I imagine that women in the palace are—"

Katarina raised her hand. "Do not try to imagine a woman's life. You could never understand. You could never know. If you do not don a corset and bleed, you can never speak for us."

Johann swallowed. He looked to the ground. This might be a king's daughter, but she had the fiery words of someone much different than he had expected.

"I have not spent time with many women, not after my mother's death." There must have been something kind, sorrowful, in the way Johann said the word *death*, for Katharina softened.

Katharina paused. She bent to the basket and held out the oldest looking book to Johann. "I do not know what I would do if my mother was not here. I am sorry you've lost your own."

"Thank you. I'm sorry, for...for assuming. Please, call me Johann."

The Porcelain Menagerie

"Well, then, Johann, what do you want to sketch today?"
"Both times I have come, you have been near this lion."
"He is an old friend of my mother's, nearly twenty years of age."
"How did he lose his eye?"
The lion rested, twitching its ears at the flies.
"That's a question for my mother, and her story to tell, not mine."
Johann tucked the old book under his arm and got close to the cage. Katharina stood by his side. She smelled like melon and sweet dessert.
"Last time I saw you, you asked me about my divorce," said Katharina.
"I am sorry, it was not my place, I spoke out of turn and..."
Katharina hushed him, looking pleased at his apology.
"My father has to grant it. It's complicated, as he is supposed to be Catholic and I am protestant. I have to get permission from both the church and my father. My husband is angry. He will lose lands and titles without me as his wife. I want to be rid of him. He is unfaithful and mean, a man of disgusting habits and bastards, nearly thirty years my senior..."

Johann thought but did not say that the man sounded an awful lot like her father the King, whose rumored bastards numbered in the hundreds. Katharina was one of them.

"Your father must grant your divorce? And the church? It is legal here, yes?"

"The church waits on Augustus. My church understands my reasons, though the Catholic church might not. My husband is cruel." Katharina folded the sleeve of her cloak. On her forearm, a pink scar bubbled. Johann recognized the type as the kilnsmen in Albrechtsburg shared such scars. It was from a burn.

"Why do you show me this?"

"As proof. Others spread rumors about me—that I am the one who's taken a lover, that I have wronged my husband. I do not know if you gossip, herr Johann, but spreading the truth would not do me harm. The poker he held to my arm was cooling as he did this. I cannot imagine what will come next."

The lion yawned. Johann gripped the small, gray book. Katharina turned away, folding her sleeve down. As soon as the burn scar was covered, she lifted her head, shaking her braid.

"I will leave you to your work, porcelain maker. I trust you. Do not put your hands between the bars. I won't tell my mother you're here. Perhaps I will see you again at the lion's cage." She gathered her things and left, surprising Johann with a smile. His face grew hot. Her long lashes darted to the menagerie path and he watched her walk, her red cloak now clean though it still gathered leaves at its hem. The sweet perfume cloud she left behind momentarily paralyzed him.

He exhaled loudly, snapped back to the world and the lion waiting in its cage. He lifted the moldy book, bound in dented gray suede. The pages were stiff and brittle, but it would do. Johann wiped its mildew-spotted cover with his sleeve and brought out a black kohl stick from his overcoat pocket.

He opened the old book, scanning it for a blank page or empty margin.

But in the margins of the Latin text were hand-written notes. He skimmed them, straining to see the faded kohl. Only whispers remained, but Johann made out numbers. He recognized some of these things. His gut churned.

These were firing times. He flipped the pages: there was a listing of clay beds, chasms in the earth that yielded bad clay and good, and ratios for clay-to-alabaster. Things that made porcelain. Notes on redware. Scrawling across the page: CRACKED! FAILED! SUCCEEDED! And line after line of how much clay, how much alabaster, how much crumbled shards to mix together...

What had he been given by the King's bastard daughter? If anyone found Johann with this book, his career and his life were in jeopardy. The formula was here, even if it was fractured, and as his eyes danced from page to page, he realized with every word he read, the dangerous knowledge leached into him like poison in a well. He shut his eyes and the book. His pulse rippled through him.

What was he to do? Should he turn it in or keep it secret? If Hao or Samuel saw the book, even flipped through a few pages, Johann did not know what would happen. Hao would assume Johann knew things he was not supposed to know. Would Samuel protect him? Would he be chained to the floor of Albrechtsburg, like that fool Böttger, whose life was ruined there?

The lion rumbled, opening its one yellow eye. Caged, powerful, handsome. His corded mane tangled, dense. The kohl trembled in Johann's hand, and instead of allowing panic to overcome him, he drew the lion's panting mouth.

On the bay mare on the way home, Johann tried his best to avoid thinking about the book and the anatomist, but he could not erase the images from his mind. His illustrations of the lion in the old book covered some of the porcelain formulas. Perhaps if he filled the book, he

The Porcelain Menagerie

would not be punished if it was found. Then he realized he may have well doomed himself: his drawings were easily identifiable, and there was no denying now that he had seen the book's contents.

He soon crossed the stone bridge over the Elbe, where the waters reflected olive light, and Johann realized with relief the day was nearly gone. Silvery puddles dotted the road. The sun sank behind the buildings. But ahead at Albrechtsburg, the King's carriage waited, led by six white horses.

He had forgotten Augustus was coming.

Chapter 12
Fatima
1706

The grand foyer of Albrechtsburg was nearly empty. Böttger led the way, and turned to Augustus and Fatima with a pained look as they stepped through the threshold. The feeling of heat was abrupt, like stepping into a stove, and Fatima's breath caught in her throat. The air was thick and sticky, with a smell she could not identify, undercut by the damp, earthy scent of stone.

The castle was a vast, never-ending cave—coffered ceilings in plaster and wood, red and white tiled floors. Star-like structures held the ceiling aloft, not unlike a cathedral. A wide spiral staircase led upward, and a rumbling came from below.

"The kilns," said Augustus at a particularly loud shaking. "That's a place I'd love to see!" He laughed.

Böttger shook his head. "Your shoes will melt down there, Your Highness. Many have succumbed to blindness, burned beyond recognition. The fires, sometimes they burn uncontrollably. If I could stay here a few weeks to regulate—"

Augustus interrupted Böttger. "I cannot have my alchemist going blind. Yet another reason you stay in Dresden under careful watch."

Böttger turned away from Augustus. Fatima curtseyed as he acknowledged her.

"You remember my lady Maria, from far away."

Far away. He could not say she was taken from her family of Turks as a child, removed from her only friend Aurora, stripped of her religion, and forced to remove her identity, including her name. *Maria, from far away.*

"She is impossible to forget, Your Majesty." Böttger's blue eyes met

The Porcelain Menagerie

hers. Fatima's lips quivered. He remembered her. "Welcome to Albrechtsburg. I can show you more of the redware you liked so much."

Böttger held her gaze. Fatima realized he expected her to respond, but she was stuck in the imaginary world where he was hers.

"It would give me great pleasure to see it."

"Show us everything, Böttger. You and Maria have something in common. She is in charge of my menagerie and its living animals. You are in charge of my porcelain—you both have things not seen elsewhere in Saxony."

Fatima longed to tell Böttger that Maria was not her name, to whisper the word Fatima to him, to feel the roughness of his dry, strong artist's hands. He smiled gently at her and his eyes darted to her pink mouth. She blinked wildly. Böttger motioned her onward, holding her gaze. Realizing Augustus watched, Fatima's pulse quickened.

She followed Böttger, and he gestured to the old murals, faded on the walls, stained glass windows, broken and melted from the excess heat. He told her of the lions illustrated on the tiles below her feet, about the expansive and stunning ceiling, and that the room used to be for dining and entertaining.

"Do you need this large of a manufactory?" Fatima asked, becoming so engrossed in Böttger's tour that Augustus seemed to fade beside her. A fireplace larger than she was framed the three of them, its hearth cobwebbed.

"Yes," said Böttger. "We are making hundreds of redware pieces, working on perfecting the white, and perhaps in the future, the largest white porcelain collection made in Europe. I wish to use the upper rooms to refine my gold making."

"An alchemist," she said.

"Yes, I am."

Augustus stepped closer and put his finger in Böttger's chest. "Don't make me a liar, Böttger. You still tell people you are my alchemist, though I have not seen gold. Do not call him an alchemist, Maria."

Böttger turned his face to the floor, and fell still. Fatima blinked at King Augustus, who showed quick rage with a scowl. Augustus kicked ashes from the massive long-cold fireplace onto Böttger's feet. Chains rattled, attached to the stone hearth.

Böttger did not move, keeping his eyes on the floor. Dirt piled at his worn, burnt shoes. Augustus reached down, picked up a filthy chain, and smiled wickedly. Augustus drew the chain between his hands, as if measuring its weight. He threw it over Böttger's neck, and Böttger nearly collapsed to the floor.

Fatima did not move. Her ears rang. The urge she had to rush to him, to release the chain... but instead she sucked in her gut and squirmed. Augustus took a step back, laughing, as Böttger slid the chain off. It left marks of rust and dirt on his shabby clothing. His face blazed with embarrassment. King Augustus pointed, coughing at the end of his chortle.

"Tell him of the little menagerie I gave you, Maria," said Augustus, as if nothing had happened. He reached for Fatima's hand. She shrugged him off, anger and embarrassment forcing tears to her eyes. He grabbed her hand roughly. The same hand he had given the key to her menagerie with, and her beautiful jewels, and a safe place to sleep, and a factory for artists to work on their craft. This man was complicated and imperfect and while he had made her dreams come true, he had also taken so much from her.

"It is my place of happiness, the menagerie," said Fatima. Her voice trembled. "I should hope you will visit, Böttger."

"Oh, call me Friedrich, my lady." He said this so casually.

Augustus scoffed. "She will not. Show us the stores, the completed pieces." The King abruptly pulled Fatima's waist.

But the way Böttger said his name, *Friedrich*, echoed in Fatima's mind and she curled her mouth around the word without putting it into the air.

It stayed, close and careful, on the broad part of her tongue, and she'd hold it silently until she was alone, when she'd say it loudly, when the early morning vapors of fog on the menagerie paths obscured all people and she felt safe. *Friedrich*.

Chapter 13
Johann
1732

Johann skirted the bay mare around the turning mineral wheel and slid off her back quickly. She exhaled loudly as he undid the cinch too fast, and turned her head to bite him. Johann dodged, sliding the saddle down her slicked sides and leading her quickly into the small stables where a young black gelding and the draft horses who ground minerals lived.

He blew out several fast breaths of air and wiped salted sweat from his temples, running to Albrechtsburg. Hao and Samuel would have his neck for being late to the audience with Augustus. The new prized porcelain maker, missing? He could imagine their panic.

Johann rushed up the servant stairs near the kitchen, his heavy body stomping. Near the stony hallway to the unused dining room, he heard the booming, low voice of Augustus, and a response from a lighter one. It sounded female.

Johann ran down the hall, nearly colliding with clay-dusted workers at the end of their day, and stopped firmly in front of the modeler's room. He pulled his tunic, wiped his brow, and descended the spiral staircase.

Augustus, Maria, Katharina, and Samuel stood peering down the blackened staircase that led to the kilns.

Samuel turned and in seeing Johann, excused himself.

"I'm so sorry," said Johann.

"Tell that to Hao, he's searching the castle for you, boy."

"I will. I was sketching in the menagerie. Katharina was there, too, I..."

"Don't tell anyone that. Play like you've been working upstairs this whole time. Make it sound like something special just for Augustus."

"It's *all* special just for Augustus, Samuel."

Samuel nudged his shoulder, then wrapped his hands around the backs of Johann's arms and pushed him to Augustus and the women.

"Your Majesty," Johann said, bowing low.

"Ah! My god of creation." Augustus took heavy steps away from the black, burned walls of the stairwell.

"I apologize for my tardiness. Perhaps you'd like to see what I've been working on? I would love to show you the most secret of rooms here."

"Surely that's the kilns, where we cannot go?" Augustus said, his eyes gleaming.

"No, Your Highness, it's the place where I mold your animals, where the water troughs on elevated tables sit for the makers, where tools and hands make kaolin into art...where—"

Augustus was suddenly by his side, and pressed his wide, salty hand over Johann's mouth. "The secrets should remain secrets. Show me this room, but speak no more."

Johann's breath grew moist and hot under the King's hand. Augustus pressed, hard, pulling his hand away, sending Johann reeling backward. The King smiled, showing no teeth, and Maria approached, eyes wide.

Katharina stayed behind several steps, hands clenched into fists. Johann steadied himself. He clenched his teeth, boiling with threatening anger.

Hao broke the silence. "Up the stairs, then, to the modeler's workshop," he said, waving a thin arm in the right direction.

Johann followed last, wanting to lick his lips but feared tasting the King's hand. He wiped his mouth with his sleeve. He wanted to feel anger, to strike out, to scream and stomp his foot. But his father's voice from the pulpit came to him: *"He that is slow to anger is better than the mighty..."*

Herman's voice emerged, a ghost's dialogue: *"Proverbs 16:32..."*

Keep me calm, he thought, and proceeded to follow Katharina's trembling form up the spiral staircase tower. Samuel waited ahead.

"Johann, you must watch yourself!" he said, whispering with fear in his eyes.

"I was trying to help distract him from the fact that I was late."

"Revealing secrets of the arcanum will get you chained to the floor or worse."

Johann felt his breath, hot in his nose. He sighed, forcing his anger out, uncurling his fists.

The Porcelain Menagerie

"Make your wares. Deliver them. Improve the manufactory. Make your money. Keep your mouth shut."

They reached the top of the tower, white stairs below curling like a shell. Augustus, Hao, and Maria were led onward. Katharina paused, mouth pulled into a thin line, waiting for Johann. "Are you alright?"

Johann was surprised at her care.

"I am." He wanted to tell her he was angry, embarrassed, ready to fight her father the brute king, but he felt as though Herman held his tongue, felt his brother's twisted hand on his shoulder, holding him back. He managed a small smile.

"You feed my father's obsession, porcelain maker. You hold more power than you think."

Johann paused, looking at her face that was so like her mother's. Her eyes were steady on his, unwavering. Her mouth parted, as if she had more to say. Augustus' voice boomed from the top of the stairs, calling them upward. What was she asking him to do? Surely she didn't think Johann could help with her divorce.

"Perhaps, Katharina, *you* should plainly tell your father what you need."

They ascended, Johann behind Katharina by one step. The staircase was long, their conversation whispered. Her black braid dangled in the air. She glared and let out a single "Ha!"

"I have. Over and over. But he arranged my marriage, and sees no reason to acquiesce with my request. Even if my husband arrives at court with an army behind him, my father will not budge."

"Separating complicates your future and your father's past."

Katharina stopped and Johann met her on the white marble stair. They were halfway up, the others far ahead of them now. He breathed in her rose perfume, an underlying saltiness of nervous sweat.

"I do not have to explain myself to you. My husband is cruel. And despite the fact that his father was my father's best advisor in Poland, I do not see the benefit of remaining married to him."

"King Augustus of Poland." Johann sighed. Though Augustus was King, he did not live in Poland, and was made King by a controversial vote that involved drunken nights of threats, uncountable monies, and coercion. Though many knew the story in Saxony, few openly spoke of the controversy it brought.

"So you are sure. How do you plan on getting your father to betray an advisor?"

"I hope my mother can help me. She can get him to do things no one else can. She got him to open her menagerie. Somehow got him to accept the red porcelain as a gift to the people of Saxony, which in turn led us here, to Albrechtsburg, where many people make money and the wares are sold."

"Without your mother, you're saying I wouldn't be here?"

"Before I was born, she had some influence. But she was married off to please the queen."

"The queen has not lived in Dresden for many years, this is known."

"Her rebellion against Augustus and her dedication to her religion are..." Katharina smiled. She hitched her skirts and began ascending again. "Admirable." Johann raised his brows at the chosen word.

"All you have to do is ask your father, Katharina."

"I already have. If it were that simple it would be done. What I need from you, porcelain maker, is for you to use your power."

"What power do you think I wield?"

"The power of desire. He paces his chambers thinking of what's coming next from you. He can think of little else. Give him a tease, a rest. Let my problem become his focus, let his hand take the pen and sign."

Johann paused before they wrapped up and around, each spiral like a shell preventing them from seeing Augustus and Samuel, already at the top of the stairs.

"I will keep with my schedule, my lady. I cannot rush this."

Katharina twisted her mouth.

They came to the hallway where the stairs dumped, both short of breath. Samuel extended a hand to guide Augustus, leading them into the modeler's room. Maria leaned cooly against the wall.

"Becoming acquaintances or...?" she said. Johann blushed.

"Mother, Johann can help us. If he pleases King Augustus, father will be more likely to sign the documents."

Johann pursed his lips. "I have to tell you, ladies, that I do not think my production schedule will sway your King one way or the other. I believe the only thing I will do by rushing is risking my own neck."

Maria stood upright, fingers pressed against the cool stone wall of Albrechtsburg. "It is good that you fear him, porcelain maker."

Johann looked down at his leather shoes.

"But let me tell you—we have more fear in us than resilience now. Help us and we can make sure you have access to the menagerie and all the other tools you need to thrive here."

"I believe Hao can arrange those things for me, madam."

Maria narrowed her eyes and Katharina swept over to her side. They were nearly identical. Samuel's head appeared in the doorway.

"Hello, tour continues this way, ladies, Johann," he said.

The Porcelain Menagerie

Johann clasped his hands behind his back and waited for the mother and daughter to cross under the wide, curved door. Inside he imagined he'd find Augustus, staring at the water troughs, spinning wheels, carving stations, honey-combed ceiling that felt like a cave of wonders.

But the ladies didn't cross through. They stared at Johann, pleading yet venomous, until Augustus appeared and grabbed Maria by the arm. He pulled her into the room. Johann followed. Samuel waited by a table filled with Johann's molds, ready for pressing precious porcelain clay into.

"In two days time, these molds will be filled with clay and taken to the kilns," Samuel said. "We're refining them now. A thrill to see essentially the skeleton of the porcelain menagerie. Come look, get close, you can see the detail."

The three visitors dipped their heads and examined. Samuel pantomimed to Johann, telling him to stop his conversation with the women and keep his mouth shut. A wave of fear rushed, and Johann bit his lip.

"What's this?" Augustus said, snapping Johann from his state. He pointed to an unpainted, matte piece.

"Ah, some are unfinished yet, Your Highness. We're presenting both to you, painted and unpainted."

"This muddy, dull white is what our old friend Böttger could not make, rest his soul. Look at you now. I cannot wait to see it gleam!" He spat, turning quickly. The women lingered around the molds, turning their ears lightly to the conversation.

"Women, come," Augustus said, heading for the door. "I want to show you the stores of perfect porcelain, something that took decades to perfect."

"Without Böttger, it never would have even started," Maria said under her breath as she walked past Johann. He tilted his head. How did she know that? He followed.

Chapter 14
Fatima
1706

Fatima settled into her broad, soft bed after scrubbing herself in a cold tub. She stared at the coffered ceiling and clenched her legs together. The day blurred by her—the smell of Albrechtsburg lingered. The rolling, bouncing horse and carriage ride and her absolute fatigue made the room spin. Her neck ached, as if the chain were there...

She faded into sleep at last but was soon interrupted. She shot up at a crackling knock at the door. The cook Brunhilde appeared.

Fatima sat up, clutching the blankets to her chest like a child. Though she was brave, the last time someone had come to her in the dead of night, she'd been taken from her childhood bed.

"Brunhilde?!"

"Listen to me, child, the King has been to the kitchens."

Fatima's breath grew tight in her throat. Brunhilde shut the door, ensuring it latched.

"He's told me to stop your moon tea."

"For what reason?"

"My lady, you can guess at that."

"He wants me pregnant?"

"Not necessarily. He wants control, love. And you're not givin' it to him."

"He saw me, today, with Friedrich Böttger, and I made a fool of myself. It was punishment in his bed tonight."

Brunhilde sat on Fatima's bed, smoothing the burgundy coverlet. Fatima wanted to crawl to her, bury her face in the cook's wide, warm, yeasty arms. Instead she let the covers drop and sighed, tears wetting her face. So many times she had held them back, but now she did not.

The Porcelain Menagerie

"I do not like Augustus. Nor his bed. I do not want to be here. I miss my friend Aurora, her son, Maurice. I want my old name and my old life and to leave this place."

"You know that's not an option, Fatima. He's got his sights set on you and that's what he'll get."

"Brunhilde, how many have come before me?"

The cook shifted, and her eyes left Fatima's face.

"Many."

"How many have had babies?"

"...Many."

"What good does it do him, and why? Why not be faithful to his wife and make heirs?"

"I'm not sure he's thought it through. It's not exactly somethin' you can ask the man."

"What if I leave?"

"He'd follow. Send men after you. I've been told of the ones who've tried. Their graves are scattered throughout Saxony, some unmarked. They never make it far unless they are dismissed—assigned to marry a dignitary or member of his court, so they keep their mouths shut about what happens here. He is charming and kind and brutal and wild, and you never know which version of him you will get. But I know what version exists for those who flee."

"Why are you telling me this? Do you tell all of the mistresses?"

"Most of them had other ladies to tell them. But you're here alone, with naught but a handmaiden and me to help you. I'm sure Marianne tried her best to explain before she left?" Brunhilde shifted closer.

"She left in a hurry."

"You know from Aurora?"

"I know Maurice is Augustus' child, and that she sends letters to the treasury asking for coppers for his care," Fatima said.

"Does he pay it?"

"Most times, yes. Sometimes, no. He has at least claimed the child as his. A rare thing."

"Likely he has a marriage match for Aurora, someone who'll accept his son as his own and take the bills on himself."

"What will happen to me, if I get pregnant?"

"Well..." Brunhilde hesitated.

"Will you do as Augustus asks? Remove my access to the moon tea?"

Brunhilde looked down at her plump hands in her lap. Fatima realized then she asked a lot of this woman, who should not be in her chambers, who risked so much by telling her these things. She also realized that if other mistresses went to her for moon tea, there was no telling of what was actually in their cups. The monkey stirred, chirped a strange sound, jumped on the bed and into Brunhilde's lap.

Böttger, chained to the floor of Albrechtsburg, flitted across Fatima's mind's eye; the many workers of the porcelain factory, the caged menagerie animals, the women. She thought of Marianna, the King's former mistress, and how she left on Fatima's first day in Dresden. Off to marry someone she'd never met. *Would it be so bad...?*

Perhaps a husband would treat her kindly or call her by her real name without malice in his mouth. She could leave Dresden, see Europe, maybe go back to find her mother and brothers in Buda. Her imagination wandered there—where waving grasses expanded on the outskirts of the city she'd been taken from. The towers there were taller and older, and she could close her eyes and walk the city with little guidance. Home.

But then she thought of the menagerie. Augustus had given that to her. No...she earned it. A thought that made her mouth quiver. Without earning it from Augustus, she would not know the place she loved most in her life: the flickering sunlight through the trees, the black cages, the wandering beasts, the clip-winged birds. The empty enclosures that waited for new arrivals and creatures from far, far away. Could she risk what she had built? People worked there now; they'd lose their positions if it were abandoned. What would become of the place if she were gone? Despite her desperation, she wondered, too, what kind of life waited for her outside of Dresden. If she truly wanted out, she had to devise a plan to keep her sanctuary place safe.

"You understand, Fatima, the gift of having a bastard of his means your body likely won't be found in the Zwinger moat. If you end up there, it was likely your own decisions that made it happen," said Brunhilde.

The gift of a bastard? Fatima's heart beat wildly. Was that what Brunhilde saw this as?

Friedrich Böttger's defiant face emerged...The sounds of chains on Schloss Albrechtsburg's floor...

"I think I can make these decisions on my own, Brunhilde. Thank you for coming to my chambers."

Fatima slid from her bed and peeled Amar from the cook's lap. She ushered the cook out into the dark, cool hallway. She shut the door slowly, watching her through the crack. Amar twittered. Her only friend in the castle was trying to control her. She locked the door, pulling the key from the hole and putting it by her bedside.

She could not sleep, despite the long day. Each time she closed her eyes, rapid dreams came to her of the many mistresses of Augustus the

The Porcelain Menagerie

Strong. Fatima felt angry, unusually so. Little was in her control. She desperately wanted to change that.

She rose and slipped on a soft cotton gown, pulling a red overcoat around her shoulders. Amar stayed asleep. As the first rays of dawn cascaded over the parapets, she darted from her room to the stables, where a sleepy, startled boy saddled her a black mare. As she crossed the long stone bridge she knew Augustus had named for himself, she looked back. The howling of the she-wolf in the menagerie broke the silence of the sleeping city.

Fatima steered the black horse to Friedrich Böttger's chambers, a sturdy, deep-gray tower near the kilns she'd visited months ago, where the pulsing red pottery felt like a river stone in her hands. Those kilns were now cold, replaced by the rumbling basement of Albrechtsburg.

In the tower, a window shone with a single golden candle. It was surrounded by a garden. It was beautiful. Why did Friedrich have such luxury if he was a prisoner? She hid in an alcove and waited until she was sure no footsteps sounded on the yard, then darted up the stairs, and into the first open doorway on the right.

The small foyer was gray with dawn; the curved windows showed the King's castle and the nearby woods that hid her menagerie. She paused, watching birds turn and glide away. The smell of a damp night garden mixed with something burnt.

She rapped on the door, heard stirring inside. Second-guessed herself; sour slime rose to her throat. But before she could dart away, Friedrich answered, in a dressing gown white as the moon, feet bare.

"Frau Maria?"

She flared her nostrils and stepped inside, pulling his cap from his head and pushing her body into his.

"Call me Fatima."

Chapter 15
Johann
1732

Johann was late to start his day, plagued by long dreams in which his brother and mother were both alive, trying to escape the anatomist's chamber. In the dream, Hao carried Herman, and Johann carried his mother. When they arrived at the carriage pulled by the bay mare, it had no wheels. He woke with a start when the bay mare's face morphed grotesquely into that of his father's.

Dawn had blossomed hours ago over Albrechtsburg. Johann hurried, and his thighs burned on the winding stairs of the factory as he ran, breathing in the vapors of the dragon's belly.

Voices came from the sculpting room and he hurried to the doorframe, stopping short like a cliff's edge waited. He didn't want to be singled out for his tardiness and needed to gather himself, but the conversation inside the room made him pause for longer than intended.

"When did this happen?" Hao said.

"Must have been within the hour," said Samuel. "Poor lad will be devastated."

Samuel and Hao stood a few steps inside the room. Johann hurtled in. All seven of his molds were smashed on the stone floor in the opposite corner, nearest the window. His face burned, his throat tightened.

"Check the visitor logs," said Samuel. "The guards at the front sign in every guest. We will find who did this."

"No one should have access to this room except those who work here," said Hao. Samuel gave Hao a worried look. Johann could not breathe. He felt as if he were choking, his body rocked. Who could have done this and why? He was so new, surely none of the workers had a vendetta against him...

The Porcelain Menagerie

Johann watched Hao turn from the room and followed to see him hurry down the spiral stairs, dodging workers hauling sacks of precious white clay coming up and pausing for the workers who carried porcelain bowls and cups on boards, ready for firing, coming down. They were all surprised at his urgency—which meant they were not responsible for the destruction of the molds.

Samuel pulled Johann back into the mold room and the men dropped to their knees, picking up remnants of Johann's precious molds. He could not swallow properly. His throat was dry, but his eyes welled with furious tears. He could hear nothing but a ringing in his ears. *Who was responsible?* These molds had taken him weeks. Now, he would have nothing to show the King at his demanded audience with him in two days. He wanted to cry out but found he could make no noise.

"Johann," Samuel said, trying to get his attention. Johann was deaf to anything but his racing thoughts. Samuel grabbed him by his shoulders, pulled him to his feet.

"Was it the painter?" Johann said in a mere whisper, pieces of his work in his hands. "Was it Christian Herold?"

"I don't believe so," said Samuel. "He is at court."

"Then who? Hao? You?" Johann walked to the nearest window, open and blustering, and threw the pieces out. They soared over Albrechtsburg, becoming birds. They shattered to nothing on the cliff face below.

Samuel froze, turning to Johann. He narrowed his eyes.

"You believe I would do this? Destroy something that a friend has created?"

"I am not sure what I believe. Someone is trying to undo me," Johann said, still staring at his broken molds on the green cliffside. "You call me a friend, but do those exist in Albrechtsburg? You said no one should have access to this room but those who work here." He ran a hand through his thin hair. It came back damp with sweat.

Samuel's eyes widened. "You think I did this?"

"Whoever did it knew they were here."

"I did not destroy your work, young man. Think, Johann, use your mind. What reason would I have to betray you? You keep the King from breathing down my own neck."

It was true. Samuel had no real cause to ruin Johann's molds.

"Go help Hao, he's checking the logs. It had to have happened recently, maybe your culprit is still in the castle."

Johann hesitated, but Samuel pushed him out the door, perhaps eager to be rid of Johann in his state of panic.

Johann hurried down the narrow hallway, his mind racing, jaw tight with anger. First Katharina gave him a book that could lead him to the gallows, and now his work was destroyed. Remaking those molds was not possible. Each one was perfectly unique. He'd never be able to bend clay in that exact manner again, even if he made the same animals.

He took deep shuddering breaths, on the verge of tears, and stopped dead. A crimson-draped figure was touching the blooming moss on the walls of his hallway. Johann recognized the color of her skin, her graying hair.

"Frau Maria?" Johann said.

Maria turned, hood up, eyes wide, and fled. Johann ran after her, through the halls and stairs, his legs burning with his urgency. He ignored his body. Maria was small; his steps longer, and he grabbed her cloak's billowing sleeve. She turned and ducked, like a creature that had been hit before, a motion that said nothing and everything.

"Maria!" Johann cried, not letting go of her cloak. "What are you doing here?"

She struggled but Johann did not let go. White dust hemmed her sleeve.

"It was you," he said. "*You* destroyed my molds."

He drew closer to her and picked her up, holding her arms to her sides. He carried her back to his room. She weighed the same as Herman. Maria screamed, but the door slammed, and Albrechtsburg swallowed her voice.

"Stop! Now!" Johann said.

Maria tried to escape his grip, but he held firm. He had no intention of harming the woman and held her until she calmed. "Why, Maria? Tell me, and I'll let you go."

"You have no idea what awaits you, porcelain maker!"

"And you do?" Johann said.

"I have seen this before. Your success will bolster him, he'll become even more obsessed, and so distracted he'll forgo all responsibilities. He will never grant Katharina's freedom!" Maria shrugged him off at last, and darted, quick like a cat, to the door. Johann blocked it, his large frame impassable.

"And yet your daughter asked me to rush my sculptures to him! You are the King's consort. There is no reason for you to destroy his happiness."

"I have not been his consort since before Katharina was born. There is every reason for me to destroy his happiness," Maria said. "You do not know the evil of Augustus the Strong."

The woman in red paced the room. Her eyes stayed on the floor, hands curled into fists.

The Porcelain Menagerie

"Tell me," he said. Johann lowered his gaze, and she stopped, taking him in.

"There is too much in the past that you cannot understand."

"Why destroy my molds, Maria?"

"Not to hurt you," she said. She lowered her crimson hood. "To protect Katharina. You know what she needs."

"She needs the King, her father, to grant her divorce."

"Yes," she said. "And she needs it now. If Augustus has a distraction, in you, young porcelain maker, he will wait. He will have to organize new places for your work, have parties and dedications, dinners with foreign princes to show off his new porcelain menagerie. He loves nothing more than to show off."

Johann shook his head. He noticed the book peeking out from under his bed and tried not to look at it. Maria still paced, his work's dust on her cloak.

"I have nothing to do with this, yet you have harmed me, Maria. I am not responsible for your daughter, nor Augustus; I am responsible for my own life and art. I will turn you over to the guards so they ensure the rest of my work is safe. You understand, your daughter thought the opposite? She thought delivering would save her."

"It will not, Kändler," she said. "You are all Augustus talks about. I need him to do this for Katharina, then I will leave you alone. If he sees no porcelain delivered, he will have to focus on her."

"My art has nothing to do with this!"

"It is hard to understand, porcelain maker. I have seen the King's obsession and how it grows and consumes people. I have seen others like you, and their fates."

"What others? The men here don't leave Albrechtsburg but on rare occasions. There are no others."

Maria shook her head, her mouth twisted. The wind whistled through the sizeable arched window; bright light illuminated her graying black hair, tangled in a braid.

"There was one who was once special to me. The things that happened to him are unimaginable. My focus now is making sure my daughter can leave Dresden, and leave her husband, and I need a few weeks of no activity from you to get there."

"I have also lost those I love," said Johann. Herman's bright, crooked smile flashed in his mind's eye. The smell of his mother's milk-warm skin filled the room, and his breathing slowed.

"Let me go."

"You destroyed my work," said Johann. "And you'll do it again. I will turn you over to Hao."

Maria let loose a shuddering breath. She was trapped, Johann knew, and there was no right thing to do. He imagined her life: the King's bedchamber, a shadowy existence as a handmaiden, a person in a foreign land, her daughter's unknown problems. Her existence was one of fear. He understood her desperation.

"I am sorry, Frau Maria, but I have no choice," he said.

A loud crash sounded outside. Maria and Johann both shifted, startled. Johann rushed to the window and opened it to see a raven spiraling downward, black feathers careening to the cliffside. The bird struck the glass.

Maria gasped, watching the bird glide. Its wings caught the wind, and it coasted gently to a ledge below. It was alive, black eyes cast upward to the window, feathers shining brightly in the sun. Johann watched silently, thinking of the eagle feather, the destroyed bird molds, and now, the raven.

"A sign," Maria said. "Perhaps you are supposed to help us."

Johann let out a short laugh. "If I don't make the King's porcelain, I cannot help you at all. What if Katharina was right, and delivering early will help? He will fawn over the porcelain menagerie so much so that you could have a moment to persuade him. You didn't think any of this through."

Maria swallowed, considering. "We need this divorce granted now. Katharina is in danger."

Johann thought of Katharina: her surprising kindness, the book, the menagerie path where she swept her red cloak. The bubbled scar. "I shouldn't care but I do." He hesitated. "What danger is she in? She is away from her husband now."

Maria turned away from the window.

"If her husband makes it to Dresden before the divorce is granted, she will not survive his rage."

Johann raised his eyebrows. He forced himself to take deep breaths as he stepped toward the bed and the book.

"And if he makes it here to see the divorce decree? How would that quell his anger?"

"He will lose all claim to cross the city gates. The guards will not allow him to pass."

"I do not know, respectfully, if what you say is true about his rage, that papers will stop him. Nor the guards, as they likely tend to favor men's wishes. And his relationship, as an advisor to Augustus is—"

The Porcelain Menagerie

"A complicated one. You're likely right. I expect we will be long gone by the time he arrives from Poland, porcelain maker, and Augustus will be left to deal with his anger. All I care about is Katharina."

Johann hesitated. "I spoke to her in the menagerie, and during your tour."

Maria held his gaze. "Alone? If you are caught together, it could mean her divorce will not be granted on grounds of adultery."

Johann sighed, his gut turned. "We were not together in that way, madam. I was there to sketch, without paper, and she gave me a book. A rather strange one, if we are telling secrets."

He grabbed the gray book, felt its spine shift with decades of use, and held it to Maria. Her face paled. She did not reach for it like Johann presumed she would.

"She should never have given you that."

"I am aware. And I am aware, now, that you know what this is and what danger it puts me in. Was this your plan the whole time? To destroy me, my work, so you could get the King's attention and keep it?"

"I do not believe Katharina knew what that was."

"But you do."

Maria nodded. "It is Böttger's book. Full of secrets that cannot be released."

"And how, pray tell, do you know Böttger? And why did you not destroy it?"

"Keeping it with me was as good as destroying it." She reached for the book. Johann tucked it under his arm.

"Then there's no reason to give it back to you."

"Despite the fact that it is mine. Give it back."

"Why would he give this to you? You cannot give my molds back. Anything relating to the arcanum should remain in Albrechtsburg, under guard. I shall give it to Hao."

Maria jolted forward, panic on her face. "No!"

"Then tell me how you came to own this book."

She pursed her lips. "I was a young woman, newly the King's mistress, when Böttger made his first porcelain. All others had failed. Augustus smashed their work in front of the entire court. Most were already crumbling, yellow-white, gray-white, green-white. Imperfect. Cracked. Böttger brought in something close... Augustus' celebrations were days long. But those celebrations didn't compare to his reaction when you brought that perfect damn eagle. Your work is distracting him, Kändler. It will boil the water, and Katharina and I shall succumb to the heat."

Johann thought. She had not answered his question, of why Böttger gave her the book. He did not want to delay his work. "You have slowed me down enough. Destroying my molds." He hesitated, thinking of the many pieces drying in a windowless chamber nearby.

Maria raised her chin and looked satisfied. "Please consider Katharina. Do what you can to help her."

"She showed me her scar. I believe she is in danger. But consider," Johann said, "if I deliver many at once, the King's joy will be so great, while he's planning his celebrations, he'll sign anything you ask."

"His porcelain sickness does not allow him to see Katharina's need. When he says he wants a menagerie, he means it."

Johann sighed. It had taken him more than a month to make the seven molds Maria had destroyed. But this woman was before him, draped in sorrow and pain. He memorized her face and nodded. He wanted to make a whole menagerie, as many animals as possible, for the King with an insatiable appetite for women and glass. If he failed, slowed down, the King might have him thrown out, or worse.

If he delivered, and believed Maria, then Katharina's life was at risk.

"The lion," said Johann. He hesitated, wondering if this was a fool's errand. Did Maria and her daughter blind him so much that he could forgive the destruction she'd caused? She turned to leave. He blocked her way.

Maria tore her eyes from the door and narrowed them at Johann. "The lion?"

"It's on the list of porcelain animals the King wants. I'll need to finish sketching your lion in the menagerie, without escort. These things take time."

"It will help our cause?"

"Tell the King I'm sketching your beast. Excite him. Perhaps then you can convince the King to grant the divorce, get Katharina away from her cruel husband. And perhaps, too, tell me how the lion lost its eye."

Maria nodded. "That lion..." she said the animal's name quietly under her breath as if disbelieving it existed. "Fine. You won't be interrupted."

"Let's get you out of Albrechtsburg." Johann put his hand on her shoulder. She shrank back. He touched her again, eyes steady. He needed her to follow him closely. She acquiesced, allowing him to escort her quickly through his chamber door.

Albrechtsburg and its hundreds of rooms swallowed them. Around every turn they ducked into hallways at the sound of rushing feet but found many doors swollen shut by heat. The spiral staircase was out of the question, constantly heavy with flowing persons. No one could be

The Porcelain Menagerie

a witness to Frau Maria in Albrechtsburg. They went carefully, winding down ancient servant staircases, through rooms jumbled with porcelain shards and finished art, drying on racks.

Half-painted teapots and dishes, figurines of people with pug dogs, a wildly huge, impossible bird cage scattered with flowers, a chandelier, and broken things Johann could not recognize were all made from white gold, marked with cobalt swords, waiting their turn to be painted or sold. Brick colored, old pieces with shining facets cut into them rested on shelves, labeled with the same scrawling handwriting of the book Johann had tucked in his pocket.

The sheer amount of items made him pause. Many were layered with dust, waiting for payment or shipment for months or years. They were essentially gold coins held tight in a dead man's hand. Albrechtsburg held too many undelivered promises.

Johann's damp palms betrayed his fears: he imagined Hao finding them and taking them both to the heat splashed dungeon, throwing Maria in the massive kiln.

Below, the kilns rumbled, and the castle tinkled with the chiming sound of porcelain colliding. Something had collapsed. Urgent voices signaled a gap in the guard. Johann and Maria locked eyes and ran. They finally made it to the ground floor. Johann signaled for Maria to leave through a large gaping window where the ground didn't drop off as steeply. Maria climbed out, leaving a tuft of red thread behind on the chipped sill. She ran. Johann pocketed the thread and turned toward the noise.

A secondary kiln had collapsed in the dungeon. Smoke rolled upward, clouding the stairs and the lower level. The workers rushed, hair blackened with soot, around a kilnsman on the ground. By his shining flesh it was clear that it was better if he did not wake. If he did, the last thing he would feel before death would be white pain. The image of Katharina's burn scar conjured forth, and Johann blocked his mind from hearing her screams.

Samuel was halfway down the stairs when Johann stopped him, coming up. Johann shook his head, telling him to descend no farther. Samuel shielded his eyes and turned. They left the burning flesh smell of the dungeons, knowing their presence was not helpful. The team of kilnsmen would mourn their own.

"Did you find your destroyer?" Samuel said from the corner of his mouth, not turning his head. Johann tried to block the cries of the kilnsman's friends.

He nodded. He knew now that Samuel was trustworthy, that he was not responsible for the smashing of his molds. Maria and Katharina were the problem, but he dared not reveal them. Why did he feel protective of someone who sought to destroy him? Because of Katharina's past, and perhaps because, unlike his brother, they were strong enough to fight for themselves, even if they might not win.

"You found something?"

Johann diverted. "I have a plan to keep my position here strong, despite all obstacles. I will deliver his menagerie in its entirety. I shall continue without hesitation."

"And how will we protect your pieces? A snake is in our midst, Johann, and your molds are easily destroyed. They were large, too large to hide!"

"The snake has left Albrechtsburg."

Samuel stared at Johann. But, used to secrets, they did not say more as they climbed farther up the spiral staircase that led to their workshop.

Two of Johann's molds were untouched, hidden, drying on a wooden shelf in the back of the room. They were both birds. He wanted to abandon them and start on the lion. Perhaps Katharina would be in the menagerie, waiting.

"Hao," said Johann, hours after the kiln collapsed. "I need to visit the forest or a hunt, and especially the menagerie, to see more animal models for the King."

Hao breathed deeply in through his nose. He was seated near the entrance on a tall stool, back straight, clearly wary after the kiln collapsed and molds destroyed.

"You will not go to any of those places unescorted," Hao said. "You will go to the royal menagerie, where Maria and Katharina have escorts waiting. I shall prepare for you to go tomorrow, documenting all exits and arrivals. I am sorry, Kändler, that I did not find your vandal."

Johann nodded, knowing he was no longer subject to be guarded at the menagerie. He felt ashamed that he could not help Hao by revealing the culprit but relieved that he would leave the halls of Albrechtsburg, in which the smell of burning flesh now wafted. The number of secrets he kept grew.

Johann left Albrechtsburg at dawn on the bay mare, saddled by Hao himself, in a show of watchfulness. If Johann so desired, he could climb down the dirt-marred staircase to Herman's grave. He could sit in the pew at his father's church. He could gallop away into the countryside. He could knock on Katharina's door... this last thought stopped him. Why would he want to do that? When she was focused on leaving another man?

The Porcelain Menagerie

He could leave and be free of the gaping fires of the porcelain factory, but the feeling of the slippery white clay in his hands and the King's face when he saw the eagle propelled him forward. He thirsted for more acknowledgment, to prove himself, and dreamed of a room full of porcelain animals, all made by him, dripping in diamond bright glaze.

Before he knew it, the mare had wound its way to the menagerie near the palace, and Johann abandoned his chance for escape. Animals cackled in the distance, and the book with the arcanum pulsed in the pocket of his leather greatcoat. Would any other patrons be here? They were only welcome if they were dressed to palace standards. He dismounted, pushed open the black and gold gate. Overhanging trees blocked the sky above.

The menagerie felt otherworldly. Large black cages with narrow bars held exotic birds. Johann had never seen such colors—blue parrots, red macaws, yellow songbirds. They flitted from branch to branch. A rainbow macaw sat on a perch, turning its head and yellow eyes toward him, then flipped upside down as Johann drew near. It flapped its wings in warning.

Johann sat cross legged on the gravel path and pulled out the book. He flipped past the kohl-marked margins and began to sketch. The texture of the feathers, the bulge around the bird's eye, the grip of its claws on the branch. Time melted as he watched the bird hop, scuttle, but not fly. Its wings had been clipped.

The bird gave him so many angles that he drew over printed words and old, scribbled arcanum symbols. The macaw hopped away, and Johann stood with stiff legs and wandered the menagerie, book open, kohl ready.

He rounded a shaded bend, listening to the rustling of the world around him. The path opened to pens and cages, and a peacock appeared, stretching its enormous tail feathers at him. Johann doubted he could create a sculpture that would survive the heat of Albrechtsburg's kilns in such grandeur. He sat again, waiting for the bird to fold its tail so he could see the mechanics of narrowed feathers.

Johann shook his head, sure that any attempted porcelain figure of this peacock would shatter if he made its outstretched tail. Nevertheless, he sketched, focusing on the plumage and shape of the bird's small body. The creature's tail diminished and, within seconds, became magnificent again. The peacock walked, bobbing its head, and Johann reveled in the silent steps of its pressing feet onto the dirt path: three toes, a non-existent weight, yet impact.

Onward were the mammals. Johann's list from King Augustus ordered over thirty types—some of which Johann could never hope to see:

Jillian Forsberg

unicorns, dragons, sphinxes, rhinoceros. Yet here he was, staring at boars and a porcupine and a small, white-faced monkey, all of which were on the list. The lion's cage was around the next bend.

The massive beast paced, and when it saw Johann, rumbled, mouth open to show broken yellow teeth. Its one eye gleamed.

Johann heard footsteps approaching and quickly closed his book. Someone had circled the numbers on the page margin four times in earnest—the word *kaolin* scribbled next to it. An unmistakable arcanum formula. He swallowed, diverting his eyes from the numbers, but his memory saved them.

If Johann's heart beat fast from the stolen formulas in his book, it doubled now. Katharina rounded the bend, wearing purple, a sash tied at her waist, a flowing silvery skirt, and white pearl-shined slippers. The neckline of her ensemble was low. Though a ruffle of lace covered it, Johann looked for the scar.

"Johann!" said Katharina.

"I'm here to sketch the lion."

Katharina raised her skirts to show white slippers, abruptly at his side.

"I find it convenient that you have arrived here precisely as I have," she said, eyes darting. He assumed she sought another Albrechtsburg worker. "Are you following me? Having me watched?"

"That is Hao's duty, not mine," Johann said. "What reason would I have to watch you? I have over three hundred animals to deliver to your father, remember?"

"My father cannot think of anything but porcelain," Katharina said. "I need him to think of me."

"Did your mother speak to you?"

"She speaks to me constantly, as we wait for the final word on my divorce."

"Your mother is causing chaos in my life."

Katharina ignored him, stepping across the path. A family of monkeys leaped from the floor to the bars of their cage, reaching hands toward Katharina.

Katharina rotated her cinched waist toward the cage. A monkey took a currant from her hand, withdrawn from a pouch by her hip, warily staring at Johann while it ate. Johann longed to draw the creature as it stayed still, tiny paw outstretched—so human like! But he hesitated.

"Why do you stare at her so?" Katharina scratched the monkey's neck.

"A monkey is on the King's list."

The Porcelain Menagerie

"She is the daughter of my mother's monkey from years ago," said Katharina. She ate a currant, eyes on Johann, though her face was turned to the creature, in protection. "Draw her."

Johann turned to a page with faded numbers, praying Katharina wouldn't recognize them. He brought his kohl and sketched, walking around the cage. The monkey hopped from one bar to the next, following Johann. Katharina laughed at the animal's speed: a low, unexpected chuckle. The monkey settled, turning its gaze plaintively upward, like a child seeking comfort, and Johann drew its face.

"A look of longing," said Katharina. "This is what the King wants. Porcelain with life, though the sculptures have none."

"He wants many things," said Johann. Katharina's eyes met his, and she subtly nodded. "But Katharina...your husband? What is it he wants? Why would he harm you?"

Johann reached out to touch the monkey, who bared her teeth gently. But Johann moved slowly, white clay under his fingernails, and it sniffed him, looked down, and submitted to a gentle touch of the porcelain maker's hands between the bars.

"My husband wants nothing but power," she said. "To be the next king, the elector of Saxony, like my father, who had no blood right to Poland's throne. He thought by marrying me, he'd raise his status. But he was never going to be any of those things."

Katharina turned to Johann and raised her chin.

"I am a bastard," said Katharina. "I should not exist, as my life only causes problems, complications for my mother and the King and my husband, who realized after trying to gain more for himself that marrying a king's daughter means little when she's a mistake. I would have a better life if I were a man. My half-brother, Maurice, leads armies in France. I am nothing."

"I am glad you exist, and I am sure these animals are, too," said Johann.

"You have not seen the anger of a man with lofty dreams that will forever be unfulfilled. I am sure if he explained why he harmed me, many men in his position would agree. I am not fit to have married someone like him."

Johann held her gaze. "You should not be subjected to such cruelty, and he should pay for what he did. Have you shown your father the scar?"

Katharina twisted her mouth and shook her head. "He is quick to anger, my father. And though I do not wish to be married to Michal any longer, I cannot say I want the man executed. I... I don't know what my father would do to him..."

Katharina began to cry. Johann gently took her hands in his, wiped a tear from her face with his kohl-smudged thumb. He knew he shouldn't have touched her, for if anyone saw… She stepped away from the monkey cage to a waiting bucket of meat for the lion, who still paced. Johann followed, watching the lion turn in the distance, mouth open, waiting for its easy meal. The lion did not turn its gaze from Johann, and he sat to resume his sketching, letting Katharina move on with her duties. They said nothing more to each other.

Back at Albrechtsburg, after the sun had set and the night cried with humming insects and the howling of wolves in the fields nearby, Johann paced the modeler's room. Samuel was examining Johann's rough white-clay sculpture of a finished monkey. After refinement, the mold-makers would cover it, halve it, pour in porcelain, fire it.

"It's nearly perfect," Samuel said. "And, I think, small enough that we can paint it, and it won't explode in the second firing."

Johann exhaled brightly. Though the painter and much senior worker, Herold, frightened him, he knew he needed the man as an ally for the King's menagerie. He wanted him to paint the monkey, so he could begin to form an alliance. Though the King's list did not specify, he knew delivering all of the menagerie pieces in white would not suffice.

The monkey held a small box and sat in almost human-like contemplation, a belt begging for golden paint around its waist. It sat on a mushroom-covered log, its fur delicately modeled in great detail. It stared into the distance, and in its paw was a currant, one second away from being gobbled.

"Refine it once more," said Samuel. "And then we'll allow the mold-makers to do their duties. Johann, I have something to show you."

He led Johann to a far corner of the room, by tables stacked with white clay. He lifted a canvas cloth from a low, large piece. Johann gasped. It was a large cat, lying down, paws curled under, its face mournful. It was enormous.

"Samuel!"

Samuel grinned, running a hand through his graying auburn hair. Pride? Excitement? Both.

"A far cry from the teacup, eh?" Samuel said. "It's a lion, or what I remember about lions, anyway. I figured you'd need some help. Forgive me for snooping, but I saw the King's list. Three hundred sculptures with no delivery date? You'd work 'til you're old, boy. Thought I'd try. Not as good as your work, but…"

The Porcelain Menagerie

"You're wrong, it's brilliant!" Johann said. If he split the work with Samuel, they could complete the King's menagerie.

"You really won't tell me who destroyed your molds, will you?"

"No, I won't."

"And what loyalty do you have to someone like that?"

Johann touched Samuel's sculpt. He knelt and looked it in the eyes.

"I understand people may make decisions we will never understand. It is not my place to condemn them when I cannot change the past. I can only grow, much like you have, from a teacup to this."

Samuel twisted his mouth. "I am not completely satisfied with that answer."

"Truthfully," Johann said. "Neither am I. But I am satisfied with this cat...tell me, though, why the eyebrows?"

"An homage to King Augustus."

Johann let out a single "ha!" "We do this together, then?" he said.

Together. The black knot in his gut loosened a bit. He was on his way to greatness, with Samuel by his side.

Johann slept fitfully that night and dreamed of the monkey and Katharina in her swirling skirts, carrying an abundance of currants, scraping her arm clean of the burn scar. He woke with a fright, remembering the King smashed unsatisfactory porcelain pieces and that Samuel's lion had the eyebrows of a man.

Chapter 16
Fatima
1706

Through her window on the third story of Augustus' palace, Fatima watched a large crate on the back of a wagon rumble by, heading toward the menagerie. Sailcloth draped the load. Fatima strained to hear the voices of the large, ruddy-faced sailors who led the horses. The wagon disappeared into the copse of trees that marked the menagerie's border, and Fatima darted from her chambers. On slippered toes, she took the stairs, heaving her petticoats around her ankles, catching bits of cloth on the rail.

Her gown fit her beautifully, and she felt like a glowing flower, golden-yellow in the gloom of the darkened hallways. Dripping pearls adorned her earlobes, and her dark hair was pulled into a low, twisted maze of braids and curls, a style that Friedrich said he liked. He made her feel wanted, fair of face.

The first floor moved with early morning preparations—servants and noblemen paid her little mind, for their daily tasks awaited them. Soldiers stood in the courtyard, short swords drawn in practice.

The soldiers were always there, though Fatima did not understand why. The King had personal guards who rarely left his side. The soldiers kept busy practicing drills, sharpening their weapons, wandering the yard after too much ale. But their primary duties came when Augustus had visitors, and they lined the halls in a show of prowess. Porcelain and soldiers and books and art and musical instruments and gilded statuettes and her... all things King Augustus used to show his immense wealth.

Eyes watched Fatima as she crossed the courtyard where soldiers socialized. Their conversations silenced as she walked by. She glanced their way unabashedly, and all but one turned their eyes to the ground. He stared openly, and she lifted the edge of her lips in a half-smile, blossoming pride reverberating in her belly. Why flirt with this one? She had the attention of the porcelain maker and of the King. She had no reason to catch his eye. But she did not look away. It gave her some kind of power.

Her path took her toward the men, into an open air portico that melted into the yard and down to the menagerie. The soldier opened his mouth as she passed by, and took half a step toward her, then lowered his arm and stilled. She'd seen this one in the King's courtroom, advising Augustus. He was handsome. Perhaps in his late twenties, he had a dark, close-cropped beard and light eyes. His uniform clung crisply to his narrow-hipped frame, and Fatima swished her skirts, unfurling frankincense perfume his way. She heard him inhale.

Mouth in a complete smile now, she raised her chin and exited the courtyard. Her rendezvous with Friedrich made her feel invincible. Catching another man's attention seemed a small, trivial thing now. A narrow, outdoor hallway that connected the stables to the castle was the final structure before the menagerie.

The stone floor was slippery, and she kept her eyes locked, from window-to-window, craning her neck to see the cart and cage, perhaps now unveiled. She wrapped her hand around a stone column and propelled herself out of the palace to the grounds.

Her red cape furled in the gray morning light. Dew caught the edges, turning it deep, blood red. Her hair gleamed, raven-feather black, loosened from the thong that tied her braid. Her movements were sure, determined. There was no stopping Fatima—the King's lady, queen of the menagerie animals but of nothing else.

Fatima ran, joy in her legs, though they were sore, pushed to her limits by the porcelain maker. The lawn dotted her rebellious bare legs with cold dew, and her leather slippers were soon soaked through, stretching around her feet. The smell of the morning woods ahead greeted her: pine needles, animal droppings, hay.

From the back of the menagerie came the shouts of men and rustling beyond the trees that hid black cages. She paused, looking back at the palace for a moment. The bearded soldier watched her from a stone column. She raised her red hood, knowing it showed her more clearly to him, and smirked again, disappearing from his view into the menagerie woods.

It was like stepping into another world. The tree canopies overhead creaked in the wind, leaves dancing, blurring the sunlight and dropping, signaling early autumn. In the distance, she heard her exotic birds saying good morning to each other in their particular ways—croaking, cawing, and from the parrots, foreign words learned from former owners or sailors cast high in the damp air. She wished she knew what they said, though she realized it was likely the word "hello" in whatever language they absorbed.

She paused by a large pine, its bark rough and scaling, trying to get the perfect view of the wagon with its cage. Fatima took a moment to settle her breath from her run down the hill. When she closed her eyes, she saw two things—Friedrich's face, and the face of the promised animal that was supposedly in that wagon.

The wagon sat on the lawn near the wooded section behind the palace, nearly hidden. It was pulled by two draft horses, mealy-looking things that needed good grooming and rest. Their ears perked at cages rattling in the distance, partly obscured by saplings and pines. Fatima pushed her aquiline nose around the corner and waited for the sailors to pull the sailcloth from their load.

"Show me," Fatima whispered to herself.

Something let out a low, rumbling guttural noise. Something large. The merchant crew, dressed in brown breeches and once-white tunics, meandered. They had no hurry in them. Fatima stepped eagerly toward the wagon, desire outweighing her anxieties about being seen. They'd send her away if they saw her, certainly not aware of a woman's role in the menagerie. The animals in their cages warbled in response to the growling.

The peacock approached the gate and shook its feathers, crying loudly as the men began to unload. The creature inside shook the cage, and the draping, stained canvas over it fell. The men backed away, shouting warnings to each other.

Fatima had never seen one—a lion. But the letters Augustus read to her told her she'd get what she dreamed of, what she'd worked for. Augustus was many unpleasant things, but he was a man who kept his promises. She gave him things he wanted, and he gave her menagerie animals.

The young lion bared its teeth, too large to stand in the wooden cage. It lunged as the men replaced the canvas. Its fur was tawny-tan, like dusk, its short mane tangled and sectioned by the wind, glowing mahogany. Fatima inched closer, sticking to the shadowy corners of the trees. The lion growled again, attacking the bars as the cage lowered to the ground. The men scattered after they placed it down, wiping sweat from their brows.

Their hands were on their knees, and the canvas drew inward. The lion had hold of the cloth and was ripping it, pulling it inside the crate.

One man tugged the cloth back out, but the lion persisted. The game of tug-of-war was not a game at all. The lion bared its teeth, lunged again, and pulled the cloth into the cage, biting it wildly, claws brandishing. The men would have to move it uncovered, risking their fingers and faces if they wanted to haul the beast to its menagerie cage.

Fatima could no longer stay in the shadows. She rushed forward, stepping into the sunlight, pulling her hood tight over her head. "Feed it," she said.

The men turned, hands on their knees in worry and exhaustion. A snarl came from the cage, the beast startled by Fatima's sudden appearance. The man in charge, a thick-chested, scarred sailor, stood from leaning on the wagon.

"Off with you, woman," he said. "Man's business here."

Fatima stepped closer, scoffing and smiling snidely. This was her menagerie. She dropped her hood. She smiled, knowing her power. Her long hair gleamed in the sunlight. "Feed the beast," she said, "and you might keep your hands. How long since he's eaten?"

The younger man glanced at his superiors, turning to the wagon's seat, where a travel bag held salted beef, no doubt from a cask that floated the sea not long ago. These men were straight from the port, and so was their cargo.

Animals panicked in their cages, rustling, cawing, shaking, whimpering at the sounds of the battle of the lion and the sailors. Fatima was keenly aware of them all and their subtle language that revealed their fear of the new beast.

She could not deny her own fear, but her purpose propelled her forward: to examine the new animal, take a record for Augustus for a later report, and describe to him the wild he'd captured for her. She was grateful, for him, for giving her this. A pang of guilt hit her, unexpectedly, as she pictured the lion on a plain in its homeland, certainly forgotten now by its family.

Was it her right to own these animals...? Was it Augustus' right to own her? The menagerie felt like it was tucked under her arm. Once her request came true and the letters started leaving asking for animals, she felt power. She *could* get the King to do some things. And even though Fatima was essentially captive, knowing she had a place to call her own felt like a shackle released. But she was not free. How could she hate the man when he had made her dreams live? How could she call owning these animals a dream when she understood what it felt like to be owned?

The younger man slid strips of salted beef between the slats of the lion's cage. The lion ate furiously, eyes on the humans surrounding him. One of the older men reached into a pouch in the back of the wagon and produced a soup bone, which he lowered into the cage. The lion grabbed it, teeth bared, eyes glowing, and lay down to gnaw.

Fatima allowed herself a small smile. She had an intuition about animals, and feeding this lion felt like a pulsing need. Clean, young teeth on bone, the lion calmed. The men lifted the cage, and the beast barely moved. They hauled him, keeping their heads and fingers away from the open spaces between the bars, into the woods where his cage waited.

Fatima followed, counting cages as she wandered the thickly laid gravel. *Seventeen, eighteen.* Bright birds. Cawing wild crows seeking leftover feed. Black cages lined the path—some small, suspended in the air for birds, some large, with gleaming padlocks dangling. The peacock called again, an echoing cry that startled the lion from his bone. He raised from his haunches and lunged, pupils turned into knife edges.

The six men carrying the cage jostled; two in the front fell to their knees, and the lion slid, too. He clawed at the planking, fur pressing between the wooden rods of his crate, mouth open. The men climbed to their feet, groaning as the weight of him pressed on their collarbones. They hurried now, seeing the animal's anger, and slid the entire cage into the largest black metal gate.

The large, bearded older man shut the wooden cage inside, clicking the padlock. With one finger, he beckoned the younger man to him. Fatima leaned in to hear.

"Open the wooden gate, lad," he said. "We'll be done with this one."

The lad dug his leather-soled foot into the gravel, steadying himself, keeping distance, and extended a shaking hand. Fatima held her breath. The lion rumbled. The lad attempted to free him, to extend his quarters beyond the small travel crate, though he would still be caged. Fatima stepped forward. The lad freed the wooden latch.

The lion lunged, and Fatima gripped her hands around the black bars and shook. He turned, bright eyed, brown and gold like a field in fall, distracted from the boy, and Fatima jumped back. The young man was unharmed. The cage opened. The lion exited, pacing, padding around the black metal cage.

"How will you retrieve our crate?" said the lad.

The bone rested inside the wooden cage. The bearded leader shook his head. "We won't."

The animal noises around them resounded, and the menagerie's life pulsed. The sailors took the wagon away, horses snorting in relief when they realized the smell of the lion no longer followed them.

They'd left Fatima the cask of salted meat. Fatima ignored it. Instead, she went to the shed where butchered rabbits, dotted with flies, waited for the wolf and the foxes. She took a dagger and sliced the flesh

The Porcelain Menagerie

clean from the bone, making strips of meat for her new animal. Fatima sat by the beast's cage, red cape spread around her in a rippling pool.

The lion was young, mane not grown in fully, giving him a shaggy appearance like a man who'd avoided taking shears to his beard for many months. He kept his distance. She gently tossed a slice of meat between the bars. It took him many moments to stand and step toward it. Perhaps it was Fatima's red cloak that startled him? She took it off.

She tossed another piece. He sniffed the first, ate it. Found the second, draped it between his teeth and swallowed it. Fatima held a piece on the dagger and held it between the bars. Her hands shook. The lion waited, eyeing the meat, and eventually, powerful paw after powerful paw, huffed at the skewered rabbit and plucked it from the blade. Fatima opened her mouth and tears threatened. Trust began with the basic things: food, shelter, kindness. She fed the lion the remaining rabbit. The menagerie grew still and silent.

"I shall call you Buda."

When she left several hours later, she noticed the bearded soldier was still in the courtyard with his comrades. Feeling emboldened by the lion, forgetting that Augustus gave it to her, and prideful in her guidance in connecting with Buda, Fatima strolled by on the gravel path, unbuttoned her cape from her neck, and curtsied to the handsome soldier. His eyes blazed. She practically danced away and did not look back when she heard his companions wildly whoop, similar to the birds in the menagerie at the arrival of the lion.

"Frau Maria!" he called, beckoning her over. She flinched, remembering she could not fully be herself with the illusion Augustus painted of her to others.

"Yes, soldier?"

"What beast did your menagerie get today, Frau Maria?" He did not have permission to speak to her. But Fatima did not care.

"A lion."

The soldier's eyes widened. "Male or female?"

"Male, young. Handsome thing."

The soldier raised his mouth. "Perhaps I shall visit and see it for myself."

"Ask King Augustus to take you. It shall certainly be his new favorite thing."

"I believe the role of King Augustus' new favorite thing is already taken, madam."

The soldier bowed and swept his arm. Fatima did not know how to feel. She was glad that Augustus liked her, but what did that mean if she faltered? She turned her back to the soldier, aware of how foolish she'd been. She needed to watch herself carefully. From the menagerie, the lion's strange and deep bellows echoed.

Chapter 17
Johann
1732

"There's a letter for you, Johann," Hao said, lingering in the doorway of the modeler's room. "Sealed from the castle."

Johann rose from his seat, wiping his hands. In front of him was a pair of half-sculpted doves. When brought close, they would settle into each other so their breasts touched lovingly. He reluctantly paused refining their feathers to read Hao's delivery.

Johann opened the letter:

"Kändler-

I have not had a delivery from you in many weeks and expect you have seen and understood my order for the Japanese Palace menagerie. Upon my wishes, I request immediate delivery of your works or your resignation from Albrechtsburg.

Signed,

Augustus II, by the grace of God, King of Poland, Grand Duke of Lithuania, Ruthenia, Prussia, Masovia, Samogitia, Livonia, Kiev, Volhynia, Podolia, Podlachia, Smolensk, Severia, and Chernihiv, and Hereditary Duke and Elector of Saxony."

The words trailed at the end, becoming smaller to fit all of Augustus' titles. Johann swallowed hard and turned to Samuel, who was working on another lion. She was the mate to his first one, which was being fired today, modeled from the one-eyed beast in the menagerie. Johann handed the letter over and watched Samuel's face. He looked up, stoic, and nodded firmly.

"We'll take him your birds," said Samuel.

"But they're not all ready."

"You have five—the peacock, the macaws, the second eagle. Take them to satiate him."

This was not the plan Maria had laid out for him.

"I'll take him just one. Tease him, make him know we're working."

"Kändler, you're risking everything. Why not allow the King his pleasure?"

That word caused Johann's stomach to drop and twist. *Pleasure*. He knew that was precisely what Maria used to be to King Augustus; what Katharina likely was to her husband. Visions of Maria's red cloak dragged through Albrechtsburg haunted him. He either had to tell Samuel or come up with a blatant lie.

"If we tempt him, we allow ourselves more glory when we deliver in full," said Johann. He turned to Hao. "Reply that tomorrow he will have a special delivery. And we'd love payment in advance to make more."

Samuel narrowed his eyes, confused. Johann risked even his only friendship.

Christian Herold walked in, as usual, dotted with pink-gold paint, with a crate in his hands.

"Your monkey, Kändler," he said.

Samuel, Hao, and Johann gathered around the crate in anticipation. Herold lifted out the spitting image of the menagerie monkey, painted and gleaming in the mid-morning sun. The head, feet, and tail were brown, the belt rosy-golden, the jewel the same purple as Katharina's ribbons. Johann smiled and raised his gaze to Herold's. The four men had the same look on their faces, like boys discovering a nest of baby birds: wonder, delicate joy, and the undying urge to touch.

They resisted and left the monkey with its gilded jar in the crate. The following day, the King would get more than a macaw. He would get Frau Maria's monkey in porcelain.

Johann, Samuel, and Christian poured into a tight black carriage. The morning was thick and heavy. The horses harnessed to the large wheel on the side of Albrechtsburg pulled, and Johann watched their stomping hooves and imagined a kiln large enough to fire a porcelain horse. The draft horses shone copper in the sunlight. Hao brought forward the same bay mare that took Johann to the menagerie and harnessed her, hopping onto the carriage seat and urging the horse onward to the King's palace.

The palace bustled with activity, but not in a way that Johann saw last time. Military men in uniform huddled in groups, standing upright with their small swords, speaking in whispered tones with furrowed

The Porcelain Menagerie

brows. Johann and Samuel gave each other worrisome looks, but Hao urged them to the throne room.

A long, winding hallway shaped like a snail's curved shell led the way. There was no way to avoid the collection rooms stacked with porcelain. Meissen in its finest, in addition to Chinese and Japanese porcelain, waited around every corner. Johann found it impossible to move quickly. He longed to pick up the pieces and feel their weight. He could not understand how the Chinese masters made such fine, translucent pieces while he still had the clunkiness of European paste. Johann lightly shook his head.

"It is hard to comprehend," said Hao, watching him. "How the Chinese, my people, were able to make this a thousand years before you. And harder still to comprehend how, with European knowledge of natural philosophy and alchemy, the arcanum is still flawed in Dresden."

"Your people?" said Johann. Hao nodded and smiled—rare for him. "They are masters, Hao, and I cannot tell you what I would give to learn from a master's hand and seek help to make our factory better."

"I did not expect you to say that," said Hao. "Many in your position would torture them and read their writings, looking to steal the arcanum and keep it for themselves. But you would be hard-pressed to find a master."

"Why is that?"

"In Jingdezhen, where I am from, there is no single master. Each of the seventy-two steps to make porcelain is carried out by a master of that one process. Therefore, the collective seventy-two people become a master only together."

"Seventy-two steps, each carried out by one person? That is what we do at Schloss Albrechtsburg, isn't it?"

Hao nodded. "On a smaller scale. Back home, the trade is passed down from generation to generation. If your father painted one dragon face, you learn to paint that dragon face."

"And then the process is never fully understood by the collective."

"The people must work together or it fails. You see now how we have kept the arcanum secret for a thousand years," Hao said. "We try to hold Albrechtsburg to the same standards, but it is like tying feathers on a bird."

Johann stared at a large blue and white vessel, the last flanking the doorway before the throne room. He thought of the seventy-two steps to make it and how many hands had touched it. The magic spell of Chinese porcelain gripped him: these pieces were brought around the Horn of Africa in a ship that traveled farther than he could have dreamed, made by hands whose father's fathers had taught them their one piece in the puzzle of the arcanum. Here he was, hauling a single imperfect monkey down the cobbled street. He reached out to feel the blue, slick-smooth surface, but the door to the throne room opened.

The booming voice of Augustus filled the hall. Johann cringed. He could not tell if it was anger or excitement. His fellow workers filed in beside him. Samuel's hot-sweet sweat filled the air next to him, and Johann took a shuddering breath. Maria sat next to the King, dressed in deep-sea blue. She caught Johann's eye and held it. On a chain near her feet, a young monkey made a chirruping noise. The same monkey he had sketched—what had Katharina said? The daughter of Maria's monkey from long ago? He could not have been more pleased that the monkey was at court today. His heart thrummed. They'd see the likeness for themselves.

He tried not to look at Katharina, not wanting to give away their knowledge of each other, or his excitement, and instead turned his attention to the crate by his feet. Hao urged him forward.

"My modelers and their latest attempt at my happiness," said Augustus. He gestured to the crate, raising an eyebrow, clearly impatient.

Johann opened the crate, and Samuel gently lifted the monkey, hesitating. Johann dropped to a knee, and Samuel followed suit. The King rose from this throne, the living monkey still peeping nearby.

"What is this?" Augustus grinned. Johann had not noticed how thick the man's legs were. He had swollen ankles and wrists and quivering jowls. As a young man, he must have been rippling with muscle. But his muscle was collapsing into the heft of rich food and laziness.

The King grabbed the porcelain monkey from Samuel's hands and practically tossed it in the air as he turned it to view each side. Johann swallowed. The fur and flesh monkey, seeing the movement, strained at its chain. The King made the connection.

"Is this my exotic lady's companion?" he said. "Let that thing go, Maria, so that it can see itself in white gold."

King Augustus' double chins folded as he bent to put the priceless porcelain on the ground. Johann cringed. Maria let loose the delicate gold chain, and the monkey sauntered up, bare paws skimming the marble floor. She cocked her head at her likeness in porcelain and bared her teeth. After a sniff and a quick tap, she rushed back to Maria's side and buried her face in the crook of Maria's arm.

King Augustus had a sly, ornery smile on his face. His thick eyebrows wagged. Johann watched his chest heave with each breath. He could not tell Augustus' emotions: pride, lust, joy? A combination of the three?

"This porcelain is beautiful. It is a perfect likeness of my first

The Porcelain Menagerie

monkey, Amar. Her daughter sits with me today," Maria said.

"This pleases me," Augustus said. "And should please my mistress, who has never truly understood my collection. Perhaps now she shall, as her beloved animal is cast in porcelain for eternity. How many more do you have?"

"More in the works, sir; it takes time. We work more quickly without interruption. We can deliver a dozen more to you in six weeks," said Johann.

"A dozen," Augustus said. He climbed the dais. "My order to the factory was three hundred."

"We will fill Your Highness' order," said Samuel, still on his knee. "We work as a team now, the three of us, and the work moves quickly, but your white gold dries slowly. And, Your Majesty, in all due respect, we have not yet been paid for these deliveries."

Augustus smiled again, sending a chill down Johann's spine. Maria watched him; the monkey's small face turned toward the porcelain likeness. The chain jingled.

"Your Majesty," the herald interrupted, leaning in toward his King with news. "The soldiers are assembled, ready for counting."

King Augustus stood, rubbing his hands together. Samuel, Christian, and Johann collectively took a step back. Hao stayed still, closest to the dais.

"My fine Meissen men, I have to tell you, I appreciate your work. But in vessels, you cannot compare to the work of the Chinese," he said. He raised his arms to make an announcement. "I have a plan to gather one hundred fifty vessels from Friedrich Wilhelm I of Prussia. Master works!"

Maria exhaled, perhaps too loudly. "And how, Augustus, will you pay for that? The coffers do not support..."

"The wealth of Saxony is not all gold, Maria."

"What will you use in your bargain?" she said, her hands folded primly on her lap.

"You hear them now, don't you?" Augustus stood, raising his arms, palms up.

Hao's eyes narrowed. Johann saw his hands clench. Samuel, Christian, and Johann drew in their breath as the realization struck them. The windows muted the noise of a commander giving sharp orders. Augustus planned to trade soldiers? For porcelain? *What madness?!*

Soldiers were in the courtyard, scattered through the porcelain-filled hallways, and the King skipped laboriously down the dais to gesture to them. His heavy feet were clumsy, and it was painful to watch him smile—six hundred men to be sent away from their homelands and families for the King's addiction. Johann couldn't wrap his head around the thought. He glanced to the dais where Maria sat. Katharina's chair was now empty.

Maria's wide brown eyes said something—but what? She looked at Johann with fervor, a desperation, a knowing. Where was Katharina? Johann needed to speak with her. Surely this was a detriment to them all.

"I hope your monkey makes it safely back to the menagerie tonight, where perhaps Katharina will tend to it, Frau Maria," Johann said. Maria tilted her chin to the direction of the living menagerie, understanding. Johann and the other porcelain makers bowed deeply to King Augustus and backed away.

Johann picked up the empty crate where the porcelain monkey once sat. The figure balanced on the throne, a shining glaze catching the light. The living monkey studied it, tiny paws reaching toward it.

Johann listened for a faint goodbye, but Maria remained quiet. He heard her tug gently on the chain of her monkey, who followed her out the wide door to the courtyard where the King's men waited, congregating. Traded for blue and white porcelain.

Chapter 18
Fatima
1706

Fatima waited for Brunhilde, but the cook was not in the kitchen. She needed her moon tea. She tried to read the scrawling labels on the many stoneware jars in the kitchen, but even if she knew what they said, she did not know what went into the tea that presumably kept her un-pregnant. The monkey by her side pulled its golden chain.

Now, Fatima was in danger—in many ways—by frequenting both Augustus and Friedrich Böttger's beds. She much preferred Friedrich, whose garden-scented chamber and clay-stained hands were now familiar.

She sighed and gently pulled the monkey's chain, knowing she could wait no longer. She was heading toward the tennis courts where Augustus was entertaining a high-ranking member of the military. She considered mixing a concoction but remembered Brunhilde's skillset was of life and death. She dare not take herbs that could kill her, not now, when she and Friedrich were growing so close, and she wanted to say she loved him.

The word made her pause, and she thought about it as she left the kitchens and out into the bright sunlight, shielding her eyes.

She loved her white-faced monkey, Amar. She loved the she-wolf, untouchable and wild, even caged. She loved the tawny lion, Buda. Their rumblings echoed in her mind even when she was far from the menagerie. The animals called her there—her place of comfort.

Augustus sometimes made her flinch. But she had no specific reason to deny him her company. She reminded herself that she owed many happinesses to this man. His nature was overbearing and sometimes cruel, but he gave her so many good things that she would never have known without him. She did not love him, though he longed for her to do so.

Amar was thoroughly attached to Fatima, like a clinging fruit to a vine. The tension in Fatima's face and heart eased because of the creature—it lightened her life to care for something so tenderly. Amar often stayed in her bed, though she had claim to a small enclosure in the menagerie, where Fatima deposited her for formal occasions or while she fed the beasts of prey in the menagerie.

Fatima walked through the dewed grass to the tennis courts, where Augustus' grunts and the clacking of the ball on the leather-bound rackets echoed. Fatima watched from a distance for a moment, waiting for the game to end. Augustus was well matched by his opponent, who played from the sunny side of the court, to Augustus' advantage.

Fatima found a seat by the few courtiers under a blood red and gold tent. Ottoman, she realized, likely stolen from her home country at the same time she was taken as a child. She touched the fringe with her fingers and Amar did the same.

A cheer from the crowd made Fatima look up as Augustus' opponent let a serve strike the court. Augustus' winning point echoed—a thwack, pock. His opponent turned to the King and bowed. He looked toward the crowd with a nod and Fatima's stomach clenched. It was the handsome soldier. She smiled politely, realizing she had not placed him in a high enough position to play the King at tennis.

Augustus sauntered up to her, dripping in sweat, his muscles outlined in dampness.

"My lady Maria," he said, kissing her hand. Fatima leaned into him. She could reciprocate when he was kind to her, and he seemed in a fair mood after winning.

"Who is your sorely defeated today, Your Grace?"

"This is Georg Spiegel, one of my finest soldiers."

Georg bowed from a distance, his eyes not leaving Fatima's face. "Pleasure, lady Maria."

Her stomach clenched. "Have your games ended, then? I am going to the menagerie to check the animals."

"They're over," said Georg. "Until I am called again to get a whooping from the Elector. I've never beat him."

"He is a strong man."

Augustus smiled at Fatima, narrowing his eyes in admiration. "You have plans after dinner, my lady?"

Fatima shook her head, well aware that she had no moon tea, but no excuses. Augustus bit his lower lip. Georg nodded and walked away.

"I'll complete my duties at the menagerie, Augustus, so I am yours later."

Augustus helped her to her feet and they stood under the

The Porcelain Menagerie

embroidered tent. Amar leapt to Fatima's arms, and the King balked. "God that creature stinks, Maria."

Fatima laughed, and said teasingly: "No worse than you, my lord."

Augustus lowered his eyes at her. He yanked Amar's chain, hard, and the monkey hit the ground.

"I'm sorry, Augustus," Fatima said, blood pulsing in her head. She should've known better. She should not tease the King.

"You'll pay for it later."

Fatima curtsied and left him, rushing to the menagerie. She let her tongue get the better of her. What a stupid mistake to insult Augustus like that! She had to watch herself. Ahead was the small shed where stable boys and servants went about their duties. The animals' care was organized, and Fatima fed them according to their plaintive cries. She learned much from the crews of men who delivered the animals from port, and the husbandry men who normally worked with horses and cattle. They all adjusted to the exotic.

She chopped piles of meat for the beasts of prey, sometimes graying and green from the kitchens, sometimes the weakest chicken from the coop, neck twisted, tossed into a cage. She measured grains and vegetables for the softer creatures, held the wings of parrots whose beaks needed trimmed, even cleaned the cages of feces and wet straw. Though at first the husbandry men stared at her in confusion as she dirtied her skirts, they eventually accepted her help, especially after noticing the solid, sure way animals regarded the King's mistress.

Fatima gathered hay, grasses, apples, and grains, in a wheelbarrow, tossing the contents in the mangers, strewing handfuls through the paths of the menagerie for the animals who wandered. The peacock lingered, watching her near the wooden troughs of food. It snatched a mouse from a hay pile, downing it quickly. Its sharp beak and black eyes gleamed when the wheelbarrows meandered the paths, searching for prey.

The servants and grooms running the menagerie had little knowledge of all of the animals; each really only knew how to care for just one creature. This, in turn, helped the place thrive. The stable boy who knew of dogs cared for the she-wolf and taught Fatima and three others how to feed her without the baring of teeth turning into snapping jaws. Fatima knew about the small mammals and monkeys' care, and another servant from the kitchens knew about birds. Together, they established a plan of care for the creatures there, and routine fell into place.

When she was done with the wheelbarrow, Fatima headed to Buda's cage. The lion's mane was growing in, darker now than when she'd first met him. He came up to the bars, rearing up on his hind legs at Fatima's approach. She skewered meat for him and held it to his face. Her arm strained. Her face came to his chest. He hit the dirt with a whump, rounded ears twitching.

He did not rush to the cage for anyone else. Fatima lowered her chin, prideful in her taming of the most stunning animal in the menagerie.

"Buda," she said. "I am trapped just as you are my friend. And if I open the cage door, would you be able to find your home? Or would you simply lay there, knowing a life of ease is yours?"

The lion turned his golden head and closed his eyes slowly.

"You get everything you need. But are you happy? Does happiness even matter in life? Or are we both content with a bed and a meal, regardless of how we must pay for those things?"

Fatima sighed.

"You don't pay for anything."

Buda flicked his tail.

"Perhaps you do, I'm sorry. They pulled you from the wild and this is your fate. I feel you are the only soul that understands."

He stood and came to the bars, and though her hand trembled, Fatima reached her hand through and touched him. He rubbed his mouth on the metal, flickers of fur danced in the air. A zing, something dangerous and lightning-like, crackled through Fatima's palm.

Buda allowed the touch, even seemed to enjoy it. She held his warmth, pressed her hands into his dense fur. Risk melted away for the impossible feeling of connection, understanding. The lion leaned into her hand. She scratched the delicate space behind his ears. He turned his teeth to her but she did not fear them.

When Fatima withdrew, Buda closed his eyes at her and flopped to his side. She loved him. They smiled at each other in the way people and animals do. She lingered for many more moments.

Fatima headed back to the castle, thinking of her menagerie.

The animals crowded the cages, earned names, and became living treasures. But the auspicious feeling of them belonging to Augustus was overwhelming. She owed a visit to his chambers tonight. And he was unhappy with her. She hadn't meant to upset him. Fatima's gut roiled, and her palms grew sticky. She pulled hay from her shirtsleeves and slowly made her way to the palace to wash.

The Porcelain Menagerie

The next morning, Fatima's thighs were marred with teeth marks. Her spine was bruised. The back of her head was tender where her hair was pulled. She felt empty, helpless. But she was out of bed, though her knees trembled and her throat screamed with pain.

Fatima pulled her own corset strings tight and made plans to catch Brunhilde in the kitchen. Perhaps the cook could make her tea. She desperately needed it. But a knocking at the door shook Fatima from her thoughts, from the wicked memories of last night in Augustus' bed. *Women must learn to ignore bad moments, to mask them, to push them aside, when they must.* She learned that from Aurora, and Fatima despised it. She wanted to scream, claw, fight her way from this so-called privileged position. But she was a woman. How could she fight?

Amar stirred from her small, curled form from bed, her paws delicately padded, to see who had made her mistress gasp. Fatima exhaled and rubbed her hands together and patted the swollen pockets under her eyes. She opened the door.

Georg, the soldier Augustus had beaten at tennis, face framed by his close-cropped beard and light eyes, swept his helmet from his head, grinning in the dawn-warm hallway.

"The King sent me," he said.

"Did he now?" Fatima scooped Amar from the floor. The monkey clung to her arm, grinning at the soldier. The feather-light chain around her waist jingled a small song. "And what more could he want?"

Georg's green eyes flashed at her, and he fingered his gray lapel. Brass buttons gleamed, catching candlelight from an ensconced cavity near the door. He held his helmet in one arm, and slung over his back was a leather satchel. Letters peeked from the opening, corners bent.

"He wants you to come to the Green Vault," said Georg. "There's to be a delivery of some kind of porcelain."

Fatima lowered her sculpted brows. Friedrich would be in the Green Vault, then. Along with Augustus. And handsome Georg was at her door.

"Forgive me, my lady, should I apologize? I've been asking after you. I am curious about your origins, but no one seems to know them. I cannot seem to get you out of my mind. You curtsy and feed lions, spend hours in the King's chambers."

"I prefer one of those things over the other, but am not allowed to deny any of them."

"The King's requests are not dismissible, as I've seen from experience. And yet, you do deny him sometimes. I see you in the menagerie, dreaming and working."

"My denials of him are not unpunished."

"I figured that."

"Well, Captain," Fatima angled her body to block her chambers, "are you simply interested in my origins because I defy the King?"

He shook his head and shifted his helmet from one arm to another. Fatima did the same with Amar, who stretched a small, dainty paw to the helmet's horsehair plume. The monkey leaped in a delicate arch, landing on the Captain's helm and forearm, and he startled, quickly jostling his armload to catch her. His muscles rippled, broad hands and fingers deftly holding the small, soft creature. She cooed at him, a high-pitched, loving sound.

"Amar!" Fatima said. Augustus would not have caught the creature, and would have dropped the lot in his avoidance of Amar. Georg stepped into her chambers, holding the monkey. Fatima's breath grew short.

"Thank you. I will take her, and head to the Green Vault."

Georg looked at her neck, which was mottled with bruising. He turned his face to the floor. Fatima looked down, too, nerves spiking.

"You could go slowly," said Georg. "We could...walk together to the kitchens, get something from the cook, and then make our way?"

Fatima blanched. Did he know she needed tea from Brunhilde? She considered. This soldier was kind to her. Perhaps it was a coincidence. But this soldier was known to Augustus, and Friedrich waited with his wares. She shook her head. She did not need another man in her life.

"No, thank you."

"My lady, Augustus has asked me to look in on you," Georg said, shuffling his feet. "I think he is concocting a plan."

Fatima narrowed her eyes.

"My name... What has he told you it is? And where has he told you I am from?"

Georg tilted his head, much like a dog. "Maria. From... from far away."

Fatima nodded her head and clutched Amar closer.

"I am Fatima Kariman, from Buda. If the King has a plan, it is *me* he must discuss it with." Fatima lifted her chin.

Georg lifted a corner of his mouth. "Then off to the Green Vault you go, my lady, to see the deliveries."

Amar pawed at Fatima's sleeve and Georg backed out of her chambers. Fatima's satin slippers made silent padding noises down the stone hall. He walked beside her, one hand behind his back, the other gripping his war helmet. They were silent together.

They crossed many rooms to get to the Green Vault, where, according to Augustus, in generations past, the jewels of Saxony were kept secret

The Porcelain Menagerie

and safe. Now, waves of people came through to view the wealth and prowess of the state, and Augustus began calling the place a word Fatima rolled around in her mouth but had a difficult time saying, due to its strange pronunciation: *museum*.

Augustus wore blue, with his red satin sash, and black shoes with golden buckles. He smiled so broadly at Fatima. He loved her. If Fatima's bruises had mouths, they would wail. Georg swept his free hand to the Elector of Saxony and bowed, leaving Fatima to her King and the promise of Friedrich.

There was a small gathering of people, including many beautiful court ladies Fatima had seen before but had not tried to speak with. They jostled their fans and smirked at her, knowing her favor with Augustus was, perhaps, as temporary as the many mistresses before her. Fatima's face grew hot. What would happen after Augustus was done with her?

Augustus extended an elbow to her, wafting that familiar, nose-wrinkling smell of armpit, and she placed her hand on his arm. Perhaps his anger toward her was gone? He got close and smelled her hair. She shivered. He led her across the room, where part of the wall was draped off, obscuring whatever treasures lay underneath.

Fatima watched her feet for a moment, waiting for the tittering of the ladies behind her to subside. Someone cleared their throat. She looked up. Friedrich, with a glossy new wig and clean clothes, met her gaze. Her heart galloped. She smiled and leaned forward, then back again. Would he see her bruises and react?

"Excited to see the porcelain, my lady?" Undoubtedly, Augustus had felt her shifting body language. She had to play into his assumption.

"Very. Perhaps I have fallen into porcelain sickness, like you." She turned her face to his. A bead of sweat dribbled down his cheek, pulling powder with it. His wig was bright black, nearly blue, and looked heavy, far more ostentatious than the porcelain maker's chestnut one.

Böttger cleared his throat. His hand was on the draped cloth, ready to unveil his porcelain to the small crowd. He stared at Fatima. She swallowed heavily, palms sweating, hoping Augustus wouldn't somehow feel the cramp in her lower belly when Friedrich looked at her with such fervor.

He carefully lowered the cloth, so not to jostle the precious wares behind it.

The crowd leaned forward. Friedrich stepped away, becoming a piece of the background in his green doublet. Though the eyes of the people of Augustus' court were on the redware, shining and glossy, diamond-cut, black-lacquered, sharp-edged, smooth and hard and whisper-delicate, Fatima turned to Friedrich and held his gaze; they both inhaled, raising their chins ever so slightly, to perhaps catch the exhaled breath of one another from across the room.

She signaled to him, with a low hand, to meet her in the hall. As Augustus fanned the flames of his porcelain obsession, picking up each small piece in his large, swollen hands, Fatima played that she felt weak.

"The beauty and richness makes me need to find a chair, Augustus."

"And your weakness after last night?" His voice was not dissimilar to Buda the lion's low, guttural growl.

Fatima's mouth soured, but she let out a laugh. What strangeness, to outwardly express the opposite of what she felt inside. She fled to the hall, where she leaned against the stones and waited until Friedrich walked by, crate in his hands, looking determined to leave the palace and load his cart and go back to his tower of isolation. But he turned the opposite way of where the carriages waited and Fatima, on soft, sure feet, followed.

"How long ago did he do this?" Friedrich asked, taking the warm candlelight down her body. Fatima's gooseflesh rippled and she shuddered, her ribs careening toward her spine.

"Last night."

"I cannot look at him the same. I knew he was...he was—"

"Say it out loud, Friedrich."

"Vile. Cruel. A million different words that do not convey his actual beastly self."

"Words don't come close to last night."

"May I bathe you? Take away some of this hurt?"

Fatima closed her eyes, but could still sense the hovering glow of Friedrich's candle. She did not answer him. He picked her up, his strong carver's hands gentle, though they still frightened her. Friedrich lay Fatima down on soft cushions near her fireplace. He stepped away.

"It's cold," he said. "The water in your tub. I'll warm it in the fire for you."

He heated water in a kettle, took a soft cloth and drizzled a spoonful of honey on it and got it wet, steaming, and dripped the cloth down her back. Fatima's wounds did not leave her, but her heart began to heal. She let her lover bathe her, whisper kind words to her, and she felt like Buda the lion. Given small things to soothe her and her trust slowly, slowly, grew, and she relaxed.

Fatima fell asleep. Friedrich took her to the bed, and in her half-daze, she remembered his hands wrapping her in her dressing robe, clothing her, placing Amar by her side, and tucking the blankets gently around them both.

The Porcelain Menagerie

Many hours later, Friedrich's back was to her, unclothed. He was far away, keeping his distance on the other side of the bed. The curtains around her large, carved bed were drawn tight, turning day into darkness. His soft, rolling shoulder muscles descended into the shallow canyon of his back, dipped in golden candlelight, curved low. Fatima moved Amai to the foot of the bed and grew close to Friedrich. Salt and clay and a faint scent of beeswax, lingering with her frankincense perfume and the healing honey, settled around her, held close to the canopy bed's warm, covered cloche.

Fatima traced a finger down Friedrich's spine, and he turned his head slowly to her, smiled, and lifted his body to face her. She touched his smooth face, watched his lips form a smile, and kissed him.

"Are you alright, Fatima? Will you stay here? I believe you are in danger."

Fatima exhaled through her nose and pushed her body closer to his. His hands found hers.

"I have nowhere to go but Dresden," she said, voice raspy and low. "But you and the King keep me alive. Him by feeding me. You by...feeling me."

"I am so angry."

Fatima ran a finger down Friedrich's chest, swallowed. "I know, Friedrich. He is not gentle like you."

"Yet he is the King. And we betray him. If he found me here..."

Fatima put her hand to his mouth. He kissed it.

"If he found you here, we'd die together."

"I am not sure he'd kill *me*. I am the arcanist. His valuable secret-keeper."

"Do you think I'm at risk from his wrath, if we're found out?" Fatima's dressing robe slid from her shoulder, exposing the curve of her breast. Her heart hammered beneath it.

"Yes. More than me, perhaps. But I've seen many women take his arm at an unveiling, at a court processional. I have not wondered, until I met you, what happens when they're released from his—"

"From his obsession."

"I was struck by lightning the moment I saw you. Like a bolt of it coursed through me, and my hair stood on end. You have not left my mind since. I thought at first it was your beauty, which I see when I close my eyes and in waking dreams. But I see you. You do some small thing for another person or those animals you've curated, I realize you are special. Even if you were not the King's lady, you are the creature of my desires. I am in love with you."

Fatima could not get close enough and wiggled toward him, feeling his heat and the soft places of his belly. She felt tears prick her eyes. How desperate she was to hear this from him, how many times she had imagined it...and here he was, the porcelain maker, saying he loved her, outside of her imagination and dreams. He not only loved her. He cared for her.

"May I always use your real name? Your family given one?"

She nodded eagerly, pressed her mouth to his, and felt warm tears build in the corners of her eyes. When he said it, she heard the world unfold and listened to the she-wolf and lion murmur to her in the depths of her mind. When he said it, she, too, felt lightning course in her body.

"Fatima."

Chapter 19
Johann
1732

As Johann, Samuel, Herold, and Hao left the Dresden palace, they studied the six hundred soldiers slated for trade. They were fully equipped—rifles, short swords, and the stomping feet of horses. Six hundred horses, helmets, trained men…enough to start a small war, and the King planned to give them away for Chinese porcelain.

"Does this sit well with you?" said Johann to Herold. He had not said a word since their arrival.

"Do not speak," Herold said, eyes scanning the crowded halls. "Not until we are inside the carriage."

Johann tried not to make eye contact with the soldiers. These men were pawns in a larger game. He could not help but hear their souls whispering; his pastor's son's mind churned. Each of them meant so much to their individual families—their wives, their children, their siblings, their mothers. And yet, as they were unimportant, insignificant, they were traded. For what? For breakable wealth?

The men milled around, waiting for their turn to be counted and tallied, their equipment and supplies notated by the court scribes. Johann had an urge to stand guard around the porcelain that lined the halls—surely they could have done this elsewhere? But the wealth Augustus wanted to show was inside the walls of his palace.

Johann was relieved that his monkey and eagle were not there, not vulnerable to the quick turns of soldiers with packs and small swords and loud guffaws. Johann turned his back and loaded into the carriage with his companions. On the way back to Albrechtsburg, they talked in hushed tones.

"Six hundred soldiers in exchange for porcelain?" Herold whispered.

"It is not a new practice," said Samuel. "Soldiers are traded quite often, but...not for porcelain. Does Augustus not see the risk? Porcelain does not add tangible wealth to the kingdom like gold or an army."

"He sees nothing but shining white, lads. Think of it!" Samuel quieted down with a hiss from Johann. "No sense in his head. He is blind to anything but women and white gold. What good does it do us now to make his menagerie, when he has masterpieces coming?"

"If we do not, imagine the results." Herold shook his head. "If he gives fully outfitted dragoons to a rival Elector in exchange for porcelain, what would he do to *us* for not delivering? We have no choice. We have to make the menagerie, the entire order."

"How many pieces have we made so far?"

"Eleven, if you count your lions, Samuel," Johann said. His mind flashed red at the thought of Maria's destruction of the seven molds. Seven steps closer to the King's wishes completed, and they were lost.

"Eleven!" Herold scoffed. "We must work tirelessly now in the hopes that what we do satiates his appetite and he does not trade his women for porcelain. Or us!"

"You mean to say you think more people's lives are at stake here?" Johann said.

"If the King trades his dragoons, who could have gone on to be lords, captains, generals, who had families here and legacies, too, I put nothing past him," Herold said.

"We haven't been paid in weeks," said Samuel. "He asks us to make him the impossible, and with this trade, it is unlikely we will see anything good. He'll be too busy fawning over his new wares to care about what us paupers in Albrechtsburg need."

"I fear it may be worse than that," said Johann, watching the stone sculptures of Benjamin Thomae roll by. "I fear he has lost all his senses, and no matter what we do, we shall never satisfy King Augustus."

The carriage rattled on, the empty crate where the porcelain monkey sat an ominous thing—they must fill it or face the King's irrational wrath.

Back at Albrechtsburg, Johann was startled to see his father's mule. He rushed out of the carriage, and she whinnied at him. He took her soft muzzle in his hands and smiled. The comforting smell of home hit him, and it took all of his strength not to bury his face in her neck. She's the last remaining member, besides me and Da, of the Kändler family, he thought.

His father rounded the corner. It appeared he'd not been allowed

The Porcelain Menagerie

inside and was exploring the grounds and nearby Lutheran cathedral near the enormous castle. Johann felt a flicker—perhaps his father had been assigned to this close church. Marten gave his son a half-smile. Johann grabbed his shoulders. He had not seen him since he'd moved to Albrechtsburg. His father felt smaller than he'd remembered. Perhaps Johann had grown. Perhaps the lack of boys to feed had made his father shrink. Johann held the thought in his mind that his father was growing old.

"Johann, I need to speak with you," said Marten. He gazed upward at Albrechtsburg as if wondering where they could be undisturbed.

"I'm sure you'll be allowed in my quarters, Da," Johann said. He would need to ask Hao if they could be left alone. He suddenly doubted if Hao was his friend, as he had implied lately, and wondered what he would say to the request. Surely, Hao knew his father would not steal the arcanum.

Samuel approached. "Pastor Kändler?"

"Samuel Kirchner," Marten said. He shook Samuel's hand and gave him a warm smile. "It's been many years since you've sat in my pews."

"Too many," said Samuel. "I cannot find the right words to tell my employers that traveling to your house of worship is my preference for Sundays."

"Seems they have a different god here," said Marten. Johann raised his finger to his lips.

The men quieted as Hao approached. Christian Herold lingered by the doorway, warily watching to see if the guard of Albrechtsburg would let Marten inside.

"What business have you with the porcelain factory?" Hao said.

"I am Johann's father," Marten said. He clasped his hands in front of his body, an expression of innocence and gentility. "I need to speak with him about his brother."

The black ball of worry in Johann's stomach grew. His brother was a ghost, a lingering laugh in his mind. What could he possibly need to tell him? He raised an eyebrow and waited for Hao.

Johann's worry must have registered because they were swept inside, flanked by Hao, directed up the stairs to Johann's room. Hao bent to fill the ledger as they walked by. Herold protested. No one else was allowed visitors like this. Crossed-armed, Herold followed them, only stopping when Hao whirled and grimaced at him.

The mossy hallway bloomed. White florals crawled down the wall. Like his son, Marten Kändler touched the moss as he waited to enter Johann's room, bright and dry compared to the damp hallway. The expanse of the Elbe unfolded below the window, and Marten let out a short whistle as he leaned partway out.

"Quite a view," he said. "Is that my church?"

"You can see all of Meissen and much of Dresden from here. Quite a view for what some call a prison, Da, but I am not unhappy. My comings and goings are monitored, documented. I have little freedom, but that is not why I am here."

"It is not," said Marten. "You are here to make the King whatever he desires in lasting porcelain."

"Ah, porcelain can break, as I have discovered," Johann said. "A fragile fortune. Father, why have you come here with news of our departed Herman?"

"The church is changing, Johann, and I fear I may not be long for my assignment. They want a pastor with a family in my place, a wife to lead the women's groups and help with the poor. I cannot say I disagree with them. I am to retire to the Lutheran preacher's college and teach others how to spread the word of God."

"But what do we do with Herman?"

Marten nodded, the wind ruffling his hair at the window. Church spires were visible in the distance, black against the summer sky. The city was green and plentiful. But Johann's mind was solely focused on the deep, dark root cellar where his brother rested.

"I fear the worst," said Marten. "When my assignment is announced we will have to move your brother. It occurs to me that it was never our home to begin with. We shouldn't have...we shouldn't have buried him there."

"How certain are you that you'll move on from your church? Could you be reassigned to Meissen, closer to me?"

"The deacon is coming in three days to speak with me. There is no word that any change will happen to the cathedral near Albrechtsburg." So near, if Johann wanted, he could touch it from the castle windows.

"So it is done," Johann said. He pursed his lips and took a shuddering breath.

"What will we do? Bury him near Ma?"

"It's too late," said Marten. "The congregation thinks we've already done that."

In the distance, a large bird rode a thermal high over the city. Johann knew the answer, but the thought made him fearful. "Albrechtsburg has over three hundred rooms, Da."

"We couldn't," said Marten. "How would it be possible?"

"I cannot imagine the things hidden here that we don't know

The Porcelain Menagerie

about," said Johann. "I can find a place unseen. Hopefully, the deacon gives you time. But I must tell you, Augustus is behaving dangerously."

He told his father of the six hundred soldiers and the porcelain vessels and, though he hesitated, of the King's daughter, longing for freedom from a cruel husband.

"Why are you involved in this, son?"

"Wasn't it you who taught me to look out for those who need help?"

"Yes," said Marten. "But this is not your brother. This is the King and dangerous situations."

"I cannot abandon anyone needing rescuing, even if danger awaits," Johann said. "I will work on my menagerie and pray the trade of soldiers for porcelain affects nothing."

"And what of Herman?"

"We must protect him, as we always have," Johann said. "I will send you a sign when I've found a place. Then I will come retrieve my brother." Johann did not say that his brother was with him, always, in dreams and waking visions and a voice in his head. Perhaps it would be of no consequence to have his remains nearby.

"People will be watching," said Marten. "Perhaps follow you."

"Da, the people who wanted him before don't want him now. We're more at risk from the congregation realizing our mistake. Besides, Albrechtsburg will eat them alive before they can find him." But he doubted himself. Perhaps the Leichendiebe did not care how old a unique body like Herman's was.

Da turned. Though the warm room feigned kindness, they could hear the shouting of the workers, the rumbling of the kilns and feet running clay up and molds down the winding, wobbling staircases of Schloss Albrechtsburg, and sensed the unspoken strangeness of the place.

"It's not as beautiful here as it seems, this castle on a hill," said Marten.

"What is in the cellar? I felt the soles of my shoes warm as I walked the main level."

"Kilns," said Johann. "Though I think of them more as hellfire."

"Those kilns bring your porcelain to life, yes?"

"Indeed, though I do not know how many men have died in pursuit of it. When they go, their bodies do not leave."

"Then perhaps this is the place for Herman after all," said Marten. "A place where even a permanent resident cannot find the bodies."

The Kändlers grew silent, both of their minds on the what-ifs: If Herman were not moved, who would live above his body? Would the anatomist still pay silver coins for his remains, even if he were reduced to a skeleton?

Johann thought, too, of removing Herman from his resting place and disturbing the deep, dark slumber of their broken boy. How would the warmth of Albrechtsburg feel to a soul buried in a cold cellar? At this, he saw Herman's smile in his head.

Johann looked to his father, resolute. They would move Herman to Albrechtsburg. He just had to find the proper place.

Chapter 20
Fatima
1706

Fatima's red cloak hung on a hook in the small, chill menagerie shed. She left the door partly open, hoping the rising sun would warm the space. The single window illuminated her work space. Amar picked bits of lettuce and seed from the dirt floor. White light hit a thick table, and Fatima picked up a wooden bucket, inhaling the scent of hay and animal musk. She knew it was unusual for a woman of her standing to feed the animals. She didn't care.

Her time alone here gave her freedom to untense her shoulders. She hid many secrets, and it felt like they were creeping up on her, threatening to spill out of her mouth at any moment. She thought of the risk of Friedrich in her chambers. The risk of no moon tea for three weeks now. The risk of King Augustus the Strong finding that she loved the porcelain maker.

Fatima startled, thoughts of redware and damp clay pushed from her mind. Georg the soldier appeared ahead on the menagerie path. She dropped the bucket with a clatter. Amar leapt to her back then clambered around her shoulder, hiding in the crook of her arm as was customary.

"I'm sorry to scare you."

Fatima put Amar down, prying away the clinging paws. Her heart thumped so heavily she thought it visible on the outside.

"I've just left the King," Georg said, shifting his feet from side to side as he peered in the little shed.

"How is our majesty this morning?"

"Full of questions about you and this place, and the way you look at the porcelain maker, Friedrich Böttger."

Fatima blanched.

"I look at...whom?"

"Don't worry. I've persuaded him that you're only interested in the treasure Böttger creates."

"And why would you offer this to the King?"

"Because he asked me, and he trusts me."

"And why have you sought me out?"

Georg laughed sadly. "Because you need to be careful."

Fatima swallowed, her throat wobbling.

"He is not stupid, Lady Maria. Tricky, you are. The whole castle thought you were a passing obsession of Augustus'. Now, it seems he actually cares for you, perhaps even loves you."

Fatima was too afraid to look up at him, but Georg reached over and lifted her chin. Augustus did not love her. It was not possible to love something you hurt.

"Do not anger him," said Georg. She pulled away from his touch.

"I don't want to, but I'm afraid..." She would not reveal what she was afraid of.

"If he's asking me questions, he already suspects that your bed is not empty every night. But you must be careful."

"Why are you trying to protect me?"

Georg said nothing for a moment, then reached his hand to Amar, who gently took his finger.

"If I were the King of Poland and Elector of Saxony, I would give up everything for you. I would fight for you. Try to win your love and affection. I believe Augustus will do the same."

Fatima stepped back. Amar pawed at her sleeve. Georg did not fully realize what Augustus did to her when he was angry.

"Perhaps you're the one who is dangerous."

"Perhaps I am, but I won't show it to the King. And neither should you. You're putting Böttger at risk, too..." He parted his lips and left his mouth open.

Fatima swallowed. "Leave me to my task."

Georg nodded, reluctance in his eyes showing his hesitation to leave. "Perhaps you could show me? How you feed them? Innocent enough, I promise."

The cries of the animals waiting for their food penetrated the conversation. She shook her head, brusquely, and bid him farewell. Georg left the menagerie.

That night, Fatima could not sleep. When she was in Buda, her brothers, then children in bed with her, had hot, long limbs that crawled like growing tree roots, anchoring her to one place, and now, she cried, feeling their absence even after many years. If Augustus dismissed her, and she went back to Buda, would she ever find them again? She wiped her tears.

Earlier, in her haste to leave the strange conversation with Georg behind, she put Amar in her menagerie cage and left her. Amar was still there, and now, Fatima could think of little else but her warm, soft fur. The monkey was fine, and sometimes even preferred her outdoor space, but she needed her.

Fatima dressed in a blue robe, sighing as she realized that everything beautiful she owned was a gift from *him*. She shrugged off the feeling of Augustus' hand on her waist and clicked shut the chamber door. The parquet squeaked under her slippered feet, and she clung to the corners, fingers tracing the plaster walls. Few candles were lit at night, sending fans of golden light into the hallways.

The castle was still, with pockets of chill air in the corners. The world felt closed in at night when the servants and Augustus were sleeping, leaving only night guards and a cacophony of small insects chirping. The kitchens rumbled early, as did the stables with the sounds of animals, but no place was louder than the menagerie at night.

The moon was waning. She wanted to speak to Friedrich, to warn him that Augustus was onto them, and that perhaps they should run away together. The thick, earthy smell of a slumbering wood cascaded over her. Her feet grew cold. Fatima unlocked the gate with Augustus' gifted key.

Inside, the menagerie stirred with the sounds of animals. Nocturnal, she realized, remembering the word from the sea captains' letters. Moon and star lovers—especially the she-wolf, silhouetted by the half-moon, seen through the gaps in the heavy-trunked trees. The path wound from birds to where Amar was likely furious from her night outside.

Fatima came to the mammals, where a camel dozed, unfazed by her arrival. A fox chittered. A boar snorted and turned over in its leaf-covered cage. In the near distance, the she-wolf's eyes glowed white-green. Fatima lowered herself to the ground in the pea gravel. The wolf was silver-gray, enormous. Her ears reached upward, fringed in fur, turning at each slight sound. She paced. Ten steps was all she could take. The she-wolf had made a nest where the bones of small creatures and femurs of her dinner gleamed.

"You've made yourself at home, then." Fatima sat in stillness, sighing deeply, hearing a long-lost song from her childhood in her head, and sang into the darkness.

An abrupt rustling sounded behind her, and Fatima stood, wary. The she-wolf pointed her ears and pawed at the edge of the enclosure. Fatima turned to see the peacock, nearly black in the gray morning light, rustling its feathers at them. It cawed, a piercing, startling noise, and Fatima shook herself free from the trance of the wolf. She remembered Amar and rounded the bend, leaving the cage behind her.

Fatima's feet crunched in the gravel, and she stopped suddenly. A man sat before Amar's cage, closing a cloud-colored book. Amar perked up, opening her tiny mouth, white teeth bared, and clanged gently against her post.

Fatima inhaled, startled, and hesitated. Amar chattered, and the man turned. It was Friedrich, hair a mess, cloak lazily tossed on the leaf-strewn path. He rose to his feet, not taking his eyes from Fatima. Friedrich smiled slowly.

"Seems neither of us could sleep." He reached for her. Fatima took his hand. She unlocked Amar's cage, freeing the creature who melted into her like an attached limb. She smelled sharp but musky, sweet from fruit.

Fatima attached Amar's chain to her wrist. "It is bold of you to come here when you're not to leave your tower."

"As long as things are going well, and I'm creating and delivering, I can sneak out at night. The guards have more treasure to watch over, and less the treasure maker."

"We're known to Augustus, Friedrich. One of his military advisors told me today..."

Friedrich stood, and his breathing grew fast. Fatima told him what Georg said.

"We should never see each other again," he said. Fatima blinked, putting Amar down.

"You say that quickly, and with fear on your lips. How do we know Georg spoke the truth?"

"How is it you know him so well to call him by his first name?"

Fatima's eyes pricked with tears. "You're scaring me."

"You know what he will do?"

"I know better than you do."

"That is in his bedchambers... that was not punishment, not to him."

"Not that you could understand!"

"I might love you, Fatima, but I cannot do this any longer."

He *might* love her? Did he mean that? It wasn't the right phrasing, the way he said it.

"I am harmed every night I am with him, Friedrich. You know that.

The Porcelain Menagerie

I don't... I don't want to lose you. I've thought of you endlessly since I saw you first. I cannot be without you, just as you cannot be without your wares."

Friedrich laughed, a wry sound, and shook his head, tucking his book under his arm.

"The two cannot be compared, love and my work. I am good at what I do. I have not been doing it long, yet I can make art and feel mastery. I can see my future—a road paved in white gold. This is my legacy, Fatima, and I cannot abandon it."

"But you can abandon me? Many women would do anything to be in my place—to have the favor of the King, and his jewels and attention, his bed, his bastards. They know not the terror! You must help me."

"I cannot. I cannot run away with you, or defy the King for you. No matter where I go, they will follow me. As a secret keeper, I cannot be safe. I know too much. They will not let me go. If we flee together, we will be caught as I am too valuable to lose."

"Then I will stay in the King's favor and we will stay together, secretly."

Friedrich sighed. Fatima did not know if he wanted that. Her throat closed.

"This obsession has gone too far," he said. "It's too risky."

"Obsession? The King's obsession with porcelain...or?" She looked around the menagerie, swallowed, and took a rattling breath. She steadied herself.

"Your obsession with me, Fatima."

Fatima opened her mouth as if to correct him, to tell him it wasn't obsession, it was love, that she was a prisoner, too, that her captivity was not her only lot in life, but she stopped. He did not want to abandon his trade for her. He wanted to abandon her. She swallowed, giving him long enough to change his mind.

"It's over," he said. "For both our sakes." Friedrich left, and the chill night touched Fatima.

Chapter 21
Johann
1732

Sixteen porcelain animals were packed in crates on the table before Johann and Samuel. They had each made eight. They had no more room to work.

"Where shall we store them for now while the others dry?"

"There's likely a place downstairs, near the stables, so that we can load them easily. I'll ask Hao and explore there," said Johann. "If we stack the crates, we only need one room."

"Out of three hundred rooms, there is surely one not used," said Samuel, fixing the lid on a wildcat with a pheasant in its mouth. The wildcat's eyebrows were raised in a surprisingly human expression.

"How can I make these look...less human?" Samuel said.

"Study the animals," said Johann. "This is why I go to the menagerie and spend so much time in the fields. They do not have expressions like we do. My book is full of sketches so I can sculpt from life."

"I find myself searching the room and my mind for human expressions. It is true," said Samuel. "But still, the King will like our menagerie no matter who has made it. He may not tell the difference between your work and mine, though I certainly can."

"No worries, brother," said Johann, putting a clay-stained hand on Samuel's shoulder. "We're partners in this."

Johann helped Samuel stack the remaining crates and counted the spiral stairs as he sought Hao and an empty room. He knew the space would house more than crates if lucky. He was looking, specifically, for Herman's resting place.

Hao was near the entrance, watching other guards shuffle about in their morning exchange of duties. He brightened slightly, turning his

The Porcelain Menagerie

face with a smile. Hao's presence, once frightening and stiff, now made Johann feel comfortable, as if nothing could go wrong when he was near.

"Hao, I'm looking for a place to safely store the menagerie before we make a delivery to the King in bulk," Johann said.

Hao stepped side to side, a usual dance on this castle level as the kilns were directly below them, and Johann, too, felt his feet grow hot. Hao motioned for him to follow.

"Why not deliver now if you have some ready?"

Johann hesitated. "Ah, we thought the King would enjoy a full menagerie at once, displayed in his Japanese Palace and Green Vault according to his wishes, rather than one at a time." A lie.

Hao raised an eyebrow in an expression, not unlike Samuel's many animals. They crossed the great hall where kings once dined. Johann sensed the flickering of laughter, memories, and meals shared...there were indentations on the stone floor, echoes of a large table that was no more.

"I understand," Hao said. "It gives you time to make sure the King does not change his mind if he sees a single piece and dislikes it."

Johann breathed heavily through his nose. Hao was right. "We were hoping for a ground floor room, perhaps something near the stables so we can load easily?"

Hao shook his head. "Sublevel would be better. Empty rooms there."

"But the heat, Hao? I don't think that would be good for the porcelain..."

"There is a room far from the kilns under the kitchen. It was once a root cellar, easy access but closed off. I don't think the temperature is too hot."

A tingle crawled down Johann's spine. A root cellar, just like Herman's current resting place. He eagerly followed Hao down a narrow staircase. It was opposite the castle from the wide stairs that led to the kilns. Johann had never been in this part of Albrechtsburg.

Hao lit a torch, and Johann followed the bouncing fire to the cellars. Moisture settled on his skin, the air chill and clean, fresh, a crumbling dampness of earth. It felt starkly different from the side of the castle with the kilns, almost peaceful, as if the stone walls were a night-cool, heavy blanket.

"There is a way out over there," said Hao, pointing to a distant prick of light. "Leads to the stables, but it's a ways to walk. The door is locked."

"Is there a closed room? Where we could lock the crates?"

Hao rounded a corner where the ceiling dropped lower. Though the men were not so tall, they crouched.

"Here." Hao pushed open a small door, which creaked with disuse—a proper root cellar: narrow, with shelves on either side, a dark dirt floor.

Herman's small casket would fit perfectly. Johann breathed a sigh of relief. He imagined stacking the crates on top of his brother's second grave. The door was heavy and could be easily equipped with a padlock. It was perfect.

"This will work," he said. "I'll want a lock for the door. And a sworn secret that you won't reveal this room to anyone. Not even Samuel or Herold, Hao."

Hao nodded. "Seems you're starting to understand that Albrechtsburg's secrets are many. Congratulations on your first one."

Johann swallowed. The book in his pocket trembled. If only Hao knew how many secrets he was keeping.

That afternoon, Johann modeled a mother wolf and two pups. He worked as the orange sun slid down, casting rays onto the Elbe. The flat river cut through Saxony like a tool on fresh clay, and he watched the water from the window of his workshop. Samuel left, seeking ale and bread, hours ago.

Johann worked the white clay repeatedly, using a dull knife to cut a face and eyes, the gentle curve of a furred neck. He remembered the dead animal slung over the King's shoulder. He remembered the look of panic on Katharina's face each time he saw her. He remembered the kindness of his mother's eyes and Herman's gentle laugh.

In the face of his wolf, he found Maria and his mother's expressions. Her eyes would shine with white-moon porcelain. He did not draw pupils. Below his mother wolf's feet, he carved two pups. Innocent, protected. One curled like a lamb under the feathered tail, the other with its face pressed between its mother's paws. Katharina's face. The she-wolf's mouth parted, revealing sharp teeth. She held her ears back, searching for sound.

Johann carved deep into the night. Stars filled the windows, and the Elbe turned to a black shining sheet, guiding water onward and away. Johann thought of where the river drifted and turned, who was drinking its waters, and what lovers bathed in the moonlight. He longed to rinse his clay-smudged hands off in the water but stayed inside his castle prison and carved the King's menagerie.

The next morning, before the delivery to the King, Johann strolled the live menagerie, hoping for news from Katharina, of both her divorce and the trade of dragoons for porcelain. Perhaps someone had talked sense into the King, perhaps the trade was off.

The Porcelain Menagerie

She was where he imagined her to be—by the old wooden shed near the back. The place held animal food and buckets, its roof green-tinged. Katharina was pacing, and looked nervous. She stopped at Johann's approach.

"I assume you have reasons to be this nervous," Johann said.

"He is restless," she said. "Focusing on everything but the papers that have been at his fingertips for weeks now. My husband has sent word that he's on his way, coming with some kind of large delivery for Augustus. Chinese vessels."

"Your husband is making the porcelain delivery?"

"Does this affect you?"

"It puts our usefulness at risk. We cannot make Chinese porcelain, no matter how we try." He had it on his lips to tell her why: that the clay was wildly different, that the thousand years of practice in China meant they succeeded more than they failed, that they simply couldn't perfect the craft...yet. But Johann kept Albrechtsburg's secrets.

"My husband is one of his favorite advisors. That is one of the reasons I was married off to him. If he makes it here with Chinese vessels in tow for my father, I fear he will never sign off on the divorce."

"Do you not see the bigger problem here, Katharina? That Augustus sends men, humans, souls, away from their families? In exchange for something breakable? Something that will not last?"

"He does not care. He has porcelain instead of gold, instead of an army, which actually strengthens his power. He chooses breakable things, even though they can shatter, and the kingdom's wealth is gone. There are still gems and gold and other valuables, but..."

"People, Katharina. We need him to think about people." He looked hard at her.

"I am a *bastard daughter* of a mad King."

"And he married you to someone important. Augustus must care about you."

Katharina laughed, her head thrown back. "No, no, you are wrong. He cares about himself. About the offspring I produce being higher blooded than me. About the man I marry being of value to Saxony, to Poland; but he does not care about me."

Johann pursed his lips and looked down. "I truly didn't understand. I'm sorry. He does seem to listen to your mother."

"He does."

"Why?"

"I cannot answer you. When she agreed to help me, I knew I had a better chance. She holds some kind of power over him."

"Is it love?"

"Perhaps. Or perhaps lust."

"If Lady Maria hadn't loved my work at first sight, I don't know if I'd be making porcelain..."

"I should push one more time for my mother to ask him for my freedom."

Johann shook his head, unsure. Maria was unpredictable, and he wasn't sure Katharina knew her mother destroyed his molds.

"It might work. But it won't convince Augustus to make smarter decisions."

"You certainly speak boldly to the daughter of the King."

Johann bit his cheek.

"Do not fear me, porcelain maker. I am the same level as you in this place."

"We have the same desires, Katharina. Freedom to be who we want to be."

"And who do you want to be?" Katharina said. "The world you live in will be protected more than anywhere else."

Johann thought of Herman. He thought of the cold night, years ago, when the merchant and his white horse stopped outside the parsonage. No matter how much he longed to, he could not go back to that time or place. He did not answer her with the resounding words in his head: he wanted to be a brother. Johann gazed upward. To Katharina, it surely seemed he was dreaming. But he was blinking the ghost of Herman from his mind.

"I want to leave a legacy, to be able to express myself and craft masterworks."

"You get to do that now."

"I do not. Not with impossible orders, not with chains in the cellars for those who fail."

"If you stay the course, you'll find those opportunities in Schloss Albrechtsburg, eventually."

"And what if my impatience matches your own?"

At this, Katharina smiled. "I believe it does. Ambition, Johann, can be dangerous."

"Let's both of us ask your mother today, before I deliver, to beg Augustus once again for your divorce and be done with this."

"It didn't work the first time."

"She wasn't holding the most exciting crate of porcelain he's ever seen from Albrechtsburg."

Katharina raised her chin in a way that made Johann realize she, too, had hidden hurts. She, too, had experienced loss. Johann fell silent. They stared at each other for a moment, sharing internal thoughts of suffering that neither dared speak aloud for fear of revealing too much. If they spoke of their entanglement, Johann might be forced to admit he cared for her.

"Are you afraid?"

"I am. But if you hold the key to the crate, perhaps he'll sign. And then we can go our own ways."

Johann saw the reflection of tears in her black eyes. He thought them grateful tears. They threatened to spill, and he rose. They stood ten feet from each other. He did not care what she would do; he strode quickly toward her and embraced her. Katharina fell into Johann, and he felt her weight like Herman's—small, strong, singular.

She wept, and he let her, smelling the deep spice scent of her black hair. Her kohl eyeliner tumbled down her face, and he wiped it, leaving white clay smudges. She was beautiful, but he did not tell her so. Instead, he smiled lightly at her and turned her wrist, the scarred one, toward himself.

"My reminder every day that he could kill me," she said. "I am terrified, Johann. I do not wish to be anywhere near him."

Katharina began to pull away, but not before patting his pocket where his book was kept, filled with sketches and secrets. Katharina, swift as a fox, grabbed the book from Johann's coat and backed away from his arms. It fell open. The margins were full of arcanum formulas.

"This is the book I gave you."

"It is the arcanum formula. You should never have had it."

"It was in my mother's trunk, buried under a false bottom. I searched there for papers confirming my father is the King. I found what I needed to prove he could sign the papers granting my divorce. Who wrote in this book?"

"Confirming?" said Johann, more forcefully than he intended. "Who would doubt that you're...? Maria is his...was his..."

"Mistresses can have many beds."

They held each other's gaze, many thoughts left unsaid.

"Böttger," said Johann. "The man who wrote this, his name was Böttger. He died, poisoned, from what I hear, chained to the floor of his room. Dead from years of breathing in Albrechtsburg. He is the one who wrote these formulas."

Katharina flipped to the beginning of the book, and there were the initials FB, FK. Next to it, his sketch of a monkey and the wolves covered the page.

"FK?" She ripped the page from the book. On the backside were scrawling numbers of arcanum formulas.

"You cannot show anyone," said Johann, worried.

"Those are my mother's initials," said Katharina. She folded the paper. "FK. Fatima Kariman, her birth name."

Fatima? Johann knew the initials FB were Friedrich Böttger's. His mind tangled with questions, but he looked at Katharina in silence.

Chapter 22
Fatima
1706

A week after Friedrich told her she was no longer wanted, Fatima woke to a quiet, repetitive knocking at her chamber door. She was slow to rise, and even more slowly, she turned the brass handle, expecting Augustus. But it was Friedrich, heading away from her room, looking disappointed. Her throat tightened.

She hissed his name, and he turned, looking both relieved and nervous. Fatima held a finger to her lips and reached out to grab his hand, leading him inside. She looked both ways down the dark hallway to ensure they remained unseen. Friedrich grabbed her hand, and she pulled him inside.

"What are you doing?" she said.

He looked sheepish. "I…I made a mistake. I cannot create anything, for the depth of the pain of losing you has gripped me, heart and soul. I am nothing without you. Nothing."

She'd longed to hear him say this over the past week. Each day, her stomach felt clenched, her whole body dry and drawn out, as if she'd been chained to some faraway rock, with only the hot sun as her companion, mean and ever-burning. She kept to her chambers, ate nothing but broth. She had little energy to even crawl from her bed after he told her they were done. But now, suddenly, she felt her blood in all her limbs, full with both energy and life.

She pushed his crossed arms down and kissed him. A cramp hit her belly—she could not determine if it was fear—fear of losing him again—or her body releasing the suffering of this week without him. Friedrich's hand cupped her chin, lifted her off her feet and carried her to the bed. He lay her down gently, and Fatima could not stop the tears that trickled down her cheeks and slid into her dark hair.

The ornate clock on her mantel said it was nearly three. Dawn was still hours away. She hesitated giving herself to him, thinking of the absence of Brunhilde from the kitchens. "Would you be satisfied simply sleeping beside me?"

Friedrich shed his coat and soft black shoes, leaning onto the four poster. He said nothing, but drew the blankets up around her. Tears pooled into her ears and she turned her head. Friedrich walked to the opposite side of the bed and untucked the covers. He slid in.

"Was this place created for you?" His eyes darted to the ceiling and corners, an artist taking things in.

"Well. This was the chambers of other mistresses, but now, besides the help I have to dress and brush my hair and bathe, it is mine and Amar's."

"Your monkey is a lovely creature."

"Yes, my little darling. She's in the menagerie tonight. Rumors of a male monkey arriving soon means she needs to get used to staying there. I want her to have babies."

"What about the other animals? Are you as close with them? Weren't you part of the King's hunt when you first arrived?"

"Yes..." She turned her face away. He did not know her well, and yet they were entangled...

"You didn't like it."

"No, I did not. Part of the menagerie's creation was born of it, of a desire of mine to ensure that even the most common beasts had a place to live here, instead of the walled-in courtyard where they're caged and released to be shot."

"I'm sorry you had to do that. Many things Augustus does seem unreasonable."

"And ridiculous. I saw him hold two urchins by their hair and ride his stallion last week. The ladies of the court practically fell at his feet."

"And how did you feel about that show of strength?"

"I am not impressed by that kind of display. I don't love him. I deal with him and he gives me this place and a purpose and nearly everything I ask, except peace." Fatima watched Friedrich's expression. She tested him now, seeing how badly it hurt, knowing that he could give her nothing.

"I didn't ask if you loved him."

"No, you didn't. Instead, you come to my chambers after telling me we're through for your fear of Augustus and then you ask me how I feel about him. How do I feel about him? Like he owns me. Like I am a piece of human porcelain."

He furrowed his brow. She rocked slightly, feeling a wave of nausea claw at her throat. Admitting these things to herself and to her lover had opened some kind of wound. How could it possibly be healed?

Friedrich swung his legs from the bed, his breath was sharp through his nose, clearly uncomfortable about the conversation. Would he leave? He walked around the bed and knelt at her side. His hair released a cloying smell of burning kilns.

"You are more than porcelain. You are kind and cunning, mysterious and beautiful, unable to be persuaded to change your mind by anyone."

"Some would call that stubbornness."

"Let them call it that. If you are porcelain, you are the rarest kind, made of the world's most beautiful clay, fired in a kiln far away, by a mold destroyed by its makers after it produced you. One of a kind. Invaluable. Unable to be priced, impossible to ever let go of."

He wove a hand through her raven-black hair. She pulled him into the bed, pushing aside thoughts of her moon tea and her fears and the possibility that he would leave and lock himself in his tower and deny her entrance to his heart and his life.

After they untangled, they talked. She told him of Buda, of the red tent in the tennis courts that felt so familiar to her, and how foreign it was here in the clean court of Dresden. She had never told this to Augustus, but she swore she could smell the market spices when she leaned close to it.

He told her how, when he was a young man, he conned a crowd of people into thinking he'd turned a silver coin into a gold one, and the King's man saw, and bid him come to the court out of intrigue, and how he was conned into staying in Dresden until he did it again. But he couldn't make gold. It was all a performance, a facade. He called himself a foolish boy.

"I wish I'd never learned that trick. Who knows where I'd be now if I'd have kept my hands still and my ego calm."

"Well, there'd be no porcelain in Dresden if you hadn't turned that coin to gold."

"I never turned it to gold, it was all a farce, like me claiming to be able to make Chinese porcelain."

"Chinese porcelain isn't important. Dresden porcelain is. And that's what you make."

Friedrich rose from the bed. Fatima wanted to ask him to stay, to sleep, to wake together, and realized the complications of the porcelain maker going back to his quarters at dawn. She held her tongue. The clock read six. They'd talked for hours.

Friedrich wandered the room, touching every decoration. He stroked the silk wallpaper, the ornately carved marble mantle, and stopped at her jewelry box.

Should she explain the diamonds, the baubles, the pearls given to her by Augustus? What would Friedrich think of the vast wealth in that box, when he made treasure, too, and yet had little to his name?

Her delicate feet hit the colorful rug and she took the box from him, opening it to pull out a diamond necklace. The largest jewel swung heavily. When she wore it, it completely filled the dipping hollow on her throat. Friedrich choked, coughing. She pressed it into his hands. She pulled a string of wildly asymmetrical pearls next, each one thick as a drop of honey, pale as the porcelain Friedrich tried to create. She layered it, clinking, on top of the diamond in his hand.

Next was a brooch, a bow dotted in small stones that sparkled in the dying embers of the fire. Last was a crescent moon, which could be fastened to a chain or worn at the jointure of her bust on her gowns, encrusted in diamonds.

Friedrich pulled his lips together tightly as she filled his hands.

"They mean nothing," she said. "They are things."

"No. He's given you this, without a promise of marriage or loyalty, or future or even knowing your past. He gives it to you, with no consequence. Can you name the people who made these treasures? Or are they invisible, and the things they make take the value?"

Who made them? Whose hands and eyes and creative minds? She blanched. Friedrich gently placed the lot back into the box and rubbed his hands on his trousers as if to rid himself of the feeling of the objects' weight. He turned to the opposite side of the fireplace, where the hidden room's door was barely cracked open. He reached for the small metal ring, nearly hidden on the wall.

The door emerged, wholly obscured by the fabric floral wallpaper. Friedrich's face brightened, curious, and he slid his head inside. The room was dark, windowless, and small, but the fireplace outside warmed it. A single stub candle on a mirrored table was cold.

A sharp rap on the door sounded. The rap of a cane. Fatima jumped. Only one person rapped on her door with such fervor. Augustus' voice sounded from the hall: "Maria!"

Fatima shoved Friedrich inside the hidden room and pushed the door shut. A small whimper escaped and she shushed him. The door latched with a click.

"Maria! I have news! We must go to the menagerie for a surprise."

She swallowed, trying to make a noise, but could not speak. Fear gripped her. She took a few steps toward the door and grabbed her

The Porcelain Menagerie

dressing robe, tossing the blanket on the floor over Friedrich's jacket.

"Coming, Your Majesty," she said, feigning nerves for slumber in her voice.

She clicked open the door.

Augustus was dressed for the day, no footmen in sight. Today, he had a plain cane with a brass top instead of ivory. It clashed with his white stockings. He wore a simple, fine green overcoat. He must have been overly excited about something to be alone and dressed at this hour. Augustus pushed the door open wide and stepped in, whispering loudly.

"A special delivery was made at the menagerie last night, and you should be the first to see it with me."

"Perhaps the monkey I asked for?"

"Perhaps you should wait for the surprise." Augustus looked down at her like she was a child, roughly grabbing her chin.

She bit her tongue, grimacing. Friedrich's black shoes were looming in the corner of her left line of sight. Her heart leaped.

"I'd like to watch you get dressed," Augustus said, touching the soft cream lace of her robe.

Fatima swallowed and threw the dressing robe off without hesitation, tossing it dramatically over the shoes. There was no sound from the small hidden room. Fatima crossed her arms, grabbed the hem of her nightgown, and pulled it over her head. Augustus dropped his cane, staring at her body. She turned slowly, taking his cane from him and leading him to the bed so he could sit.

"I must thank you for the beautiful quarters, Augustus," Fatima said. She pointed her face to the corner of the room, hoping Friedrich could hear her, that he would stay put. "Forgive me for not mentioning it before now. But having my own drawing room and chambers has been a remarkable thing. I often sit here and think of you."

"My dear, you are beginning to understand what being one of my women means. You are privileged and, if lucky enough, will soon be in many other's positions. The palace staff will care for your children as you will care for me in your own special way."

Fatima grabbed a fine silk shift and tossed it over her head. She shivered under the cool fabric. Next were her stays, her stockings, and a wide pannier support that broadened her already curved hips.

"I will need help with my corset, Augustus, if you know how."

She wrapped the crimson bodice around her waist and told him what to do. He was slow. The seconds ticked by, painfully, and in the silence she found herself panicking, hoping that Friedrich stayed put, that he didn't think they'd left the room.

Fatima coughed and thought of something to talk to Augustus about. "Do you have a hunt this week, Augustus?"

"Of course. Every week we have a hunt. Almost time for the year's biggest hunting event. I'm having my military advisor, Georg von Spiegel, organize it. You know him."

At the sound of Georg's name, Fatima turned her head.

"Yes, I do. You introduced us after beating him solidly at the tennis courts. You're close, then, and talk often?"

"When we need to. He does his job, keeping tabs on things of consequence."

Fatima's mouth soured. Things of consequence, like knowing she and Friedrich Böttger shared a bed. Had Georg told Augustus? She didn't know. She wished Augustus would hurry lacing her.

"I see. You like Georg," she said.

"I trust him. He sees many things I do not. I have grand plans for the man. Especially if this event he is in charge of goes well."

"Of course. I'm sure it will. What will the event entail, Your Majesty?"

Augustus laced the last of her corset, planting a kiss on her bare shoulder as he did so. Fatima's goosebumps were not from pleasure. She turned and grabbed her petticoat and skirt.

"We call it the fox tossing."

She paused, skirt suddenly wildly heavy in her hands.

"Fox...tossing?"

"Yes, my dear. Annual tradition. Those cages in your menagerie being full of animals will make the event even easier this year."

"Surely you don't mean you actually toss a fox?"

Augustus laughed. Fatima raised her hand to her breast, laughing with him in relief.

"Oh, no, no. We toss hundreds of them! Not just *a fox*. And boars and wolves and wildcats. And this year, I'm going to throw that lion of yours in the mix and see what happens."

Fatima dropped her skirt, heard a ringing in her ears. Augustus rose from the bed to retrieve it for her. As he bent, Fatima kicked Friedrich's cloak under the bed.

"Ah, you're excited too! We'll go to the menagerie and you can choose your favorites to be entered into the event. The people will love to see if the exotic creatures will survive. I'll make a special point to taxidermy your favorites. Perhaps that little monkey of yours, what do you say?"

Fatima's breath was short and hot in her mouth. She pulled the chamber pot from under her bed and vomited.

Chapter 23
Johann
1732

Maria and Katharina met Johann and Samuel in the hallway outside the throne room. Johann had asked them there to present the latest porcelain as a symbolic gesture of Maria's (or was her name Fatima?) love to the King. In case his note was intercepted, Johann mentioned nothing of the divorce decree and the coercion that could occur, knowing Katharina would explain the plan to her mother.

Samuel was left in the dark. He fidgeted, sensing something was going on.

"I don't understand," he said to Johann, moments before the chamber doors were to be opened. "Why do we need them here? This is our work. Certainly you see how this distracts and could potentially mean a delayed payment. Augustus is easily distracted, Johann."

"I know. But the ladies are here for a short time, Samuel. It's nice to have pretty faces deliver our wares, get us men out of it."

"Seems ridiculous to me. I'm good looking enough."

"You've worn the same coat every time we've brought things from Albrechtsburg."

"No one notices that."

Johann raised an eyebrow. Samuel straightened his yellow sleeves, pulling lace cuffs down. "Do they?"

The doors opened, and Johann and Samuel hauled in the two crates. Maria and Katharina were each given small metal tools to open them, and their matching night-sky gowns swept the parquet floor. Augustus uncrossed his legs and leaned forward.

"My ladies, I thought you'd never arrive."

"We're here, Highness, for you, a special delivery. We've organized many things from Schloss Albrechtsburg, for your new collection," said Maria.

Augustus smiled at her, a flicker in his eyes that echoed the one-eyed lion staring at a leg of lamb.

The courtroom, full of lovely dressed ladies, military men, and a few foreign dignitaries, collectively leaned in while Maria opened the first box, its contents covered in fine cloth. Samuel started to step forward, undoubtedly wanting to help her, but Johann grabbed his frilly lace wrist and shook his head.

Maria stopped. She held her hand out to Katharina, who stepped forward with a rolled up document and quill, dripping with ink. Black spots dotted their path.

Augustus narrowed his eyes. His courtroom murmured. Katharina unrolled the papers. Maria pulled Samuel's lion from the box and held it precariously in one hand. The porcelain animal must've weighed twenty pounds; her arm visibly trembled. A smile crept over her face, eyebrows raised. Augustus stood, ready to grab the thing from her.

Katharina met him halfway, shoving the quill into his hands and pressing him backward to sign. She drew her sleeve up, showing her scarred arm. "Nothing should prevent you from disagreeing that my marriage should end, Father."

Augustus gaped, fishlike, and Maria leaned backward. The crowd let a collective moan escape, leaning with her. The porcelain dangled. Katharina's arm was exposed to only Augustus, up close.

"Sign it. While you have it in front of you and your former mistress and my mother hold you captive for the masterpieces in those crates."

Samuel rushed forward and Johann grabbed both his arms behind his back.

"Sign!" Maria yelled. Johann watched over Samuel's shoulder. Maria's voice made him flinch, the volume of it something he had not experienced, especially from a woman. Anger was not the right word. It felt like a warning, a bark from a vicious dog straining against a chain. Augustus hesitated.

"Your marriage is a tie between this kingdom and another. It is not something I want to dissolve."

Maria raised the lion over her head and slammed it to the floor. Shards of porcelain shot outward, hitting hard against the courtiers legs and billowing skirts and chairs and Augustus himself. Johann's gut collapsed, and he let Samuel go.

Samuel yelled: "NO!" and rushed to gather the ruined pieces, as if he could will them back together. Johann's hands were on his face.

The Porcelain Menagerie

He stood in disbelief at Maria, whose eyes were black and tortured. She turned to Katharina's crate and motioned for her daughter to hand her another piece of the porcelain menagerie.

Augustus cried out, a whimper, and quickly put the quill to paper, signing. Katharina's nostrils flared. Augustus threw the quill to the parquet, sending ink like a blood splatter, and rushed to Maria, seeking not her but porcelain. Samuel was still on his knees. Augustus fell as well, grabbing the broken bits from Samuel, who fought to keep them. Augustus held the lion's distorted, humanlike face.

Maria backed away, but not before whispering something to Augustus. Samuel looked at her and his lion, in pieces, and the crate of other porcelain treasures and raised his lip to say something cruel. Johann flew forward and helped Augustus to his feet, shushing Samuel at the same time.

Their plan worked, but it didn't. Katharina rolled the parchment. Maria wiped her hands on her dark skirt. Johann smelled sweat rolling from the King. The people in the courtroom exhaled and spoke amongst themselves, like birds after a storm.

"Thank you, Father," Katharina said.

"I hope this letter reaches him in time," Augustus said.

Johann backed away from Samuel and the King. Samuel's hands were bleeding. Johann watched the King.

Maria stepped forward. "What did you say?"

"He's on his way, slowly," Augustus said. "With my lot of porcelain vases. I couldn't trust just anyone to deliver. Michal, now her *former* husband, is on his way to help with the trade. I'm not sure where or when he will receive this letter."

He spoke low, so the ladies and lords and soldiers and servants in the courtroom could not make out his words, but the two porcelain makers and the two women could. The crowd created their own noise of disbelief and murmurs. Johann swallowed and looked to Katharina. She held the scroll in her hand.

"Doesn't matter," she said. "It's done. You've signed, decreed it over. There are many trusted messengers in Dresden."

"I hope he receives the news well, after fighting for your hand, and fighting to keep you."

"He burned me. Does that mean anything to you?"

Augustus lowered his gaze to her and said nothing.

Maria took Katharina's hand and they exited the courtroom quickly. Johann wondered what messenger, swift on horseback, they could trust

Jillian Forsberg

to deliver such news. But it's over, he thought. The divorce decree was signed.

Johann and Samuel gathered the rest of the broken pieces. They would be put back into the kaolin clay mixture, ground to make more porcelain. Samuel was silent, red-faced, brutally angry. Johann had never seen him like this. He got into the carriage with the crate of broken lion pieces and shut the door, leaving Johann to take the mare.

Johann squared his shoulders and ignored the pull to go after him. Instead, he took Albrechtsburg's mare to his father's parsonage. The narrow cobbled streets pressed in, houses fingertip-close to each other. His heartbeat slowed, though he could smell his own sweat from the stress of the meeting with Augustus and the broken porcelain. How could Maria have done that?

He supposed a mother would do anything to save her child, just as he and Marten would do anything to save Herman. But the destruction of Samuel's finest piece...it weighed on him. He wasn't involved before, but now he was, and Johann worried what the future would bring.

The horse plodded to the stone church, black spire reaching. Directly across was the small parsonage, a narrow stone building with a worn front door and diamond-paned windows. It seemed much smaller than it had when Johann was a boy.

Warm firelight glowed through. Da was home. Johann knocked. A foreign thing, he felt, to do at his childhood home. A chair scraped, and the unlocking of many mechanisms sounded, including the familiar slide of the bolt from its lock. The door opened, and his father's face went from pastor to Da, a soft smile gracing his mouth.

"My boy," he said. The door opened wider, and Johann stepped in. The place had not changed. His and Herman's bed was made neatly in the far corner, a thin layer of dust on top of the coverlet. The place where the horseshoe once rested caught his eye. Bare. Johann ached and turned away from it. He remembered then that under his feet, his little brother's body melted into earth below.

"Come, I'm ready to eat," said Marten. "I did not think you could leave Albrechtsburg, Johann."

"I made a delivery to the King," said Johann, dropping his satchel on the table and sitting in the chair that was always his. "A dramatic one, and I need your company." His sense of urgency to tell his father the porcelain trade was nigh dwindled.

"You've shrunk some, son," said Marten. He piled lamb stew thick with potatoes and carrots in a wooden bowl and slid it to Johann, who smelled it and politely waited for Da to fill his own bowl and sit beside him.

They ate synchronously, as father and son do, wordless, grateful for the food and quiet company that comes with love and familiarity. Johann cleared the table when they had eaten, and his father brought out his Bible. Johann listened to him recite a verse as he cleaned their wooden wares.

"The Lord is close to the brokenhearted and saves those crushed in spirit," said Marten.

"Psalm 34, verse 18," Johann and Marten said simultaneously.

"Want to see what I've been working on, Da?"

"Yes, my boy, I do," Marten said. He closed the Bible, and Johann produced the worn gray book, opened to the peacock. Marten leaned over to see.

"Ah, what will become of this?"

"I will sculpt it tomorrow at the factory from clay. Then, the mold maker will come through and build a mold around it. They'll fill it full of porcelain clay and fire it in the dungeons. When it's done, they'll throw it in a pot of cold water and pray it won't break. The glaze will set. They take weeks to dry, even longer if they're painted."

"Should you have told me all that?"

"Likely no," said Johann. "But I tire of keeping secrets, and you are my father. And besides, steps are missing. I do not know the clay formula. I doubt you'll sell the arcanum to the world."

Marten laughed, his thick hands rubbing together. He shook his head and motioned for Johann to hand him the book. It was gray with clay dust, messy. The pages were in danger of falling out, and he thumbed through it, not pausing at the words but at his son's animals. He stopped on a page and held it out to Johann.

It was a sketch of Katharina's eyes.

"Who is she, then?"

"The King's illegitimate daughter," said Johann.

"Will you mold her too? In white gold for him?"

Johann looked at his father in surprise. He had not considered making Katharina in porcelain. But he could. Would it please the King? Or was it too sentimental, not exotic enough?

"Perhaps I will," said Johann. "Da...?"

"Son?"

"Can I draw you?"

"Oh." Marten straightened, furrowing his brow. "What for?"

Johann hesitated. "I am beginning to forget Mother. And Herman. My memory was once so sharp I carved an eagle from memory for the King. But months in Albrechtsburg have changed me. I cannot explain it."

"Look in a mirror, boy. You are them. The only living thing left that reminds me of your mother and your brother. The same eyes. The same gold-red hair. The same laugh as Herman. Draw yourself. You don't need to draw me to remember them."

"I don't wish to draw you for their sake, Da. I wish to draw you for your own and mine."

Marten turned his face to his son, his strong black brow furrowing.

"Make it quick," he said. "I've no reason to be turned into some idol."

"Perhaps I'll use you for a model reference," said Johann.

"Blasphemy!"

"You could be Zeus," said Johann. "Or Hercules or Moses."

His father laughed at this, and Johann bid him be still. He sketched his father over the book's text, no longer caring about the arcanum formulas in the margins or the scrawling, decades-old handwriting. And in an hour, a detailed portrait of his father took up the whole page. Johann had no worries of Hao or Samuel coming after him. They were likely pacing the modeler's room in Albrechtsburg, their thoughts far from Johann, lamenting the loss of the lion.

He finished and took a deep breath, turning the page to his father.

Marten smiled at him and leaned forward.

A strong brow. Wide set eyes, black hair. A narrowing mouth, lips lost from age—pain, dictated on the page by lines on Da's forehead. Laughter told in lines near his eyes that crinkled as he smiled at each parishioner, at his boys, and the sprinkling of gray star-dusted hair through his temples.

Marten said nothing. He looked up at his son and grabbed the back of his arm.

"A model for your porcelain or your mind's eye?"

"Both, Da," he said. "If you're alright with it."

Marten nodded. Johann closed his book and told his father about Hao's secret room.

"How will we get Herman there without people seeing us? My time here is almost up. The bishop will come soon, and I cannot haul a dirty casket through the streets."

"The right time will reveal itself to us."

"I am wary, son...You keep a lot of secrets, don't you?"

The Porcelain Menagerie

Johann nodded. "I hope to confess them all to you one day."

Da rose and held a finger aloft, bidding him wait. He went to the kitchen cupboard and withdrew something, rubbing it with the heel of his hand. The horseshoe.

"I have started. And though I never forgot this was on the top, I still could not help but...when I saw it again I..."

He held the horseshoe to Johann. He'd cleaned it well, but still scrubbed at it as if it held grave dirt in its crevices and holes. Johann took it and so quelled his grief by immediately drawing the horseshoe and his hands under the table. A ringing in his ears overwhelmed. He swallowed.

"Keep it, for now."

Johann nodded but did not look up at his father.

"We'll replace it. In Schloss Albrechtsburg."

The Kändlers made a promise to each other that night, with Herman below their feet. They would move him to a fortress where he would not be found. And they would tell no one.

Chapter 24
Fatima
1706

Someone unlocked the menagerie in advance, something Fatima did not typically experience. Footmen waited by the black gates. Augustus' face turned to her, proudly taking in everything as if it were new—it was clear he had not been here since the menagerie's opening months before. He had taken her here for a surprise.

Familiar sounds greeted Fatima's ears—the whirl of feathers on exotic bird wings, the huff and chuff of waking animals, and the creaking of the trees in the wind. In the distance, she heard the cooing of Amar and rushed around the path to her favorite animal's post.

Amar looked cross: disheveled fur, pacing. Fatima unlatched her chain and opened her arms. Amar leaped up, the weight of her comforting. Fatima took a moment to breathe, smelling the sharp scent of Amar's soft fur.

"Ho there, girl, don't pull my hair."

But the monkey held tight as if dangling from a cliffside. Fatima tucked the small creature under her arm, pried her braid from her tiny paw, and uncurled the fingers. Amar did not want to let go.

"You're mad I left you again," she said. "It's practice for your future husband, love. I'm sorry. He's on his way and you won't be alone much longer."

Amar cooed. Fatima curled her hand under her rump, settling the monkey. Augustus, footmen following, rounded the bend.

"I have not seen any new animals, Your Majesty," said Fatima. "Why have you bid me come here?"

He pointed his cane behind her toward the closed back gate.

"There," he said. "Out in the yard."

The Porcelain Menagerie

Fatima furrowed her brow and squinted to see through the lines of trees and cage bars. There was nothing there, no movement, no creatures making noise. Augustus held his arm to her. She took it, causing Amar to hiss gently. Augustus did not hear.

He led her to the gate. Beyond were dozens of empty cages, wooden and small, all portable, scattered in the bottom with evidence of animals: feces, fur, white slaps of saliva now long dried.

"No new animals? Just cages?"

Fatima turned her face toward him. Her mind flickered back to the courtyard full of animals she encountered upon arrival in Dresden—the caged and screaming beasts.

"These are for you to fill for the fox tossing. You love animals so much! Georg will help you, of course, but you will curate the creatures, the food, the celebration. Quite an honor. The servants have done it before and will help you. I am certain you can instruct a squadron on collecting the creatures for the party in three weeks."

"It's considered a party?"

"Of course. We invite all of Dresden, and the surrounding state electors, to come experience the fun. And you'll have Georg! I can see you're excited. He'll guide you."

Excited? A drum filled her chest. Georg, the betrayer, who knew her secrets, was to help her gather animals for this horrendous thing.

"Alright, then," she said quietly. How could she escape this? "I'll gather the men. You said, curate creatures...?"

But Augustus was still talking and hadn't heard her question. "Some of the soldiers in the courtyard helped last year, and Georg is their commander. You won't need to lift a finger. Each cage must be filled. With what animals and from where I leave to you. Last year we had hares, foxes, boars, wolves, wildcats...But surely your menagerie here is a bit overrun. Add some of those exotic ones."

"Is this needed? Surely we can have the people come here, see how the animals live? Fill the cages and then release them without harm?"

Augustus stopped and looked at her. He misinterpreted the look on her face, he laughed, a rumbling noise. "It is an honor and I understand you're not the Queen. Don't worry, I give you permission to organize it."

Fatima trembled. Her animals! Even the wild ones who appeared near the shed to pluck leftover feed from the grass were special, precious, innocent. Amar sensed her nervousness and buried her face in Fatima's gown sleeve.

"During a fox tossing, dear, we *toss foxes*. It's a sport! To see how high we can get them and then...well...!" He pantomimed something hitting the ground. Hard.

Fatima's mind raced with questions: How could she be expected to fill these cages with the intention that the animals would be harmed? She nodded at the King, feigning comprehension, masking her fear, and began to count the cages.

"How many...?"

"Last year, we had twelve hundred animals. All gathered from the countryside. I'm sure you can manage that amount. The creatures here are abundant. You'll also have pfennigs to give to the farmers in return for their captured beasts. They're always happy to rid their lands of foxes and wildcats to protect their flocks."

Twelve hundred. The number resounded in Fatima's ears as she counted, now realizing the cages were stacked three and four high, drawing outward at least the length of the menagerie or more. Her mind turned. All the animals would die if she let anyone else take on this task. But she could find a way to care for them, perhaps free them.

Fatima smiled at the King, fighting another wave of vomit. "I will accept with honor, Your Majesty."

The King tapped his cane into the menagerie's path, grinning broadly. He scooped Fatima by the waist and brought her close.

"My Maria," he said. She clenched her fists.

Chapter 25
Johann
1732

"What is this, Johann?" Samuel said. He leaned over the table, hand on Johann's shoulder, examining the wet clay sculpture before him. "Not menagerie pieces?"

"Centerpieces," said Johann. His horseshoe rested nearby, a token the other makers had not asked about. Johann hadn't let it out of his sight. "The King's advisor requested them for state dinners. I feel pressured to complete these quickly. Sugar bowls, if you look closely enough, you can see the lids. Vinegar, for this one. This clay was made from your shattered lion."

"I am glad it's being used, but I cannot forgive that woman. Your work might make me smile for the first time since, lad."

An elaborate, maze-like thing, the first sculpture was gray-wet and slick. Johann was carving a face, a small one no bigger than a man's thumb. It was a woman's face, and Johann prayed he had made it small enough that Samuel would not recognize Katharina's features. She held a telescope and leaned on a globe.

"A woman of worldly pursuits?" Samuel said.

"No," said Johann. "A woman of other-worldly pursuits. See how she leans on the globe like she owns it? Gazes to the heavens in search of something else?"

Samuel smiled. "The King will love this, and so will Christian Herold, for the opportunity to successfully paint it," he said.

"Yes," said Johann. "He's been sour lately. None of us could have predicted that the larger animals would shatter upon second firings."

Three of the menagerie pieces, in fact. After Christian elaborately painted them and they were fired again to set the glaze, they exploded, sending priceless colored shards at the kilnsmen. Was it bad luck, after Maria ruined the lion, to have three more of Samuel Kirchner's explode in the kilns?

Broken pieces were tossed in a corner, where a pile of white glaze crunched into sand—beaks, ears, tails, teeth—a graveyard of porcelain animals, soon re-worked into the porcelain clay they used. All of the damaged work was ground to dust by the booted feet of kilnsmen. The cuts on their arms from sharpened corners and broken edges told stories of the pieces that failed. Singed hair and lacerations, all for the King's obsession and the glory of Saxony.

"When will we deliver to him again?" said Samuel. "How many new pieces are ready, now?"

Johann paused. He knew the delicate timeline of delivering this porcelain. He didn't want to compete with the large porcelain vessels arriving soon, delivered by Michal, Katharina's brute ex-husband. Johann also waited for news from Marten, of when he would move from the parsonage, of what the bishop's letters said to him.

"Samuel," said Johann, carefully choosing his words. "I believe the soldiers will be traded within a week, that our work will be directly compared to those rumored masterpieces of Chinese porcelain."

Samuel nodded, rubbing his stubbled face, eyes telling, as if he knew more than Johann.

"There's never peace here. As you've seen with the dramas of the King's women, and now this porcelain trade. But Hao and his guards have been busy, back and forth to the King more often than expected," said Samuel.

"Will Hao tell us?" said Johann. "He knows the arrival date?"

"Perhaps he'll tell us," said Samuel. "I believe there are ways to flatter Hao that no one has attempted."

"Flatter him?"

Samuel motioned to the vinegar display. Five blank faces waited for Johann's hand, ready for sculpting. The rough outline was done, and Johann caught on.

"You want me to preserve Hao in porcelain in exchange for information," he said.

Samuel nodded, a wicked grin spreading across his face.

"Another of the King's closest made permanent," he said.

"Another?"

"You think I do not recognize Katharina?"

Johann balked.

"You are too fine a sculptor to try and hide your real work, lad. I

The Porcelain Menagerie

knew it was her from the profile. Beautiful work. Don't change it. If I recognize it, so will Augustus. It will make him happy."

Johann sighed and rubbed the rough edge of his work. It *was* good. He was proud. He smoothed the figure's delicate arms.

"I'll sculpt Hao," he said. "We can present it to him after the firing before seeing Augustus."

Samuel nodded in agreement and asked what he could do to help. Johann pointed to the nailed up list of menagerie animals the King had ordered. It was battered, crinkled, clay-stained. Samuel sighed and walked over, reading out loud the completed works so far: lions, lionesses, leopards, dogs, foxes, billy goats, eagles, owls, peacocks, macaws, monkeys.

"Shall I take on the unicorn or the dragon, then?"

Johann wiped his hands and went to the list. Samuel pointed, and Johann shook his head. "We cannot sculpt those from life," said Samuel.

"All the more reason for you to make them and not me," said Johann. "You're better at those expressions—the fantastic ones that make people wonder if they're seeing a beast or a person."

Samuel gave him a look of appreciation and sat down to model the dragon, curled around in a protective sleeping position as if it had treasure to guard. The two worked together for hours, bantering and talking about their favorite works in the Green Vault and what they thought the King would say of the faces of the lions and the feathers of the peacocks. Johann realized that Samuel was the closest thing he had to a friend, and through the genuine smiles and eagerness to help smooth an angle, give an opinion, and point out a flaw.

Hao made a throat-clearing noise from the doorway. It was nearly nightfall.

"Gentlemen," he said. "You've gotten a lot done today."

Two dragons were ready for their molds. Johann's vinegar and sugar services also waited, and Johann beckoned Hao forward.

"Come see, Hao," he said.

Hao's black slippered feet silently padded. His face decorated the vinegar service. He leaned in, hands clasped behind his back, and drew back quickly.

"Is that..."

"You, Hao, in porcelain." Johann wiped his hands and stood back with Hao, admiring the fine details.

Hao gave a half smile and chortled. "Will Augustus approve of this?"

"He will have no choice if he wants this fine vinegar set," said Johann.

Samuel came up beside them. "I hope this will satiate his appetite, especially after my lion was ruined."

"It will. I'm sorry, still, my friend."

"It might've shattered here. We still have the lion's molds. We just continue forward. Christian can paint your new piece with his fancy gold colors and bring you to life, Hao. But I have one sad piece of news for you," Samuel said. "You likely won't wear black in your porcelain masterpiece."

Hao's face crinkled upward instead of down, an unusual sight. He laughed—a short "ha!" The walls of Albrechtsburg absorbed the sound, and it stayed in the room. Down the stone wall, no noise made it to the kilns where fires bloomed and heated the earth beneath. The floor was soft where Johann planned to bury his brother, warmed from the heat of treasure making.

When they were ready for presentation, Johann loaded the sugar and vinegar services into a crate and hauled them into the black carriage. He worried; even though this was one of his finest pieces, surely it would not compare to the Chinese vessels the King traded for. Would he ever be good enough?

Hao drove silently. Johann, alone in the small black carriage, fiddled with the horseshoe. Samuel stayed behind, working on the menagerie. He had no reason to join Johann in this particular presentation as King Augustus believed Johann had made each piece himself. He would give them an unnecessarily critical eye if he knew Samuel was responsible for the molding. Johann prayed Maria would be absent.

Despite his fears, Johann swelled with pride as he hauled the crates, heavier than the last. He carefully walked through the Chinese porcelain displayed in the palace halls, at last passing by his eagle. Hao and Katharina's faces stared back at him from his vinegar service, and he waited for King Augustus to arrive.

The noise of the palace was steady. The sounds of bustling servants and royal court members permeated the walls. Katharina, Maria, and Augustus were not there. Johann realized he'd been waiting for a while. Hao shifted from foot to foot even though the heat of the kilns was not present. A habit by now.

"Shall I seek him out?" said Hao.

"I suppose," said Johann. "He knows of our arrival?"

Hao nodded. "Unlike him to be late to his favorite event."

But the door opened, and King Augustus' party filtered through, dressed in their finery—furs draped over their shoulders despite the late summer heat. The place smelled of overdressed bodies. Augustus entered, and Johann paled.

The Porcelain Menagerie

The King's brow furrowed, his skin dotted with beads of sweat. His mantle shrugged off his shoulders. His steps were slow and dreary. His ruddy face was white as if powdered, but the slick sweat of it told Johann he was not sporting the latest French makeup. Johann glanced at Hao, and they shared a knowing look. The King did not look well.

Johann cleared his throat, and instead of leading the King to the table, he carefully picked up the vinegar service and, kneeling, held it out to the King, seated on his throne on the dais.

"Your Majesty," he said. "I present to you a vinegar service as a gift of goodwill while you wait patiently for the delivery of the porcelain vessels for trade." Johann tried not to tremble, but his kneeling made the presentation difficult. The horseshoe weighed his left side down.

Augustus motioned to his footmen, who picked up the porcelain piece and placed it in his lap. He chortled, choking a bit, and let out a phlegmy cough. Fever glazed his eyes. But Johann could not mistake the bloodlust in them. He was still, under it all, obsessed.

The King smiled, sickly sweet, and turned the piece in his hands. He raised his thick eyebrows at the figures made from Hao's likeness.

"Kändler," he said. "Is this Hao?"

Johann bowed, hands clasped in front of him, and nodded.

"Your Majesty, I find making your porcelain from real people more compelling."

"Come forward," said Augustus to Hao. Hao approached the dais silently and, in one smooth motion, ended on a knee, head bowed.

"Raise your face to me," Augustus said.

Hao raised it. Johann had immortalized this man in white gold forever. Had he made a mistake? He did not know his story, childhood, or mother's name. He did not understand why he was in Saxony and not in Jingdezhen. He did not know how he had gotten to Albrechtsburg or where he lay his head each night. And yet, he put his face on the King's service. Johann's palms grew damp.

"My friend from Jingdezhen," Augustus said. "My shipwreck survivor, lone soul. Now, made into porcelain yourself. How ironic."

Hao nodded. *Shipwreck?* Johann turned his ear, listening intently.

"Tell my court the story. Our entertainment." Augustus smiled coolly.

Augustus motioned for Johann to take the vinegar service. He placed it back in its crate, hands trembling. The King crossed his legs and leaned forward, jowls jiggling.

Hao spoke:

"When I was a boy, I was on a trading ship that sank to the bottom of the South China Sea. I am here because of the Dutch. They were supposed to trade with the *Lorcha* boat for its porcelain. But the ship and its fifty thousand pieces were gone, under the waves, before we hit open sea. I managed to survive, clinging to wreckage."

Augustus' eyes flickered at the mention of fifty thousand pieces of porcelain.

"And what did you bring me when you begged at my door?"

"One piece and my father's knowledge," Hao said, looking at the floor.

"Your father's knowledge."

The King rose, smiling again, though his breath was labored. He stepped down the dais. Johann saw a tiny shift; Hao's body silently screamed in discomfort, but he did not move. He raised his chin at the King's approach and swallowed.

"Without that shipwreck, the arcanum may not exist in Saxony. And yet, you claim you cannot remember where the ship sank to recover the fifty thousand pieces free for the taking under the sea."

"I told you all I can remember, Your Majesty," Hao said.

"Now your face is forever on my porcelain," Augustus smiled, dripping with disdain. "It's fitting that both your deed and likeness are immortalized. Perhaps, Hao, you will remember why you are still alive."

"When I remember, Your Majesty, I will gift you with the knowledge."

Johann felt a chill rise in his spine despite the heat in the throne room. His brain rang with questions for Hao, but he said nothing. He stepped forward, hauled the second crate, and cleared his throat.

"I have one more thing for you, Your Majesty."

Augustus shifted his gaze from Hao to Johann. It permitted Hao to slink back into the shadows.

Johann opened the crate and, head bowed, walked up the dais to put the King's sugar service, with Katharina's likeness in porcelain, in his lap. The King smiled, a wicked expression, and a bead of sweat dripped slowly down his pallid face.

"You are, Kändler, a master. No one will touch this but me."

Hao and Johann left the King's throne room through a long, marbled hall that held some of the porcelain menagerie. Already displayed were unpainted animals Johann had brought to Augustus, their eyes dead and white.

"You are a prisoner, too?" Johann said to Hao.

"Yes."

The Porcelain Menagerie

"Why would you guard a place you are held captive in?"

"What is the alternative, Johann? Kilnsman? I cannot be a modeler like you. I do not have the skillset for mold making. I cannot paint. So I compromise."

"Augustus said your father…"

"My father is dead. Drowned with that damn porcelain boat, bound for India."

"India?"

"Do you know much of Chinese porcelain?"

Johann shook his head.

"Jingdezhen is the home of the greatest porcelain in the world. They transported it to India, Batavia, and Europe, where people paid a fortune. My ancestors have been part of the creation of it for a thousand years or more. How do you think Meissen knows how to make it?"

"Some say a man named Böttger…"

"Böttger tried and failed and failed some more. He died of poison fumes from his mismade concoctions, his lungs burning to ash in his body. Chain marks scarred his ankles. It wasn't until I arrived as a boy, sneaky as I was in Jingdezhen, to see the families that held the secrets that I told him what he was missing."

"What was he missing?"

Hao stopped dead and turned to Johann, hands holding his elbows. He set his mouth in a thin line. A beat passed between them, and he turned on his heel to exit the hall. They passed Johann's outstretched eagle.

"I do not wish to risk my life again by telling you what I told Böttger."

Johann shielded his eyes from the late summer sun as they walked to their black carriage, where the bay mare stomped, impatient.

"I was a child. And saw my father sink to the bottom with a crate of blue and white porcelain in his arms. What I told them, in my innocence, was an attempt to cleanse my memories. I do not understand why I was the sole survivor."

"The shipwreck was not your fault."

"The shipwreck was not my fault, I acknowledge. But the contents of the wreck, the location, it became an obsession for them. I was the only one who knew where it was, so it was also an obsession for me. To prove where my father was, that what I said was true. That the porcelain waited beneath the waves. For weeks, nearly out of supplies, the Dutch searched the waters. We found remnants, but no one could dive deep enough to find the crates. But they knew I was a risk. I could show others the location and perhaps knew more about porcelain than I let on."

"So they brought you here."

"They sold me to the King. Promised him the arcanum, the formula they swore I knew, and the location of the shipwreck, lodged somewhere in my memory. Because of my ancestry, and that memory, I became permanent."

Johann took in Hao, truly. His blue-black hair. The tight muscles of his jaw and forearm. He realized his bristling nature was necessary, and he wondered what terrors in Albrechtsburg a young boy faced. He could not release the thought of Hao growing up there, with Albrechtsburg as his mother.

"You could leave."

"A Chinese man in Saxony?" Hao laughed. "They would find me. So I stay. And now, I do not remember from two decades ago where the ship sank. The waters have changed. I would never find it."

"You told them everything?"

"I told them what I knew, and Böttger was so desperate, he was kind. He filled in the gaps with my knowledge."

"Böttger. He needed you."

"He was a fool. He played a trick on Augustus to show him he could make gold from lead. The King believed him, imprisoned him, and when his falsehood was discovered, Böttger turned to the next most valuable thing."

"White gold."

Hao nodded. "And now, we face the repercussions of my input. He did not know the formula, and his porcelain was thick, cracked. But as a boy in the streets of Jingdezhen, my life was spent wandering between each of the homes of the seventy-two makers. I knew things a child should not know. So, to save my skin, I helped him."

"Did he tell the King of your input?"

"I don't believe so. He took the glory for himself or faced execution. You cannot trick Augustus twice."

"Then how are you still at Albrechtsburg if you cannot tell him exactly where the shipwreck is?" Johann said.

"Do you believe the King would allow me to leave? Somewhere in my memory is the last resting place of thousands of pieces of porcelain, free for the taking. I know the entire arcanum, just from observation, too. He would never allow another to draw my memories from me. He tried his worst, in many ways, to get me to tell him where that shipwreck is."

"How does he know if you'll ever remember?"

"It doesn't matter, as long as the promise is there. He will keep me from anyone else. It is like keeping me keeps the secret safe."

The Porcelain Menagerie

"The obsession is unfathomable."

"Speak nothing of fathoms to me." Hao slid onto the driver's box of the black carriage. His black robe rose as he did, and Johann saw an old, curved scar on his calf. It looked like a hook drawn from the depths of the ocean.

Hao wiped his brow, settling into the seat.

"We are not enemies, Hao. I am not the one keeping you captive."

Hao sighed, staring into the distance over the red tiled roofs of Dresden. "I know that, Johann. You and I are held here, though we do not make much effort to leave."

"We could," Johann said, testing.

Hao turned his body to Johann, reins and whip in his hand.

"And go where? We are well known, not in a way that brings us riches and good things. We are well known as the King's porcelain prisoners, and nothing will change that."

"Hao, the six hundred soldiers..."

"Do not think long on them. They have no choice."

"Neither do we, it seems."

"You must understand, Johann, that your ability to stay alive is tied to the existence of the porcelain you make. If it is gone, so be it. But if the kilns, the clay stores, and the arcanum are harmed, you will have no lasting legacy. You are tied to this, and your work is, too. If you leave, no one will know what you created. Your work can last beyond the obsession. Your *existence*, lad, can last beyond."

Johann could not perform his art anywhere else but Albrechtsburg. Hao was right—leaving here would mean abandoning his art, his toil, his joy. He did not know how to make a porcelain kiln. He did not know the formula for porcelain clay. He knew how to carve, make a porcelain model, and where it went after. But that was all.

"We are in a precarious situation, Johann," said Hao, motioning for Johann to enter the carriage. "So far, the menagerie animals have pleased Augustus. But it will not be long until he sees the finery of the wares from Jingdezhen and we are scrutinized. What a foolish thing to have porcelain instead of gold or jewels. At least those things are not easily broken. At least we are protected by Schloss Albrechtsburg."

"Part of me is glad we live in a dragon's mouth," Johann said.

"We both call it that. The dragon," Hao smirked. "She is old. Guardian of treasure and keeper of secrets. Fire in her belly, down her throat. The ceilings look like scales and wings, do they not? I have always seen it as a dragon."

"A living, breathing creature."

"Can you make that for the menagerie?" Hao smiled wickedly.

"No. But a dragon was on the list. If I deliver the castle instead, only you and I would understand."

Hao stared at him, hooded eyes wild. "I think more people than you know consider our castle alive and angry."

Johann clambered in, Hao shook the reins, and the carriage careened toward the fire-warm factory and its secrets.

Chapter 26
Fatima
1706

Fatima's skirts clung to branches in the woods outside the palace. The thin ones broke before her, crunching to the forest floor, but the thorned plants grabbed the egg-colored linen of her simple country dress and pulled snags through it. She could not find the same path she'd taken last week. Her mind was too distracted then or now, and she cursed herself for not being more observant.

By the time she reached the clearing, pink scratches crisscrossed her hands, and the threads of her skirt loosed from their weaving. She pulled a thorny stick from her low, dark braid.

Fatima interrupted birdsong and knew she should keep quiet but could not quite manage in her heavy boots. The noise of traipsing through the woods annoyed her. She was hunting, but not in the same way as Augustus and his many courtiers. Her goal was to trap as many creatures as she could for the fox tossing, to take place in less than a week.

The cages near the stone castle walls were already filling: hares, three boars, and foxes. So many foxes. The squirrels she let go. They were too difficult to keep. Farmers and hunters also brought live animals for a pfenning, and the cages grew in number. Each morning she counted, a dozen more appeared.

Fatima did not know how long a fox's legs were until she saw the animals in the cages, gangly and skinny, panting in fear. Her least favorite part was checking the live traps in the forests near Dresden. Augustus told her she did not need to accompany the hunting parties assigned to the task, but she insisted. She had to keep track of the animals. But her mind was elsewhere. Since the close call in her chamber, she had not heard from Friedrich. Fatima's heart ached, and her stomach flipped each time she came to another strategically placed cage with an animal inside, its job complete.

Sixteen animals had come from the clearing she approached now. And the cage in the distance rattled, a brown creature inside desperate to escape. To her surprise, it was not a fox.

She approached, hiking her skirts up to reveal dirt-smeared boots. Surely, when Augustus charged her with this task, he did not realize she would do it herself. The creature rumbled and hissed.

A wildcat. Fatima crouched several paces away, brow furrowed. The cat resumed its pawing.

"Not unlike me," she said. "Desiring something you cannot have. Not yet, anyway."

The cat hissed again. Fatima heard her entourage clambering toward her, carrying an empty cage to replace this one. Snapping branches and the sounds of men's voices filled the clearing.

"What's this one?" said Georg. "Another fox?" He set the empty trap down.

Georg wore a soft suede hunting tunic that protected his arms and legs but left him sweating. The sweet smell of leather filled Fatima's space. She stood.

"Wildcat," she said, not making eye contact. She felt his eyes cascade down her body, and heat rippled up her spine.

Three other men wandered the woods nearby. Fatima stepped toward the cage, a baited trap. Upon entrance, the wooden door swung down, containing the animal inside. The wildcat darted its arms out of the wooden bars, searching to hurt her and protect itself.

"How many more do we need?" Fatima asked Georg.

"Maybe two dozen. We're nearly there. If we check the cages in the five-mile radius, we could complete it by tomorrow, provided the farmers in the area also drop off a few."

"What of the empty cages we're leaving out then? Do we abandon them?"

Georg shrugged.

"Last year, they did. Came upon poor creatures reduced to skeletons when we put out the new traps this year."

Fatima turned to him, angry. "That will not happen this time."

Georg raised his hands to the sky, frustrated. "Fatima, the results will be the same. The festival will happen. These animals will die. There is no change here, even though you are in charge. This is a man's job, Fatima. It's close to insulting that a King's woman takes this on. It would be best if you were inside, fawning over the table decor and organizing the food vendors and prizes. The animals will die."

The Porcelain Menagerie

"They will not. I have a plan."

"And who to help you execute it, when a hundred people know what fate awaits these animals?" Georg lowered his voice to an angry whisper.

"I...I hoped you might."

He narrowed his eyes. "Why would I help you? I cannot risk it."

"You already know my secrets. This gives you even more power over me."

"What makes you think I want power over you?" Georg said.

"You know about...about Friedrich."

"And I have kept it to myself. Though I could reveal you and Böttger, I protect you."

"My role has an ending," she said. "You know full well my place here is temporary. Augustus trades women like we're the balls of his tennis matches. It is the same story every time. He moves on, leaving women behind, assigning them elsewhere."

"Assigning them husbands, you mean, to keep them quiet and his bastards fed."

She shook her head, yanked her arm from his grasp. "If you do not help me, I will find another way."

"You think your porcelain maker will help you? He's under lock and key, now, after producing something the King wants, he'll never let him go. He's a captive, Fatima, with no future."

He turned from her, walked a few steps away into the golden-green light of the clearing. She followed him, placed a hand on his shoulder. He did not shrug her away.

"You feel anger toward me. But why?"

"You understand that you are special," he said.

Fatima's mouth parted and she felt her heart rise. Why was he saying this to her?

"The King has told me he loves you. I have seen a dozen mistresses come and go, lasting mere weeks, or a few nights in his bed. And you're still here. And he still calls to you, and smiles at you, and brings you things you want."

Fatima sensed a strange tone in his voice.

"You're jealous."

Georg raised his chin. His eyes were nearly green in the light of the woods, dappled just the same. Flecks of gold, ringed in black. Fatima leaned back a step. He rubbed his stubbled chin and looked away. "I cannot deny I am attracted to you."

"I am the King's mistress."

"I am well aware, and I believe he knows, too, that many in his court find you...irresistible. Another reason to keep you longer and keep you close."

Fatima turned and began to walk away, nervous now of Georg's intentions.

"But if it makes a difference, I simply want to keep you safe. To leave with you is my ultimate desire. My dream. But to know you're content, for a second, a day... I would rather allow myself those feelings of happiness and never have you. I can keep you forever in memory, but only if we create the memory."

She softened. Was he serious? Or lust-driven?

"What is your plan, lady? I cannot say I will help you. But I must know what your brilliant and beautiful mind has come up with, or I will wonder the rest of my life."

Georg could not help her without risking everything, she knew. But still, he asked. The wildcat in its cage hissed. She thought of the menagerie, of the animals in their cages, pacing in the courtyard, waiting for their doom. She thought of Friedrich Böttger and his clay-stained hands. How she loved him.

She leaned into Georg and whispered her plan. He backed away and stared at her. She could not read his expression. He turned from her.

"We've another cat here!" He called into the woods, ending their conversation. The other soldiers crashed through the underbrush to gather the creature, leading it to its fate. He nodded at Fatima. She inhaled and smiled. The cat's cries in the cage faded, and they went deeper into the golden woods to find the last of their traps.

When Fatima returned to her room, she shed her overcoat and tousled her braid away easily with her fingers. The dull scent of dust and woods clung to her, as did leaves to her skirts. She dropped to the bed.

Something cream-colored flashed near her bedside. A note. She sighed. It was on the tray only delivered by Augustus' messengers.

"Tonight, the menagerie."

She rubbed her face in exhaustion and sat up, her boots muddy, waiting by the door, the bottoms and sides wearing thin from many walks through the woods.

"I will end his waiting for my own sake," she said to herself. She slid on her slippers, threw on her red cloak, and left her chambers. Fatigue clung to her bones, and she exhaled deeply, blinking away the urge to lie down and drift into a dreamless sleep.

Through the palace, Augustus' treasures were scattered. Works from

The Porcelain Menagerie

goldsmiths, Chinese porcelain, and Böttger's redware made her pause... was she risking Böttger's life by loving him? She cursed, closed her eyes, and stayed close to the castle walls to avoid getting too close to the things her lover made for the King who supposedly loved her.

The golden, gray light of evening guided Fatima to the menagerie. She was so used to watching her feet on this familiar path, but because of the brilliance of the lavender hued sky and the darting, full-bodied clouds, she instead turned her face upward. The urge to leave the complications of the castle behind and the subtle rustle of animals ahead in their confined but safe homes drew her onward. Perhaps being caged wasn't always bad.

The animals were cared for, loved by her if by no one else, and fed each day at the same time. They were tended to by the farrier, and the doctor who tended cattle came to check the mammals frequently. They had soft beds and shelter from rain and wind. They were given treats and playthings and had companions, even if they sometimes quarreled. The world of the menagerie was small but safe, and Fatima felt safe there, too, when the canopy of trees enfolded above.

She considered what would happen if she freed an animal from here—the lion padding slowly down the streets of Dresden, the peacock unfurling its feathers to reflect in the Elbe at sunset, Amar darting in the trees making chirping noises. They'd be foreign. Unsure of where to go or how to feed themselves. Indeed, they'd be caught or maimed or dragged away with chains about their necks to serve some other master.

The gates of the menagerie were closed, and Fatima pulled the black metal toward herself, then turned to see Augustus' palace backlit by the setting sun. The last rays had warmed the gate, and her hand absorbed it. She stepped into the menagerie, knowing where she'd find Augustus: near the small cage of the creature she loved most, Amar.

She closed the gate behind her and cast her eyes downward to the path, feeling the rough ground beneath her slippered feet. Two bends, a dozen cages, and a large tree ahead signaled where she'd find her monkey, and her reluctantly claimed King.

Without him, she thought, this menagerie wouldn't be here. She stopped, gripping her red cloak tightly to ground herself: Friedrich, Georg, Amar, Brunhilde. Without being here, without Augustus, she'd never have met them. These animals would be somewhere else. *She* would be somewhere else, without ever having fed a currant to a monkey.

The she-wolf in the cage ahead stood when it saw Fatima and began to pace, mouth closed and eyes glowing in the gathering darkness. Fatima hurried past, suddenly aware of her singularity and the darker clouds as night expanded.

Fatima rounded the bend to Amar's tether and cage. The creature chirped, and on the bench beside her was Augustus, something large on the ground beside him. Amar kept her distance, though Augustus held a single currant in his fleshy hand.

"Your Majesty," Fatima said, dipping low. Her red cape skimmed the ground.

Augustus pulled a white cloth from a gilded cage. Inside was a male monkey, Amar's new mate. Fatima could not help herself, she gasped and ran forward. Augustus smiled, quite pleased. She freed Amar, who leaped to the cage to greet the new arrival with no leash tied around her middle.

"I should have known," Augustus said, holding the golden links in a swollen hand. "This creature has no need for a chain. It would never run away."

Chapter 27
Johann
1732

Johann and Hao made their way through Dresden's winding stone streets. The entirety of the porcelain menagerie was at risk. Though he did not love the King, he loved the art he made, and the destruction of it by any means made his heart pound. Could he save it by hiding it in the depths of Albrechtsburg until the threat of invasion by the traded soldiers subsided?

He worried about Katharina and Maria. Though part of him trusted them as adversaries to Augustus, his mind went to the shattered pieces of porcelain. Maria was dangerous. He had to meet with her and tell her his worries about Albrechtsburg and the soldiers, but the night was falling fast in the city, and the coolness of evening brought people out of their homes to finish their errands. He could not simply seek out the King's women.

The palace of Augustus reflected dimly in the Elbe, mirror-like, glowing with lanterns and fire and the warm orange sunset. Bright clouds scattered, the gates to the menagerie lay ahead. He signaled to Hao to stop.

"I need to see if someone is here," he said. "Will you wait for me?"

Hao narrowed his gaze and frowned. "After everything I have told you, I don't believe I should be kept from your secrets."

Johann was silent but gave a curt nod. Perhaps Hao would give pity to the animal captives of Augustus the Strong.

Johann pushed the black iron gate forward, trees enveloping them. Johann stopped. Hao left the gate swinging. Johann rushed back to shut it.

"They will escape."

"What will?"

At the rounding of the first bend, a flock of parrots erupted from the trees like green leaves in a windstorm. Hao ducked and covered his face, but the thin, crisscrossed bars stopped the birds.

"They're caged." Hao leaned close.

"You've never been here." Johann meant it as a question, but it came out differently. Hao reached a finger into the cage, and a parrot waddled down to see what he offered.

"Why would I come here?" The parrot nipped his finger. "I don't draw. You do."

Hao withdrew his finger. The birds stared at him, turning their heads curiously. Johann and Hao turned at a rustling nearby. It was the peacock, spreading his feathers and shaking wildly at the unexpected visitors.

Johann motioned for Hao to follow him deeper in. The peacock followed, fanned fully out, the evening sun reflecting on his feathers. The path ahead could lead to Maria, Katharina, or both. But when they rounded the bend to the one-eyed lion's cage, they stopped abruptly and jumped smoothly into the shadows. Katharina and a man Johann did not recognize stood, their bodies tense. They moved around each other like buzzards and something long dead. The lion was nowhere to be seen.

Johann put his finger to his lips, and Hao slunk behind him, silent in his black slippered shoes. Johann crouched down low in the nearby brambles. The man was older than Katharina—perhaps twenty years older. His shoulders sloped, his nose a beak, his face drawn and pale. His voice was startlingly loud.

"You cannot be serious, Katharina, after all the things I've promised you."

"King Augustus has signed," Katharina said. "You've delivered my father's porcelain and now you'll leave. Our ending is legal, Michal."

Her husband, newly divorced. A prickle of guardianship touched Johann, and he let out a deep, heaving breath that made Hao kick him gently and motion for silence.

"And you expect me to leave without a fight?"

"I expect you to leave with six hundred dragoons and nothing more."

"Your father made a promise to mine. That I would have land and title, and you, the King's bastard daughter, would bear my children to be royals, even if he never claims you as an heir. You take that from me."

She swallowed, looking down. The man's graying hair gleamed in the moonlight. His fine military clothes couldn't be tailored properly to his small, paunchy belly. Katharina stared at him, raising her chin, showing the length of her neck. She looked so much like her mother.

The Porcelain Menagerie

Johann saw her scar, flickered his eyes back to Michal. His anger rose, like sparks above a fire.

"When you burned me, you lost me, Michal. I am no longer yours. Even an army wouldn't bring me back to you."

"Oh, but that was an accident. An oversight. You know the accident with the poker was unintentional, Katharina."

"That's a lie," she said.

Michal reached out to touch her brutalized forearm, tenderly, and she drew back, gasping. Johann leaned forward. Hao caught his shoulder. Katharina shoved Michal's shoulder, forcing him away. Suddenly, he rushed toward her and smashed the heel of his tall black boot into Katharina's foot. She cried out in pain and kicked him in the shin. The one-eyed lion emerged behind her, letting out a low growl.

Michal startled, noticing the one green eye in the near-dark. "This stupid beast! This filthy, disgusting place of your mother's. I'll burn it and you."

Katharina fell behind the bench and put her back to the bars of the cage. The lion rose, legs trembling with age, and began to pad her way. The lion roared, eyes focused on Michal. Michal paused, pointing at Katharina. The lion vibrated, a threat, and Michal retreated. Johann let out a sharp exhale. He should have rushed from the bramble he hid in and fought for her. He caught himself. If he emerged now, what would Katharina do? She, and the lion, defended themselves.

Johann slowly crept back through the bushes but was a larger man than Hao. His back and arms scraped the branches. As he emerged from the bramble, the peacock cried out from the path ahead, feathers unfurled. Hao ran toward the carriage, and Johann followed.

"This means the Chinese porcelain is delivered," said Hao.

"If Michal is their commander, the six hundred will now leave. Hao, what foolishness is this?"

"You cannot call the King a fool. To do so is to undermine all of Albrechtsburg."

"And what if I want to?"

"Call yourself a fool, then, for delivering these things to him today. Things that make him thirst for more."

"And what of Katharina? She is not a fool, yet she's drawn into these complications. He deserves to lose her if he harmed her like that," said Johann.

Hao nodded. "Daughters often receive the same treatment as their mothers. Seems Katharina is trying to break that pattern."

Hao raced the carriage through the streets. The horse shook her head at the speed. But Johann could not form a thought beyond Michal stomping on Katharina's foot. He should have run to her side, helped her. Though his mind should have been on his art, his brother and his father, the treasure he delivered to the King, instead, he thought of the cry of pain from the King's bastard daughter.

He made up his mind to protect her.

Hao and Johann parted ways abruptly at the ascending staircase of Albrechtsburg. The rumbling of the kilns and heat below their feet felt surprisingly welcome after the scene in the menagerie.

Johann played it over and over in his mind's eye, and when he reached the mossy, humid hallway that led to his chambers, his shoulders were tensed about his neck. He patted his pocket. The horseshoe.

With a jolt of fear, he realized he did not know where his book was. The weight of it in his pocket had been replaced by the horseshoe.

He unlocked his room and checked the usual hiding places—the small stone shelf near his window, under his bed, on the wooden desk that held a small amount of clay for when inspiration struck. But the book was not there. He tightened his thin ponytail and walked out of the room. He must find it.

The studio where he carved his clay sculptures was across the castle—a long walk. Johann made it quickly. The almost hot floor pulsed under him, propelling him forward. The upward spiral staircase was clogged with men taking sculptures and teapots, cups and saucers, plates and dishes, all to be fired in the kilns downward. He had to wait to go up. His hands curled to sweaty fists.

He pushed his way through and found the carving room, with its wide water basins and lumps of clay, the ceiling beautifully honeycombed, empty, minus the painter Christian Herold, sitting on the floor in the corner, back pressed against the stone wall. In his hand was Johann's book.

Herold rose, trembling.

"Herold, I can explain," Johann said.

"This is a risk, Johann."

"I could ask you how you came to have my book and accuse you of sabotage and theft, but I dare not. I know you better than that and trust you. I ask you now to trust me in return."

"You have Böttger's book."

"I know, but I did not know until recently whose book it was."

"We must burn it, or lock it up tight."

The Porcelain Menagerie

"We cannot. My sketches are in it. It holds my work that I cannot replicate in time to make the menagerie."

"If you are caught..."

"We won't be. The arcanum is safe. We don't even know if the formulas in this book are correct."

"I know who does."

"You cannot ask Hao."

"I can, and I will."

Johann held his hand out. He was not going to let Herold walk out with his book, his only reference for the hundreds of animals he must make, his only piece of leverage for power over Albrechtsburg. He could reveal at any moment what he knew, and though he knew he would not sell it, his mind filled with riches and a fleeing horse that would take him far away if he chose.

Herold stared, nostrils flaring, the book clamped tightly in his hand. Johann was torn—how to reconcile this world: one of captivity and the singular freedom to be an artist? How to combat the power and anguish equally? He could not win here, and he realized Christian Herold could not either.

The men regarded each other. Johann's pulse steadied. Herold loosened his grip on the book and held it out to Johann. Slowly, Johann took it and flipped it open to the page on which Böttger had written the most. He began reading:

"Number five: 149 dot A dot 2 dot 9 dot ut dot I dot ad dot 7."

Herold shook his head. "It doesn't make any sense to me."

"My exact point. We may have Böttger's book, but we have no actual idea what he means. The ramblings of a madman, I tell you." The jagged edge of the page remnant where Katharina ripped her mother's initials stood upright.

"But how does the factory keep going if you and I, who spend our lives here, cannot decipher his formula?"

Hao's voice sounded from the doorway.

"Because, like in Jingdezhen, each man knows his place and his one step to create porcelain. Regardless of if you know the step before you or the step after, one single person cannot complete the cycle," Hao said.

"Therefore, Böttger's book..."

"Böttger's book, Johann, is worthless to anyone but Böttger."

Hao held his hand out, asking for the book. Johann gave it to him, and Hao thumbed through it. He shook his head lightly.

"We cannot know what he meant by any of it," said Herold. "But we still need to protect it. Though someone may not know how to use it, they may still try to steal it from us. Three of us know it exists."

"And Katharina. And Samuel. And Maria."

Herold made an exasperated noise and stared at Johann. "Maria and Katharina? They are no longer friends of Albrechtsburg!"

"They know the book exists, though I am not sure they know what's inside beyond my drawings. I drew Katharina and Maria's monkey for the King's porcelain." He did not say what he wanted to: that something more resided inside. Some proof of a relationship between Böttger and the King's mistress.

The three men did not have answers. The kilns below rumbled, indicating that the fires were being stoked.

"We continue our work," said Johann. "We finish this. We deliver the menagerie, whether or not the delivery of Chinese vessels will be all the King will ever want again, and better than our own work ever could be. We finish this."

They nodded, and Johann left the room to take his book to his chambers.

Chapter 28
Fatima
1706

Fatima stepped into the Japanese Palace, seeking out her favorite redware porcelain. Most of the vessels on the walls and floor and shelves were blue and white. They were not the work of Böttger.

"How many, Amar?" she said. The monkey's soft chain jingled as she reached toward a large vessel, curious about what was inside. Fatima pulled her back and looked. The vessel was empty.

"Nothing in there, darling," Fatima said, moving through the narrow hallway. Up the columns, resting on delicate stands, were plates decorated with scrolling blue clouds on bright white backgrounds. Large and small vessels of every shape, size, and gentle feminine curve sat on pedestals and seashell-shaped shelves.

"How do you see wealth and worth when you have so many?" Fatima said to Amar. "Would it not be more impactful to have *one* piece, Amar?"

Amar smelled of soft fruit and musky ammonia. Her padded feet were warm on Fatima's arm. The first room on the ground floor was all blue and white. Fatima wandered to the next, where vessels of red and white reigned. The next room held green. The small room beyond held only five pieces; unlike the others, they were painted solid yellow.

A bowl so thin it glowed like a turning disk of sun, its tall edges curled gently like an opening flower; a teacup, translucent and smaller than the palm of Fatima's hand, rested on a saucer, both lemon-yellow. A vase, smaller than the bowl and fluted at the top, its neck wrung by an invisible hand. The last dish was a shallow bowl, unparalleled in its evenness. Smooth as starlight, unblemished. All the yellow pieces were on a single marble stand, the room empty otherwise. The place echoed. Unlike other rooms, there were no empty, waiting shelves.

"These must be of great worth, Amar, if Augustus only has five and expects no more. They are perfect."

Amar reached to touch the narrow-necked vase, and Fatima drew her back. The shining surface reflected the monkey's paw. Fatima paused, then leaned into it. Amar grabbed it, put it to her mouth, and when she drew back in disappointment, the monkey threw it to the marble floor.

Yellow shards rocked back and forth. The piece shattered, leaving sharp sundrops, revealing its white insides. Though a pit formed in Fatima's belly, it was only because she realized the porcelain maker would be ashamed of her. She shook the feeling and smirked at the thought of Augustus finding this precious piece destroyed. Destroyed like her relationship with Friedrich, her life in Buda, her friendship with Aurora, who had not written to her in months. It felt good to control something.

A broad stone staircase led to the first floor. Here, were familiar shapes: slick, glass-like red porcelain pieces, gathered in groups. Compared to the thin and delicate Chinese porcelain Amar had destroyed, they were cumbersome, dirty.

More pieces of Böttger's wares gleamed in the bright daylight streaming in through tall windows. One vessel was black lacquered, painted delicately with a scene set somewhere faraway. The spout of the small pot was a bird of prey, feathers leading into the body of the vessel; gold paint skirted over the thing. Its sharp corners folded gracefully into a wide, curved bottom. Fatima picked it up. It was light, smooth. She knew Böttger had made it.

"He has improved," Fatima said to Amar, pointing out the delicate details of the feathers and eyes of the bird. A voice from the doorway startled her.

"Fatima! It's you!" said Brunhilde. "I'm here to present something to Augustus…"

Fatima rushed to her friend's side. She was dressed for travel, and her face speckled with red, thinner than it had been when they last spoke.

"Brunhilde! You've been gone weeks, I've missed you and needed you and—"

Brunhilde shushed her.

"I've been at the docks waiting for something special to arrive. Something Augustus paid for, and as I've been loyal to him in the past, he tasked me with gathering it. I must say, my lady, that I have never been so scared."

"Brunhilde? Why does Augustus ask a cook to gather a treasure?"

"Treasure indeed. Likely because no one would recognize me. Dangerous business I'm in. If I'd been caught…" Brunhilde wrung her hands.

The Porcelain Menagerie

Fatima hiked her many layers of skirts with one hand and put Amar down. Her friend was scared. Fatima embraced her, breathing in sage and rosemary and the sour scent of bread yeast.

"Come see. You'll understand."

Fatima nodded, shivering lightly. What was it? A thing to make even Brunhilde tremble with something close to panic?

"I've been asked to do many things for Augustus and his mistresses. Steal their babes away to wet nurses who won't ever bring them back. Give them moon tea if they're not in his favor. Brew concoctions of untold ramifications, delivered to the King's lover's lovers. But this...this is the strangest. I fear it reveals Augustus' true nature."

Fatima furrowed her brow. She was unsure how someone could not see the true nature of Augustus immediately upon meeting him. Perhaps the allure of growing closer to a King distracted many, but not her. Brunhilde continued.

"Augustus banished his wife, you know."

"This isn't news to me, Brunhilde. All of Dresden knows his wife is safely away from him."

"But he asked me to help, when that happened, and I grew closer to him, and did his bidding, and he paid me so well you see, that I didn't think to ask what things would come next and..."

Brunhilde grabbed her chest and pulled her hair, chaotic and wild. Fatima grabbed her friend by the shoulders. "Brunhilde! Calm yourself. He is not here. You are safe."

"He is on his way. To see his treasure. But the boy doesn't know, he doesn't remember anything."

A boy? Fatima let her go. What was this, Augustus collecting people like objects? She shook her head slightly and narrowed her eyes.

Brunhilde took small turns around the room, her drab skirts damp with road dirt. Amar followed her, eyes darting rapidly from her hem to head.

"What boy, Brunhilde?"

"The boy that I bought from the Dutch, the boy who knows where the ship sank."

"Brunhilde, you make no sense."

Brunhilde stopped pacing and her pink face turned red. "I have held many sins to God's ear. But this one, this one may be unforgivable."

"Brunhilde."

"He sent me to Rotterdam, where the Dutch were coming with a load of porcelain for Augustus, to see what was on the ship. It held many things for the kitchens, and I know what his intentions were." She licked her lips and heaved her breath from her chest. "But they were late, by many weeks, and when they docked, they had with them a boy from far away. He was on a ship that sank, full of treasure, in a sea across the world. Such a small boy, he speaks no word of any language I ever heard. But the Dutch sent a letter onward and Augustus responded and told them he'd buy the lad from them, the poor darling, to squeeze the place of the treasure ship from him. He's been hurt, he's sick. So thin. He looks like no one I have seen, and I am to get the place of the wreck from him."

"Brunhilde, why are you tasked with such a thing for the King? Turn the boy over to the advisors and be done with this! You are a cook, nothing more, and you cannot burden your heart with such a torturous task."

"Torturous is right, my lady. I didn't know what they'd do to try and get him to speak their language, to reveal his secrets."

"You are not to blame." Fatima raised her hands to Brunhilde's face. "You are following orders."

"I have done many things," Brunhilde said, "that I cannot erase from my mind. And God will not forgive this."

Brunhilde raised her eyes. Fatima gave her half-smile. The cook messily wiped a tear away. Her face was blotched with pink.

"Let me meet him."

Brunhilde nodded aggressively and grabbed Fatima's hand. She pulled her through a nearby door, Amar closely on their heels. The door slammed shut and they were cast into darkness.

"We could be caught," Brunhilde said. "There's no possibility we won't be caught." Amar's paws made scrabbling noises down the stone-walled hallway.

Ahead, a dim light, a single candle flickered. There were no windows.

"What is this place? I have never been here before."

"This connects the Japanese Palace to the kitchens below. No one of your status comes this way."

"My status," Fatima said harshly under her breath, but the stones of the hallway echoed them back. Brunhilde stopped. Amar clattered onward.

"That is a knife's edge, Fatima."

Fatima collided with her. The candle ahead, on the right, tucked into the gloom-spattered wall like a glinting eye, caught their wind and gasped, nearly extinguishing.

"Your status is that of a King's woman, no matter how you complain. You have jewels, a bed, a warm room. Dresses, food in your belly and likely a baby, too."

Fatima's gut roiled and sour spit filled her mouth. But Brunhilde kept going.

The Porcelain Menagerie

"You complain and whine and seek somethin' other, but we see through you. The whole of Dresden knows how miserable you are, while people starve, watching the King flaunt his wealth and his treasures and this place, where one simple piece of it would change their fates. And yet you long for somethin' else, somethin' more, even though the most you could be given, born foreign, from far away, is what you've been given."

Fatima's face was hot. She uncurled her fists, sweat pearling from them. She smelled her fear, as strong as Augustus' odor, and swallowed, hard, hating herself.

"It is not..." Amar pawed at Fatima's hem. Fatima ignored her.

"Watch yourself, girl."

"It is not the life I want, even though it may seem easy to you."

"That's it. Tell me what easy means. You've seen nothing."

"Then show me, Brunhilde."

Brunhilde walked past the flickering candle and shoved her shoulder into a metal-clad door. "He cannot understand a word you'll say," she said. The door scraped against the flagstone floor.

Inside, a single window cast a beam of white light into the room. A small cot, covered in brown and gray blankets, was empty. A small and ragged stuffed doll was face down on the stones.

"Boy?" said Brunhilde. A small figure stirred in the distance, and slowly stepped into the light, limping.

Fatima lowered to her knees, her dress catching around her legs like a net. Amar continued forward, meeting the boy in the square of sun. He squatted to reach out to her, and let out a sound of pain.

He was bone-thin, dressed in a tunic that looked as if it had been soaked in brown water and wrung roughly to dry. He had slanted, narrow eyes, a sharp pointed jaw. He could not have been more than seven. The boy was barefoot; one swollen calf wrapped with a dull red, deep wound shaped like a fish hook.

"Boy," Brunhilde said again, holding her arms out to him. He stood from his squat and rushed past Fatima to Brunhilde's arms, leaving Amar in the pool of sun. The monkey pulled her tail around her body.

Fatima stayed on the cold floor, turning to see the boy crumble into Brunhilde's broad embrace. The boy's back was laced with fresh red whip marks. Salted saliva filled her mouth again, but this time she could not swallow it down.

Chapter 29
Johann
1732

Johann practically skipped down the steep, golden hill to the countryside surrounding Albrechtsburg, breathing in the sweet, deep scent of the wheat harvest. A flock of small blackbirds turned as one in the air, somehow avoiding collision. A mile downriver was a bend, a lagoon, where he thought he might find his mission: a heron.

He tried not to think of the list of porcelain that bound him like shackles to the King's menagerie. But the names of animals echoed in his mind. How could he successfully give the King an auroch, a rhinoceros, a unicorn... How could he make them believable and real, let alone lifesize, when anything larger than the billy goat had shattered in the kilns?

His feet folded the high yellow grasses that followed the Elbe, scattering insects that flew like splattering clay with each step. He could make grasshoppers and flocks of small birds. They'd be easier than lifesize herons or billy goats. Perhaps the King would accept an alternative menagerie of small things.

The grasses ahead wheezed with insect songs, the little armies of crickets protecting their homes by becoming silent when he was near. At last, he drew close to the water's edge. A tall, gray bird stood, legs blending with the reeds. Johann dropped to the ground slowly, retrieving the book from the large, square pocket of his overcoat. In his other pocket was the horseshoe.

Early morning sunlight draped the bird, illuminating its edges. The soft textured feathers near its neck were sprinkled with water droplets.

The bird's beak was sharp, orange, weapon-like. Above its small eye was a black cap of color, similar to a monk's hood. Gray feathers of varying shades draped down its body, each folding gracefully over the other.

The Porcelain Menagerie

Johann dreamed he could carve hundreds of individual feathers for the animal, sharpen their hollow shafts from clay, and insert each one into a porcelain body.

Each piece, each shape, was separate from the whole. He filled the margins of his forbidden book with the heron, drawing over the printed words, ignoring their meaning. He smudged Böttger's formulas, written in wobbling hand, and ignored the arcanum secrets he destroyed by drawing the heron. The heron's bright, lively eye covered a wobbling map showing a clay bed nearby, hand drawn by Böttger, forgotten by time. Johann drew. The bird stayed still.

Johann's slow breath caught in his throat as the heron saw its prey in the deep, clear river. The bird plunged its head and beak under, retrieving a silver fish, and Johann drew quickly, eyes on the bird and not on the page. The bird swallowed. Johann saw the completed porcelain piece in his mind: a heron with a fish—a king with a prize.

The bird crouched, bobbed, then extended its wings to a length unbelievable, and Johann rose from the ground. He dusted his brown breeches, stained with white clay, and closed the book. Albrechtsburg loomed in the distance, his home, and his prison. His entire existence was torn. Why did he return now when, like the heron, he could disappear to the surrounding wilderness? But he had an unfinished vulture in the modeling room. The vision of the completed heron itched to be sculpted. If he left, his menagerie would haunt him, and his work would remain incomplete. He could not let his legacy be destroyed. And besides, he had a hole to dig for Herman. His legs took him to Albrechtsburg.

He entered the castle from the kitchen and took Hao's staircase to the opposite end of the subterranean levels, stopping by the stables for a wooden shovel first. The kilns were far away, though the sounds of them rumbled. Herman's future resting place was fifty yards away. Johann approached the narrow door, almost hidden in shadow around a corner. There were many hallways and storage spaces here, where grain and preserves, beer kegs, and wine bottles were once stored for royalty. Dusted bottles and broken barrels made the place uninviting, as if the party was long over.

A new lock, black and shining, dangled, unclasped. The key was with Hao, and Johann knew he would give it to him unquestionably. He pushed the door open, rough on the unfinished floor. There was no light here. He knelt, the dirt cold to the touch, black and fine, as though no feet had ever touched it, though it was the rumbling of the kilns that had smoothed any footprints from years ago. He gathered a handful of the fine silt and let his eyes adjust.

Shelving lined the room, stacked with a few earthenware jars. It was narrow, small. It took three significant strides to reach the opposite wall. Johann walked in, settling into the total darkness and silence so loud his ears filled with whispers. He stayed for a while, waiting to see if anyone came by. No souls approached. The room, like a monster's heart, was buried deep.

Johann took the wooden shovel and began to dig.

Many hours later when Johann emerged, the factory was oddly still. Johann crept up the stairs, and the usual raucous cries of men traipsing up and down the narrow passageways with white gold in their arms were absent. A subtle dripping was all he heard. He peeked into the many rooms that housed painters, sculptors, organizers, kilnsmen, and saw no one. Johann felt a chill creep up his spine and quickly headed toward the looming carved front doors of Albrechtsburg.

Hao sat at his usual perch on a wobbling black stool, head leaning against the wall, mouth open, asleep.

"Hao?" Johann shook him.

Hao leaped to his feet, hands ready for a fight. Johann quickly side-stepped and dodged, heart pounding.

"Johann, why are you still here?" Hao put his hands down.

"Where else would I be, Hao?"

"With the other porcelain makers at the arrival of the Chinese vessels for trade."

"I was not told of this."

"Everyone was told of this."

"Not I."

"Yes."

"Hao," Johann pursed his lips, "I was not told."

"I told Christian Herold to tell you."

Johann inhaled deeply through his nose and tilted his head slightly toward Hao. Hao raised his eyebrows, understanding now that Christian Herold did not tell Johann the vessels had arrived.

"Is there a mare left for me?" He did not know what consequences existed if he missed the ceremony.

Hao shook his head. "Only the draft horses pulling the mill, but you can saddle one of them easily enough."

Johann pulled the heavy doors shut behind him. He followed the winding, narrow dirt path around the castle to the mill where the draft horses pulled, grinding the minerals that made porcelain clay. Johann slipped the harness off the larger horse and led the animal to the stables, where he found the largest saddle he could and cinched the horse tightly.

The Porcelain Menagerie

He had to climb on a bale of straw to mount the towering animal.

The nearly-black horse had feathered feet, pink nostrils and inner ears, and a penchant for shaking his head. Johann urged the lumbering beast toward the castle, waving goodbye to Hao, though he was not visible. Leaving his friend behind felt strange, but he knew Hao was the least likely to believe good things about King Augustus and want to join in a celebration, and someone had to guard Albrechtsburg.

The winding cobbles on unshod hooves were slow, and Johann did not push the horse. Instead, he enjoyed the new perspective. He had never ridden so large an animal and could see on top of the buildings of Dresden. The creature's warmth radiated through his legs, and he began to sweat. The crowded merchant street parted for him. On the roofs of many buildings were doors, ladders, and balconies—alcoves, secret spots, hidden places. He had lived here his entire life but never knew of these hideaways. It was possible to move from rooftop to rooftop, unseen. He tucked this information away and soon approached the castle.

The grooms took the horse after Johann strained and reached the tips of his booted toes to the ground to dismount. He was led hastily by a footman who was clearly perturbed by the late arrival. The courtyard had a short layer of verdant green grass flanked by pea gravel bordering walkways. The place was full of people—kilnsmen, stableboys, modelers who only made teacups and plates—all Johann recognized or knew quite well, including Herold's small team of painters and Samuel.

He gave a short wave to Samuel and joined him, settling in beside, sweat making a line down his temple.

"You're late," said Samuel.

"Herold did not remember to tell me."

Samuel shook his head and sighed. He gestured to a dais near the King's tent. The tent towered, red and gold and embroidered, art in its own right, but the threads were wearing thin. The breeze puffed the top, sending golden pewter tassels bouncing. Stakes held it firm. Johann counted seats: one large for Augustus, and three more set beside him, of smaller size, but all matching.

The dais, broad and narrow, held what he presumed were the vessels, draped with thin white cloths. The dark blue of Chinese porcelain pulsed through, and Johann raised his chin, squinting to get a closer look. The other members of Albrechtsburg's makers stood nearby, straining and whispering amongst each other. They were provided no chairs. This was what their work was compared to, this was the level of art their King desired. Johann exhaled loudly through his nose and twisted his mouth. To be compared to thousands of years of perfecting an art form...

A trumpeter began, announcing King Augustus, and the crowd, hundreds of nobility and wealthy merchants and citizens of Dresden grew still. The people closest were dressed finely, not a poor one among them, but one section of faraway people were clad in the grays and browns and creams of peasantry, and Johann realized with a sour gut that they had to be the families of the six hundred dragoons who left in exchange for Chinese porcelain. The crowd wiggled with small children on mothers' hips, with young puffy-eyed men now tasked with moving their lives or unexpectedly saying goodbye to their fathers. They stood with women whose faces were gaunt and shimmering with wetness, from tears or sweat or both. Six hundred lost their Da. Johann swallowed, swiping dirt from his brow.

Augustus took his seat, closely followed by Fatima, Katharina, and to Johann's surprise, Michal, who sat by Katharina with a devilish look on his face. Samuel stepped closer to Johann.

"Why's he still here, if the divorce is final?"

"He's in charge of taking the six hundred back to Prussia."

"Is that safe?" said Samuel.

No, thought Johann. "I'm sure it's fine. He wouldn't violate Augustus' orders, would he?"

But the look on Michal's face was one of power, one of control, and the smirk he held sent fear into Johann's chest like a dull punch. Katharina was stoic, and Michal played with the sleeve of her red gown, though she did not turn to him. He snapped his fingers at her. She glared, facing the other way.

The ceremony began.

"The unveiling of the greatest porcelain in all the German states! A link between Prussia and Saxony! We bid farewell to soldiers and hello to masterworks! A show of the wealth of both Electors!"

A dwarf and his family, finely dressed, somersaulted onto the stage and gently flipped the sheets from the vessels, which stood as tall as them. The crowd cheered. Heat swept Johann, and then goosebumps ran up his arms. The vessels were massive, impressive, glowing blue and white and thin and perfect: no cracks, no fissures, no bubbles on the surface.

Samuel shifted. "We cannot make things that large."

Johann turned to his friend. "Not yet, Samuel, but soon. We can. We certainly can."

"How will our work compare when he has masterworks? Why would we need to even continue? He'll be done with us. We haven't been paid in months as it is, Johann, and now I fear his appetite for white gold will be satiated."

"I hope you're wrong, Samuel. Now that he has these, surely he'll want ours. More. Desperately. He'll want us to make things better, stronger, so that Saxony can claim the greatest porcelain factory in ten thousand leagues. The menagerie is unlike anything made in China, unlike these vessels, we have the imaginations to go beyond pots and jars." Did Johann say these things to reassure himself or to reassure his friend and fellow porcelain maker? He bolstered himself, straightened his spine though his body trembled. "We make living things in white gold."

Johann nodded. Living things. He turned to where the soldiers were lined up, breaking rank to say their goodbyes, fully outfitted with swords and muskets and packs full of supplies. Their war horses waited, gleaming outside the Japanese Palace. Six hundred men for porcelain vessels. If Augustus gave lives in exchange for porcelain, what would he take if Albrechtsburg faltered?

He rose from his throne to examine the pieces, rubbing his hands on the one closest to him like it was a woman. Johann flinched. The noise of the soldiers and trumpets overwhelmed whatever King Augustus murmured to himself. The sun beat down, and his powdered face dripped, his many layers of clothing heavy and damp from sweat. Katharina and Fatima came to the dais, skirts spread wide by nearby ladies.

Michal stayed in the shade of the tent, whispering something to a well-dressed courtier, who nodded briefly and left the courtyard. Katharina swept around the dais and paused near Johann, who took a few steps closer, hoping to see the inside of the vases, which stood as tall as his chest. The crowd filtered from their seats into the courtyard, lining up to see the vessels before they were locked away inside the Japanese Palace.

"Dragoon vases," she said, barely close enough for him to hear. "That's what my father's calling them."

"He loves them," Johann said, coming closer but keeping his eyes on the vases so not to draw attention to their conversation.

"Obsession and love are two different things."

"Indeed. I do not know if our work will compare."

"It doesn't. But it doesn't matter. He seeks singular things, you know, and will want yours even if they're flawed as no one else can make them. Did you consider giving up? That this was his final acquisition?"

"It felt that way when I saw them unveiled. No matter how hard I try, will it ever be good enough for him?"

"You make your art for him? Him alone?"

Johann swallowed. No, it wasn't just for Augustus. But could he admit that to the King's daughter?

"I have a brother, who died not long ago. He asked me to make something everlasting, and I carve his face onto figures—"

"Still another person. Do you not make things for yourself, Johann? To feel like you're good at something? To know you have purpose? To leave a legacy?"

"Indeed. Though I am surprised to hear you say those things to me, as I am not a high ranking—"

She interrupted him again. "Your rank means nothing. When I am gone, nothing of me will remain. Bones, ash, a lock of hair. When you are gone, your art will last forever. Leave them for centuries, and even when all of your descendants are buried, your art will be uncovered and longed for."

"My art will only last if it's not destroyed by your mother."

"That act helped me escape my husband. I plan to leave Dresden in a fortnight, and you'll be rid of me and my mother. This drama, this band of six hundred will leave and disperse. He will be gone by then, too, attending to them, and you'll be rid of me."

"Where will you go?" He didn't want her to leave, but he could not tell her that. He clenched his jaw.

She turned to him, dark-eyed and red-lipped, and her voice quivered. "I will not say."

He held her gaze. She did not turn.

"Thank you, Johann, for helping me. Without your push, and my mother's bravery, I don't think he would have signed the papers. I'm sorry your friend's work was destroyed. I am glad it wasn't *your* lion."

Augustus was heading their way, after boyishly flicking a vessel to make it ding. He smiled eerily, his face covered in rivulets of makeup and sweat.

"My porcelain man," he greeted Johann, who bowed.

"Your Majesty must be pleased," Johann said. "I'd love to study these once they're installed in the Japanese Palace. Perhaps Albrechtsburg can learn something from them."

"Indeed. Unlike my dear daughter who learns nothing from example." Augustus laughed, but Katharina did not return it. She turned, curtsied, and left.

Samuel approached. "Your Majesty holds the best in the world now, and I am honored to be part of your artisans."

"You're the one whose cat Maria destroyed, Samuel Kirchner? The other one making my menagerie?"

Samuel nodded. His chest puffed a bit, and he leaned toward the King. Johann caught a lilt in the word "other" and held his breath.

"They're too human-like, you know," Augustus said. "Unpleasant to look at. Glad it was yours she destroyed and not Kändler's here. How long have you been at Albrechtsburg?"

"Ten...ten years, sir."

"I think that's long enough, don't you?"

Johann's ears seemed filled with dust. Samuel's face grew pale. Augustus flitted his hand at him. "Perhaps they'll find room for you somewhere else. I'll make sure Hao knows you're no longer welcome."

"Somewhere else?"

"I hear the anatomist could use assistance."

Johann bit his tongue. Samuel shrank beside him.

"Kändler, you'll join me tonight. At the reception, the party. I want people to meet you, to praise you." He drew out the word praise, trilling the r. Johann's eyes grew large, but he could think of nothing to do but nod.

Samuel turned on his heel and before Johann could reach him, his yellow jacket disappeared into the crowd. The army was departing from the courtyard, a long fanfare of trumpets echoing, and Samuel was swept into the wave of people. Johann raised on his toes, pushed through the soldiers and their families, seeking Samuel's graying hair, a glimpse of his potter's hands, the lace cuffs, his kind eyes... but Samuel was gone.

Chapter 30
Fatima
1706

Faraway cages on a green lawn rattled in the distance. On the pea-gravel paths farthest from the castle walls, people lined up, bending to see into the wooden crates full of pacing animals. The creatures were distorted from Fatima's distance, and she hurried. She thought she recognized... yes. Ahead, much like Augustus on his throne, settled in the center of the woodland creatures, was the wooden cage of her lion, pulled from the menagerie and still on the rolling cart. Buda paced, angry in his cage, clearly distressed.

The other animals whined, squealed, yelped, panicked, both by the presence of the largest beast of prey they had ever seen or smelled and by their own narrow quarters. The sound of their claws on wooden cages scraped a percussion that became the undertone of the musicians on the lawn.

Fatima grimaced, squinting at the cages. She turned to go to them, but Brunhilde pulled her arm. Paces away, the young Chinese boy stood stiffly, dressed in fine clothing with jeweled details. They started calling him Hao, a shortened version of the name that he'd told them, repeated slowly. Brunhilde only gathered the longest syllable. He was a novelty, as no one else had seen a Chinese boy in Saxony, the King claimed him as a rare and usual specimen. Hao might as well have been put in a cage, too. Brunhilde leaned into the boy, explaining things in a loud voice:

"This is a fox toss. This is how the King shows his strength. He will form teams, each flanks a *prellgarn,* and the foxes will be released. As they run across the *prellgarn,* people on each side will pull as hard as possible and see how high the foxes will fly."

The boy looked puzzled. He understood little, so Brunhilde

mimicked the actions. Fatima inhaled, sharp.

"And then the judge, the King's woman, that's Fatima there... I mean Maria, will tell us who won. The winning team launches the fox the highest."

Fatima did not want Brunhilde to tell the boy what happened to the animals, but she continued. "They die on impact with the ground but if they're not dead, they're clubbed to death by the court dwarves or children. You could give it a go, I can get you one of the clubs!"

Fatima blanched. Brunhilde turned to her.

"They won't let your lion out, will they? I shake to think of it. The boars found the ladies' petticoats last time. I can't imagine what a lion would do if it got loose. I see a few other mean ones—wildcats, vicious things."

"We are not safe, and neither are the animals."

"I'd like to tell you it's normal, but somethin' feels different in the air this year..."

"Tell me it could change, Brunhilde? Surely not all of these animals will perish?"

"Maybe not all. My lady, I thought you were in charge of this celebration?"

"How is this celebrating anything?"

"The power of King Augustus the Strong, who lifts a fox eight feet up with one finger and a net."

"We are foxes, aren't we?"

Brunhilde said nothing but shifted side to side as if she were on the lower level of Albrechtsburg.

"What if I feign illness? Go back inside?" Fatima could not force her voice to more than a whisper.

King Augustus was beginning to form teams, choosing laughing courtiers and soldiers and artisans to pit against each other. He was a few paces away when he saw Fatima and broke into a wide grin, his jowls wobbling, his face red and puffy.

Fatima whimpered slightly, and Augustus approached with a silver scepter. He smelled of meat and cloves and man-garlic; flowering herbs tied to a string around his neck were meant to mask the stench of sick and sour beer on his breath.

"Ah, my judge!" said Augustus, swaying slightly. "You must be overjoyed to see your lion here." Fatima curtseyed, a bead of sweat careening off her forehead to the pea gravel.

"I am here to please you, Your Highness." Her mouth moved before her thoughts. There was a presence beside her. Georg, dressed in a fine dark uniform. He gave her a small smile and his eyebrows knit together, a gentle show of concern.

"You'll be with me, Georg, on my team. Surely we can beat last year's seven feet, six inches? It only took me forty animals to get that number! I would have gotten there sooner had that boar not gutted my footman. Really put a damper on the celebration."

"What if we spare the boars this year, Your Highness? I'd like Maria to keep one in her menagerie."

The King turned his head slightly, mouth curved in an expression unlikely to be called a smile. The whites of his eyes looked like freshly glazed porcelain, shot through with pink veins so delicate a fine Chinese artist could not have painted them with anything more than a single-strand brush.

"A boar is on my list. Undelivered. So is a fox, and a male wolf for my she-wolf, and a wildcat," Fatima said. "You can deliver them from here to my menagerie and I will find space for them."

"Those animals are too stupid to have escaped me. Now they'll meet their match, thrown to their doom. And if they survive, I've had my carpenters create lovely little clubs of hardwood, some laced with metal nails, to help end their suffering," Augustus said. He ignored Fatima's plea to save the creatures.

Fatima inhaled sharply and tried to make her expression neutral.

"You see, Maria, I own them. In life and death, they are my subjects. It is their own fault that they were caught in the wild and didn't fight hard enough to escape. It is their own fault if they don't die on impact. They belong to the kingdom. If they weren't caught, they might still be alive. It's your fault they're here anyway."

Fatima looked up, the sun scalding her view of Augustus, and felt deeply the scratching claws of the waiting foxes, the strange call of the wildcat, the rumbling plea of Buda.

"Your Highness, give them to me. Alive. To remind me of you. Choose the best so that your menagerie may hold the specimens you deserve."

"No," said the King, cackling wildly, his booming laugh echoing. The courtyard joined in, not knowing why they laughed other than that the King had started it. "Give me the fox that is tossed the highest, Maria. Dead or alive. *That's* the one you'll keep in a cage."

Fatima swallowed.

"As you wish, Elector," she said slowly, waiting for the crowd noise to die. Augustus cackled again, nodded, and motioned Fatima to the canopied risers where the court ladies sat.

The Porcelain Menagerie

They stood, fanning themselves, panniers rippling. Fatima, dressed in red and gold, raised her gaze to Georg. He held her eyes. Around her, the courtiers whispered. She might have been the King's current favorite, but she knew they, too, frequented his bed and that they wore jewels he bestowed upon them. She had no special place anywhere.

"Ladies," Georg bowed, extending an arm. "The King has commanded you judge fairly, and tell us which animal goes the highest so his lady Maria may take it for her menagerie."

"Dead or alive," said one of the women mockingly.

Fatima fanned herself, ducking under the broad red tent that was stolen from her homeland, and the other ladies followed. The tent held others from court, a few Fatima recognized, and Brunhilde and Hao, too, found seats under the broad shaded area.

Then, as the heralds below blew through golden trumpets, signaling the first tossing was upon them, Friedrich stepped into the tent. Fatima leaned toward him, surprised, but he gave a quick hand signal that told her to ignore him.

She looked away. The expanse of the courtyard, including the cages, unfolded in front of her. Green yard, gray paths, brown cages. The animals rattled and trembled, screaming high-pitched notes that disordered the low, even trumpet sound. Her lion's low grumbling echoed in her roiling gut.

The King took his position. In the middle of the field, a net-like *prellgarn* laid out in front of him, stretching the length of three carriages. Fatima strained to see the figures near the cages.

There were men, shaking, with darkened burns on their arms. Friedrich had come close to the raised benches where the ladies sat.

"Those are my workers," he said, barely moving his mouth. Fatima raised her fan to her face.

"We must do something to stop this. I will be ill."

Georg had left the tent, his handsome profile watched by the ladies who murmured and giggled amongst each other. He turned at their chittering and bowed deeply. Fatima could not bear to watch as he strode to a *prellgarn*.

Friedrich's porcelain workers were stationed near the cages, bent low, hands on the latches of the first few. Dozens more cages shook behind them. The first line of foxes was released when the King raised his arm and shouted, sending his large body quivering. The animals darted, terrified, through the yard. Fatima opened her eyes.

Six of them, fast orange and brown blurs, long-legged and haggard, crossed the first *prellgarn*, and the pairs of people on either side lifted the nets and launched. Two foxes were caught, feet falling through the netting, faces smashed to the ground before they were lifted. Their bodies dangled mid-air before they landed.

A yelp sounded. The first fox was still alive. The second fox landed on its back, a hollow-warm whump resounding. Fatima squeezed her eyes tight. There were four more *prellgarns* to get through. She could not believe any of the animals would survive.

"Mr. Böttger," said Fatima. "You must watch to know which fox I am to take back to the menagerie." Amar sat, chained, under her skirts. The sounds of fearful animals frightened her.

"None of these animals will live, Fatima."

A dripping worry of nausea in her stomach grew to her throat and she choked, nearly vomiting, as the next two rounds of *prellgarns* stopped the foxes. One screamed, primeval, before a court dwarf dressed in purple silks clubbed it, sending flesh spattering. Two foxes remained. Brunhilde held a trembling Hao, who had let his club drop from his small hand.

The crowd cheered, bells ringing in their hands, clapping and dancing to a fiddler's musical accompaniment. The King's *prellgarn* was next. The foxes were lightning-quick, trying to avoid the people on the sides of the courtyard, which forced them directly into the nets. Augustus' large arms flickered, moving the net upward, smoothly. The people on the other side of the net did not move nearly as quickly, and one fox was thrown sideways into the audience flanking the courtyard on the gravel path.

The fox was not injured, only startled, and latched its small, rapidly biting teeth onto a man Fatima recognized from the kitchens. He fell, trying to shake the animal off, but lost his balance, skidding sideways on the gravel, hitting hands-first. The fox latched onto an outstretched palm and ripped, taking fingers with it. The man screamed, and the fox continued to bite. Suddenly, Hao darted from the tent, seemingly trying to head back to the castle.

The fox turned, mouth bloodied, and lunged at the boy. The crowd gasped. King Augustus began to run, a stumbling, mad looking gait, and the court dwarf scurried upward on saddle-wide legs. Augustus got there first and grabbed the fox by the throat with his massive bare hands. He clamped down hard and choked the life from the animal before taking it by the tail and catapulting it over the wall of the courtyard. The crowd bellowed.

King Augustus picked up Hao from the gravel and cradled him like a baby. The boy's hands were scraped, puncture wounds pierced his forearm. The kitchen man was not moving. His wrist was spurting blood. His pallor grew white. Fatima kept down bile. Friedrich grabbed her hand, keeping it low so no one else could see.

The Porcelain Menagerie

Then she heard a strange sound from the opposite end of the yard. The remaining foxes began to scream.

Fatima stood slowly. The ladies ceased their chattering. Fatima turned to Friedrich. His chest heaved with breath and he let go of her hand, exiting quickly from the side of the tent. She looked ahead, standing. Amar clutched her petticoat.

The lion was loose.

Many in the crowd were watching Augustus cradle his new Chinese novelty, Hao. Was it she that screamed? Perhaps it was—but her ears felt clogged and her throat raw and the noise that left her was more of fear for what would happen to her lion than what the lion would do next.

Buda leaped over the cages, clawing them crazily sideways, seeing the small creatures inside as screaming threats. The crowd shifted its attention and more screaming echoed. They ran. The ladies in the tent followed Friedrich's path out the side, under the Turkish tent. Fatima darted straight out, feet tangling with one of the nets. Amar could not keep up.

The lion jolted from cage to cage, shoulder muscles rippling, its safe enclosure now far away. Fatima ran toward her beast but was caught around the waist by Friedrich, who wrestled her down.

"You cannot!" he cried.

"They'll kill him!"

"He's stronger than you think! Let him be!"

She fought, still, as Augustus shoved the boy he held into Brunhilde's waiting arms, then motioned for his armored guard to take Buda down. The King looked at her, fighting against Friedrich's grasp, and unsheathed his sword.

"No!" Fatima's throat could not bear another scream, yet it came.

Augustus hunted her animal, standing as large as he could, waving his swollen arms toward it. The lion saw him, and changed its course.

Friedrich let Fatima go. She rushed forward, her destination the lion's cage, where she hoped she could lure it back. But she could do nothing if the King killed Buda first.

They met in the center of the courtyard, stepping cautiously around the *prellgarns*, equal matches, the King and the lion.

The back of Fatima's neck prickled with sweat. Heat rose up her face. She stopped running and stood, still as one of Benjamin Thomae's sculptures, watching the lion walk slowly and deftly toward Augustus. Buda's eyes were solidly black.

Augustus bent low, sword pulled under his body like a third arm, ready to strike. The lion charged. Augustus jabbed, missed. The lion missed, too, and they spun. Fatima ran a few steps closer and Augustus turned to hiss at her, primal and large and fearsome, all humanity gone from him.

The lion lunged as Augustus did, and they caught each other. The blade of the King's jeweled sword, hilt carved with an outstretched eagle, sliced across the cat's face, its left eye hit. The lion lunged forward and sliced its vicious claws through the King's opposite palm. They both roared, injured, turning from each other. Fatima sprinted.

She darted past the fighting pair, aware that Amar was left behind and Friedrich was close on her heels, and slid to the waiting cages. She began opening them, all of them, avoiding bites and scratches by sheer luck. Friedrich joined her, and dozens of animals poured from their prisons. The lion was soon overrun by foxes, boars, wildcats, and dozens and dozens of hares darting closely by.

Women cascaded from the tent like parrots leaving their perches, screaming. The King's palm was crisscrossed with red. He held it to the empty stands and laughed. Loose animals were everywhere; the people panicked, running like rabbits before a dog.

A wildcat darted close by Augustus and the lion, foxes following. Chaos reigned, and the people rushed to find a way out before angry teeth nipped at their heels. They'd all been released.

Augustus retreated, chased by a boar who likely weighed more than the King's new prized Chinese child, his hand dripping with blood. The lion caught a rabbit, easier prey than Augustus, and pulled it in close. Fatima signaled to Friedrich to help her, a bright whistle that made him run.

They hauled the lion's cage, still on its wagon, toward the center of the courtyard. Animals had found escape in the stands and the open pathways and under the shade of the Ottoman tent, but many still fled in circles, too frightened to save themselves.

Chaos surrounded them, wild and piss-filled, and still they hauled. Fatima's skirts ripped from their seams, the satin of her bodice puckered and split. She did not care. She pulled her creature's safety net toward it.

The lion held the rabbit in its mouth, panting around it, panicked, blinking, pawing blood from its face. Georg suddenly appeared beside Fatima and Friedrich and helped them haul the heavy cage from the wagon. Fatima picked up a dead rabbit, likely perished from fear, and threw it in the cage. The lion growled.

If this did not work, they would have to kill Buda. The King was nowhere to be seen. The crowd was gone, fled from fear and injury and disgust and every other emotion Fatima could not name for the task at hand consumed her. She saw nothing but her animal, the poor young

The Porcelain Menagerie

thing not even full grown, now faced with doom and death if Buda did not return to his cage.

She tossed another rabbit in the cage. Georg stepped back, signaling to surround the lion. Fatima followed. Friedrich motioned to them, hands behind his back, tailing the lion to scare it into its cage. Something dropped from his overcoat to the grass. He watched it, but left it, focusing again on the beast. The lion pawed at its eye, considering its options. Fatima saw Buda's working mind, much like hers: should it attack, or retreat?

The creature chose its cage.

Georg closed the gate. Fatima could not still her heart. She bent to pick up what Friedrich had dropped: a gray book, thick and tightly bound.

Fatima turned her dark eyes to Georg's pale ones, frowning. "Who let him out? Who would risk his life?"

"I did," said Georg. "To save the rest of them."

"To maul the King?"

"It was always a possibility that someone would get hurt but I..."

"You chose this for me."

Georg nodded. Friedrich looked between the two of them, opened his mouth to speak, but was silenced by Fatima's scream. Rage settled in her chest. How could Georg have loosed her lion in the crowd like that? Many people could have been killed. Buda could have been killed.

"It's over. Get your troops to take him back to the menagerie," said Fatima.

"The King will have him killed now," said Friedrich.

"The King likes unusual things. A one-eyed lion with whom he met his match might qualify for unusual. I will do my work. Now go do yours, Fatima," said Georg.

She turned from him. Georg left, sweeping his fancy tailcoat behind him. Fatima could not keep her anger from her body and let out a third scream, this one muffled by her closed mouth.

Fatima scanned the courtyard for Amar. Most of the remaining crowd kept their distance. The people around the beer man cheered as creatures scattered, wondering if the festivities would resume. Böttger stood by her side.

"Where is Amar?" said Fatima, fingers wrapping around Friedrich's forearm, gripping him tight. "Where is my creature?"

The animals filled the courtyard, stomping on the torturous *prellgarns*. Others found their way once a wolf leaped over a low stone wall. Drunken members of the crowd chased the creatures, some of which turned back in anger, snapping their bone-white teeth.

Amar was nowhere to be seen. Fatima did not know it was possible to feel the level of panic that cascaded over her. She ran back to the tent, praying her beloved had not been snatched up by a wildcat or a fox.

Friedrich ran ahead, faster on his long legs, scanning the benches under the red tent. He pulled cushions aside and pulled the trembling monkey from a soft pile. Fatima cried out and leapt forward, embracing the shivering creature. She let her tears come, and turned to Friedrich, weeping.

He embraced her, and she saw from over his shoulder Georg and his soldiers hauling the caged lion across the yard. Georg watched her. A thrum went through her body and she pulled away from the porcelain maker, who then swept her off of her feet and, staring at Georg, carried her toward the palace kitchens, away from the chaos.

Chapter 31
Johann
1733

Candlelight, like a close galaxy, lit the hall from above. The mosaic floor depicted Saxony's coat of arms, blurred by the dozens of feet traipsing their way into the grand party room. Johann's throat was dry and though he would normally have looked around at the carvings and statues to guess which were Benjamin Thomae's, instead he gazed at the people, hoping Samuel was among them.

But the people were too loud, too beautiful, too well-dressed to be from Schloss Albrechtsburg. Johann's coat, though his finest, felt shabby amongst the royals and dignitaries, the high generals, and the ladies of the court. The candle flames moved as they walked past, like they were delicate fingers stretching out, hoping to be included.

Dresden was visible through the massive windows, the church spires and statues creating a strange, otherworldly cityscape. Hao suddenly appeared by Johann's side, barely recognizable in red silk.

"Hao? Where is Samuel?"

"Gone. I expected something dramatic to happen but not that. Kirchner has been valuable to the King for years. I am here at the King's request to enhance the presentation."

"Enhance the presentation?"

"I am Chinese, and so are these vessels. He wants me to authenticate them in front of his crowd. To show his wealth and his intelligence. He has done this before; there is a script for me to follow."

Hao wore a traditional Chinese outfit, one Johann had never seen before. Creatures embroidered in gold crawled up its sleeves.

"Dragons? May I use this for reference, my friend?"

"For the menagerie? I thought you'd deliver Schloss Albrechtsburg as your dragon," Hao said without a smile. He did not look at Johann.

Johann followed his gaze. Hundreds of tapered candles glinted off crystal glasses in hands and sapphires in ears. The buttons of the generals flickered. Swords on their sides and jeweled brooches on their throats caught fragments of light.

"One hundred fifty one pieces of porcelain are being brought through the halls," said Hao.

"I am overwhelmed, Hao."

"I was asked to read the symbols on the documents. The pieces are the size I was when I arrived in Saxony, and likely heavier."

"How is it they make them so perfect? And I cannot."

"You try to force thousands of years into one, Johann. Remember that perfection is the perception of the person who sees it, not the person who made it. The person who made it will always find a flaw."

"As large as a child, though, I..." Hao raised his hand to silence him, his face forced into a smile. He ended the conversation as others began to recognize them both: porcelain makers from Augustus' manufactory. Whispers flitted about.

Musicians played grandly from the corners of the room. The air was perfumed by some kind of incense that made the smells of Albrechtsburg on Johann's clothes and hair melt away. Servants better dressed than he raised small pastries and meats on silver trays, glasses of Riesling matched the candlelight. The room warmed, swaying with silk gowns.

Someone tapped loudly on the floor. The crowd stilled. The musicians halted. The procession began: white-gloved servants hauled in Chinese porcelain, blue and white gleaming gold in the firelight. Waiting pedestals received their treasures. Then, a fanfare.

"Meine Damen und Herren! It is with unbridled esteem that we present to you His Majesty, Augustus, King of Poland, Grand Duke of Lithuania, Elector of Saxony, Sovereign of many realms! A monarch whose grandeur surpasses that of the heavens! A ruler whose reign is marked by boundless ambition! Behold our great leader, whose courage and strength have marked his name in the annals of history! Let us welcome him! For without him, tonight, we would have no light!"

Johann's heart beat in rhythm with every syllable of the herald. He could not help his mouth from curling in distaste. Hao drew a step closer to him and they stood, shoulder to shoulder, nearly touching. Their chests rose.

Augustus came from the back of the room, parting drapes for drama, clad in a fur-lined cape and bright, shining blue satin. His snow-white tights showed the swelling of his ankles. Sweat, like the candles, languidly dripped down his face.

The Porcelain Menagerie

Maria waited for him at the bottom of his dais. She wore green-silk brocade, the waist dropping low and panniers broader than any other woman in the room. Johann knew little of gowns and court ladies, but he knew this gown must've cost just as much as a porcelain bowl from China. Maria curtsied to him deeply and Augustus took her delicate hand.

"I remember them doing this when I first arrived here," Hao said quietly. The whole crowd hushed as they watched them. Maria's silk skirts swished and waved and her jewels, including a thumb-sized diamond that rested in the hollow of her neck, momentarily blinded Johann.

They strode to the first porcelain pedestal and Hao cleared his throat and stepped forward.

Hao stopped directly in front of Maria and Augustus. He dropped to his knees, then bowed to them as if in worship. Augustus touched his head with a scepter and Hao rose. He spoke loudly in a language Johann did not understand, but some of the merchants in the room nodded and raised their Riesling.

"I shall reveal the wealth of King Augustus," said Hao. "In a display of porcelain, you see the strength of Saxony. One hundred fifty one pieces, each from the perfect kilns of Jingdezhen, so far away we shan't see the place for half a year if we set out now!"

The crowd laughed and marveled at Hao, especially his foreign language and his clothing. Johann did not know how to feel. His friend was helping Augustus in this spectacle... this strange exchange of soldiers for porcelain. People for wealth.

Hao continued, and Johann fiddled with his hands in his pockets. In one pocket was the book, the other, the horseshoe. Hao bowed deeply again, and backed away, allowing the King to see his guests and flick open his gold-lined jacket to the people.

"See the glory of Saxony!" King Augustus yelled. Maria flinched, closing her eyes momentarily. Johann saw this for what it was. He saw the King's deepening sickness, both physical and mental, and his skin crawled for him to leave.

Instead, he watched. The people clustered around the porcelain masterworks, touching them. The bolder men reached their hands inside the vessels and knocked, sending a discordant note into the room. They handed the lids to the women, whose faces matched the white interior.

"So, porcelain maker," said a man Johann did not know. "Tell us of the quality of these vases. Was it worth trading people for? I question the King's ability to see reason here..."

"Sir, surely you do not doubt the judgment of King Augustus?" Johann said. "Surely you misunderstand this art. My art. Let me show you."

Johann lifted a lid. It was the same weight as the forbidden book in his pocket; smooth, stunning, deeply cold. He flipped it over to show the bone-like quality, the delicateness, the intense surface like unrippled water.

"I see white," said the man. "And something breakable." He wouldn't be able to understand, Johann realized, no matter how he tried to explain, unless he saw the contrast. Unless he saw the failures, fissures, and imperfections of the porcelain Johann himself made. Shame burned his face.

He dare not mention the many failed pieces, the worthlessness he felt, the comparison of his eagle, his vulture, his monkey, his delicate carvings of Hao and Katharina and the face of Herman on vinegar services... he could not make anything like this. He could not make perfection.

Heat crawled up Johann's limbs, and his scalp burned with sweat. All of his flaws felt on fire, visible to this stranger, who looked at him with a puzzled gaze and slowly backed away.

Just as Johann inhaled, trying to still his breath, the ruddy, thick hand of Augustus landed on his shoulder. The lid in his hand nearly dropped and Johann's knees trembled.

"Your Majesty," he said, replacing the lid and dropping his neck, exposing his spine like prey.

"My porcelain maker," said Augustus. His breath was sharp and strange, sweet but not with wine. "What say you, lad, of these pieces? Worth the lives of six hundred men, yes!?"

This was a call for Johann to agree. To agree that lives were worth less than objects. People gathered around, desperate to hear the praise from Saxony's newest porcelain star creator. Johann placed the lid back on the vessel. A perfect fit, like a joint and a bone, made by God.

He inhaled, put his hands in his pockets with book and horseshoe, and tried to gather his words. The audience looked to him. Maria's diamond shone. Katharina stepped forward and Johann's thoughts blew out like one of the candles, extinguished. She wore dark blue, the same color as the coiled dragons on the porcelain in front of him. The fabric shimmered as she walked.

Johann saw nothing but her. Her black hair, the way her ears escaped her coif in a way some might call imperfect, her slightly parted mouth, the way the corners of it turned up when their eyes met. Johann inhaled and held his breath.

"Well!?" Augustus cocked his head and stomped. Johann's attention snapped to the King and he swallowed, eyes sweeping the floor before the crowd. He released his hands from his pockets. Too quickly.

The horseshoe clattered to the gleaming floor.

The Porcelain Menagerie

Johann bent to grab it, but it skittered, just in front of Augustus. The King snapped his fingers and the nearest guest picked it up, offering it to him.

"They are..." Johann began, hoping to turn the attention back to the Chinese porcelain. But Augustus began laughing.

"Who here was lucky enough to witness my feat of strength, so many years ago?"

Maria raised her hand, as did many of the dignitaries. Most hands remained gripped around crystal glasses. What feat of strength was Augustus referring to?

Augustus raised the horseshoe. It did not catch the golden light. It was dull, worn, dirty, stale. But it held so many memories for Johann. Herman. The merchant with treasures in his cart. His brother, his father, his mother, the small, narrow bed in the parsonage... the new grave that waited for Herman's casket.

Columns cast shadows that suddenly overwhelmed the firelight. Darkness crept toward Johann. The room swam, people became gold-tinged blurs. A flash of red silk, Hao, dripped to the floor, though nothing truly moved. Johann's knees stammered beneath him.

King Augustus took the horseshoe in both hands and stepped to the dais. The crowd began to cheer and followed him. The ladies hopped excitedly, save Maria and Katharina, who flanked Johann so closely that their skirts touched his fists. Katharina turned slightly to him and made the lightest shushing sound. It matched the whisper of anger running through him.

The King cried out, a warrior's noise, and held the horseshoe to his massive thigh. He twisted, wrenching it between his hands, then showed the crowd its bent, malformed change.

Augustus moved it to his other thigh and wrenched again. The snap of metal and small spark sliced through Johann's daze. He screamed.

The crowd cheered, and though some turned to Johann in surprise at his reaction, their eyes did not stay on his face.

King Augustus threw the horseshoe onto the dais and stepped into the crowd where many hands reached to him and touched his silk and satin, like he was their savior. They followed him, like ripples behind a swan, and he picked up a woman from the crowd, hoisting her onto his shoulder. He wobbled. She grinned.

"His strength is not what it once was," said Maria.

Johann released his feet, which seemed nailed to the floor, and rushed to the dais. The pieces of horseshoe had jagged edges. He grabbed them both. He did not care if he looked like he was saving a trophy of Augustus'.

Katharina's hand was on his shoulder. Hao was by his side. Maria stood, looking fervently between Johann and Augustus, who was balancing the woman on one shoulder and hoisting a new porcelain vase in the air with his other hand.

"This balancing act is dangerous," said Maria. "That look in his eye... I have seen it before. He will lose all sense."

"The people are distracted, are they not?" Johann said. The horseshoe grew hot in his hands.

"They are very distracted," said Katharina.

"I will take my leave," said Johann. He looked to Hao.

"You need to stay, the King has need of you, he will ask again what his new prized porcelain maker thinks of the new arrivals and..."

But Johann held his hand up, stopping him. Red tassels swung from Hao's hat and he turned to go. Johann would not, could not speak on the Chinese porcelain. But before he could leave, Michal stepped toward them.

"There you are," he said. He grabbed Katharina's arm. "I've been seeking you." His words were slurred with wine. He stank of alcohol and a sharp tang of metal. A sword hung from his side.

"I am free of you," said Katharina. She shrugged him off. "I do not have anything to say to you."

"And instead you speak to this person? Lower than you? No title, no ranking?"

"You mean Johann Kändler? Porcelain master? Lower than me? The bastard daughter of a King who forced his way to his title, killed his elder brother for the princehood, bedded hundreds of women, fathered countless children he will never know, and shows his strength through breakable items? A man who takes a woman against her will? Low has many definitions, Michal."

She turned to leave, but Michal grabbed her arm. Johann, fury blazing, chest large with a powerful inhale, gripped his wrist like a shackle.

"Do not touch her."

Michal snarled, veins standing in his forehead, and wrenched his way out of Johann's grasp. "Do not tell me what to do. You are no one."

Katharina backed away and disappeared into the crowd. Johann held Michal's stare. Suddenly the horseshoe pulsed in his pocket, and the book, too, reminding him of the many things he held secret and safe for others, for himself. Johann's shoulders fell and Michal, scanning the coiffed heads and bejeweled necks, departed, seeking Katharina.

The Porcelain Menagerie

Augustus motioned for the musicians to begin again and a frantic tune resounded from the corners, the party resuming full force. Why had Johann not stopped him? He could not answer that, but instead turned to Maria.

"She is in danger."

"She will try to escape him. Find her, Johann! I can do nothing now, not as Augustus expects me on his arm. It is as if he is reliving his past tonight. I did not think he had the strength to...to..."

"To showcase the brutal man he is?"

"It's just a horseshoe." She narrowed her eyes at him.

"It is not." Something in that moment passed between Maria and Johann, and perhaps the ghost of Herman, whose voice sounded loudly, like a scream, in Johann's mind. He clenched his jaw.

"I prefer the name Fatima," Maria said. Her mouth was a thin line. "Go," she said. "Find her, get her out."

Johann nodded and swept his shabby coat away from the gleaming bodies of King Augustus' party. He knew where he would go, where she likely was. The menagerie.

The castle grounds were dark. The party grew distant, music and cacophony of delight faded. Johann's mind screamed for silence. He could not slow down. Not when Katharina's life was on a cliff's edge. Johann had to reach her. He urged his feet as quickly as they would go.

The menagerie was five hundred paces from the palace, but it felt like miles. The gate was ajar. Katharina always shut the gate, to protect the peacocks. Birds chattered inside, ruffling their feathers at the nighttime disturbance.

He quietly traipsed the now-familiar path of the menagerie, thinking of his brother, now cold and unrecognizable under the parsonage floor. Thinking of his mother, how he shared the color of her blood-straw hair. One life he could save tonight. Katharina's. He would not bury another one he loved.

The word startled him—loved? He hardly knew her...and yet, the pained look in her eyes, the captivity she endured, he *did* know her. He knew her as her story, though foreign and privileged, was like his mother's and Herman's, cut short. And his, tied together in the cage of a menagerie, with a living, breathing woman who would rather be made of porcelain than stay here, chained and barred by her husband, or her father, Augustus the Strong.

A crackling of a branch ahead, of someone who did not know the paths, snapped him from his thoughts. Someone shouted. Something rattled. Johann raised his eyes, sucked in a lungful of air, and ran.

Chapter 32
Fatima
1706

Friedrich placed Fatima down inside the kitchens, kissing her hand. Amar darted away to the pantry she knew existed. Friedrich knelt to the floor with Fatima, hands on her shoulders.

"I have to leave, I cannot be seen here…"

"Georg watched you pick me up, Friedrich, and many people saw you touch me like we are lovers."

"We are lovers. Georg protected all of us back there. We owe him something, though I am not sure what a man who stands at the right hand of Augustus could want."

But Fatima knew. Georg wanted her. Georg did all of this because he was infatuated with her. Friedrich did not know they had spent so much time together in the woods, gathering animals. Friedrich did not know the strangeness of being wanted by three men, none of whom knew how to properly be her match. Friedrich looked at her with eyebrows drawn upward, as if sensing she had many things to say. To Fatima's surprise, he stood.

"You should go to the menagerie. Look in on Buda. I will try to meet you there, tonight. But if I am delayed, do not wait for me," he said. He rubbed his fingertips together, as if ridding them of touching her.

Fatima tried to stand, her urgency to make him stay rushing through her. If he left her now, she'd be alone. She could not quell her trembling. The heel of her hand tapped the floor, though she did not move it of her own accord. Friedrich saw this, and turned, then walked with great speed to the door. And for the second time, he left her.

Fatima's knees and legs ached, and a settling low in her gut cramped. She swallowed, though her throat was parchment dry, and brought herself to her hands and knees, and then her feet. She inhaled, tightening her belly to settle herself. A noise sounded by the ovens.

Using every hold she could, Fatima slowly wound her way through the massive kitchens to the warm corner. Brunhilde and Hao, the Chinese boy, sat there. Hao was nestled in Brunhilde's arms.

"Fatima!" Brunhilde said. Hao wiped his wet face. Fatima knelt to the boy.

"Is he badly hurt?"

"A puncture wound, and his old one opened up, nasty thing on his leg."

"It will scar now."

"Indeed, but with luck and herbs, the bite won't do nothin' but burn for a bit. Ach, he's been through enough, poor lad."

"What will happen to him now?"

"King has special orders for him." Brunhilde said this abruptly, as if she knew the King's decision was a questionable one.

"Brunhilde, what do you think happened?" Fatima asked this with great intention. Georg could be implicated.

"Chaos," said Brunhilde. "Did that lion break its own cage? I doubt that. What scheming took place there? Something seems peculiar, mark my words... But you should know, bein' responsible for the beast. What did happen, Fatima?" She doused Hao's brittle, thin forearm with a poultice and patted his cheek. The boy cried.

Fatima could not give away Georg, nor Friedrich. She feigned innocence. "The cage must have been faulty, Brunhilde. Perhaps Augustus ordered it in his wild mindset out there, hollering at everyone like he... like he—"

"Like he's King. You say you had no part in this, Fatima?"

"No. And besides, Brunhilde, many escaped unharmed because my lion was released. These creatures have souls, I swear." Fatima closed her eyes, protecting herself from the scrupulous look of Hao and Brunhilde. "I see it in the menagerie and the fields. They feel things like we do. Buda knew to return to his cage."

"You'll need to see to your animal, now. Where's Amar?"

"Hiding in the pantry. I shall fetch her. Brunhilde, what could help me with Buda? I shall need help attending to his wounds and I—"

"You're a right remarkable person, Fatima. Most would have the lion destroyed."

"Most lions would not stand up to King Augustus II."

"Most creatures on this planet would not, not even me."

"Me neither, Brunhilde, but we are—"

The Porcelain Menagerie

"We are women, Fatima, but without us, the world crumbles."

Brunhilde lifted Hao off her lap and onto a nearby table, and brought Fatima close. She paused, inhaling. Fatima settled into her, trembling. Brunhilde embraced her wholly.

Hao sat, somber faced, while Brunhilde snipped herbs from the ceiling, her great wide bottom swaying from a stool. She threw the herbs into a large stone bowl and ground them to a mash, adding boiling water from the ever-orange fire.

Brunhilde then grabbed the carcass of a rabbit and slid the steaming concoction inside. Fatima thought she might be sick again, and held the back of her hand to her mouth.

"My lady?" Brunhilde held the rabbit out to Fatima to take, but Fatima hesitated.

"Yes, Brunhilde?"

"Have you been sick often?"

She had been.

"When's the last time you had any moon tea?" Brunhilde said.

"I...I am not sure," Fatima said. "Before Hao. Before...before the animals were brought in from the fields."

"When's the last time your blood flowed?" Brunhilde looked deeply at Fatima's face.

Fatima set her mouth in a thin line. The rabbit's fur grew damp from her clammy palms. She felt a pulsing in her body that was not wholly hers.

"We'll wait a few more days, my lady. Just to see."

"I am terrified, Brunhilde."

"I understand, love, havin' a baby is quite an ordeal but—"

"No, no, not of birth."

"Then what, Fatima?"

She shook her head, unable to voice it. She begged her body to begin bleeding, so she'd never have to answer the questions: Was this Augustus' child? Or Friedrich Böttger's?

Fatima stumbled to the menagerie, tears flowing. The courtyard and grounds were empty. The crowds had fled with the animals, and Fatima wondered how long it would take the wildcats and foxes to find their dens. She imagined them warm and small, careening through the wilds to their waiting holes.

Night threatened, and with it, strange sounds warbled from the menagerie cages. She hurried, despite her body aching and her clenching gut. The rabbit, with its insides replaced by the warm draught for Buda, grew cold in her hands.

The cage bars cast linear shadows broken by beasts whose shapes were ill-defined, strange, frightening now that the fox tossing had broken all bond between human and animal. Buda was locked in his small cage, the same one he was brought here in, which meant Fatima had a choice.

She could leave the animal, blood dripping down its proud face, paw raised to its tongue, smearing the wound in a rhythmic, compulsive beat. Or she could open the cage and let him free. She stood, cold rabbit full of herbs in her hand, and thought. Buda knew her, but his damaged eye might cause him to confuse her for an enemy.

Fatima considered her options. It did not surprise her when the violent trembling that swept her body all day stilled. She opened the lion's outer cage. Leaves, sticks, bones crunched under her feet. She had never been inside here.

Buda turned to her and put his paw down. Fatima stepped closer, fear replaced by something else, something quite undefinable, and slid the rabbit into the smaller cage. She let her hand linger. Fatima touched his shoulder. The lion opened his mouth and whispered a desperate moan. Buda considered, too. The rabbit or the woman?

But the cat flicked his fur like Fatima was a fly. He switched from licking his paw to licking the rabbit's fur, and grooming turned to a bite. Soon enough the rabbit was gone. Buda licked his paws until he could lick them no longer, put to sleep by the powerful concoction made by the King's cook.

Fatima ran to the shed that held the menagerie tools and withdrew a sharp needle and thick, black thread. The husbandry men and sailors had sewn up cuts on themselves, the flanks of horses, and now, in the dead of night, with only the stars and moon as her light, Fatima would sew the wound of her lion.

She entered the smaller cage. Buda's breathing was slow. His eye was mutilated, and Fatima felt another wave of nausea overwhelm her. She wiped clean his face and sewed.

Chapter 33
Johann
1733

"Frau Katharina," Johann called into the darkness. The glowing eyes of beasts surrounded him. A whimper sounded from near the lion's cage but Johann did not know if it was beast or woman.

"Frau Katharina!" he cried again. More snapping twigs. He ran, twisting around a corner to see a terrifying sight.

Katharina had loosed the lion. Her back was to its open cage, the lion between her and Michal. Johann was behind them, watching the scene full on. Michal was on his knees, hands up, his neck exposed to the beast. The one-eyed lion, though ancient and old, bared its teeth and warbled, a demonic sound.

Johann's presence did not startle the animal. It twitched an ear in his direction but did not lose sight of its focus, its prey. Michal. Katharina slid silently, hands clinging to each of the bars. She motioned to Johann to go to the darkened shed to the right.

The lion roared, showing its yellowed teeth. Its age did not matter. It crouched, making its way to Michal.

"Katharina...!" he cried through clenched teeth. "Call off your beast!"

"I don't know how." Katharina's voice was level, unphased. She did not move her gaze from the lion and her former husband. She reached the shed.

"Johann," she said. "Please come this way."

Michal turned his head and Buda lashed out a paw, keeping Michal dead centered.

Terror coursed through Johann, who skittered to the shed, sliding on wet leaves, colliding with Katharina as she wrenched the door open.

Johann slid inside just as Buda lunged. A shrieking sounded from outside, the muffled voice of man and beast combined. Though Johann tried to shield Katharina from the door, she pushed him aside and watched.

To his surprise, she let out a gasp and opened the door once more.

"Mother!" she cried. Maria, or should he say Fatima, was there, and quickly grabbed a bucket, buzzing with flies, from the ground.

She threw the meat into the fray, where Buda and Michal blurred, and called out the lion's name.

"BUDA!" She banged the bucket with her hand but it was not loud enough. Johann withdrew the broken horseshoe from his pocket and handed one half to Fatima. She rang it, loud, on the metal brackets.

Johann hit the stone doorframe of the shed with the other half. Katharina stood, fists clenched. The lion turned, recognized its easier meal, and snatched it. Fatima threw another bloody reward into his open cage door.

The lion, still in hunting mode, slid through the opening, meat in mouth. Michal lay, trembling, cut and bleeding. Fatima shut the rattling cage.

"You, you Dreckspatz!" he said. "Filthy little sparrow! You nearly killed me!"

"No, Freiherr Michal," said Johann. "The menagerie nearly killed you. No one will believe that these ladies pulled a lion off you, no one will believe you. No one will want to hear that you followed your former wife into a dark corner after the King signed the papers granting her wish to divorce you. You had better take your six hundred soldiers and leave Dresden. I do not think you want the rest of the animals here unleashed."

Buda murmured from his cage, deeply savoring his kill. Fatima and Katharina stood, arms locked, beside Johann. Michal got to his feet. His heavy military cloak was shredded, wig lost, hand dripping blood.

Johann swallowed. As he turned back to Buda, the lion gave him a strangely human look. Michal fled, limping, back through the dark menagerie path.

Katharina trembled and collapsed into her mother's arms. Fatima handed Johann his brother's horseshoe. Broken. He put it in his pocket. It thudded against the book.

Johann brought it forth, held it to Fatima. Katharina looked from the book to her mother.

The Porcelain Menagerie

"I am sorry," he said. "I have no right to this book, and I return it to you now."

"It was my fault, Mutter, and I—"

Fatima raised her hand to silence them both. She took the book, opened it, thumbed through the pages.

"You know whose book this was by now. But it seems it is no longer Friedrich Böttger's...you've drawn all over it. Keep it. It's done, what happened with him. He's gone. But...this is missing a page." She thumbed the rough edge of the ripped page.

"That was me, Mother, I...I saw your initials together and the rumors I heard...It seemed you and he..." Katharina said.

"Augustus knew what happened between us. He chained Böttger in his chambers in Albrechtsburg, where he died. He never knew about you. I mourn him. Albrechtsburg sends ghosts to me."

So it was true. Böttger and the King's woman knew each other beyond simple recognition at court. Johann swallowed his many thoughts. Maria grew quiet. She stood in her menagerie, thin moon shining through the trees, and held the book back to Johann.

"Katharina, if you choose to leave tonight, so the lion and your husband cannot be put on you, I can help you," Johann said. He put the book back in his pocket.

"I do not want to go back inside my father's walls," Katharina said. "If he is indeed my father." Johann studied her face. She looked so much like her mother.

"If you promise to keep quiet about the journey you go on, my father will protect you. He is a good man."

"I have a hard time believing in good men."

Johann wrapped his hand around the back of his neck. "I understand. I hope I have proven myself to you."

"Go with him, Katharina. Write to me in Goslar when you get to safety. I will attend to King Augustus," Fatima said. She shut the shed door, grabbed her daughter tightly, and released her.

Katharina rushed past Johann as if she did not go then, she would not go at all. She grabbed a lantern and led Johann through the dark menagerie. They trudged through a grassy path back to where Albrechtsburg's draft horse waited patiently, obscured by the tent where they watched the porcelain trade. The horse whinnied, and Johann rushed to soothe it. He swung up, helping Katharina. Johann sped off, away from the palace, toward a black church spire.

They came to a halt in front of the Lutheran church. Johann stepped into an alley where the Leichendiebe used to wait, pipes in their mouths the only light, hooded and evil. He shuddered, hesitating to leave the draft horse, but he'd be helpful.

"Katharina, this is my father's church. We must retrieve something from my father's parsonage, and he can lead you to safety. Please don't be frightened by what you see."

Katharina looked at the porcelain maker. He extended his hand to her. Johann was responsible for priceless, fragile things; King pleaser, maker of friends, and carver of her own precious face. He was gentle with things in the menagerie. He wanted her to trust him. Johann saw her expression change in their silent exchange. He hoped she wouldn't panic at his task.

Johann wondered where Da was. He knocked on the heavy wooden door of the parsonage and jiggled the handle after Da did not answer. It was locked, and he lifted on his tip-toes to grab the iron key hidden above the door's threshold.

The beamed ceiling was low, black with fireplace soot, but the hearth was cold ash. The cellar door loomed ten feet in front of him, its outline invisible to those who did not know it was there. He could not pry his eyes from it. Fear swept him. He heard a small voice in his head and did not force it away. He dropped Katharina's hand.

"Brother." The voice of a child. *"It's cold."*

Johann's breathing quickened. Despite the early autumn chill in the room, Johann wiped the sweat from his brow.

"They are coming."

With a sudden snap, the door behind him opened, startling Johann out of his vision. Da stepped in, pastor's robes folded over an arm, and the voice of Herman was catapulted to the wind. Marten practically collapsed into Johann's arms. Katharina stepped back.

"Johann, what are you doing here at this hour? I've returned from the Lutheran school, and nearly ran into an army on the way here. Hundreds of men waiting to leave the city."

"I know, Da, that's why I'm here. We're moving him tonight. And her."

Katharina emerged from the shadows.

"This is Frau Katharina, daughter of," he hesitated, "daughter of King Augustus, Elector of Saxony, and she asks for sanctuary."

"I ask, Pastor Kändler, to be removed from Dresden and taken somewhere safe."

"The Lutheran college, Da."

"My child, if this is your wish, it shall be granted," Da said. Johann sighed in relief. His father was a good man.

The Porcelain Menagerie

"Tonight, I have a task that might disturb you, lady. I apologize for it. We made a mistake so many months ago and—"

"We're taking my brother to Albrechtsburg. He rests under the floor. The Leichendiebe sought him, and we only wished to keep him safe."

"This is your secret, porcelain maker. If you move him to Albrechtsburg, you cannot leave." Something painful registered in Katharina's voice.

"I know. And I accept that fate."

Katharina looked as if she'd like to say something, but looked to the floor. Johann was suddenly aware of the worn furnishings, the cracked panes, the dust, the sole book. The narrow bed with its thin coverlet. They did not match, but they did.

"I think you're best outside while we do our work. Can you ride, lady?"

She shook her head no.

"Do not worry," said Marten. "I can ride the draft horse and you two can take the mare cart. Once we are through at Albrechtsburg, Frau Katharina and I shall depart."

Johann led Katharina outside to the lean-to where the mule slept. The chickens clucked their disapproval at waking.

"I'll be fine here," she said. But she trembled.

"We won't be long," said Johann. "You are safe."

She grabbed his face, her hands cool on his skin. "I am safe."

Johann put his hand onto hers and settled, feeling his heaving chest calm. "Katharina, I..."

She looked at his mouth and kept her hands on either side of his face. She opened her lips to speak, but Johann leaned in and kissed her. A fiery rush cascaded through him. Her tongue flickered in his mouth, and she drew closer to him. The rustling sounds of animals surrounded them.

Katharina drew back, resting her forehead on his. In his very soul, Johann knew it was a goodbye kiss. Johann left her. As he turned back, he saw her rubbing the neck of the mule.

Marten crouched down to the faintly visible crack below which his son's body lay. He sighed and ruffled his black hair, streaked with silver.

The two men opened the cellar door, plagued with the soft stench of death muted by the soil and long-abandoned roots. Marten had done work in the last few weeks, and the casket waited to be hauled out of its hole.

Johann had to tell him, then. He removed his jacket and the two pieces of broken horseshoe.

"What...what is this!?" Da's face crunched with anger.

"The strength of Augustus. During his party tonight. I...I couldn't stop him."

Da turned his head, the sinews of his jaw tightening. Johann cringed, nearly crying out, but Da grabbed one piece.

"Fine. Seems Herman has come up with a clever way of each of us getting a piece of it before we're separated."

Johann bit his lip to still his words. He had so many things to say but held back.

"I could do almost all of it," said Da. "But I couldn't get it out alone."

Johann and Marten pulled up Herman. While they did so, Johann told his father everything. He told him of the porcelain menagerie list, the real menagerie, and the stifling furnaces of Albrechtsburg. He told him of Hao and Samuel and Christian Herold. He told him about the look in King Augustus' eyes that he knew was sinful and could not be called anything but obsession.

And though he hesitated, he told his father of Katharina.

"She was married off, Da, and divorced, when she was too young, and her vile husband is back to get her," Johann said, shoveling, dripping in sweat. "She has to get out."

"I will see her to safety."

"Perhaps this is why you were called to leave Dresden now. God saw that you needed to help her, and help me, and help Herman."

Marten nodded, considering. "Saving souls as my son becomes a god of his own making."

"It is not of my making. King Augustus is the one who called me the god of creation. I do not claim that title for myself."

"Then what do you call yourself, boy?"

"Simply a porcelain maker, Da."

His father's pale face shone across the room, wet with tears or sweat, Johann did not know. He stayed seated as Johann climbed the cellar stairs.

Muffled from the depths of the last few steps, Johann heard a stirring in the street. He emerged, paused by the thick window, but the glass was too wavy to see out of clearly. Shouting, singing, trumpeting, a rustling of bodies and feet. He licked his lips and opened the heavy wooden door by its black handle. A few people ran by, heading in the direction opposite Albrechtsburg. In the distance, a crowd grew, and Johann craned his neck to see.

The Porcelain Menagerie

People stopped at a large intersection, cobbled stones beneath their feet, the army leading a procession through Dresden. He had an opening. If he could get Herman onto the cart and away, the city's focus would remain on the departing soldiers. He pictured the small storage room in the dungeons of Albrechtsburg and slammed shut the door.

"Da!" he shouted. "Now! Let's go!"

Marten Kändler struggled to his feet, and from the steep stairs above, Johann saw him clutching at his chest. He was breathing shallowly, and Johann clambered down to help him up. His father's face was pale and filled with fear. He needed air and rest, and the trip to Albrechtsburg only promised one.

"I will need your help to get Herman up the steps, Da. Stay down here and hold him steady, and I can pull, yes?"

Marten nodded, breathing heavily, and Johann shoved his brother's casket toward the stairs, moving quickly around it to haul it up, one steep wooden step at a time. Marten pushed, Johann pulled, and clunk by clunk, their beloved boy rose, leaving soil behind him. Johann returned to his father, helping him up, and shut the cellar door.

They hauled Herman's casket to the cart. Johann swept around the corner and led the mule to its cart. Katharina loaded into the front. Marten covered the coffin with an oilcloth.

Marten donned his preacher's hood and raised onto the black draft horse. Johann slammed the reins against the mule. The cart rattled. People ran by them, paying them no mind, eager to see who paraded through the streets at this hour.

"Michal wasted no time leaving, then," said Katharina. "Perhaps his wounds weren't too deep."

"Not the physical ones anyway," said Johann.

The cobbled streets below the wagon were old, and Johann drove the cart too quickly for the journey to be smooth. They rattled, as did Herman, and Johann's teeth clicked together over the wavy intersections.

"What gods watch out for us, porcelain maker?" said Katharina, watching the tips of flickering torches down the side streets.

"The one in my father's sanctuary does, my lady."

Johann hurried the mule, slippery with foamy sweat. They made it to a high point in the city. The valley of the Elbe extended below them. In the distance, a line of fire moved like stars had fallen to earth in dropped constellations. The six hundred left the city.

The mule slowed down the hill, and both Johann and Katharina held a palm to Herman's casket. They were nearly there, crossing the stone bridge over the Elbe that led to Meissen, onward to Schloss Albrechtsburg.

The soldiers were gone, disappeared from view, as well as Augustus' many palaces. Eventually, they climbed the massive hill to the castle.

Albrechtsburg was pitch black. Johann wondered if Hao had returned, in his red silks, from the party.

Johann urged the heaving mule around to the kitchen entrance. Katharina leaped off first, her cloak a leaf in the wind. Marten slid from the draft horse, pushing Herman's casket while Johann unlocked the kitchen door.

"I have a place prepared," he said, rushing back to grab his brother's casket with his father. Katharina stood at one side. She extended her arms, her fine gown like liquid.

"Don't ruin your dress, Katharina," said Johann. But Katharina shook her head and pushed the soft wood.

Albrechtsburg slept. They padded quietly through the massive kitchen and directly down a narrow stair. Johann and Marten hauled and Katharina held the lantern aloft.

Down they went, away from the belching fires of the kilns, into the dark, dry room three hundred paces from the narrow stairs. Johann produced the key to the iron padlock from a leather cord around his neck and opened the creaking door with difficulty. The mound of dirt he'd made was close, the gaping hole ready for Herman.

Marten and Johann slid the casket into the bottomless belly of Albrechtsburg, and Marten grabbed the shovel to rebury his son.

Johann and Katharina stared at each other, both on their knees by the open grave of Herman. Johann held his half of the horseshoe. Marten held the other. As father and son do without saying a word to each other, they considered dropping them into the grave.

Perhaps it was selfishness that made them keep them. Perhaps it was memory. Perhaps it was connection. But both Kändlers pocketed the horseshoe split in two by Augustus, Elector of Saxony, and buried Herman in the depths of Albrechtsburg.

Chapter 34
Fatima
1706

Fatima tossed the gray book Friedrich had dropped during the fox tossing onto her spindly-legged bedside table. It was dawn. Her night was spent cradling the head of Buda, hoping he would wake. He did. His eye was stitched, and she prayed he'd be alright.

The gray book's contents were confusing. It was filled with scribbles and numbers and words like *kaolin* and *quartz* and *feldspar*. She understood none of this. But his initials were inside it, and she drew her own beside his. FB. FK.

Amar had found her way to the chambers, likely let in by a footman or Brunhilde, and the monkey cooed at her, clinging to her desperately, but backing away once the strange, sweet smell of lion met her. Sweat, dirt, blood, fur covered Fatima. She fell into her bed.

A small knocking sounded through Fatima's chambers. She'd slept for what felt like days. The clock on the mantle read nearly noon. The smell of Amar's droppings and the stifling, unaired room filled her breaths. Head pounding, she opened the door. A messenger with a letter on a silver plate bowed. She took it.

To the ladies of the court, it read.

She wrenched it open.

Ladies,

I am pleased to accept a position in Augustus' court alongside you. I will be arriving in two weeks hence, to no great fanfare as my father settles his debts. Augustus' kindnesses have allowed me to travel a distance to join you.

I look forward to meeting you and the King in person....

Fatima did not finish reading. It did not matter who signed the letter. She was being replaced. She knew her place in Dresden—foreign, chosen for her uniqueness, as a temporary plaything for Augustus. She was glad for the letter. It gave her clarity. She longed to talk to Friedrich and Georg... but she had to choose whom she would share this information with.

She threw the letter to the floor and readied herself for what remained of the day. She must check on Buda, and on the rest of the menagerie. The wild animals that were freed yesterday were likely fine, but which menagerie animals were set free and not returned to their cages? Animals whose fragmented memories of life before captivity meant they would not survive outside of their cages. Would she survive it? Life outside the cage?

Fatima stopped short as she opened her chamber door, her red skirt belling about her. Another of Augustus' messengers waited, like he had been standing there for hours, leaning against the wall. "His Highness waits for you, Frau Maria."

Fatima's belly clenched; she followed, shutting the door and picking up Amar, who chattered. The advisor pursed his lips at the monkey. Fatima did not care about his opinion of her companion.

Darkness enveloped her in the hallway, and despite her cloak, she felt the chill of autumn and the heaviness of a fog-filled day. A small meeting room awaited her. Inside, Augustus sat, a pair of small glasses perched on his nose, leaning over a table, reading something.

"Ah, Maria," he said. He did not stand. His hand was thickly bandaged.

"How is your hand, Highness?"

"It will scar, but I'll keep my fingers. How fares your lion? Many times I have thought of marching to the menagerie to shoot it in its cage."

"Please, no, Augustus, I—"

"But I won't. I plan to keep it. The lion and the King who matched in battle and both survived...quite a story. The court performers are working out the details for the their next play, in a version where I win."

"You have won."

"And how's that?"

"It's back in its cage."

Augustus chuckled and picked at his bandage. "I have good news for you, my lady. You'll be quite pleased. I've chosen a husband for you."

The room swirled. A husband? But...Friedrich waited for her in his tower, where he was going to dry her tears with his artist's hands and she would tell him she was pregnant, and in her mind's eye he kissed her navel and they curled together in his low-slung bed. But a figure stepped out from behind the door. Through tears, it was unclear who it was.

"Lady Maria," said a man, her future husband. She closed her eyes.

"I think you'll be well suited." Augustus' chair scraped back. Her face was suddenly cupped by a hand, a rough thumb wiping a tear away. She tried to imagine she breathed in the smell of clay. But she didn't.

She opened her eyes and saw Georg.

"Is it you?" she said, trembling. "Not a stranger?" She twisted her hands. How did she feel? Could she accept this? Did she have a choice?

"Not a stranger."

Augustus clapped Georg on the back.

"I've spoken to Brunhilde and to Georg, and they both agreed this is best for you. Servants are packing your things from your chambers. You'll go far away. Now."

"You've spoken to Brunhilde...and we're going far away," she repeated slowly.

Far away. Fatima's mind whirled: she'd leave Dresden, and her animals in the menagerie. She'd leave Buda, Brunhilde, and vulnerable Hao... and her porcelain maker. *Böttger.* So Brunhilde had told Augustus that she was pregnant. And likely had also told him that she did not know who the father was. Instead of throwing her in the Zwinger moat, Augustus had given her to Georg. Why had he not punished her?

But he had. She was leaving now, without telling Friedrich she was pregnant, without saying goodbye. She trembled, heartbroken and relieved simultaneously. She left with so many untied knots and unraveling secrets that her mind felt stiff and her heart hardened. She nodded at Augustus, gathered up Amar's chain, and grabbed Georg's hand. They left, taking the same hallway that led to Augustus' dangerous chambers.

"Georg...may I, please, before I go, see my menagerie one last time?"

He hesitated. "I was instructed to take you, quickly, from the city before you speak to anyone. I know who Augustus suspects—"

"Friedrich Böttger. So you know, then? That...that I betrayed the King...and I might be—"

"Carrying a child. But it does not change the King's orders for me."

"You're disappointed."

"I cannot say otherwise. I am happy to have you as my wife, please understand. But I hoped...I hoped for a cleaner start."

Fatima looked at the ground. She turned left, leading Georg to the path near the menagerie.

"Please, Georg. I will not ask for much. But this...let me say goodbye." Amar's chain glistened. He nodded.

"Make it quick. I'll wait for you at the ridge before the gate, so I can see the castle. If someone comes, I'll call for you. They expect us at the carriages."

She hurried, and before she opened the gate, paused, listening. Something rustled. She knelt to see between the bars of the black iron gate and gasped.

The she-wolf was loose. Her green eyes flickered in the shade beyond. Perhaps in the chaos of the previous day, the feeders left her cage unlocked. She lay on the path, eating something between her paws, tearing it with small, delicate bites. Strewn feathers dotted the path, and as Fatima scrambled backward, one caught the air and flew through the gate bars. A peacock feather. Hundreds of them. Downy white and green and blue iridescent feathers, smeared with black-red blood, made a macabre line to the she-wolf and her prize.

Fatima rose. She rattled the gate like a cage door. The wolf stood and bared her teeth. Fatima twisted herself behind the gate, protecting herself. How had she not attacked last night, when she was in the menagerie with Buda...? But the answer came to her: Buda himself.

The she-wolf bolted, grasping the limp bird in her mouth. Its tail feathers skimmed the path as the wolf fled the menagerie and disappeared into the streets of Dresden.

Fatima felt the beast fading. She imagined the she-wolf crossing the bridge over the Elbe, running to the wilds beyond the city. Fatima began to cry. Perhaps it was only her exhaustion. Perhaps it was that her life was, once again, not chosen by her. Her belly cramped again, low and dull. She closed her eyes and traced the path on the palm of her hand and on her heart, begging to never forget this place and these animals and the feeling of freedom she felt when the she-wolf's wind crossed her. From the back of the menagerie, Buda let out a low, mournful cry.

Chapter 35
Johann
1733

Johann breathed deeply for the first time in hours. Katharina and Marten sat like father and daughter at the top of the basement stairs. Marten's arm was around her.

"Time for you to go, then," said Johann.

Katharina's eyes scanned Johann's face. There was sorrow.

"I feel I shall cry," she said.

Marten straightened. Johann grabbed her hand, his filthy.

"No one need disturb him ever again. No daylight. No fire. No evil men. Not you or I. We know where he is, in the belly of this beast. He is safe here, forever, with you, Johann."

"I will never leave him, Da."

"I know."

A voice sounded from the kitchen. Hao. Johann blanched.

Hao removed his red silk hat. "Do you know what they call a secret keeper here? One who knows every mark on the porcelain and every stone in this castle?"

"Hao, I...I can explain everything."

Hao held his hand, silencing Johann.

"They call them arcanists."

"He is one," said Katharina. "An arcanist."

The book, the horseshoe, his brother's grave, Katharina's departure. Added to the secrets he kept of his own trade, of how to make white gold. Yes, Johann thought, I am an arcanist.

At dawn, Katharina stood by the Kändlers' wagon with Marten. The wooden bed behind them had a dirt imprint of Herman's small casket.

"Porcelain maker, arcanist," she said. Her eyes were downcast.

"I claim that title. But you could claim a different one, if you like," Johann said. "Your mother revealed you might call yourself a porcelain maker's daughter."

He put his hand under her chin, forcing her to look at him. Her nose scrunched, eyes closed, and she collapsed into his arms. He lifted her into the wagon.

"Two days to my new assignment at the Lutheran school," said Marten. "I will send a letter when we arrive. Come see us if you are allowed."

Johann smiled, thinking. He did not know if he was. Dawn crested over the Elbe, casting golden green, and he rubbed the mare's ears, bidding his father goodbye. Katharina sat up, raising a small, delicate hand.

He had saved her, and his brother, and his Da. He could not claim that he had saved himself but had work to do.

Johann resumed sculpting that evening, keeping his hands and mind busy.

"I cannot make up the time, Hao," said Johann. "I need Samuel badly to help me start again."

Hao was studying a letter.

"I believe that may be possible now," he said.

Johann looked at him quizzically, rising from his seat where his latest sculpture, a dragon, rested, waiting for refinement.

"The King is dead," said Hao. "Found in his bed this morning after the party."

Johann's eyes grew large. He settled into his seat with a whump, raising his hand to rub his temples.

"What does this mean for us, brother?"

"We continue," said Hao. "We are the porcelain makers, the keepers of the arcanum. With or without a King to urge us onward. You make what you want. Menagerie or none. It is your legacy now, Johann. Will you stay?"

Johann's mind's eye flickered to the castle's depths where his brother's laughter echoed in his dreams, resting without disturbance.

"Yes," he said. "I will stay."

Epilogue
Fatima
1733

Fatima opened the hidden door in her chambers after sounds of Katharina and Johann had long ago faded. She jingled the chain of a small monkey and it clambered up her dressing robe. The creature smelled so much like her beloved Amar.

She readied the herbs gathered from the kitchen, hidden in her jewelry box inside a fat, egg-shaped pearl that opened with a hingeless secret. She tapped the contents into a yellow porcelain cup and carefully opened the door to the hallway.

It was empty, but the sounds of the remnants of the last partygoers sounded in the distance. She hurried. The monkey clawed at her, not as agile as Amar on a shoulder. She knew well the way to Augustus' room.

The torches in the hallway swept toward her, flickering tips of fire nearly touching her billowing robe. She did not knock at his door.

He was in his massive bed, the sight of which sent a chill down her spine, a second figure beside him. Fatima woke the woman first. She was barely twenty, wide-eyed, fair skinned, blonde hair piled high on her head. Augustus knew no boundaries, even at his age.

"Go now," said Fatima. "To the kitchens. Ask for moon tea."

Fatima pressed a finger to her lips to silence the girl, and pulled her out of the bed. The woman clutched her clothing to her chest and ran, bare bottomed, out the dark door. A nearly-empty bottle of Riesling glowed near the fire.

Fatima poured the remnants of wine into the porcelain cup, stirring the herbs. The dusted liquid swirled, nearly black. Augustus stirred, the scars on the palm of his hand raised from the lion so many years ago.

"My King," she said.

"Maria?" He was suddenly wide awake. "It has been many years since you have been in my bedchambers late at night."

"This will be the last time I fear."

"On your way then, in the morning? Come, warm my bed. Georg is dead, he won't mind."

Fatima's hand shook as she handed him the cup. Her late husband was dear to her, and she hated hearing his name on Augustus' lips.

"This is my favorite kind of porcelain. Nearly translucent, perfect, crisp. So thin, so delicate. So powerful. It will not stain with this wine, either. Thank you, my love."

He drank. His eyes closed, and in the dying embers, his age showed on his face: jowls quivering with sour wine, unwigged hair a shorn mess, waggling eyebrows graying.

"You know, you were my favorite."

"I have heard, but did not believe it."

"Of all the mistresses, I believe I might have actually loved you. But it was not to be."

"You were married."

"Divorce is legal under the right circumstances."

"So the circumstances were not right?"

"No, they weren't. You loved that damn porcelain maker. Don't think I didn't know. That's why I sold you to Georg."

"Sold me?"

Augustus downed the rest of the wine. In moments, herbs from the kitchen eaves would hit his gut. "Yes, but I've made amends. When I die, you're in my will. Eight thousand thaler for you, the same amount he paid for you."

Fatima's head pounded but she held steady. Her husband, who she knew had loved her, had secrets, too.

"Shall you warm my bed, love?" His words slurred.

"Yes, Augustus," she said.

He began to cough, and his eyes widened.

"Maria? Fatima? What have you done?"

She said nothing.

The King clutched at his chest, sat straight up in his wide bed.

"Forgive me!" he cried. She shook her head, fearful tears welling. "Forgive me! My entire life was one sin!"

She swallowed, tried to quell her trembling, and climbed in, leaving the monkey on the floor. She grabbed his scarred hand. Fatima waited until he made no more noise, and left the King's body behind as morning rose over the Japanese Palace.

Epilogue
Johann
1747 - 14 years later

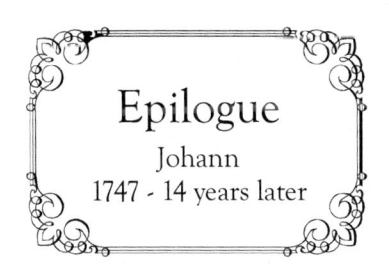

A knock sounded at the door of Albrechtsburg, though it blended with thunder, and Johann could not discern one from the other. Hao woke him.

"There is someone outside," he said. "He has been there for several hours. He is not a vagrant, judging by his clothing. He is persistent."

"What does he want?"

"He says he has a rare animal for you to sculpt," said Hao, running a hand through his graying hair. "It is bothering me that he has not yet left."

"Let me go meet him. Perhaps he really does."

Hao opened the door, and Johann descended, rubbing his eyes. His hands were dry, stained with white kaolin clay. The moon was bright, storm passing quickly. Johann went to the door, sighing, shaking the deep sleep from which he had emerged.

"Good evening, sir," said the man. He was handsome, with a tricorne hat in his hands. Rain soaked his clothing and clung to his form. It was threadbare but elegant.

"I appreciate you letting me in, as the night has grown cold."

Johann stepped out, and Hao closed the door behind them, standing next to Johann. The man hesitated, clearly uncomfortable.

"I...have an animal in my possession and find it most prudent for you to sculpt it," he said. "I believe your depiction of her species is currently incorrect."

Hao looked at Johann, who allowed a half-smile to creep onto his face. What did he have—something dead and stuffed? A false unicorn? A gryphon? A dragon?

"It's a rhinoceros," said the man. "So rare there is no scientific name yet. The only one in Europe."

Johann's mind flickered to the list King Augustus had given him years ago. The rhinoceros puzzled him—only known from a single drawing of Albrecht Dürer in 1515. There was no way of knowing how large the animal was, nor if the drawing was accurate. He rubbed his hands together, dusting clay.

"Alive?" he said. The man nodded.

Hao and Johann looked at each other, passing unspoken thoughts. Augustus the Strong's son with his wife the exiled queen, Christiane, his only legitimate child, Augustus III, told Johann he could leave the castle at the promise of a new species, but he had not done so for nearly a year. He would love to go. Hao's eyes permitted him.

Johann nodded at the stranger and turned back to the castle, smiling. A rhinoceros. In Dresden. Of all things.

Author's Note

Real history often brings complications in fiction. One of the funniest things I encountered while writing this book is that I had to rename almost every male character. They were nearly all historically named Johann.

Johann Joachim Kändler is the only one who retained his name. Johann Friedrich Böttger is called Friedrich in this book; Johann Gregor Herold is called Christian Herold; Johann Georg von Spiegel is called Georg von Spiegel, and Johann Kändler's father, Johann Kändler, is called Marten in this book. I hope readers will accept this changing of their names—the confusion would have been quite dreadful to navigate.

The art of Johann Kändler can be seen in museums and collections around the world. Stunning porcelain portraits of people, animals, mythology scenes, chandeliers, dinner services, and more exist by the thousands with the crossed, dark blue swords of Meissen porcelain painted on their bases. If you ever go antiquing with me, please don't be alarmed when I pick up porcelain. I'm checking for Meissen's crossed swords!

Even though Kändler made hundreds of pieces of art, I have only been able to locate two portraits of the man himself. His life is well-documented, but his own visage is not. I find this a strange contradiction for an artist who carved so many faces.

Johann's dedication to his craft, his meticulous attention to detail, and the refinement of the porcelain molds mean that his art is still considered some of the finest porcelain ever made.

In the early eighteenth century, porcelain was more valuable than gold. Royalty around the globe coveted porcelain for generations. Meissen was the first in Europe to make hard-paste porcelain, breaking the Chinese and Japanese monopoly. The factory guarded the secrets of kaolin clay, kiln temperatures, molding techniques, and paint formulas in the gothic walls of Albrechtsburg for over 150 years.

Albrechtsburg was originally a wooden fortress, constructed in 926 CE. Once a grand medieval castle, it was essentially unused before Johann Friedrich Böttger started the rumbling kilns in the lower levels. I fully consider the castle itself a character in this work.

Today, Meissen operates in a factory setting full of artists and makers and Albrechtsburg is a stunning museum. Without Kändler, and without Böttger and Augustus the Strong, the art of Meissen would not exist.

This secret formula, called the arcanum, was one way kingdoms could control wealth; especially after alchemy, the turning of metal into gold, was proven impossible. Porcelain, according to Johann Friedrich Böttger, satisfied three human desires: beauty, rarity, and usefulness. He finally succeeded in its discovery by first making Böttger redware and then, finally, white porcelain, in 1708.

But the fiery kilns and chemical experiments turned fatal for many, including Böttger himself, who was held in varying degrees of confinement for around thirteen years. Toward the end, he was almost always drunk. Sadly, Böttger died at age thirty-seven, seemingly due to his high-stress work, toxic chemicals, and alcohol.

These things are very well documented in several books, but my personal favorite is *The Arcanum* by Janet Gleeson.

The life of Augustus II of Poland is best documented in the biography by Tim Blanning, which I was lucky enough to get an early copy of to help with my research. *Augustus the Strong: A Study in Artistic Greatness and Political Fiasco* tells the story of a second son who never knew he'd be king, and when he got the chance, seized it. Disastrously.

His famous womanizing, terrible decisions, unsightly behavior, brute strength, and downright disgusting treatment of animals make him one of the most despicable royals in early modern Europe. On the flip side, Augustus created Dresden's most stunning buildings, collected art like no one else in Germany, and created a legacy of porcelain, goldwork, sculpture, and paintings. He is a contradiction, a real human, an imperfect leader, a brilliant collector.

He died in Poland, however, for the ease of narrative, the main story takes place in Dresden. His last words were recorded after a drunken night of debauchery.

Sadly, the fox tossing was a real court event. Hundreds of animals were killed. In the audience of events like this was Fatima Kariman.

I scoured every source I possibly could to find information about Fatima. And when I read Blanning's book, he summed it up as best as anyone could: "Accounts of her origin and early life are so various that almost nothing can be believed."

What we think we know: She was likely captured during the Siege of Buda in 1686 as part of the spoils of war. She was given to Maria Aurora von Konigsmarck and was baptized and renamed Maria Aurora herself. You can understand why I called Maria Aurora, Aurora, and Fatima,

Maria. Repeated names can be very confusing. Fatima was educated in etiquette and French, and became Aurora's companion.

Fatima took the place of Aurora as Augustus' mistress and birthed two of his children, Katharina and Friedrick Augustus. The drama that must have existed as a companion took the place of a high-born lady as the King's mistress is one of the reasons I wrote this book.

The most interesting thing about Fatima's story to me is that Augustus acknowledged both of her bastard children as his, and left her an 8,000 thaler allowance in his will. He did not do this with any of his other mistresses.

This means Fatima may have held more than just Augustus' attention. She may have actually held his heart. Regardless of this, Augustus married her off to Johann Georg Spiegel in 1706. Love triangles abounded, but the one between Böttger and Fatima, I have no proof of.

At one point, it is rumored that Augustus had over 300 bastard children. Historians think that number is actually eight to ten. However, him bedding over 300 women would be no surprise. He had one legitimate progeny, Augustus III, with his estranged wife Christiane.

Katharina and her husband Michal did get divorced, but I have not found a reason why. That piece of this history is something I will continue to search for my entire life. I hope someday I find it.

The story elements of porcelain animals, visiting menageries for inspiration, steaming castles, stolen bodies for the anatomists, broken horseshoes, one-eyed lions, monkeys on chains, shipwrecks, prisoners, traded soldiers for porcelain, and egg-sized jewels are all real.

Any mistakes in this book are my own, and as with any historical fiction, I took liberties where necessary to hold the audience captive. Much like the porcelain wares in this book, all history is subject to smashing when new sources are found.

To read more of the porcelain maker's story, pick up a copy of the companion novel, *The Rhino Keeper,* in which you will discover the life of the rhino in the epilogue.

Acknowledgments

A massive thank you to Colin Mustful, founder and editor of History Through Fiction, who I told about this book when we had our first meeting for *The Rhino Keeper*. I remember specifically telling him: "I have another one." Thank you for trusting me, believing in me, and telling me I can do this. You're awesome, dude.

Thank you to historical fact-checker Grace Turton, whose kindness and expertise allowed for some incredible additions.

Thank you so much to the Meissen porcelain factory staff for their kindness and willingness to stalk the archives for me. Thank you to the curators and historians at Albrechtsburg for sending me both hand-drawn maps of the castle and documents that describe the grounds as early as they could find them.

Thank you to museum curators Kit Maxwell and Mairead Horton at the Art Institute of Chicago for showing me behind the scenes. Seeing the porcelain menagerie pieces in person was overwhelming and outstanding, but seeing a teapot that Böttger made was chilling. Thank you, too, to Vanessa Sigalas of The Wadsworth for an early discovery call.

Thank you to porcelain artists Tricia Zimic and Joseph Rincones for explaining the art to me. Thank you to the Meissen porcelain Facebook group for schooling me on how to recognize Meissen without flipping it over!

Thank you once again to the staff at Tanganyika Wildlife Park. Ben Valencia, the lion keeper, let me sit with the pride for many hours. The observations there helped me with Buda. Thanks, too, to LynnLee Schmidt.

Thank you to Jenny Quinlan for your editorial services. My early readers: Sandee Lee, Susan Wiedner, Kayla Jordan, and Sara E. Leslie.

My writing people, I could not do this without you: Kate Khavari, Jess Armstrong, Paulette Kennedy, Sarah Penner, Elise Powers, Molly Greeley, Ian Tan, Rose de Guzman, Libbie Grant, Bianca Miller, Diana Giovinazzo, and the Kansas Author's Club.

Thank you to my people: Cody, Phoebe, Beth, Grant, Claire, Annika. You are my heart and soul. I love you more than porcelain.

About the Author

Jillian Forsberg is a historian and author with a master's degree in public history from Wichita State University. She will always write animal historical fiction. In addition to her historical fiction novels, Jillian is a dedicated small business owner. She lives in Wichita, Kansas, with her husband, child, and pets.

About History Through Fiction

History Through Fiction is an independent press publishing high quality fiction that is rooted in accurate and detailed historical research. As publishers of historical fiction, we seek to provide readers with compelling narratives that also act as valuable historical resources. Our books, though fictionalized, include important primary and secondary source materials that are disclosed to readers through a variety of traditionally nonfiction elements such as footnotes, endnotes, or a bibliography. This way, readers may enjoy a fictional narrative while also examining the historical foundation upon which that narrative is based. By combining elements of fiction and nonfiction, our authors provide readers with an immersive experience that is both entertaining and educational.

If you enjoyed this novel, please consider leaving a review. It's the best way to support us and our authors. Plus, you'll be helping other readers discover this great story.

Thank you!

www.HistoryThroughFiction.com